Keri **Arthur** won the *Romantic Times* Career Achievement Award for Urban Fantasy and has been nominated in the Best Contemporary Paranormal category of the *Romantic Times* Reviewers' Choice Awards. She's a dessert and function cook by trade, and lives with her daughter in Melbourne, Australia.

Visit her online:
www.keriarthur.com
www.facebook.com/AuthorKeriArthur
www.twitter.com/@kezarthur

D1380188

DARKNESS HUNTS

A DARK ANGELS NOVEL

KERI ARTHUR

piatkus

PIATKUS

First published in the US in 2012 by Signet Select
an imprint of New American Library
a division of Penguin Group (USA) Inc.
First published in Great Britain as a paperback original in 2012 by Piatkus

A CIP catalogue record for this book
is available from the British Library.

ISBN 978-0-7499-5775-9

Printed and bound by CPI Group (UK) Ltd, Croydon, CR0 4YY

Papers used by Piatkus are from well-managed forests
and other responsible sources.

MIX
Paper from
responsible sources
FSC® C104740

Piatkus
An imprint of
Little, Brown Book Group
100 Victoria Embankment

An Hachette UK Company
www.hachette.co.uk

www.piatkus.co.uk

I'd like to thank the following people:

my editor, Danielle Perez; copy editor Jan McInroy;
and the man responsible for the fabulous covers,
Tony Mauro

A special thanks to:

my agent, Miriam Kriss; my crit buddies—
Mel, Robyn, Chris, Carolyn, and Freya; and finally,
my lovely daughter, Kasey

DARKNESS HUNTS

Chapter 1

"I need to speak to a ghost."

Adeline Greenfield paused in the middle of pouring tea into her expensive china cups and looked at me.

"I was under the impression you already could." Her voice, like her appearance, was unremarkable. With her short gray hair, lined face, and generous curves, she reminded me of the grandmotherly types often seen on TV sitcoms. It was only her blue eyes—or rather, only the power that glowed within them—that gave the game away. Adeline Greenfield was a witch, a very powerful and successful one.

"No. I mean, I *can* hear them, and sometimes I can see them, but they don't seem to hear or acknowledge me." I grimaced. "I thought if I was on the same plane as they are—if I astral-traveled to them—it might help."

"Possibly." She set the teapot down and frowned. "But didn't you help relocate a ghost that was causing all sorts of mischief at the Brindle?"

The Brindle was the witch depository located here in Melbourne, and it held within its walls centuries of knowledge, spells, and other witch-related paraphernalia. "Yes, but it wasn't really a ghost. It was actually a mischievous soul who was undecided about moving on."

"Souls are usually incapable of interaction with this world."

"Yes, but the Brindle is a place of power, and that gave her the ability."

She nodded sagely. "It is still odd that you cannot speak to them the same way as your mother, because I'm sure she said you had the skill."

I raised my eyebrows. "You knew Mom?"

She smiled. "Those of us *truly* capable of hearing the dead are few and far between, so yes, I knew her. We had lunch occasionally."

That was something I hadn't known. But then, there was probably a whole lot of stuff I'd never known about my mother—and never would, given she'd been murdered. Grief swirled, briefly touching my voice as I said, "Well, no matter what she may have believed, the dead *won't* speak to me."

"Ghosts *can* be vexing creatures," she agreed. "And they often have no desire to acknowledge their death."

"So how is ignoring me helping them disregard the fact that they're dead?"

She placed a couple of sugars in each cup, then gently stirred the tea. "We're talking about the dead here. Their minds are not what they once were, especially those who have been murdered."

"I didn't say he'd been murdered."

"You didn't have to. Trouble, my dear, darkens your

steps, and it's not such a leap to think that if you want to speak to a ghost, it's because he died before his time. Otherwise, your reaper would have been able to find out whatever you needed." She handed me a cup of tea, then glanced over my right shoulder. "I would prefer it, by the way, if you'd just show yourself. It's impolite to skulk on the edges of the gray fields like that."

Heat shimmered across my skin as Azriel appeared. Of course, he wasn't strictly a reaper, as they were soul guides. He was something much more—or, if you believed him, something much less—and that was a Mijai, a dark angel who hunted and killed the things that broke free from hell.

But what he hunted now wasn't an escapee demon, daemon, or even a spirit—although we certainly *had* been hunting one of those. We'd gotten it, too, but not before the fucking thing had almost killed me. Which was why I was moving like an old woman right now—everything still hurt. I might be half werewolf, but fast healing was one of the gifts I hadn't inherited enough of. In fact, I couldn't shift into wolf shape at *all*, and the full moon held no sway over me.

Of course, I *could* heal myself via my Aedh heritage, but shifting in and out of Aedh form required energy, and I didn't have enough of that, either.

"That's better," Adeline said, satisfaction in her voice. "Now, would you like a cup of tea, young man?"

"No, thank you."

There was a hint of amusement in Azriel's mellow tones, and it played through my being like the caress of gentle fingers. Longing shivered through me.

Adeline picked up her own cup, a frown once again marring her homely features. "Why do you wear a sword, reaper? There is no threat in this house."

"No, there is not," he agreed.

When it became obvious he didn't intend to say anything else, Adeline turned her expectant gaze to me.

"He wears a sword because he's helping me hunt down some—" I hesitated. For safety's sake I couldn't tell her everything, yet I couldn't *not* explain, either. Not if I wanted her help. "—rogue priests who seek the keys to the gates of heaven and hell so they can permanently close them."

That raised her eyebrows. "Why on earth would anyone want that?"

"Because they're not *of* earth." They were Aedh, energy beings who lived on the gray fields—the area that divided earth from heaven and hell. Or the light and dark portals, as the reapers tended to say. While the reaper community had flourished, the Aedh had not. They'd all but died out, and only the Raziq—a breakaway group of priests—were left in any great numbers. "And they've decided it would be easier to permanently shut the gates to *all* souls than to keep guarding against the occasional demon breakout."

She frowned. "But that would mean no soul could move on and be reborn."

"Yes, but they don't care about that. They just see the bigger picture."

"But surely the number of demons who break out of hell is minor when compared to the chaos that closing the gates permanently would cause."

"As I said, I don't think the priests care." Not about the human race in general, and certainly not about babies being born without souls and ending up as little more than inanimate lumps of flesh. "They just want their life of servitude to the gates ended."

Which is how I'd gotten involved in this whole mess in the first place. The Raziq had developed three keys that would permanently open or close the gates. The only trouble was, my father, who was one of the Raziq responsible for making the keys, had not only stolen the keys but had arranged to have them hidden—so well that even *he* knew only a general location. And as he could no longer take on flesh form, he now needed me to do his footwork, since only someone of his bloodline could detect the hidden keys.

In fact, *everyone* needed me—the Raziq, the reapers, the high vampire council. And all of them wanted the keys for very different reasons.

Adeline said, "And this is why you wish to speak so urgently to this ghost? He knows of the keys?"

I hesitated. "No. But he might have some information about a dark sorcerer who could be tied up in all this mess. We questioned our ghost when he was alive, but someone very powerful had blocked sections of his memories. We're hoping death might have removed those blocks."

"It's a rather vague hope."

"Which is still better than no hope." I took a sip of tea, then shuddered at the almost bitter taste and put the cup down. Tea had never been a favorite beverage of mine.

"When do you wish to start?" Adeline asked.

"Now, if possible."

She frowned again. "Your energy levels feel extremely low. It's generally not considered a wise—"

"Adeline," I interrupted softly, "I may not get another chance to do this."

Mainly because I'd been ordered by my father to retrieve a note from Southern Cross Station later this morning, and who the hell knew what would happen after *that*? But if past retrievals were any indication, then hell was likely to break loose—at least metaphysically speaking, if not physically.

She studied me for several minutes, then said, "If you insist, then I must help you, even if it is against my better judgment."

"Must?" I raised my eyebrows. "That almost sounds like you've been ordered to help me."

"Oh, I have, and by Kiandra herself, no less." She eyed me thoughtfully. "You have some very powerful allies, young woman."

Surprise rippled through me. Kiandra—who was head witch at the Brindle—had helped me on several occasions, but only *after* I'd approached her. That she was now anticipating my needs suggested she knew a lot more about what was going on than I'd guessed. "Did she say why?"

"She said only that your quest has grave implications for us all, and that it behooves us to provide assistance where possible."

Which suggested that Kiandra *did* know about the existence of the keys and our effort to retrieve them. And I guess that wasn't really surprising—surely you couldn't become the head of all witches without *some* working knowledge of the fields and the beings that inhabited them.

"Which is why I need to do this now, Adeline."

She continued to study me, her expression concerned. "What do you know of astral traveling?"

"Not a lot, though I suspect it won't be that dissimilar to traveling the gray fields."

"It's not. Astral travel is simply your consciousness or spirit traveling through earth's realm, whereas the gray fields are merely the void through which your soul journeys on its way to heaven or hell. But there are a few rules and dangers you should be aware of before we attempt this."

Having traveled through the gray fields many times, I knew they were hardly a void, as they were where the reapers lived. But I simply said, "There usually are when it comes to anything otherworldly."

"Yes." She hesitated. "Thought is both your magic carpet and your foe on the astral plane. If you want to go somewhere, think of the precise location and you will be projected there. By the same token, if you become afraid, you can create an instant nightmare."

I nodded. She continued. "Be aware that any thought related to your physical body will bring you back to your body. This includes the fear that your physical body may be hurt in some way."

I frowned. "If I can't speak or move, how am I going to question my ghost?"

"I didn't say you can't move, and you think the questions, the same as you think of the location. Clear?"

"As mud."

She eyed me for a moment, the concern in her expression deepening. "The astral plane is inhabited by two types of spirits: those who cannot—for one reason or another—move on spiritually, and other astral travelers. And just like walking down the street, you cannot control who's on the astral fields. But you *can* be certain that not all will be on the side of the angels."

"So I should watch my metaphysical ass?"

"Yes. At your current energy levels, you could attract energies who are darker in life, and they may cause you problems on the astral plane *or* follow you onto this one."

"I can handle unpleasant energies on *this* plane. And if I can't, Azriel can." I paused. "What of the dangers?"

Her expression darkened. "While you cannot die on the fields themselves, it is possible to become trapped there. It is also possible to become so enraptured by whatever illusion surrounds you on the plane that what happens there can echo through your physical being."

I frowned. "So if I somehow imagine getting whacked on the plane, my body can be bruised?"

"If the illusion is powerful enough, yes. And if you find yourself entrapped there, you risk death."

"Why?"

"Because," Azriel said, before Adeline could, "flesh cannot survive great lengths of time without its soul. And while the astral body is not the entirety of the soul, if you find death when your astral being is not present in your body, then your soul is not complete and cannot move on. You would become one of the lost ones."

"And here I was thinking it would be a walk in the park." I swept a hand through my short hair and wished, just once, that something was. "Let's get this done."

She glanced past me briefly, then rose. "Come with me, then."

I followed her out of the living room and down the long hall, my footsteps echoing softly on her wooden floors. Azriel made no sound, although the heat of his presence burned into my spine and chased away the chill of apprehension.

Adeline stopped at the last door on the right and opened it. "Please take your shoes off."

I did so as she stepped to one side and motioned me to enter. The room was dark and smelled faintly of lavender and chamomile, and my bare feet disappeared into a thick layer of mats and silk.

"Lie down and make yourself comfortable."

I glanced over my shoulder at Azriel. Though his face was almost classical in its beauty, it possessed the hard edge of a man who'd won more than his fair share of battles. He was shirtless, his skin a warm, suntanned brown and his abs well defined. The worn leather strap that held his sword in place emphasized the width of his shoulders, and the dark jeans that clung to his legs hinted at their lean strength. His stance was that of a fighter, a warrior—one who not only protected me, but had saved me more than once. And would continue to do so, for as long as I was of use to him.

Still, I couldn't help mentally asking, *You'll be here?*

I'll be here to protect your physical form, yes. His thought ran like sunshine through my mind. I wasn't telepathic in any way, shape, or form, but that didn't matter when it came to Azriel. He could hear my thoughts as clearly as the spoken word. Unfortunately, the only time I heard *his* thoughts was at times like now, when it was a deliberate act on his part. *But not on the plane. Astral travelers are of* this *world, not mine, so you are basically little more than a ghost to me. I cannot interact with you in any way.*

Reaper rules?

Reaper rules. He hesitated, and something flashed through the mismatched blue of his eyes. Something so bright and sharp it made my breath hitch. *Be careful. It would be most . . . inconvenient . . . if you find death on the astral plane.*

Inconvenient? I shucked off my jacket and tossed it to one side with a little more force than necessary. *Yeah, I guess it would be. I mean, who else would find the damn keys for you if something happened to me?*

That, he said, an edge riding his mental tone, *is an unfair statement.*

Yeah, it was. But goddamn it, if *I* was an inconvenience to him, then *he* was a vast source of frustration to me. *And* on more than one level. Was it any wonder that it occasionally got the better of me and resulted in a snippy remark?

That frustration is shared by us both, Risa.

I glanced at him sharply. His expression was its usual noncommittal self, but the slightest hint of a smile played about his lips. I snorted softly. If he *was* implying he was as sexually frustrated as me, then he had only himself to blame. After all, *he* was the one determined to keep our relationship strictly professional now that desire had been acknowledged and acted upon. Although *how* he could ignore what still burned between us I had no idea. I was certainly struggling with it.

"Risa," Adeline said softly, "you must lie down before we can proceed."

I did as she ordered, and the mats wrapped around me, warm and comforting. Adeline closed the door and the darkness engulfed us. The scents sharpened, slipping in with every breath and easing the tension in my limbs.

"Now," she said softly, her voice at one with the serenity in the room. "To astral-travel, you must achieve a sense of complete and utter relaxation."

I closed my eyes and released awareness of everything and everyone else around me, concentrating on nothing more than slowing my breathing. The beat of my heart became more measured, and warmth began to throb at my neck as the charm Ilianna—my best friend and housemate—had made me kicked into action. It was little more than a small piece of petrified wood, to connect me to the earth, and two small stones—agate and serpentine—for protection, but it had saved my life when a spirit had attacked me on the gray fields, and I'd been wearing it ever since. That it was glowing now meant it would protect me on the astral plane as fiercely as it did on the gray fields, and I was suddenly glad of that.

Though why I thought I might need that protection I had no idea.

"Let your mind be the wind," Adeline intoned. "Let it be without thought or direction, free and easy."

A sense of peace settled around me. My breathing slowed even further, until I was on the cusp of sleep.

"A rope hangs above your chest. You cannot see it in the darkness, but it is there. Believe in it. When you are ready, reach for it. Not physically—metaphysically. Feel it in your hands, feel the roughness of the fibers against your skin, feel the strength within it."

I reached up with imaginary hands and grasped the rope. It felt thick and real, and as strong as steel.

"Ignore physical sensation and use the rope to pull yourself upright. Imagine yourself rising from your body and stepping free of all constraints."

I gripped harder with my imaginary hands and pulled myself upward along the rope. Dizziness swept over me, seeming to come from the center of my chest. I kept pulling myself upright and the pressure grew, until my whole body felt heavy. I ignored it, as ordered, and every inch of me began to vibrate. Then, with a suddenness that surprised me, I was free and floating in the darkness above my prone form.

Only it wasn't really dark. Adeline's aura lit the room with a deep violet, and Azriel's was an intense gold. Which surprised me—I'd have put money on the fact that his would be the fierce white I saw on the fields. The black tats that decorated his skin—the biggest of which resembled half of a dragon, with a wing that swept around his ribs from underneath his arm and brushed the left side of his neck—shimmered in the darkness and seemed to hold no distinct color.

Only that half dragon wasn't actually a tat. It was a Dušan—a darker, more abstract brother to the one that had crawled onto my left arm and now resided within my flesh. They were originally created to protect the Aedh priests who had once guarded the gates, but we had no idea who'd sent them to us—although Azriel suspected it was probably my father's doing. He was one of the few left in this world—or the next—who had the power to make them.

Valdis, the sword at Azriel's back, dripped the same blue fire on the astral field as she did in the real world, and it made me wonder if my own sword, Amaya, would be visible on this plane, given that she was little more than a deadly shadow normally.

I shoved the thought aside, then closed my eyes and conjured the image of the area where our ghost—Frank Logan—had met his doom.

In an instant, I was standing in front of the gigantic shed that was the Central Pier function center. On the night Logan had been murdered, this place had been filled with life and sound, and the pavement lined with taxis and limos waiting to pick up passengers. Now it was little more than a vague ghost town—figuratively *and* literally.

I looked around. The first thing I saw was a man, watching me. He was tall, with regal features and a body that was as lean as a whip. *A fighter*, I thought, staring at him.

As our gazes met, humor seemed to touch his lips and he bowed slightly.

I frowned, and thought, *Do I know you?*

No, but I know you rather well. I've been following you around for weeks.

His voice was cool, without inflection but not unpleasant.

Why would you— I stopped and suddenly realized just who he was. *You're the Cazador Madeline Hunter has following me?*

I certainly am, ma'am.

I blinked at his politeness, although I wasn't really sure why it surprised me. I *had* grown up hearing tales about the men and women who formed the ranks of the Cazadors—the high vampire council's own personal hit squad—and I suppose I just expected them all to be fierce and fearsome.

He gave me another slight bow. *Markel Sanchez, at your service.*

Well, forgive me for saying this, Markel, but you're a pain in my ass and I'd rather not have you following me around, on this plane or in life.

Trust me, ma'am, this is not my desire, either. But it has been ordered and I must obey.

I raised imaginary eyebrows. *Meaning even the Cazadors are wary of Hunter?*

If they are wise and value their lives, yes.

Which said a lot about Hunter's power. She might be the head honcho at the Directorate of Other Races, but she was also a high-ranking member of the high vampire council and, I suspected, plotting to take it over completely.

I need to speak to a ghost. You're not going to interfere, are you?

I'm here to listen and report. Nothing more, nothing less.

I nodded and turned away from him. A grayish figure stood not far away. He was standing side on, looking ahead rather than at me, and he was a big man with well-groomed hair, a Roman nose, and a sharp chin. Frank Logan.

I imagined myself standing beside him, and suddenly I was. If only it were this easy to travel in Aedh form.

Mr. Logan, I need to speak to you.

He jumped, then swung around so violently that tendrils of smoke swirled away from his body.

"Who the hell are you?" He wasn't using thought, and his words were crisp and clear, echoing around me like the clap of thunder.

I'm Risa Jones. I was standing nearby when you were murdered.

His expression showed a mix of disbelief and confusion. "I'm dead? How can I be dead? I can *see* you. I can see the buildings around me. I can't be dead. Damn it, where's my limo? I want to go home."

He was never going home. Never moving on. He'd died before his time, and no reaper had been waiting to collect his soul. He was one of the lost ones—doomed to roam the area of death for eternity.

But I suspected nothing I could say would ever convince him of this, and I wasn't about to even try—that could take far more time than I probably had on this plane. *Mr. Logan, I need to speak to you about John Nadler.*

He frowned. "I'm sorry, young woman, but I can't talk to you about clients—"

Mr. Logan, John Nadler is dead—murdered. I imagined a cop's badge, then showed it to him. *We'd appreciate your helping us willingly, Mr. Logan, but we will subpoena you if required.*

His confusion deepened. "When was Nadler murdered? I was talking to him just today."

Logan's "today" had actually been several days ago. *Which is why we need to speak to you. We believe you could be the last person to have seen him alive.*

Or at least, the last person to have seen the face-shifter who'd killed the real Nadler and assumed his identity. The real Nadler had been dead—and frozen—for many, many years, and *that* was the body the cops now had.

The Nadler Logan had known had used Nadler's money and influence to purchase nearly all the buildings around West Street in Clifton Hill—a street that just happened to cross one of the most powerful ley-line intersections in Melbourne. It was also an intersection that seemed very tied up in the desperate scramble to find the portal keys. According to Azriel, the intersections could be used to manipulate time, reality, or fate, and it was likely that whoever had stolen the first key from us—or rather, from me—had used the intersection to access the gray fields and permanently open the first portal.

Suggesting that the face-shifter was either a sorcerer himself or worked for someone who was. Only those well versed in magic could use the ley lines.

Of course, *why* the hell anyone would want to weaken the only thing that stood between us and the hordes of hell, I had no idea. Not even Azriel could answer that one.

But we'd obviously gotten too close to uncovering who the face-shifter was, so he'd stepped out of Nadler's life and into a new one. Unless Logan could reveal something about the man he'd known as Nadler, our search was right back at square one.

"I'm not sure I can help you," Logan said. "He was just a client. I didn't know much about him on a personal level."

We're not interested in his personal life, but rather his business one. I hesitated. *What can you tell me about the deal he made with the heirs of James Trilby and Garvin Appleby?*

Trilby and Appleby were the two other members of the consortium the fake Nadler had formed to purchase all the land around West Street. Their heirs had decided to sue the consortium—and therefore John Nadler, who had, when they died, become sole owner—for a bigger piece of the land pie. They'd reached an out-of-court settlement the day before Nadler had pulled the plug on his stolen identity.

"I'm not sure how that deal—"

Please, Mr. Logan, just answer the question.

He raked a hand through his hair. The action stirred the ghostly strands, making them whirl into the ether before settling back down.

From somewhere in the distance came a gentle vibration, and the sensation crept around me, making the shadowy world surrounding us tremble. It almost felt like the beginnings of a quake, but was that even possible on the astral fields? Even as the thought ran through my mind, the shadows around me began to quiver, and Adeline's warning came back to me. I took a deep breath, imagining calmness. The shadowy world close to us stilled, but the distant vibration continued. It was a weird sensation—and it felt like trouble. I forced myself to ignore it and returned my attention to Logan.

"Nadler agreed to pay them several million dollars each," he said, "in exchange for them signing an agreement to accept the wills as they currently stand."

And will those payments proceed now that Nadler is dead?

He frowned. "Of course. The heirs just won't get the payment as quickly, because it'll be tied up until Nadler's estate is sorted."

And who is Nadler's heir? He has no children and he divorced his wife a long time ago. A fact, I thought bitterly, that hadn't stopped the fake Nadler from killing her.

"You know, there's a good percentage of men and women who forget to change their wills even after a second marriage, and it's not unknown for the first partner to get the estate." He paused, eyeing me critically. "Have you got a will, young woman? It's never too late to start. I can offer you excellent—"

Thanks, I interrupted quickly, and rubbed imaginary arms. That vibration was getting stronger, and it was *not* pleasant. *But I'm good will-wise. Now, Nadler's heirs?*

"How am I supposed to remember?" His tone was cross. "I haven't got the paperwork with me, and he's not my only client, you know."

I know. Just think back to the agreement. Imagine you have it in your hand.

He frowned and a second later ghostly paper began to form between his hands. I didn't move, not wanting to startle him and lose the moment.

Who is his heir, Mr. Logan?

"He's got three—Mr. Harry Bulter, Mr. Jim O'Reilly, and a Ms. Genevieve Sands."

A woman? One of Nadler's heirs was a woman? *Are any of them related to Mr. Nadler?*

"Not as far as I'm aware." He glanced up. "I still can't see why—"

Mr. Nadler was a very wealthy man, I said easily. *And it's not unknown for heirs to kill their benefactor to get hold of their money.*

"That, unfortunately, is true."

How was Nadler's estate divided among the three?

He glanced at the paperwork again. "All three have equal shares in everything."

I frowned. This wasn't making sense. Why would the shape-shifter go to all the trouble of killing Nadler off, then divide the estate he'd murdered to get control of among three people?

When was the will drawn up?

His gaze flicked down to the bottom of the paper. "The same day he signed the deal with Trilby's and Appleby's heirs."

Which suggested an on-the-spot decision, but I very much doubted the man we were chasing ever did anything without forethought. *Is there anything else you can tell me about Nadler? Any reason you believe someone might want him dead?*

He frowned. "Not really."

I sighed. Logan hadn't actually given us anything we couldn't have found out via a little subversive hacking, so maybe his death had been nothing more than the face-shifter leaving no threads behind, no matter how small.

Thank you very much for your assistance, Mr. Logan—

"You could repay me by finding my limo, you know. It seems to have disappeared."

Just use your phone and call it, Mr. Logan. He wouldn't get anywhere with it, but hey, if it made him happy, then what the hell.

He made the right motions, and a somewhat fuzzy white limousine popped into existence. As Logan happily climbed in, I turned away. Time to return—

The thought was cut short by a scream.

A scream that suggested there was a woman on the astral plane in very big trouble.

I froze, not sure I could—or *should*—do anything. Then the scream echoed again, and it was so filled with fear and pain that goose bumps crawled across my imaginary skin. I glanced around for my watcher. He was standing about six feet away, his expression unconcerned as he looked in the direction from which the scream had come.

Are you going to do anything about that?

He turned to me, obviously surprised. *Why would I? I am here to report your actions—nothing more, nothing less. But there is nothing to stop you from stepping in.*

I guess not, I muttered, then closed my eyes and imagined myself standing near the screamer.

There was no obvious sense of movement, but I was suddenly somewhere I didn't know. The building outlines, though still shadowed, were sharper here, but rubbish lay everywhere, rats ran in full view, and there were vast puddles of putrid-looking water.

Not the sort of place I'd ever want to be—on this plane, or in life.

A woman stood ten feet away. She was reed thin, with limp blond hair and an almost gaunt face. Her clothes were little more than gray rags and seemed to be unraveling of their own accord, exposing jigsaw sections of her torso and legs. She wasn't trying to pull the threads back together, wasn't trying to do much of anything other than scream.

But maybe she couldn't do anything else. The man who stood in front of her had his palm pressed against her forehead and was burrowing ethereal fingers into her skull.

He was also the source of that uneasy sense of trouble I'd felt earlier—only it wasn't coming from the stranger himself, but rather from the area immediately around him. It was as if the air were so repelled by his presence that it violently recoiled.

And the air wasn't the only thing repelled. The Dušan crawled around my left arm, its dark eyes spitting fire, as if it wanted nothing more than to be free from the flesh that bound it to attack the man who stood before us.

A man I wasn't about to face unarmed.

I imagined Amaya in my hands, and she appeared in a blaze of purple fire, her normally shadowed blade so bright on the astral field it was almost impossible to look at her.

Hey, you. I projected my mind voice so hard it shook the very foundations of the buildings around us. *Leave that woman alone.*

He didn't unhand her. Didn't react in any way that I could immediately see. Then, slowly, he turned his head in my direction.

He had no *face*.

Where there should have been eyes, a nose, and a mouth, there was nothing. It was as if his features had been wiped clean. It was totally and utterly blank.

Impossible, I thought in disbelief. It had to be a trick of some kind. *Had* to be.

Go away. His voice was little more than a whisper, crawling around me like a dead thing.

I shivered and gripped Amaya harder. *Maybe you didn't hear me the first time. I said, leave that woman alone.*

I heard.

Then do as I say or the sword I bear will sever your ethereal head from its body.

I didn't know if that was possible, especially after Adeline saying you couldn't actually die on the plane. But my sword was from neither the real world nor the astral one. She was born of a demon's death, and was far more than mere steel. She had a life of her own, a serious hunger for blood, and she could destroy demons and spirits as easily as she did flesh. Surely it wasn't such a stretch to think she could also kill someone on the astral plane?

The stranger raised his featureless face, oddly looking like he was sniffing the air even though he had no nose. After a moment, he said, *As you wish.*

He released the woman and stepped back. She collapsed in a heap at his feet and remained there. Which was odd—why hadn't she zapped back to her body? In fact, why hadn't she done that when she was first attacked?

Now leave, I said. *Get off the fields.*

He didn't react, didn't reply. He just stood there, his unseeing face pointed in my direction, as if he were studying me. The unease crawling through me grew stronger, but I ignored it and imagined myself closer to the woman. The charm at my neck burned to life, its white light slashing through the shadows. Whoever—whatever—this man was, Ilianna's magic didn't like it.

Did you hear me? I swung Amaya in warning. She reacted fiercely to the vibration pouring away from the stranger, spitting and hissing purple fire that danced across the shadowed buildings around us.

I heard. His voice remained soft and oddly free of emotion. *But you should know that what I claim, I keep. You have saved no one here, huntress.*

I wouldn't be so sure of that, stranger.

He cocked his head sideways. If he'd had features, I think they would have appeared . . . amused. *If you are so confident that you can save her, why don't we play a little game?*

There wasn't a snowball's chance in hell of me playing *any* sort of game with a featureless freak on the astral plane. I swung Amaya again, her *kill, kill, kill* chant crystal clear in the back of my thoughts. For the moment, my desire for control was stronger than her need to attack, but I had to wonder if that would always be the case, given she'd already tried to take me over once before.

I'm not interested in playing games. I just want you gone.

Ah, but this game involves saving the woman's life. We both know you are interested in doing that, huntress, or you would not be here.

He was right, of course, but I saw no point in admitting the obvious.

He nodded in the woman's direction and continued. *She has twenty minutes of life left on earth. If you can find her in that time, I will let her live.*

Twenty minutes? That's hardly fair.

Life is never fair. He shrugged. *That is the offer. Take it or leave it.*

And if I don't take it?

Then she dies as I have planned, and you will be left to wonder if you could have done the impossible.

And with that, he was gone, taking with him the uneasy sense of trouble. As the charm's fierceness died to a more muted glow, I imagined Amaya sheathed, then knelt beside the woman.

Miss? Are you all right?

She didn't respond to the soft question, so I lightly touched her shoulder. She jumped, then shimmied away from me, her brown eyes wide and staring.

It wasn't so much the fear in her expression that surprised me, but rather the mark burned into her forehead. It was raw and weeping, as if it had only just been done. It was also K-shaped, with a tail that looped, reminding me oddly of a serpent. Two wounds marred her wrists, slicing up the center of her arms. While these were neither raw nor weeping, they'd split the skin open and looked painful. Two red marks also appeared to ring her calves, but from where I stood I couldn't really see if they were open wounds or not.

Adeline had said you couldn't be harmed on the astral plane, and yet this woman *had* been injured, and one of those wounds lay right where the stranger had been touching her. I doubted it was a coincidence.

Who are you? Her mind voice trembled with the fear so obvious in her pale features.

I'm a friend, I thought softly. *There was a man attacking you—*

Attacking? She frowned. *What do you mean, "attacking"? We were having sex, for fuck's sake!*

Sex? On the astral field? How the hell was that even possible? *That's not what it looked like. Besides, you were screaming in fear.*

She gathered the remnants of her clothing. *Just because I don't like it vanilla doesn't mean it wasn't sex.*

I frowned. She was making all the right sounds, but there was something not quite right about her eyes—something beyond the fear. It was almost as if someone else was staring out of them.

I shivered. *I need to know where you live, Miss—*

Like I'm about to tell you that! And with that, she disappeared.

I swore softly, then closed my eyes and imagined myself back in my body. I whooshed back with surprising speed, my eyes springing open as I gasped in shock.

"Returning swiftly can be quite painful when one isn't used to traveling on the astral plane," Adeline commented. "Lie there and rest. I'll bring you your tea."

"No!" I jerked upright, and immediately regretted it as my stomach jumped into my throat. I swallowed bile, then added, "We don't have time."

Adeline stopped and frowned down at me. "What do you mean?"

"I mean, I came across a woman being attacked by a man with no features." I pushed to my knees, but the room spun around me, and it was all I could do not to fall back down. "He gave me twenty minutes to try to save her on *this* plane."

"Meaning she *wasn't* actually being attacked on the astral plane. What you saw was merely a reflection of what is happening here."

"If that's the case, he's branding her with a hot iron and pulling her brains out."

Adeline went pale. "Then you're definitely dealing with a dark traveler."

"Yes." I pushed to my feet, then flung out an arm to steady myself, only to catch Azriel rather than the wall. The fingers that wrapped around mine were gentle steel, and heat leapt from his flesh, warming the chill from my body and lending me some much-needed strength.

"How are you going to find him if he has no features?" Adeline asked. "Did he give you any clue as to his identity? Did the woman?"

"No, so we're going to have to do this the hard way." I glanced at Azriel. "You need to take me to Stane's. *Now*. Adeline, I'll be back."

Azriel stepped close and wrapped his arms around my waist. His scent—a scent that was both masculine and sharply electric—filled every breath as his power burned through me, sweeping us from flesh to energy in an instant. A second later we were on the gray fields, but these were very different from the ones I traveled. The fields I knew were little more than shadowed echoes of the real world, a place where things not sighted suddenly gained substance. But in Azriel's arms, I saw the fields as a vast and beautiful place, filled with structures and life that were delicate and unworldly.

We re-formed outside of Stane's electronics shop in Clifton Hill, which happened to be on the very same street that Nadler's consortium had been attempting to purchase. In fact, only Stane's building and one other— a bar—remained in private hands.

I'd known Stane a good part of my life, simply because he was Tao's cousin. Tao, like Ilianna, was a childhood friend and current housemate, and he and Stane had come from the same brown werewolf pack. Their fathers were brothers—although Tao's had died when he was young, and Tao himself hadn't actually lived with the pack; he'd lived with his mother, who was human. Stane was a whiz at all things computer related, and he'd become a rather invaluable source of information and black market technology. If he couldn't get me the information I needed in record time, no one could.

"You should have just zapped us inside." I glanced at Azriel as I pushed open the somewhat ratty-looking door. A tiny bell rang cheerily above our heads. "It would have saved us a few seconds."

"Stane does not react well to sudden appearances." He shrugged.

I guess that was true—and certainly the last thing we needed right now was Stane passing out in shock. Once we were inside, the camera above us buzzed into action and began tracking our movements. Not that we could go far—the shimmer of light surrounding the small entrance was warning enough that a containment shield was in action.

"Stane, it's Risa." Impatience edged my voice as I stared up at the camera. "I need some help rather urgently."

"Well, it's about fucking time." His voice sounded tinny as it echoed from the small speaker near the camera. The shimmer flared briefly, then died. "I've been bored as hell lately."

"What?" I said, as I ran for the rear stairs. "The black market business isn't going so well at the moment?"

He appeared at the landing and gave me a wide smile. "It's going very well. But I've grown addicted to the challenges you give me. A little subversive hacking into government databases is good for the soul."

Despite the urgency of the situation, I laughed and kissed his cheek. Stane rather looked like his building— a slender, unholy mess. With his somewhat long and scruffy brown hair, his wrinkled blue shirt, and loose, ill-fitting shorts, he certainly didn't look like someone who was in any way dangerous—until you actually gazed into his honey-colored eyes. Stane was smarter and harder than he looked.

"So what is it this time?" he said, stepping to one side and waving us through.

"We have a life to save, and precisely eighteen minutes to do it in."

"Fuck!" He scraped a hand across his bristly chin, then reclaimed his seat at the computer system that dominated his living area. He shoved a second chair in my direction. "You really *are* pushing it this time. How can I help?"

"I need you to work up an image of the woman I have to find, and then I need you to find her address."

He swore again, then stretched out his fingers and cracked his knuckles. "Okay, hit me with the details."

I gave him everything I could remember, and within a couple of minutes we had an image of the woman I'd seen on the planes. He flicked it across to another screen, and the search began.

And all I could do was wait.

I pushed to my feet and began pacing. Stane watched me for a moment, then said, "Anything else?"

I inhaled deeply, then slowly released it. It didn't do much to ease the tension growing inside me. "Well, I also have the names of Nadler's heirs."

"How the hell did you manage that?"

I grimaced. "I had a conversation with a ghost."

He eyed me for a moment, then said, "I won't even ask. What are their names?"

"Harry Bulter, Jim O'Reilly, and Genevieve Sands."

"A woman?" Stane frowned. "I can understand naming a number of men, because as a face-shifter, he could step into their lives anytime he wished. But a male face-shifter cannot take the form of a female, and vice versa."

A fact that I knew, since I was a face-shifter myself. "He obviously has a reason for doing it, but it's not like the man we've been calling Nadler is working on any logical playing field, anyway."

"True." Stane typed the names into his system, then swished them across to a separate light screen. "You want a coffee or Coke while we wait?"

"Coke, thanks."

Stane glanced at Azriel, eyebrow raised in question. Azriel shook his head and I continued pacing, pausing only long enough to accept a can of Coke with a grunt of thanks. The time continued to tick away and it seemed to be taking forever to get our answer.

Stane reclaimed his seat and watched the screens, his expression intent, as if willing a prompt response. But another five minutes passed before the screen closest to him beeped. He put his coffee down and scooted forward.

"About time," I grumbled, stopping to peer over his shoulder.

"Believe it or not, that *was* actually fast." He ran a finger across the screen to highlight some lines, then enlarged them. "The woman you're looking for is Dorothy Hendricks, from Craigieburn."

I frowned. Craigieburn was a suburb on the northern edges of Melbourne, developed before the no-larger-than-a-postage-stamp housing plots of today, and popular with families thanks to its decent enough schools and leafy environs. It wasn't the sort of place I'd expected last night's woman to live. Given where I'd found her on the astral plane, I'd been expecting a suburb far grimmer. Grimier.

"What address? And what other information have you got on her?"

"Seventeen Crockett Avenue." He paused, and quickly scanned the screen. "There doesn't appear to be anything remarkable about her. Her parents are dead, and she has no siblings. According to her tax records, she works the night shift at the Nestlé factory in Campbellfield."

That raised my eyebrows. She hadn't looked like a factory worker, but then, what was a factory worker supposed to look like?

"Anything else?"

"No record of marriage or kids, no fines of any kind, good credit history, owns her home." He paused. "She's a vampire."

I blinked. That was something I *hadn't* expected. "When did she turn?"

He glanced at me. "About thirty years ago, according to the records. No history of trouble after her rebirth, and she was released from the care of her maker about twelve years ago."

According to Uncle Quinn, fledglings could be in the care of their creators for anywhere between ten and fifty years—it just depended on how quickly the newly fledged vampire learned to cope with all the sensations and needs that came with the state of being undead. That Dorothy had been released after eighteen years suggested she'd been a reasonably fast learner. "Does it list her creator on the certificate?"

It had been law for a few decades now that everyone who underwent the ceremony to become a vampire registered their details with the Births, Deaths, and Marriages Bureau. Once they *had* turned, their creator then had to register their "birth." There were still vamps who were turned illegally, of course, but the Directorate and the vampire council—both the high council and the local council—took a dim view of this and came down hard on the turnee and the turner.

Stane glanced briefly at the screen. "Bloke by the name of Martin Cresswell. You want me to do a search on him?"

"That would be great." I dumped the empty Coke can into the bin, then said, "Let me know if you find anything else."

He nodded, his expression concerned. "Good luck."

"We're going to need it." Especially when there were only eight and a half minutes left. I glanced at Azriel. "Can you take us to Dorothy's house?"

He didn't say anything, just wrapped his arms around me again. In an instant, we'd zipped through the gray fields, reappearing on the other side so quickly that my head spun and the bitter taste of bile rose up my throat again.

"You," he said, his voice severe as he stepped back but didn't quite release me, "need to eat."

"Like I've got the fucking time right now."

"I did not mean right now."

"Good." I scanned the home in front of us. It was nothing remarkable—just an ordinary brick house in a street filled with similar buildings. I pushed open a picket gate that had seen better days and ran for the front steps. There was a doorbell to the left of the door, so I leaned on it heavily, then rapped impatiently on the door itself. Inside, the chime and knocks echoed, but there was no response. If there was anyone inside, he or she was either deaf or dead.

"There is neither life, death, nor *undead* inside. The house is empty."

I glanced at my watch. Eight minutes left. Fuck, fuck, *fuck*! I closed my eyes and tried to remain calm. Tried to *think*. "Even if she's not there, there may be some clue—"

I didn't get to finish the sentence. He just caught me in his arms again and whisked us inside. I drew in a deep breath the second we re-formed, ignoring another rush of dizziness as I sorted through the various scents in the air. Lavender and furniture polish vied for prominence with the aroma of coffee. Underneath that lay the scent of femininity, though it was far more vague than it should have been if she spent the majority of her time here. Certainly in the apartment I shared with Ilianna and Tao, the dominating scents were horse and wolf, with the tang of females coming in a close third. The masculine, incandescent scent that was Tao was a distant fourth.

But there was no male scent here. Nothing to indicate she ever had any visitors, human or otherwise.

I growled in frustration and waved a hand at the first couple of rooms. "I'll search these; you search the ones at the back of the house."

He nodded and disappeared. I moved into the nearest room—a living room that was comfortably furnished and neat as a pin. I did a quick walk around, shifting various bits and pieces, but I couldn't find anything that jumped up and screamed *clue*.

Conscious that we were running out of time, I dashed into the room opposite. It was a bedroom—the main one, if the shoes lined up neatly along the end of the bed were any indication. I scanned the nearest bedside table, seeing nothing but change, then opened the drawers. Knickers and socks. I cursed, ran around the other side, and repeated the process. Nothing. *Fuck!*

"Risa," Azriel called. "Here!"

I spun and ran down the hall. Azriel stood near the phone at the end of the kitchen counter, and as I entered, he pushed a notepad toward me. On it was a series of K-shaped doodles, some with snakelike tails, some without. And in one corner, an address—Amcor, main entrance, Alphington—and a time: midnight last night.

I glanced at him. "We have four minutes left."

He didn't answer, just caught me in his arms again and swept us across the fields. This time, when we re-formed, I staggered and would have fallen if not for the fierceness of his grip on me.

He didn't say anything—he knew me well enough by now to know the futility of it—but his disapproval swept around me as sharply as any rebuke.

We'd reappeared in the middle of an old parking lot. I swung around, searching the old buildings, seeing the grime and the many shadows that haunted the place, even in the midmorning sunlight. The air was ripe with disuse, rubbish, and rats, and the wind whistled through the many broken windows. It was very similar to what I'd seen on the fields.

"There is magic in this place," Azriel said softly.

I gave him a sharp glance. "Good magic or bad magic?"

"Neither." He paused. "It sits in between."

How the hell could magic sit in between? "What about life? Can you sense the woman?"

He hesitated. "There is someone in the end of that L-shaped—"

I didn't wait for him to finish. I just ran, as fast as I could. I leapt the remnants of the gates and bolted for the shadowed building, nostrils flaring as I dragged in the scents. Death ran underneath all those I'd noted earlier.

No, no, *no*!

I crashed shoulder first into the door, sending it and myself falling into the building. I brushed my fingertips against the concrete to steady myself, then ran on, splashing through puddles and leaping over rubbish as I followed the nebulous scent of death through the various rooms—all the while hoping it wasn't the woman's death I could smell, but something else.

It was a small hope and, as it turned out, a vain one.

Chapter 2

Dorothy Hendricks lay on a table in the middle of the little room. She was naked, her body so pale and thin that I could count every rib. Though she wore no jewelry, something stuck out from her chest, slightly to the left of her breastbone. It took me a moment to realize it was a knitting-needle-sized piece of wood. She'd been staked.

And yet she looked at peace—her expression was serene, with a smile forever frozen on her lips.

Either she'd welcomed this death or she hadn't realized exactly what was happening to her. Given what she'd claimed on the astral plane, I had to guess the latter to be true, especially since there was little in the air to suggest anything sexual had been going on.

My gaze went to the four-inch cuts on her wrists. She'd obviously been bled out, but there was no evidence of it on the floor underneath her. Which meant someone had collected her blood—or consumed it. Shivers raced up and down my spine. I really didn't want to know what someone would do with that much blood, and I really, *really* didn't want to meet someone who could consume that much.

"We had time left," I said, my voice flat despite the anger that surged through me. "But he never intended for us to save her. He was just playing games."

"Perhaps, but this death was meant to be."

As Azriel spoke, the gossamer shape of Dorothy's soul rose from her flesh. She looked happy and content, offering her hand without qualm to the white-haired, white-winged reaper who suddenly appeared beside her body. It really didn't surprise me that she'd chosen the more traditional version of the reaper. Despite her words on the astral plane, there'd been nothing out of the ordinary to be seen in her house. Certainly nothing that suggested she liked her life to be anything other than vanilla.

So why had she become a vampire?

I watched them walk onto the gray fields and disappear, then glanced at Azriel. "Why would a woman like Dorothy be the target of someone so dangerous? She may have been a vampire, but if the information Stane uncovered is to be believed, she was harmless in every other way possible."

"Perhaps it was nothing more than a weak astral spirit unwittingly attracting a darker soul."

"Perhaps." The image of the faceless man ran through my mind, and I shivered again. He'd called me a huntress, but he'd been the one hunting, not me. "But I have a suspicion that his choice of victim was deliberate, not one governed by chance."

"Yet he offered you the opportunity to save her. Even if that was never to be, it seems an odd decision for one who takes no chances."

"I know." My gaze swept Dorothy's body and came

to rest on her calves. Cuts ringed them both, the wounds gaping. I frowned. "Why would he cut her tendons like that?"

"There is a belief in some cultures that cutting the tendons in the legs prevents the soul from rising."

And he'd staked her because she was a vampire. "Then why bleed her out? It seems a little overboard."

"Perhaps he merely wished to be triple sure of his kill."

"Perhaps." I scanned the concrete again. Azriel had said earlier that he'd sensed magic, but there was little indication of it. No protective circle, no candles, nothing that in any way suggested there was ever a practitioner here.

"What do you wish to do now?" he asked.

"What I wish to do is go home, eat the biggest steak I can find, have a long soak in the bath, then catch a week's worth of sleep." I grimaced and dug my vidphone out of my pocket. "What I *have* to do, however, is ring Uncle Rhoan."

His expression, when he answered, was resigned. "So tell me where the body is."

A wry smile touched my lips, although—sadly—his presumption was all too correct. Most of my calls to him of late *had* been about the dead or the about to be dead. Still, I couldn't help saying, "Hey, I might just be ringing to say hello to my favorite uncle."

He snorted softly, amusement crinkling the corners of his gray eyes. "We both know if you just wanted a chat, you'd ring my sister. Who, by the way, is a little peeved that you missed the weekly get-together."

Damn, so I had. Mom and Riley had met for coffee and cake every week for as long as I could remember, and it was a tradition Riley and I were determined to continue.

While I *did* have a good excuse—I'd still been in the process of recovering from the fights with both my sword and the Rakshasa, the spirit who'd answered the call of ghosts desperate for revenge at one of the blood whore clubs run by the high vampire council—I couldn't exactly tell Riley that because she didn't know about my connection with the vampire council. If she ever *did* find out about it, she'd hit the roof, not to mention shove me somewhere safe while she confronted Hunter and her cronies. And as strong as Riley, Quinn, and Rhoan were, I had a suspicion it would take more than the three of them to outmaneuver Hunter.

"You need to ring her," Rhoan continued. "She's worried. We're both worried."

"Then you need to not tell her so much about what's happening."

He snorted again. "Yeah, like that's going to work. You know she can smell trouble a mile away." He paused. "Okay, I have your location and will be there in twenty. Don't disturb any evidence."

"I won't. See you soon."

I shoved the phone back into my pocket, my gaze on Dorothy's body. Why on earth would anyone go to so much trouble to destroy someone who was, it seemed, totally harmless? It made no sense, and part of me—a small, insane part—wanted to unravel the puzzle.

"Let your uncle find whoever is responsible for

this," Azriel said. "It is not something we should get involved in."

"No, it isn't." I couldn't help but look again at the woman's face, though, and there was an unpleasant suspicion in my heart that this was far from over. "We've enough on our plate as it is."

Including, I thought, with a glance at my watch, a date with a locker at Southern Cross Station in just over an hour.

I rubbed my arms, then scanned the immediate area. Rhoan might have warned me not to disturb any evidence, but that didn't mean I couldn't look. Besides, I needed to do something while I waited for him.

Water and trash lay everywhere, and the air was ripe with rotting rubbish and mold. The vaguest aroma of blood laced the thicker, more unpleasant scents in the room, but there was little else. If the stranger—or anyone else, for that matter—*had* been here, he had no distinct smell. Which went with his lack of a face, I guess.

"Someone *was* here," Azriel commented. "The air still resonates with energy."

I glanced at him. His blue eyes held echoes of the anger that burned within me. "Can you track it?"

He shook his head. "They used magic to leave."

"And yet there's no trace of magic on the ground."

"Magic can take many forms. The charm around your neck, for example."

"But this charm is minor magic compared to something that could transport a person." My gaze went back to Dorothy and I studied the wounds on her wrists again. "How can there be no evidence of bleeding when she's been bled out?"

"I do not know."

I squatted next to the table. The concrete was thick with layers of grime and god knows what else, but the area underneath her hanging wrist bore a faint ring-shaped mark. The blood hadn't been consumed—it had been collected.

Why would anyone want to do that? I glanced up at Azriel, but he merely shrugged. "I am not an expert on humans and all their eccentricities."

"So the person behind this was human?"

"I would have sensed either a spirit or a demon."

That the no-face stranger might be human somehow made him seem all the more creepy. I shivered, then rose and walked around the rest of the table. Other than a matching ring in the grime on the opposite side of the floor, there was little to see.

I retreated to a wall and sat down on the floor. God, if I didn't get some food and rest soon, I was going to end up back in bed and sick as hell.

Azriel strolled around to my side of the table. "Shuffle forward."

I raised an eyebrow, but did as ordered. He sat down behind me, then placed his fingers against my temples and began to gently massage them. Heat radiated from the epicenter of his touch, and the pain began to recede.

"Azriel," I said, somewhat reluctantly, "I thought we agreed you shouldn't be healing me. You're the better fighter, so it's more important that you keep your strength rather than sharing it with me—"

"If you can't think and move, then me being the better fighter is irrelevant." He paused, but his fingers continued to work their magic. "Besides, I can no longer fully heal you. I merely revive."

"That's splitting hairs and you know it." Not that I wanted him to stop. It felt far too good—both his touch and the sense of reassurance it provided.

"Reviving does not require the same output of energy."

I wasn't believing *that* for an instant, but I let it slide, and asked instead, "I remember Tao saying something about your inability to heal—what's gone wrong? You had no problems healing me previously."

"I know." He hesitated. "And I'm not exactly sure why this has happened."

Liar. "It hasn't got anything to do with Amaya's presence, has it?"

"No. Your sword will never harm you."

I snorted softly. "Then what do you call her attempt to gain control over my body?"

"An attempt to save your life. As she saw it, she was the stronger spirit, and therefore the logical choice to control your flesh."

And I'd agreed to that control—temporarily. I wouldn't have survived the onslaught of the Rakshasa otherwise. But once I was safe, Amaya had refused to leave my flesh, and it took every ounce of strength I'd had left to get her back into the sword. "Does that mean every time I'm feeling low she's going to make a takeover bid?"

"Only if she believes your life would be in danger if

she did not. And remember, you *did* invite the invasion."

Something I will *not* be doing again. Not unless I'm at death's door.

Ten minutes later, I sensed Rhoan's approach. Azriel rose and held out a hand. I twined my fingers through the warmth of his, and he pulled me up. We ended up standing so close that my breasts touched his chest and his breath teased my mouth with possibilities. God, it would take only the slightest movement on either of our parts for our lips to meet, but as my eyes searched his, I knew he wouldn't do it. Not this time, not yet. He was still fighting to delay the inevitable.

"Nothing is inevitable." There was a huskiness in his voice that suggested his control was closer to the knife edge than I'd thought. "And you have no idea of the risk we run—"

Behind us someone cleared his throat, and I jumped as if stung. Rhoan walked toward us, amusement crinkling the corners of his gray eyes.

"Riley will be pleased," he said.

No, she won't, I thought grumpily. Not when I was having zero luck in getting Azriel back into bed—a problem *she'd* never had when it came to men, human or otherwise. I waved a hand at Dorothy's body. "I haven't touched her, and only went close enough to the table to check whether her blood had been collected or not."

His gaze slipped to the woman on the table, and in the blink of an eye, he became the guardian rather than the uncle. It was a chilling change.

"What?" I said warily, knowing there had to be something more behind his reaction than merely this particular death.

"I've seen this before."

I briefly closed my eyes. Of *course* he had. Why I'd thought this was a one-off murder I had no idea. "How many have there been?"

"Three in three days." His expression was as intense and cold as his voice. "He normally contacts the Directorate an hour after the death."

I raised my eyebrows. "Why would he do that?"

"To taunt us." His gaze centered on me. "How did you get involved?"

I told him about the gray fields and what I'd witnessed there.

"Unfortunately, it doesn't give us much to go on." He paused, then added more severely, "You're not intending to chase this one down yourself, are you?"

It was a warning more than a question, and I gave him a lopsided smile. "No. I'm not a guardian and have no desire to be."

He grunted. "That's the first sensible thing I've heard you say in weeks."

"I *can* do sensible."

"Really?" Rhoan's tone was disbelieving. "This is the first evidence of it that I've seen, and I've known you a very long time."

I punched him lightly—though it was like hitting a brick wall—and he grinned. "Go home and get some rest, Ris. You look beat."

I raised my eyebrows. "You don't need a statement?"

"Yeah, but later will do."

"Thank you." I dropped a kiss on his cheek, then left. Once we were outside, I raised my face to the sky. Though it was barely ten, the promise of heat was in the air, and sunshine bathed my skin. But it wasn't warm enough to burn away the uneasy fear that had first stirred on the astral plane. The no-face killer wasn't my problem, but I still couldn't escape the notion that he and I would meet again. I had to hope that notion was wrong, because I needed to get back to the business of chasing down portal keys and deadly sorcerers.

"Do you wish to return home now?" Azriel asked softly.

"I wish I could." Wished he would just take me in his arms and hold me. Just hold me.

But he didn't react in any way—even though he could follow my thoughts and knew my desires as clearly as if I'd spoken them—and I sighed softly. "But I need to collect my car from Adeline's, and then we have that meeting at the rail station."

"You should eat—"

I cut him off with an abrupt wave of the hand. "I'll grab a burger and chips along the way."

"That's hardly what you need right now—"

"It's food," I cut in wearily. "And it's better than nothing. You're not my mom, so don't nag me, Azriel."

"Someone has to." His blue eyes flashed with the annoyance he wasn't quite containing. "Because you seem absurdly determined to run yourself into the ground."

"And we can't have that when there's keys to be found, can we?"

"As I have said before," he said coldly, "that is not a fair comment."

I sighed. "Sorry."

He once again accepted the apology with an almost regal incline of his head, then said, his tone still frosty, "You wish to go back to Adeline's now?"

"Yes."

He stepped close, and once more whisked us through the gray fields. Adeline jumped when we reappeared in her living room.

"Gracious," she said, placing one hand on her heart. "You could at least give some warning before you pop into existence like that."

"I thought you could sense reapers." I stepped free from the warmth of Azriel's arms, but distance did little to ease the fires his presence ignited. I picked up the cup of tea Adeline had poured earlier and gulped it down. I might not be fond of the stuff, but it was better than nothing.

"If they are on this plane, yes, but not before then." She eyed me for a moment, then said, "You didn't succeed in saving her."

"No, but only because he didn't keep his end of the bargain. He killed her too early."

"He is a dark energy, so that can be expected."

Stupid of me to expect otherwise, I suppose. "This isn't his first kill, though. The Directorate is on the case."

"At least you could provide a description—"

"No, I couldn't," I interrupted. Because he didn't have a face on the fields."

"That *is* unusual." She frowned. "How indistinct were his features?"

"Totally—he had no facial features whatsoever. It was as if someone had completely erased them."

"But that's not possible." She hesitated. "Well, obviously, it is, but it is extremely rare."

"Why?" I asked curiously. "I mean, you can change your outward appearance, can't you? Things like clothes, shoes, even hair color?"

"Yes, but it is almost impossible to change your actual features. Normally your spirit won't allow it."

"Well, this guy's spirit *did*." I paused, remembering the sensations that had rolled over me. "I actually felt him out there long before the woman screamed. It was as if the astral plane was rejecting his presence. It set up this really weird vibration."

Adeline chewed her lip for a moment, then said, "And the woman? What was she actually doing?"

I described what I'd seen, then added, "The woman claimed they were having sex, but that sure as hell *wasn't* what it looked like." I paused. "Is it even possible to have sex on the astral plane?"

"It's possible, but you have to be very careful about who and what you form such a connection with. Once you open that door, it may never close."

I shivered. "Could this guy be some form of incubi?"

"Again, it's possible, but both incubi and succubi tend to take physical advantage of us on *this* plane. It is rare for them to act on the astral plane."

"Rare means it's still possible."

"Yes, but from what you described, he was not sexually interacting with the woman, despite what the woman believed."

"Is there any way to stop him?"

"On the astral plane? Not that I'm aware of. I would think you'd have to find him in the real world."

And that wasn't going to be easy. Nor was it my job. *Leave it to Rhoan*, I reminded myself, and set the cup back down. "Thanks again for your help, Adeline."

"No problem." She escorted me to the door, then added, "I'm here if you need anything else."

I gave her a smile and headed down the street to my SUV. The Toyota wasn't my preferred mode of transport—that honor went to the silver Ducati I'd bought when RYT's, the café I co-owned and ran with Ilianna and Tao, had made its first profit. Unfortunately, the Ducati and I had a serious parting of ways thanks to a pack of demons, and she was still in the shop getting repaired. She was an old bike, and her parts were hard to get, so I was going to be without her for a while. Which was why I was seriously considering buying another one. I preferred the feel and freedom of a bike as opposed to the sedate safety of a vehicle like the SUV. Even Tao's Ferrari couldn't give the high of the bike— not on Melbourne streets, anyway.

A breeze stirred the air, cooling the early-morning heat but doing little to ease the furnace-like intensity of the man who walked close behind me. Part of me wished I could ignore him, that we could just go back to the time when the attraction was muted and he was more antagonistic. More distant. But there was no way on earth to put *that* particular genie back in the bottle.

After a moment, I asked, "What did you mean before, when you said I had no idea of the risk we were running?"

"Just that. This attraction breaks all the rules—"

"Your rules, not mine."

"Yes." He paused. "I thought we had agreed that we should—"

"No," I snapped back. "*You* decided we should attempt to ignore this. *I* had no choice."

"Because of the danger—"

"To whom?" I swung around and stabbed a finger into his chest. It felt like I was hitting steel. "Not to me, buddy boy, and don't pretend otherwise. You're protecting your ass here, not mine."

"True." His expression was as enigmatic as ever, and yet there was an undercurrent in the air that was both frustration and anger. At himself, at me, at the situation. "But you have no idea of the dangers I face."

"No, because you won't fucking *explain* them to me." I glared at him for a moment, then shook my head and walked on. "You know what? Forget it. It's not important."

"If it wasn't important, you would not be this angry."

I snorted softly and just kept moving. He was silent until we got to the SUV, then appeared in the passenger seat.

"As I said before," he commented, as I pulled out

into the traffic, "the longer I remain in flesh form, the more I take on certain human characteristics."

"So? It's not like a little human emotion is going to destroy you or anything, is it?"

"*That*," he said, his voice holding an edge that suggested he was barely holding on to his patience, "is where you are very wrong."

I glanced at him sharply. "How the fuck is that even possible? I mean, emotion *isn't* a physical force. Being emotional *can't* destroy you." I paused, then remembered Jak, the man I'd thought I would marry one day, and all the heartbreak he'd caused me. "Although sometimes it does feel like it can."

"While gaining the emotions that come with flesh form is, of itself, not dangerous to us, the fact that you and I are connected at a chi level *makes* it so."

I slowed down as the lights ahead went to red, then said, "Why?"

He hesitated. "A chi connection is a connection of life forces—"

"I'm well aware what a chi connection is," I snapped. "Just tell me why you believe it's so damn dangerous."

He released a breath that was more a hiss. "It's dangerous because it can lead to assimilation."

I blinked. "Assimilation?"

"It happens when a reaper becomes so attuned to a particular human that their life forces merge, and they become as one."

"No—"

"Yes," he spat back. His expression was as grim as I'd ever seen it. "If that happens, my reaper powers will become muted, and I will never again be able to function as a soul bearer."

"But you can still be a Mijai?"

"Yes. But this is not a position I wish to retain for eternity." He glanced at me. "And I suspect you would not wish the connection between us to strengthen any further, or become permanent."

"God, no." I liked Azriel—a lot—but he wasn't Mr. Long Term. And neither was my Aedh lover, Lucian. I wanted someone who was flesh and blood *real*, someone who could give me a family and a life on *this* plane.

The lights changed again, so I pressed the accelerator and continued. "Does that mean the attraction between us is a sign that we're on the cusp of assimilation?"

"Possibly." He looked away for a moment, studying the road ahead. "But it is never wise to play with fire."

"We knew it wasn't wise when we made love," I commented. "It didn't stop either of us."

"No." The ghost of a smile crossed his lips. "And as much as I cannot regret that moment, to continue down that path is to risk the link strengthening into assimilation."

"Then you're going to have to be the strong one, because I'm damn sure I won't be." I tried to envision being around him and not being able to touch him. It just wasn't possible.

"If I was capable of such strength," he said quietly, "there would not have been a first time."

My gaze briefly met his. Deep in his differently colored blue eyes desire burned. He might be keeping it in check better than I was, but he definitely *wasn't* as immune to my nearness as his actions sometimes led me to believe.

I swung onto Spencer Street and headed toward Southern Cross Station. "You do realize this decision of yours means that you can't object to me being with Lucian. I may not be driven by the moon's heat as most werewolves are, but I *do* have an above-average sex drive."

I didn't need to see his expression to know that his anger had just ratcheted up several notches. The force of it singed my skin and senses. "You know I do not trust the Aedh."

Yeah, I did. Just like I knew that his distrust—hell, I'd even call it hatred—left him unable to even *say* Lucian's name. It would have been amusing if it wasn't so damn frustrating.

"And we both know," I snapped back, "that your distrust stems more from the fact that *I'm with him* than from anything he's actually done."

For once, he didn't dispute it. "I am not jealous, if that is what you are implying."

"Then why do you have a problem with me being with him?"

"He is using you."

"We're using each other."

"Yes, but his reasons are not what he states. He lies, Risa. I can taste it."

"If he's lying, then he's doing it so well my internal radar isn't picking it up."

"He has been earthbound for many, many centuries. Have no doubt that he is well practiced in more than the art of sex."

That, at least, was something we both agreed on. But it still didn't mean Lucian was lying to me—or rather, I hoped it didn't. I swung into the parking lot under the Flinders Street bridge and squeezed into a spot between one of the bridge stanchions and a large four-wheel drive.

I turned off the engine, then faced him. "You can't have it both ways. Either you and I run the risk of assimilation, or you accept the fact that I will be with others. No more shitty aloofness."

"The first is not an option, and the second will not be easy."

"I didn't think it would be."

When he didn't say anything else, I climbed out of the car and headed for the Southern Cross railway station. The building's undulating roofline gleamed crisply in the bright sunshine and, as ever, reminded me of snow mounds—albeit snow mounds covered in pigeons and pigeon poop. A constant rush of people flowed in and out of the station, and the vast area under the unusual roof was filled with the sounds of chatter, footsteps, whistles, and trains.

I made my way through the interior to the main locker area, my footsteps slowing as I neared the doorway. I flared my nostrils, dragging in the air, and I couldn't smell anything out of the ordinary. But I hadn't the last time I was here, either, and that time two Razan—the human slaves of the Aedh—had been waiting for me.

"Anything?" I asked softly.

Azriel shook his head. "There is no human or non-human life within."

"Which doesn't mean there isn't a trap waiting inside."

"No." He paused. "There is no sense of magic, however."

"That's something, I guess."

I considered the doorway for a few seconds longer, then took a deep breath to fortify my nerves and headed in. The locker room was large and the air cool. There were two rows of cream-colored lockers in the center of the room, while more lockers lined the walls. The one I wanted sat about midway along the central locker row. I dug the little key out of my pocket and walked toward them. Trepidation crawled across my skin. Nothing, no one, was here, and yet every sense I had tingled.

My fingers shook as I opened the door. It was a stupid and illogical response given everything I'd survived over the last couple of weeks, but I just couldn't help it. I *feared* my father. Feared him more than the Raziq themselves, even though he'd done little more than threaten me and my friends if I didn't comply with his wishes.

And his threats were nothing compared to what the Raziq had actually done—they'd torn me apart, placed a tracker in the fabric of my heart, and then rebuilt me.

Perhaps *that* was the problem. I knew what the Raziq were capable of, and I knew what they wanted. Hell, I knew what Azriel, the Mijai, and even the vampire council wanted from me. But my father's motives were little more than murk. All I could be sure of was that what he *said* he wanted and what he actually *planned* were two entirely different things.

It was the *not* knowing that scared the shit out of me. That, and the intuition that he could be far more dangerous than the Raziq as a whole ever could be.

The locker door swung open, revealing a totally empty interior. No letter, nothing to indicate what he wanted or what I was supposed to do next. It didn't make sense. Why send me here if he didn't intend to leave instructions?

"What the fuck is going—"

The rest of the sentence died in my throat, because it suddenly felt like someone had a hand around my heart and was threatening to squeeze the life out of me.

And hot on the heels of *that* came the awareness of an approaching presence. Only it wasn't body heat I sensed, wasn't humanity, but rather the heat of a being that was all energy, all power.

An Aedh.

My father, to be precise.

Chapter 3

As the awareness of my father's presence grew, so did the ache in my heart, until all I felt was pain, inside and out.

I doubled over, unable to do anything more than gasp. But it wasn't a heart attack. It was something far more deadly—the transmitter the Raziq had placed in my heart, reacting to my father's presence.

Calling the Raziq, telling them he was coming.

And I could barely even breathe, let alone give him any sort of warning.

An instant later, I was flung up against the lockers, my feet off the ground and a band of iron against my neck.

"What have you done?" The voice was a deeper, angrier version of mine, and it seemed to shake the foundations of the room around us. "What have you *agreed* to?"

I opened my mouth to answer, but no words came out because no air was getting in. Panic surged, and for a moment I wondered if he intended to kill me in sheer and utter rage.

Blue-edged steel appeared in my line of vision, the sword's sharp point aimed at the heart of the fierce energy holding me captive.

"Tell us where we can find the keys," Azriel said flatly. "Or die now."

Deep inside me anger flared. *For fuck's sake, Azriel, I'm choking and in serious pain here, in case you didn't notice!*

He either didn't hear me or didn't care. Neither, apparently, did my father. The iron band of energy continued to squeeze my neck, and it felt like my lungs were about to burst. Tiny spots began to dance in front of my eyes.

"If you kill me, reaper, you will fail in your quest to capture the keys."

There was no hurry in my father's voice, no urgency. As the shadows of unconsciousness began to crowd close, I wondered where the hell the Raziq were. At least their arrival would break this uncaring tableau.

"As will everyone else who seeks them," Azriel replied. "That is an outcome I could live with."

It was an outcome I could live with, too. If I got to live, that was.

"You and I both know such an outcome would be unacceptable to those who sent you here, reaper." Amusement ran through my father's deep tones. "It would appear we have reached an impasse."

Azriel!

The mental shout was filled with desperation, and his gaze flickered briefly toward me. Frustration and anger burned in his eyes. "Release her. Or I *will* kill you."

And *hurry*. The spots were getting larger, my heart felt like it was about to shatter, and the need for air was so fierce my lungs were on fire.

"You won't kill me, reaper." The trace of amusement was gone from his voice. "As I've already stated, you need the information I carry too much."

"And we both need her *alive*. Release her—now!" Valdis's flames skittered across the fierce energy that was my father's presence, enveloping him in a fiery cage.

Whether it was the threat of the flames or simply the realization that he *did* need me alive, the steely band of energy bruising my neck suddenly disappeared and I collapsed to the ground. There I remained, on hands and knees, dragging in shuddering gasps of air and grateful that I could still do so.

"You bear the device of the Raziq in your body," my father said. Though the force of his anger no longer held me captive, it vibrated through the undernotes of his voice. "Why?"

Because I had no fucking choice, I thought, but the words remained locked in my throat as I continued to suck air into my still burning lungs.

God, where the hell were the Raziq? My father might have released his death grip on me, but the Raziq's transmitter had not. The pain of the device was all-encompassing, and spots still danced madly across my vision.

"It was not her choice," Azriel answered. "And if you know a means of removing it without killing her, tell us."

"There is no removal except death." My father paused, and the energy of him pulsated. "The Raziq come. I will find another way to contact you."

"Leave a damn note—" I croaked.

"No," he said.

"Why the fuck not?"

"Because I need to read your mind and understand what the players around you do."

And despite the net of fire enveloping his form, the force that was my father disappeared. I couldn't say I was entirely sorry to see him go. I might not have gotten any answers, but at least the fire in my heart began to ebb away. It left me trembling and weak.

"I'm afraid it is not over yet." Azriel tucked an arm under my arm and hauled me upright. "The Raziq come, as he said."

The words had barely left his mouth when another storm swamped me. Panic surged, but I drew Amaya and tried to ignore it. Of course, past experience told me she wouldn't be enough against the force of them, but at least this time I had Azriel by my side. Surely *he* wouldn't fall victim to the mind tricks the Raziq had used last time I was with them.

Fire dripped from the points of the two swords. It hissed and spat as it hit the concrete, and spread out in a sweeping arc, forming an incandescent barrier around us. It was almost as if the swords had drawn a line and were daring the Raziq to cross it.

The storm grew stronger, until I was being physically buffeted by it. I narrowed my gaze against the dust and rubbish flying through the air, my breath caught somewhere in my throat and my stomach churning. Every time I'd faced the Raziq, something had gone wrong.

Every single damn time.

"Not this time," Azriel said. He took a step forward, half protecting me with his body.

No protect! Amaya's protest echoed through my brain. *Want to kill.*

There is time enough for that, I snapped, my gaze on the flicker that was growing beyond the circle of fire. Once upon a time I would not have seen it, but my sight seemed to have altered fractionally since Amaya had become one with me.

Want now, she grumbled, but her voice had at least lowered a couple of octaves.

Soon. I waved her lightly back and forth. Her fire spat through the air, reaching past the wall of fire, landing near the edge of the Raziq's shimmery presence. But there was more than one here. There *had* to be. The wash of energy was too fierce.

And Azriel's readiness to attack was so strong that the force of it vibrated through every part of me, vying for prominence with the energy crawling across my skin.

"I told you my father would sense your approach," I croaked, before either the Raziq could say anything or Azriel could react. "He's far more cunning than you give him credit for."

Red flames flickered down Valdis's sides. I wondered if it was an indicator of the sword's annoyance or her master's.

"It is also possible that you warned him."

The voice was cool, without inflection or emotion, but it nevertheless sent a chill down my spine. This was one of the Raziq who'd torn me apart to place the tracker in my heart.

"I *didn't* warn him, trust me on that. I want as little to do with him as I do with you."

"That, at least, is true." The energy in the air sharpened. "Do not release your weapon, Mijai. There are too many of us here, and your numbers are few enough."

"Our numbers are irrelevant." Though his voice was as calm and cool as the Raziq's, his stance had shifted imperceptibly. He was readying for action. "What matters is my ability to counter your presence, and *that* is not in question."

The fierceness in the air suddenly sharpened, and a thick sense of impending doom swamped me. If Azriel attacked, he'd die. I was as sure of that as I was of the moon rising tonight. There was no way known that I was about to let that happen.

I stepped forward and wrapped my fingers around his arm. It felt like I was gripping stone.

The force of Valdis's flames ramped up, but Azriel didn't react. Which didn't mean he wasn't *feeling* anything. The force of it just about blew my brain circuits.

"Your presence here does nothing to encourage my father to come back," I said, trying to keep calm against the twin storms buffeting me. "If you want him, you had better leave."

"He now knows about the tracker. The point of it is useless."

My mouth went suddenly dry. If the tracker was useless, did that mean I was as well? I swallowed heavily, and somehow said, "And here I was thinking the Aedh were clever enough to work out a way around that."

He obviously didn't catch the sarcasm in my voice. "That is without question. But your father is also Aedh—he will find a means to mute the transmitter."

No doubt. "Then you'll just have to work faster than him, won't you?"

"Or develop a different way of drawing him to you." He paused. "We will be in contact, Risa Jones."

The threat hung in the air as the energy of their presence began to dissipate. Azriel wrenched his arm from my grip, then drew Valdis back and released her in one violent movement. The sword sang through the air, the sound fierce, joyous. She hit the fading remnants of the shimmer and there was a short, sharp explosion, accompanied by a shrill scream. Then there was no energy, no Raziq.

Only fury.

Valdis looped around and returned to her master. Azriel caught her one-handed, then swung to face me. His expression was as angry as I'd ever seen it.

"Do not *ever* do that again." Though his voice was flat, every inch of him seemed to vibrate. Valdis's steel wasn't even visible, so dark were her flames.

And Amaya responded, her hissing fierce enough inside my head to make my eyes water. She was ready to protect, whether it be against foe *or* friend.

"Azriel—"

"I am here to protect *you*, not the other way around."

"You would have *died*." I sheathed Amaya—although it didn't shut her up—and rubbed my arms. Not that it did much against the force still assaulting me or the chill that the mere *thought* of losing him sent through me.

"There is always the Aedh," he practically spat. "You trust him so much, after all."

Anger surged. Anger *and* hurt. "Damn you, Azriel, that was totally uncalled-for!"

I shouldered past him, blinking back ridiculous tears as I stepped over the dying embers of our swords' fire. Damn it, far worse had been said to me over the years, so why would I let a comment like *that* get past the armor?

Because, my inner voice whispered, *you care more than you should. More than is wise.*

And he *didn't*. Because he was energy rather than flesh and didn't do emotions the same way the rest of us did. I knew that. Just as I knew his mission would *always* come first, no matter what. But the knowledge didn't help ease the pain of *that* situation *or* this one.

I made it five steps past the flames before he caught my hand and stopped me.

"I'm sorry," he said softly. "I should not have said that."

"No," I answered, not turning around and still blinking furiously.

He hesitated. "I did not mean to hurt you."

My smile held little humor. "If you didn't intend to hurt, you shouldn't have said the words."

"I agree. Risa, please, look at me."

I closed my eyes and took a deep, somewhat shuddering breath, then obeyed.

"I *am* sorry." He wiped a lone tear from my cheek with his thumb. "It will not happen again."

My gaze scanned his, but I could see nothing more than regret there. Whatever else he might be feeling or thinking, he was controlling it tightly. I sighed and rested my forehead against his shoulder.

"I'm afraid I can't offer the same. If I think you're going to die, Azriel, I'll do what it takes to protect you. I can't do anything else. I need you."

And not just for protection.

He brushed a kiss across the top of my head. Warmth tingled through me, filling the spaces that had been so recently shivering under the force of his fury. "If dying is my fate, then so be it. I am here to do a job, Risa, and neither of us should forget that."

"You can't do that job if you're dead."

"As I have said, if death is my fate, then so be it. You are the important one in this equation. You and the keys."

"And I'm only important because I'm the only way to those keys." I snorted softly. "You know, if I *did* die, the world would be better off. No one would be able to find the keys or open hell's portals."

"If you think your father or the Raziq would stop searching simply because you were dead, you are sorely mistaken." Azriel's voice held a sharp edge. "Death cures nothing, Risa."

Maybe. Maybe not. I pulled away from the comfort

of his touch. "Let's go back to the car. I need to go home."

He released my hand and I walked out the door— only to run nose-first into an all-too-familiar chest.

"Speak of the devil and he arrives," Azriel muttered.

I shot him a warning glance, then stepped back. If ever there was a man who was perfectly formed in every imaginable way, Lucian was it. He was truly beautiful to look at, and yet there was nothing effeminate about his looks or his presence. He was tall, towering over me by a good six inches, and his build was that of a warrior—muscular and strong.

He had the facial features of an angel, and in the past—before his golden wings had been torn off—he probably would have been mistaken for one. Because even though reapers were the true soul guides, it was the Aedh who were the source of the angel seen in so many myths. And like many of those mythical angels, he had golden hair and eyes that were the most glorious shade of jade, but his were so full of power that it was almost impossible to meet them without flinching.

Normally, my heart rate would have leapt into overdrive at the mere sight of him, but given my recent brushes with both my father and the Raziq, I couldn't muster anything more than annoyance—though it was edged with a bit of suspicion.

"What are you doing here, Lucian?"

His eyebrows rose. "We haven't seen each other for almost a week, and this is the greeting I get?"

"It is when you suddenly appear where you're not supposed to be."

"Last time I looked, this was a public train station, not a private one." His expression was amused, despite the slight edge in his voice.

"You know what I meant."

"I do." His gaze ran past me. "So nice to see you again, reaper. And I can see by the bruises around Risa's lovely neck that you've been doing an outstanding job of protecting her again."

Azriel didn't reply, but then, he didn't have to. Even Lucian couldn't have missed the sudden jump in air temperature. I wondered briefly just how dark Valdis's flames were, but didn't turn around to check.

"Stop avoiding the question, Lucian. Why are you here?"

He snorted softly. "You were here to meet your father, were you not? I thought I might be of some use—especially since the Raziq were likely to turn up and cause problems."

"But how the hell did you know we were even going to be here? It's not like we've been anywhere near each other recently, so you couldn't have read it in my thoughts."

The Aedh generally could read human—or non-human—minds only when they were in close proximity to them. However, they formed a strong mental link with their partners during the act of sex, enabling them to hear their thoughts from a distance.

That bond was—according to Lucian—somewhat

inoperative between the two of us. In fact, he'd claimed he could read my thoughts only when he was physically making love to me. Whether that was true or not I had no idea. I trusted him, but no matter what Azriel might think, it wasn't blind trust. I knew he had secrets. Knew they were more than likely dangerous ones.

"If you do not wish anyone to know where you are," he said, "then you had better inform your friends of this fact."

"Ilianna told you?" That surprised me. I would have expected a little more caution, even though she knew Lucian was involved in our quest for the keys.

"No. I was at your home waiting to see you, and the note from your father was lying in plain view on the table. If you didn't want anyone to know where you were, you should have hidden the evidence."

That was true enough, I guess. But I hadn't thought it necessary to hide the note in the safety of our own home. Yet . . . something still niggled. And I wasn't entirely sure whether it was disbelief or Azriel's distrust flowing through the far reaches of my thoughts.

"Well, as it turns out, you've missed all the action."

He raised an eyebrow. "What happened?"

"My father was less than impressed by the discovery that I have a tracker in my heart. He left the minute he sensed the Raziq's approach."

I stepped around him, then headed out of the station. He fell in step beside me. Azriel was a seething mass of annoyance that followed.

"And the Raziq? I venture they were not pleased by such an outcome." His gaze raked me, and deep inside, desire stirred. Goddamn it, what was it about this man that called to me, even when I was annoyed with him? "Are they the reason you have the bruises?"

"No, they're thanks to my father." I stopped at the traffic lights and punched the button with a little more force than necessary. Who, exactly, I was more annoyed at I couldn't say for sure—my father, the two of them, or myself for not being strong enough to tell Lucian to fuck off and leave me alone.

In fact, right now, I wished *both* of them—and the rest of the damn circus that had entered my life around the same time—would just go away and leave me in peace.

"Your father?" Surprise edged his tone. "Violence might be one of his mainstays, but it's rarely unleashed when he still requires that person's assistance."

I gave him a long look. "And just how do you know that about my father?"

He snorted. "He's a Raziq, is he not? They are rebels and outcasts for the precise reason that they do not conform to Aedh standards—not only in ideology, but in their very natures."

He lies, Azriel said. *There is more to his knowledge than what he claims.*

Just as there's more to your dislike than what you claim? I grouched back.

And yet I couldn't dismiss his doubts, simply because I agreed with them.

"What you said sounded more like firsthand, personal knowledge than like a general statement about the Raziq."

"I said I'd ask around about your father, and I have. Aedh numbers may place us on the verge of extinction, but that does not mean there are none in this city. Hieu is old even in Aedh terms, and not unknown."

"All that sounds a little too convenient."

"Sometimes the truth *is*." He caught my hand and pulled me to an abrupt stop. "You know why I'm on this hunt. I want the Raziq."

"I know—"

"No, you don't," he interrupted fiercely. "Because I don't just want them dead. I want them burned from existence. I want them erased from the memory of the earth itself and their names never to be mentioned, even in the darkest whispers in the darkest of places."

I stared at him, for the first time seeing the true extent of the anger and darkness in him. And I couldn't help wondering just what he would do to get that revenge—and what he'd already done.

More than either of us currently suspects, Azriel commented.

Suspicion gains us nothing, I replied, despite the fact that my own thoughts were careening along the same line. *And just because he wants the Raziq erased doesn't mean he can't be trusted. Hell, I'm sure you wouldn't mind it one little bit if the Raziq no longer existed.*

I returned my gaze to Lucian. "Last time we saw each other, you were intending to hunt down information about the tracker the Raziq placed in me. Is that why you were waiting at our place?"

The anger in him faded, but didn't completely disappear. It remained in the edge in his voice, in the fierceness of his gaze.

It was a fierceness that had me trembling, because it wasn't *entirely* anger. Lust burned in the deeper recesses of his eyes, and it was growing stronger by the moment.

I might be tired, I might have the mother of all headaches developing thanks to Amaya and the events of the day so far, but it seemed even that wasn't enough to stop the growing hum of desire.

Although it wasn't like I had many other options with which to satisfy my needs. With Azriel intent on remaining a monk, my only other possibilities were Jak—the man who not only betrayed the trust I'd placed in him by writing a newspaper article about my mother that basically called her a fraud who lied about her background, but who broke my heart in the process—or I could head down to Franklin's, a private wolf club where I was a long-term member. And while I did have a regular partner there, his touch had lost some of its appeal since Lucian and Azriel had come into my life.

A smile teased Lucian's lips. Despite his claim to the contrary, he was obviously catching at least *some* of my thoughts. I tugged my hand free from his and strode toward my car.

He was back beside me in a heartbeat. "In answer to your question, yes, I have been researching ways to mute the tracker, and yes, I was at your home to discuss one possibility."

I opened the car door but didn't climb in. "And what is the possibility?"

"A dark sorcerer, but not one who uses blood magic."

"Any sorcerer who trades with darkness is not a wise choice," Azriel said. Though his voice retained its usual even tone, his distaste and annoyance still shivered through me.

Which was odd. It was almost as if the chi connection had somehow deepened, allowing me greater access to the ebb and flow of his emotions. And from what I'd gathered, that *shouldn't* have been the case.

Unless it was a sign that assimilation was a whole lot closer than we'd presumed.

No.

I glanced at him. *If it's not assimilation, then what is it?*

He gave me the mental equivalent of a shrug and my annoyance surged. Some things, it seemed, would never change.

"We haven't even had the chance to explore our options with the Brindle witches yet," I said to Lucian.

And since they were some of the most powerful witches in the land, you'd have to think they should be able to come up with something.

"What you bear in your heart is unlike anything the Brindle witches have seen before," Lucian commented. "It is Aedh in origin, and their magic far exceeds anything ever seen here on earth."

"By that logic," Azriel said, before I could even open my mouth, "a dark sorcerer will be of as little use as the Brindle witches."

Lucian gave him a somewhat scathing glance. "Except that witches rely on natural magic, whereas a dark sorcerer uses the magic of this world *and* the other. In this case, that is probably as close as we'll ever get to Aedh-strength magic."

"Which does not mean we should discount other options without even exploring them." Azriel's voice held a dangerous edge. "Risa, you cannot—"

"We have to at least *talk* to this sorcerer," I cut in firmly even as trepidation crawled across my skin. I'd heard too many of Ilianna's stories to ever be comfortable in the presence of a dark sorcerer. "Even if we do nothing with the information he gives us."

"At least someone in this little group has some common sense," Lucian said. "I've arranged a meeting for this evening."

"I'm working at the café until eleven."

He shrugged. "Shall I pick you up, or would you prefer to meet us there?"

"The latter." I didn't want to be reliant on him to get back home, simply because that was one sure way to end up in his bed rather than alone in mine. Amusement teased his lips again. I added, somewhat crossly, "I thought you could only read my thoughts during sex?"

"That is mostly true."

Azriel snorted softly. I ignored him and said, "Define 'mostly.'"

Lucian shrugged again. "Thoughts of a sexual nature are easier to pick up. Anything else is very muddy."

"Muddy" didn't mean he couldn't read them, just that they were harder to hear. Fabulous. *Not.*

"When and where do you want to meet?"

"There's a lovely little bar down the Paris end of Collins Street—Maxwell's, it's called. Shall we say midnight?"

"Fine. Now, if you don't mind, get the hell out of here so I can go home and get ready for work."

"Your grouchy side is showing, my dear." His gaze swept to Azriel. "Understandable, I guess, given the company you're forced to keep twenty-four/seven."

Azriel took one step forward, then stopped. Other than the slight tightening in his jawline, his expression remained as impassive as ever. But the emotional turmoil that exploded through my being just about sent me staggering.

Lucian was a dead man if he ever gave Azriel the slightest reason to attack.

He will not, Azriel said. *He is not that stupid. Nor am I that rash.*

You might be if you hang around me for too much longer.

Many things might happen if I hang around you too much longer.

It was a comment that sparked an avalanche of questions and possibly some hope, but before I could say anything, Azriel winked out of existence—neatly avoiding said questions—and Lucian stepped closer. His scent was an enticing mix of lemongrass, suede, and musky, powerful male.

"Until tonight." He caught my hand in his and raised it to his lips. The kiss was light and teasing, and oddly erotic. "Wear something sexy."

"I have no intention of wearing anything sexy—

either for you or for this dark sorcerer." I ripped my hand from his, but the warmth of his lips lingered, making my skin tingle.

Amusement played about his mouth. "I can't *still* be in the bad books for previous behavior, surely."

"You can, and you are." I shrugged. "It's going to take some pretty stellar behavior to get you out of the bad books."

"Ah, a challenge. I like that." He hesitated, then added, "One thing, though."

I raised my eyebrows in question when he didn't immediately go on, and he half smiled. "This may seem a strange request, but do not wear your demon sword when you meet our sorcerer. They tend to be sensitive to demon magic, and it would create the wrong impression."

I snorted. "I'm not really caring about the impression I give to a sorcerer."

"You might if you want a solution to your problem." He caught my hand again and dropped a soft, sweet kiss on it. My toes curled in delight. "I promise to protect you from any harm the sorcerer might offer."

"Yeah, but who's going to protect me from you?"

"Ah," he said, his voice filled with mock distress. "You've uncovered my evil plan to have you helpless with desire by the evening's end."

Despite the annoyance—at both myself and him—I couldn't help smiling. "Amaya's presence won't stop that from happening."

"No, but it may stop the sorcerer from helping us. Will you leave her behind? Please?"

I eyed him for a moment, then said, somewhat reluctantly, "Okay."

He bowed lightly. "Until tonight, then, when the games will commence."

He gave me another smoky smile, then turned and walked away. And I knew that if I didn't end up in his bed tonight, it would be a goddamn miracle.

It was just after three by the time I arrived at the café we'd named RYT's, an acronym for *rich young things*, which was precisely what we'd been at the time we'd started the business. Though I was a good fifteen minutes late, the café wasn't that busy, with only a couple of regulars sitting at the bar drinking Irish coffees and a third at one of the tables reading the newspaper. The article, I noticed with amusement, was one of Jak's, but I resisted the temptation to peek over the customer's shoulder to see just what he was reporting on this time. He might have stepped back into my life, but that didn't mean I now needed to keep up with everything he was doing.

Even if that wistful, not-quite-over-him-no-matter-what-he'd-done piece of me desperately wanted to.

"Hi, Risa," Manny, one of our newer waiters, said as I walked in.

"How's things going today?"

"A particularly insane lunch rush has been followed by this lovely lull."

"Enjoy it while you can," I said with a smile, "because it won't last long."

The afternoon rush usually hit between five and

seven, when werewolves hungry from the afternoon spent at the werewolf sex club Blue Moon came in to eat, and those on their way to the club came in to fuel up.

I looked around for a moment, then added, "Where's Linda?"

"Apparently one of the kitchen hands didn't turn up today, so Tao's asked Linda to help with the dishes while we're slow."

I cursed softly. If there was one position we couldn't seem to keep filled long term, it was the damn kitchen hand. It paid well enough, but it was hot, grubby work, and it seemed the younger generation weren't inclined that way—it was all middle management and high starting salaries for them, or it was nothing.

Which was a comment Mom often used to make. I smiled, even as the wistful ache that she was gone swept through me again. No matter how close I was to my aunt Riley, she wasn't Mom and never could be.

I grabbed the banister and headed up. "I've got to go do some paperwork, Manny, but give me a yell the minute it gets busy down here."

He nodded, and I continued on up to the office.

I was near the top of the stairs when the kitchen exploded in flames.

Chapter 4

There was a gigantic *whoosh*; then the kitchen doors burst open and a fist of flame punched through them. I ducked instinctively, but the flames were sucked back into the kitchen almost as soon as they'd appeared.

It *wasn't* a natural action.

The flames were *Tao's*.

He'd lost control. Had to have. *Fuck.*

I jumped over the banister, landed lightly in a half crouch, then surged upright and ran forward. The fire alarm went off, forcing me to shout as I said, "Manny, get everyone outside!"

He nodded, his face white as he herded the three customers out. I made a quick dash into the bathrooms to ensure that no one was there, then bolted for the kitchen.

I hit the doors with enough force to wrench one from its hinges. Water poured from the ceiling sprinklers and soaked me in an instant, but it wasn't doing anything to extinguish the source of the fire—Tao. He was on his knees in the middle of the kitchen floor, his arms wrapped around his chest and his entire body alight. It wasn't burning him—it couldn't, because he was now more a spirit of flame than a werewolf with pyrokinetic abilities, thanks to the fire elemental—a creature created from magic—that he'd consumed to save Ilianna's life. But his flames leapt high enough to fan out across the ceiling, and there were thick scorch marks above the stainless-steel oven surrounds—obviously, that was where the initial loss of control had happened. Yet nothing else had been set on fire, even though the intensity of the heat pouring off him had me flinching.

My gaze swept the rest of the kitchen, looking for Linda and Rachel—the other chef who was rostered on to help today. Neither of them was here, but the rear door was half open. Tao must have sent them out just before he exploded.

I scooped up tea towels from the nearby bench, dunked them in a sink that had trays soaking, then wrapped them around my hands as I approached Tao.

"Don't," he croaked. "You'll burn."

"Then fucking control it."

His gaze leapt to mine—haunted, desperate. "It's not me. It's not my fire-starting abilities—it's the elemental."

I bit my lip against the urge to say something comforting. That was *not* what he needed right now. "And you're *both* now, like it or not. You *can* do this, Tao. You *can* control it."

"If I *could*, I wouldn't have exploded," he ground out.

True enough. But all I said was, "Well, the only thing

on fire in the kitchen is you, so don't bullshit me about not being able to control it."

I grabbed him under the armpits and dragged him toward the freezer. His entire body shook violently, as if the flames that enveloped him were physically assaulting him. Heat soaked through the towels and singed the hairs on my arms, but the flames leapt no farther up my arms—he *was* controlling it, even if imperfectly.

I opened the freezer, shoved him inside, then grabbed the safety-release knob and slammed the door shut behind the two of us. The flames were so fierce it felt like I'd stepped into an oven, and I briefly wondered if he'd get himself under full control before everything started melting—me included.

He squatted on the freezer floor and hugged his knees, making the overall area of his flames small. I stepped past him and grabbed some bags of ice, tearing them open, then pouring the contents down his back. The blocks melted in an instant, but it didn't matter. What that did was get his core temperature down so that he could have some hope of regaining control.

Gradually, the flames subsided, until they were little more than fireflies dancing across his skin. I poured the last of the ice down his back, then tossed the bag on the floor beside the others and knelt behind him. I wrapped my arms around his still-shaking shoulders and held him tight. I was soaked to the skin—we both were— but I wasn't cold. The flames might be practically out, but the heat in his body was still enough to warm an entire battalion of people.

After a while, he took a deep breath and released it slowly. "Don't ever do that again, Risa."

It seemed to be my day for getting told that. But there was no anger in Tao's voice, only resigned weariness. I said, "You know it's pointless telling me that, so why even waste the words?"

"Because I keep hoping one day you'll actually listen to someone."

I snorted softly. "And how long have you known me?"

He made an odd sound that stood somewhere between laugh and groan. "Okay, point taken. But it was still one hell of a risk. I wasn't in control, and I could have hurt you."

"As I've already pointed out, you were the only thing alight in the kitchen." And that alone meant he had some level of control, even if he couldn't immediately douse the flames. I dropped a kiss onto the back of his neck, then pushed to my feet. "I knew you wouldn't let the elemental hurt me."

"Next time I might." He took my offered hand and let me haul him upright. As a werewolf he was naturally lean, but these days, thanks to what resided within him, he could only be considered skin and bone. Not abnormally so, not yet, but not far from it, either. "And the fire trucks have just about arrived."

I cocked my head a little and caught the wail of the approaching fire engine. "You want to go out the back and reassure Linda and Rachel? I'll go talk to the firemen."

His smile was a little on the wan side, but it nevertheless warmed me. He was going to be okay—at least this time. "You always did like a man in uniform."

"Most women do." I gave him a grin. "And some men."

"Not this man."

"Well, no, not unless you'd walked in on one of Ilianna's potion-making moments." I hesitated. "Once this mess is all sorted out, you'd better meet me upstairs and tell me exactly what happened."

He nodded, his expression suddenly grim. Prickles of concern danced through me, but I shoved them aside, then hit the freezer door release and headed out not only to meet the firemen but to see what could be done about the mess.

As it turned out, there wasn't a whole lot we *could* do. We cleaned up the best we could, but the kitchen itself was shut down, thanks to all the water damage, and it wouldn't reopen until everything was checked and passed by the local government council, who controlled the planning and permits for the area. I spent the next hour lining up plumbers, electricians, and the gas people, while Tao rang the insurance company, then put signs in the windows explaining the situation. I hoped we weren't closed for too long. Customers could be fickle creatures at the best of times.

I locked up, then pulled a couple of beers out of the fridge and headed upstairs.

"So, give with the details." I handed Tao a beer and plopped down on a nearby chair.

He sighed and put his feet up. His warm brown

eyes, when they met mine, were somber. "I was pulling a double shift because Jacques had his dad's funeral today, and no one was able to fill in."

I nodded. I knew all that—just as I knew that Tao could have called in a temp but didn't because he was a little on the fussy side when it came to just who worked in his kitchen.

"Lunch was madder than normal and the kitchen was its usual stinking-hot self." He grimaced. "In this day and age you'd think they'd make air-con that could function more efficiently in kitchens."

"I'm sure they do. Problem is, we don't actually own this building."

"Yeah. Might have to fix that now that the place is pulling decent money." He thrust a hand through his still-damp brown hair. "Anyway, the heat had the thing inside me stirring. The hotter the air got, the stronger it got, but both Rachel and I were working flat out and I just couldn't take time to go sit in the freezer for a while."

"And you didn't think it would get to the point that it did." I said it softly, without accusation. Tao wasn't the type to risk the lives of others.

"It's never been this bad before. I don't know why it was this time."

I drank some beer and contemplated him. The elemental's flames still burned fiercely within him—the power of it glowed under his skin.

"Obviously, the kitchen heat had something to do with it."

"Yeah." He took a sip of beer and leaned back in the chair. "I had all the jets going on the stove. It seems to feed on that sort of stuff."

It was a fire elemental, so that was logical. "It might also have been the sun. It was warm today."

He raised his eyebrows. "No sun gets into the kitchen."

"It mightn't need direct sunlight. Maybe just the warmth is enough." I paused. "At least no one was hurt. You controlled it that much; in the end, that's all that matters."

"But I almost *didn't*." His expression was bleak. "I'm scared to death it'll take me over, and I'll destroy everything and everyone I love."

I put my beer down, then knelt in front of him and took his hands in mine. "I promise you, Tao, we won't let this thing destroy you *or* anyone else. It hasn't won the fights, and it won't win the battle. We won't let it."

"I hope you're right." But his expression suggested he actually held very little hope himself.

I hesitated. "Maybe you should work at night for the time being. At least until you're more confident of your ability to control the elemental."

"Yeah." He tugged his hands free from mine and pulled me close. For several minutes he did nothing more than hug me—it almost felt like he was attempting to hold on to his own humanity by hanging on to mine. Gradually, the heat in him began to dissipate, until his body temperature was only a little above what would be considered normal for a werewolf.

Only then did the tension in him subside.

He released me and said, "Looks like we've both got an unintended night off."

I forced a smile and sat back on my heels. "I guess the fire did have one benefit, then."

"I guess it did." He scrubbed a hand across his stubbly chin, the sound like sandpaper against a wall. "I might take myself down to the Blue Moon and lose a couple hours."

And the ghosts of fear, I suspected. They were ghosts I knew all too well, because they were inside me, too. "I'll ring Ilianna and update her."

"Oh fuck, I forgot—"

"Don't worry," I cut in quickly, as the air temperature suddenly spiked. The elemental might be down, but it wasn't yet out. He needed to keep calm. "I'll take care of it. Just go have some fun and relax."

"I will." He rose and kissed the top of my head. "Thanks."

I caught my bottom lip with my teeth as I watched him walk out. Because I knew, despite my promises, that there was no guarantee he would win this battle. He had to find the strength within himself—none of us could do that for him, and certainly there was no magic or potion that would work in this sort of situation. Lord only knew, Ilianna and the Brindle witches had tried hard enough to find one.

Tao was one of the strongest people I knew, but he was obviously struggling. And I knew, deep down, that there was a very real possibility that we might yet lose him to the monster that resided within.

* 　　 * 　　 *

In the end, I decided against leaving Amaya behind. Lucian might fear the sorcerer's reaction to her, but I wasn't about to walk into the unknown without the means to fully protect myself. And if that meant that the sorcerer walked, then so be it.

Maxwell's, it turned out, was more than just a lovely little bar situated at the upscale end of Collins Street. It also happened to be an extremely discreet wolf club.

Not that you could tell from merely stepping inside the place. It appeared to be nothing more than a very stylish, very elegant bar that catered to humans and non-humans alike. The surrounds—old-world architecture, luxurious leather couches, and a stunning marble bar—gave it the feel of a gentlemen's club, although overall it was far more friendly and welcoming.

It was only the faintest trace of sex and desire stirring lazily through the air that gave the game away and, even then, it was only an occasional tease.

I briefly contemplated walking out, but if I did that, I might throw away our one and only chance to talk to someone with the skill to either stop or mute the transmitter in my heart. We needed to at least hear our options before we declined them.

Although if I was being *completely* honest, the real reason I didn't walk out was that I was intrigued. I'd never heard of Maxwell's—not even a whisper on the grapevine—which meant whoever ran it maintained extreme control. And that made me wonder why. Franklin's—the private wolf club I was a member of—was also very discreet, but it was not unknown in the wolf world, and I imagined it catered to the same sort of upmarket clientele.

A waiter approached, a polite smile creasing his pleasant features. "Welcome to Maxwell's, ma'am. Are you here for a casual drink, or would you prefer a seat in our restaurant?"

I hesitated. "I'm here to meet a friend—Mr. Lucian Dupont—but I'm not sure whether he's booked a table or not."

"Ah yes, Mr. Dupont said you might be late. He and his other guest have been here for just over an hour." Though there was no censure in his voice, it was nevertheless a gentle rebuke. Obviously, one did *not* keep members waiting. Amusement teased my lips as he motioned a waitress forward. "Amy will show you to the private dining area."

Was "private dining" a euphemism for the werewolf section? I guessed I'd find out soon enough. I followed the willowy waitress through the main bar and up the stairs. The third floor held the wolf club, if the strengthening smell of sex and lust was anything to go by, but we didn't stop there. We went on, up to the fourth floor, then along a corridor that had darkly stained wood-panel doors at regular intervals. She stopped at the seventh one and knocked politely. "Your final guest has arrived, Mr. Dupont."

"Please send her in," Lucian replied, in a cool and authoritative tone. The high-end investment adviser, not the lover.

I wasn't sure whether to be pleased or annoyed.

The woman keyed open the door and waved me inside. As the door closed behind me, I paused and looked around. I'd half expected some sort of private boudoir, but it was actually set up as a plush but comfortable dining room. A mahogany table dominated the space but, oddly, there were only two chairs. Maybe dark sorcerers didn't eat. Or maybe *I* wasn't invited to eat. He might be taking the "behave yourself" request to a whole new level.

And *that* would definitely be annoying. I mean, just because I was angry that he'd forced intercourse one time to read my mind, that didn't mean I never wanted to partake of his particular brand of loving again.

The scent of sex was heavier in the room than in the hallway outside, but it was oddly entwined with the sharpness of blood. I frowned and glanced toward the end of the room, which seemed to be the source of the scents. The entire width of the wall was covered by heavy red velvet curtains. I was half tempted to walk over to see what they were hiding but resisted, and scanned the rest of the room instead. The remaining walls were paneled in dark wood, once again giving the impression of something you'd see in a gentlemen's club. A bar dominated the other end of the room, and it was against this that Lucian leaned. He gave me a wide smile when my gaze met his, but it was his companion who caught my attention.

Because it *wasn't* a man, like I'd been expecting. And—for one fleeting moment—she seemed very familiar. But before I could figure out who it was she reminded me of, she turned fully around and the moment was gone. All I saw was a stranger.

She was a tall, full-bodied—almost matronly—woman, with angular features and dark hair cut close to her head. Her nose was large and Roman, and gave her an arrogant air. But it was her eyes that sent shivers skating across my skin. They were a blue so pale it was almost impossible to separate the iris from the white. And in those pale depths, eons of knowledge seemed to glow.

Enough knowledge to steal a portal key, perhaps? Maybe, just maybe.

And yet this *wasn't* the person who had stolen the key from under our noses. Not because the person who'd taken it had been a man—in truth, gender could temporarily be altered, whether by a glamour or by more basic means such as makeup and wigs. It was more that she didn't *feel* the same. The man—the sorcerer—who had taken the key held an energy that was dark, ungodly, and bitter. This woman didn't, although she didn't exactly feel clean, either. There was a definite taint to the energy that poured off her, but it was more an uneasy vibration of something not quite right than anything truly dark.

"Risa." Lucian stepped in front of me, effectively blocking my view of the stranger. "You look divine, as usual."

"It's just a black dress, and there's very little flesh on show."

And for a very good reason—I still had too many bruises. Old ones, as well as the new one my father had given me. Divine didn't give me enough coverage; this simple shift, with its high neckline, did.

"Ah, but it skims your curves delightfully, and teases the imagination. That is extremely sexy to those with good imaginations." He kissed both cheeks, every action overly polite.

I raised an eyebrow in silent query. He grinned and said in a low voice, "You did warn me I needed to be on my best behavior if I ever wanted to get into your bed again."

"Yes, but I didn't exactly expect such immediate and polite compliance."

"Why not? It is, after all, to my benefit if I do." He swung around, offered me an arm, then said in a more normal voice, "Let me introduce you to our guest."

He escorted me toward the bar. The stranger's gaze flickered down my body and it felt like I was standing there naked, being judged inside and out. Her expression seemed to say I'd been found wanting. And that, unsurprisingly, was something of a relief. The last thing I wanted was to attract the interest of someone who dealt with the dark forces of this world on *any* level other than that of hunting them.

Not that the man who *did* hunt them had been sighted for the last few hours. Which suggested Azriel had taken to heart my snarky wish that they'd all leave me in peace and was keeping watch from a distance rather than up close and personal.

Lucian waved a hand in the stranger's direction. "Risa Jones, Lauren Macintyre."

"Evening." Lauren's voice was mellow and soft, the

opposite of what I'd been expecting. "It's a pleasure to meet you, Ms. Jones."

She held out her hand. My pause was brief, but nevertheless there, and something flickered through her eyes. Not amusement. Something deeper. Darker.

The fingers that wrapped around mine were long and warm, her grip strong. But there was nothing untoward in her touch, no dark shimmer or foul feel, despite that flicker in her eyes and the vibrations that continued to roll off her.

"Would you like a drink?" Lucian walked around the bar. "We have wine, beer, and champagne."

"Champers, please." I propped on a barstool and returned Lauren's gaze steadily. "I'm gathering Lucian has told you the reason I wished to see you?"

A small smile touched her lips, though little amusement reached her ice-colored eyes. "A woman who gets straight down to business. I like that."

"I told you she was a no-nonsense person." Lucian slid a glass of bubbly toward me, then leaned on the bar.

Desire slithered through me, quick and hungry. I took a drink and tried to keep my attention on the sorcerer, not the lover.

And wondered, even as I did so, why the hell he affected me so strongly. He might be Aedh, and able to ensnare lovers with just a kiss, but this was something else. Something that was almost darker.

And *that* was worrying.

"Indeed," Lauren said. "So tell me, what do you think of dark sorcerers?"

"My personal opinion is that you should all be dumped in the deepest, darkest hole in hell and forgotten about." My shrug was casual, but tension rode me. I couldn't be anything less than honest, even though she was obviously ready to walk, given the slightest reason, and being honest might well give her that reason. "I'm afraid I've seen too much pain and catastrophe caused by your kind to want anything else."

"And yet here you are, wanting my help."

"Just because I hate what you do doesn't mean I won't use you if I need to."

White teeth flashed in what I presumed was a grin, though it was an oddly unsettling one. "If you had answered any other way—if you had been less than honest—I would have walked out the door."

"Then thank god for honesty." I contemplated her over the rim of the champagne glass. "So, back to my original question—did Lucian fill you in on why we wanted to speak to you?"

"Yes." The amusement died from her lips. "I know of the reapers—one such as I cannot help but be aware of them. However, I did not know there were beings called Aedh who once manned the gates to heaven and hell. Or that some fool wants the gates of hell opened permanently."

That raised my eyebrows. "Don't you trade with hellkind?"

"Of course, but that doesn't mean I want all hell to break loose here on earth. If demons were as common as ants, it would destroy my business."

I snorted softly. Consorting with demons was a business, was it? "Then you also know why I need your help."

She nodded. "However, we are talking about a device created by beings who *aren't* of this world. I will need to get the feel of it before I can say whether I could help you or not."

"That's going to be a bit hard, given that it's woven into the fabric of my heart."

Lauren gave me a cool smile. "I did not mean that in the literal sense."

"Then how did you mean it?"

"I simply need to touch you. Stand up."

I took a large gulp of champagne, then did so. She pressed her hand under my left breast, the coolness of her long fingers sending goose bumps skittering across my skin. There was nothing sexual in her touch, nothing dark or uneasy, and yet all of those things slid through me.

Lauren closed her eyes. For several minutes, she neither moved nor breathed, although she obviously *was* breathing, since otherwise she'd have passed out.

Then she retracted her touch and opened her eyes, a frown creasing her smooth features. "The device is very powerful. I'm not entirely sure if it could be stopped from functioning for any length of time."

"Damn." I sat back on my chair and met Lucian's gaze. "It was worth a shot, I guess."

"Young woman, you weren't listening." Her soft voice held more than a hint of rebuke. "I *said* I couldn't stop it for any length of time. Meaning, it might just be possible to stop it for brief minutes."

"A few minutes is better than nothing." I hesitated.

"But whether we could use it would depend on just what it takes to achieve that."

Her gaze slid down my length. Horror swamped me. Not *that*, I thought. Anything but that. Or blood.

But when her gaze met mine again, there was little in the way of desire. Just cool calculation. And if I hadn't been aware of it before, then that look alone was enough to tell me she was *very* dangerous.

"Lucian has already informed me of your aversion to blood magic—"

"I thought you said she didn't do blood magic," I cut in, glancing at Lucian.

He shrugged. "If I had said anything else, would you have come here?"

"Probably not."

"Then that explains the lie. You need to explore *all* options, Risa. It is foolish to do otherwise."

"Blood magic is *not* an option."

"Which is a shame, as it's the most powerful form of magic available here on earth," Lauren commented.

I met her gaze again. "It also taints the user in the extreme."

"That is a debate I will not get into. It does, however, lessen our options."

"At least there *are* options." Hopefully, there were some that were a little less unhealthy than blood magic. Although Ilianna was going to hit the roof either way.

"Perhaps." She glanced at Lucian, then rose and finished her drink. "I will be in contact if I uncover any possibilities."

She gave me another of those cool, thoughtful looks, then walked out. But as I watched her leave, foreboding shivered through me. She *would* find a way to mute the Raziq's device—I had no doubt of that.

Just as I had no doubt that the price would be one I'd be reluctant to pay.

I rubbed my arms against the sudden chill in my flesh, and couldn't hold back a sigh of relief when the door closed behind her.

"I'm glad she isn't staying for dinner."

"So am I." Lucian topped up my glass. "As much as I like the occasional threesome, I have this odd feeling you would not have been your usual unrestrained self."

I gave him a wry smile. "That is, of course, presuming I'll have anything to be unrestrained about."

He gave me an innocent smile. "Of course."

I crossed my legs. "So how come you know about this place and I don't?"

"A client told me about it and offered an introduction."

His gaze was on my legs and his hunger stirred the air. It echoed through me, warm and delicious. "An introduction? You have to be introduced and approved to be a member here?"

He nodded. "Franklin's caters to the rich. This place caters to the überrich, as well as those who derive pleasure from watching."

"You can watch in any of the wolf clubs. And Franklin's has private viewing rooms."

"Yes, but we are not talking about common sex here."

"BDSM?" I had no problem with that in and of itself,

but beyond the odd handcuff fantasy, I really wasn't into that sort of sexual play.

He nodded. "And blood play, fetishes, fantasies— but not all at once. Every night has a different 'theme.'"

"And the theme tonight?"

"Bondage." His gaze pinned mine, the intensity making my heart hammer. He didn't care where we were; he just wanted—intended—to make love to me tonight. And while I hungered for his touch, somewhere in the dark recesses unease stirred anew. Because while I was part wolf, and did have an above-average sex drive, this was definitely more than that. But no matter how uneasy I was feeling right now, it wasn't enough to make me walk away. Not yet. He added, "But we do not have to stay. We can walk to my place, and I shall personally cook dinner for you."

And then we shall love until you can take no more and beg for me to stop.

The thought whispered through my brain, distant and tantalizing. I wasn't entirely sure that the thought was mine, although I wasn't telepathic, and certainly hadn't been able to catch his thoughts before now. But then, did I need to? The hunger in his eyes made it very evident where his thoughts were headed.

"Isn't your place a little too far away?" I had no problem about actually walking there, but not in these heels.

A smile teased his lips. "As it so happens, I recently purchased a nearby building for investment purposes, but I'm keeping the top floor for myself. The entire place is being renovated, but I have a kitchen and bathroom in working order."

I was betting the bedroom was in working order, too. "Why arrange to meet here, then? Why not just meet in your apartment in the first place?"

He caught my hands and raised them, palms toward him, to his lips. "Because Lauren wanted someplace public, but absolutely secure. Maxwell's is certainly that."

Lie, lie, lie. But the thought died abruptly as he began to place gentle kisses on each of my fingertips, then drew one into his mouth and sucked on it lightly. My breathing hitched, then became more erratic. I might have doubts about him, but there was no denying my attraction, enhanced or not.

"So," he added eventually, "what is it to be?"

From the minute I'd walked into this room, there was only ever going to be one outcome, and we both knew it. The *where* was a secondary consideration. I raised an eyebrow, and a victorious grin lit his features.

"I thought as much, which is why I already have a lamb roast in the oven."

"And everyone knows a good lamb roast is a guaranteed way of getting into any werewolf's bed."

"Well, that and dessert. Which is a triple-layer chocolate mousse cake."

I laughed, then leaned over the counter and dropped a quick kiss on his lips. It left mine tingly with anticipation. "I might just forgive you if the food's as good as it sounds."

"Excellent. Shall we make a retreat?"

I downed the rest of the champagne, and felt its effervescence all the way down to my toes. "Let's."

He came around the counter and offered me his arm. I slipped mine through his, and he escorted me out of the building and across the road to his apartment. It was one of those grand old Victorians that Collins Street was famous for, and only five stories high, which meant his floor was at treetop level. The old lift rattled and shook as it swept us upward, then opened to reveal a vast room that was filled with building debris and smelled of paint and dust.

"Welcome to my palace." He grinned as he caught my hand and guided me through the mess of dustcovers and workmen's tools.

We walked through the remains of a wall into the kitchen area. It was very rudimentary. There was an oven, a fridge, and the bare bones of two small counters—one of which held the sink—but just about everything else had been gutted. Plates were stacked on the non-sink counter and a drawer that held cutlery sat on the floor near it. But the mouthwatering scent of roasting meat filled the air. I breathed deep, then sighed in contentment.

"God, I don't think there's a better scent in this world." I crossed my arms and leaned against the free bench.

Lucian's smile was wicked. "Oh, I can think of one or two. What would you like to drink? I have wine or champagne in the fridge."

"Champers again, thanks." I watched him pour the

drinks, then asked, "So how did you actually find Lauren?"

He walked over to the oven and opened the door. Steam billowed, and the smell of roasting meat intensified. My belly rumbled happily. "I asked around, as I said. She was the only one willing to meet me. Us."

I took a sip of champagne, enjoying the tease of bubbles on my nose. "So you've never met her before today?"

"No." He hesitated, and looked over his shoulder. "Why?"

I shrugged. "It just seemed a little odd that you'd be in a place like that with someone you didn't know for over an hour."

"Well, I did have to explain the whole damn situation." He paused, then said, "As an aside, did you leave your demon sword behind, as requested?"

I blinked at both the sudden change of direction and the fact that he couldn't sense her. "You can't tell?"

"I'm not sensitive to her magic, so no."

I frowned. "I would have thought *all* Aedh would be sensitive to anything demon-related, given their traditional role of gate guardians."

For a moment the darkness in his eyes was so intense it almost verged on insanity. It was gone just as quickly, but its mark remained, leaving me cold inside. It made me wonder why the hell I was spending so much time with him—what was the draw, beyond great sex? Why oh why did he have this incredible pull on me? Was it just a matter of Aedh calling Aedh? Or was there something else at work? Something deeper. Darker.

I really didn't know, but I was beginning to suspect it might pay to find out.

"As I've mentioned before," he said, "many things were ripped from me when they stole my wings and forever contained me in flesh."

I forced a hand up and lightly caressed his cheek. "That doesn't make you any less an Aedh in my eyes."

He grinned, and the final remnants of darkness fled. "That's because I'm still potent where it counts. Now stop avoiding the question."

I hesitated. He couldn't sense Amaya and—given that she was shadow-wreathed and little more than invisible particles right now—he certainly wouldn't feel her, so I saw no reason not to lie. Especially since I still had that niggling, deep-down chill and more than a small suspicion that he wasn't being honest with me. "Well, there was much protest from Azriel, but I did do as you requested."

"I'm glad. And thank you for trusting me."

A statement that only made me feel bad for *not* trusting him.

He closed the oven door and walked around to where I stood. His lips brushed the back of my neck, and then he said softly, "Dinner will be another hour, at least. What do you suggest we do?"

His breath teased my earlobes, and a delighted shiver ran through me. "How about we talk?"

"About what?" The sound of my shift's zipper being slid down seemed to echo through the vast space around us.

"How about why it took an hour to update the dark sorcerer, for a start. We both know that's a lie, Lucian."

"Perhaps." His fingers brushed my spine, and desire coursed through me. "These scars are new."

"They're a present from the Rakshasa I killed." My voice held a slightly husky edge. I swallowed some more champers, but it didn't do a lot to curb the rise of desire. And whether the fierceness of that desire was natural or not didn't really seem to matter at this point in time. "Explain what you mean by 'perhaps.'"

He slid his hands around my waist, linking them just under my breasts. My nipples went tight. Ached with expectation.

"When you said you wanted to talk, I didn't actually think you meant it."

"I just want an honest answer, Lucian. That's all."

"There's nothing sinister going on, if that's what you're implying. The simple fact is, no dark sorcerer does anything for nothing. She wanted payment, in blood."

Horror twisted through me. I turned in his arms. "You didn't give it to her, did you?"

"Why wouldn't I? This is just a form I'm forced to use, Risa. I do not cherish it the way you all do."

"But giving a dark sorcerer your blood? That's like giving a thief free access to your credit card. It's stupid—and dangerous."

"She can't do anything worse than what has already been done to me." His voice was both grim and dark, and again it had me wondering just what lengths he'd go to for the sake of revenge. More than I could ever guess, I suspected. "I do not fear her, Risa, and neither should you."

"Forgive me if I don't believe that statement one little bit."

We were standing so close all I could smell was musky, powerful male, and all I could feel was the heat of his desire. It took every ounce of control to just stand there in his arms—to not tear his clothes off and beg him to take me there and then. But I wanted answers. Wanted honesty, and he wasn't giving me either right now.

"She is an extremely old—and powerful—sorcerer, Risa." He hooked his fingers under the shift's shoulders and slid them down my arms. It fell to the floor in a river of soft black silk and puddled at my feet. "She didn't get there by making foolish moves. She knows a reaper protects you."

I clenched my fingers, fighting the urge to wrap my arms around his neck and kiss him. "I got the feeling she wasn't particularly scared of reapers."

"Only a fool wouldn't be wary of the reapers, and as I said, she is no fool."

My gaze searched his, but what I was looking for I couldn't honestly say. "You can't be sure of that; you don't know her."

"I know her kind," he murmured. "Just as I know your kind."

Then he kissed me, and any sense of resistance fled. I gave in to desire and just enjoyed. Somewhere in all our kisses, my bra came off, as did my panties. Then his mouth left mine, and he kissed his way down my chin, then my neck. When he licked along my collarbone, I flung back my head and moaned softly. He chuckled, and continued his downward journey, catching one nipple lightly between his teeth. A shiver that was part fear, part delight, ran through me. He teased me with his teeth, stopping just on the cusp of hurting, then swirled his tongue around my nipple, taking away the sting before he moved across to the other side. Then his lips left my breasts and moved down my trembling belly. He dropped kisses on either thigh, then gently parted my legs and kissed me, his breath washing coolness against my heated flesh. Then his tongue swirled around my clit, alternating fast flicks with long, slow strokes and driving me insane in the process. I shuddered, shook, and moaned, as the lowdown tightness spread rapidly through the rest of me, until it felt like I was on the edge of a precipice, unable to think, unable to breathe, and more than ready to fall over.

Then he was in me, driving hard, thrusting deep. I climbed up onto him, wrapped my legs around his waist, and forced him even deeper, my movements as frantic as his. There was little sound except the slap of flesh against flesh, and the heat of lust and sex was so fierce that the air shimmered with it. I came, screaming in pleasure, my body convulsing around his. Heard his answering growl, felt him come deep inside me, his body suddenly rigid against mine.

When I could finally breathe again, I wrapped my arms around his neck and kissed him, long and slow.

"Well," I said, with a somewhat cheeky grin, "that filled five minutes. What next?"

"Next," he said, cupping his hands under my butt, "we take this to a more comfortable situation."

"And the kitchen bench wasn't?" I murmured, wiggling a little against him. Despite having come only heartbeats ago, he was more than half ready to go again. The stamina of an Aedh left a werewolf for dead.

"It was suitable enough for a quick encounter, but I'm planning our next campaign to be a long one, and that always requires comfort."

He shouldered open a door to reveal another large room. A king-sized bed dominated the middle of it, but in the far corner sat the working skeletons of a bathroom—including the biggest damn bathtub I'd ever seen. You could practically swim in it.

"And what about the roast?"

"I ravish, we eat, then I ravish some more, until you can no longer take it and beg for me to stop."

Which was almost word for word what I'd heard earlier. Trepidation shivered through me, but it was quickly lost to the assault of desire as he put his plan into action.

He was a man of his word.

And in the end, I did indeed beg him to stop.

The scent of coffee stirred me from sleep. I flared my nostrils and drew in the delicious scent—one that ran through the heavy aroma of sex that still clung to the air. Hunger stirred, but it was a sluggish sensation. Which aptly described the rest of me. Deliciously so.

Footsteps approached, but I didn't bother moving or opening my eyes. "What time is it?" My words were muffled by the pillow I was facedown in.

"Nine o'clock." Cutlery clinked as Lucian placed a tray beside the bed. "I have coffee."

"I can't move."

"Not even for coffee?"

"Not even."

He chuckled softly. The mattress dipped as his weight hit it. "Your phone rang about ten minutes ago. You want to see who it was?"

"I guess I should." I made a weak "give me" motion with my hand and forced an eye open. It was Jak—he wanted to meet around lunchtime. I groaned, not sure I would even be capable of moving by then.

"Anything important?" Lucian asked.

"A reminder that I have to meet someone for lunch." I let the phone drop back to the bed and snuggled deeper into my pillow. "But I'm not sure I'll be able to do anything more than sleeping for the rest of the day."

"And here I was thinking werewolves had stamina."

His fingers began tracing lines up and down my back. While it felt nice, I barely had the energy to breathe, let alone go another round with him. And *that* was something I'd never thought would happen.

"As werewolves go, it seems I'm a poor specimen."

"But you're also half-Aedh. That should give you an advantage over regular wolves."

"Not when my partner is apparently insatiable."

He chuckled softly. "So you're telling me you're feeling no desire whatsoever right now."

"I am."

His hands slid down to the base of my spine, then over one butt cheek. "Not even the slightest stirrings."

"Not even," I murmured, stoutly ignoring said stirrings.

But the fact that the minute he touched me I seemed unable to tell him to leave me the hell alone had doubts stirring again. Not that those doubts did me a lot of good in this situation.

"Then if I do this"—his touch slid between my legs and gently caressed—"it will have no effect whatsoever?"

"None. Absolutely, totally zero."

He chuckled softly and the bed bounced as he nudged my legs open a little wider. His caress found my clit and I bit my lip against the moan that rose up my throat. "Lucian, I've only had three hours' sleep."

"And?"

"And, I'd really rather—" His fingers slipped slowly inside me at that point, and the rest of the sentence was lost as my muscles clenched around him and pleasure shot through me.

"Ah, the stirrings of desire," he murmured, his voice filled with satisfaction. "Let's see if we can get it a little stronger."

But his touch withdrew, and disappointment swirled. *So much for having no energy*, I thought, amused. Then he shifted, and something hot hit my back. I flinched instinctively, but it didn't actually burn. The scent told me what it was—coffee. It drizzled down my back, following the line of my spine, until it ran between my legs. The heat was a stark contrast to the coolness of the room, and I shivered in expectation and delight. Then his tongue touched me, swirling across the moisture, lapping it from my skin, following the trail of it down my spine and between my legs.

Any pretense of zero interest flew out the window there and then.

He chuckled again and repeated the process, until the moans were thick and constant, and all I wanted was him inside me.

And that was when the phone rang. I cursed softly, knowing the ringtone, not wanting to answer it but knowing I had to. Uncle Rhoan rarely rang unless it was urgent and it would undoubtedly mean an end to the morning's delights.

"Ignore it." Lucian gripped my hips and lifted me into a doggy position.

"I can't." I reached for the phone. "It's my uncle."

Lucian slid his cock through my slickness, teasing but not entering. "I'm sure your uncle would understand. He is, after all, a werewolf."

"Who doesn't normally ring me. My aunt normally does all the social stuff, so this has to be urgent." I hit the ANSWER button, but not the vid-screen option. No matter how open werewolves were about sex, I wasn't inclined to let Rhoan know just what I was up to right now. "Yes?"

"Risa?"

"Yes." Lucian hadn't stopped his seduction, so it came out a little more breathless than it should have.

"You okay?"

"Yeah, just busy. What can I do for you?"

Lucian slid fully inside of me and I bit back a gasp of pleasure. He withdrew, then thrust inside again, and then again, his movements becoming faster, more demanding, with every stroke. Pleasure pulsed through me, thick and heavy.

"We need to you to come down to the Directorate," Rhoan was saying. "We have a major problem."

"And why is your problem suddenly my problem?"

I have no idea how my voice came out so even. Lucian's movements had grown fiercer, his grip on my hips harder, and I responded, pushing back against him, wanting all he could give, as fast as he could give it.

Then my orgasm hit, and I bit my lip against the scream, trying to hear what Rhoan was saying as Lucian surged within me, coming with such intensity it felt like he was spearing through my entire body.

"What?" I somehow said.

Rhoan growled low, then said, "Damn it, Risa, pay attention. Our killer has contacted us again. But this time, he doesn't want to gloat. This time, he's offering a challenge."

"Challenge?" I repeated, too lost in the haze of satisfaction to understand.

"Yes," Rhoan snapped. "He offered the chance to save his next victim."

"But that's a good thing, isn't it?"

"Yes. Except for one thing. He wants you on the case, Ris. And *only* you."

Chapter 5

It took me ten minutes to shower and dress, and another five to catch a tram down to Spencer Street, where the inconspicuous green-glass building that housed the Directorate was located. Given it was rush hour, it was quicker and easier than a car.

Pale blue light swept my length as I walked into the foyer. It was the only visible indication of the vast array of scanners installed in this place, and they all had one purpose—to protect those within. Not even a gnat could get into the Directorate without security being aware of it, let alone anyone armed with some form of weapon—be it metal, plastic, or laser. Though there wasn't any sensor in the world capable of detecting Amaya's presence.

A different kind of energy shimmered across my skin as I walked toward the security officers. Azriel.

"So nice of you to finally join me." I didn't bother to look his way, yet awareness of him hummed through me.

"It would have been awkward had I joined you earlier." His voice was as even as ever. It was only the anger vibrating through my being that suggested he wasn't as calm as he appeared.

"Oh, I don't know," I said, unable to resist the urge to needle him. "A threesome can be quite fun."

"I would not know, nor do I have any intention of ever knowing."

Especially when the third is someone I would rather kill. The thought was soft and vehement, and one I suspected I wasn't meant to hear.

Which suggested that the link between us was not only getting stronger but beginning to flow both ways. And although it was something I was sure *he* wouldn't be happy about, I wasn't about to complain. Any insight into my reaper's thoughts—good or bad—was more than welcome, given his general reticence when it came to explanations.

I stopped at the desk and smiled at security. To Azriel, I silently said, *Can they see you?*

Yes.

The blond guy behind the desk leaned back in his chair, his expression courteous. "Can I help you?"

"We have an appointment with Rhoan Jenson."

"If you'd like to take a seat, I'll inform him you're here."

"Thanks." I walked over to the square of comfy chairs situated to one side of the foyer and sat, legs crossed. I was still wearing the shift dress, so a decent amount of thigh was revealed. But if Azriel noticed, he gave no indication—either physically or mentally. I squashed the sliver of disappointment and said, "Why have you been so absent?"

He half shrugged, the movement casual and eloquent. "I have no wish to be near when you are with the Aedh."

"Granted, but what about before that? When I was at the café, and Tao exploded?"

"You obviously had everything under control. I did not see the need to interfere."

In other words, he'd been too pissed off to interfere. I sighed. "Azriel, this distancing is not the answer."

"Is it not what you wished for?"

I studied him for a moment, wondering if he was deliberately being obtuse. "You can't solve a problem by ignoring it."

"Unless I try, I will never know."

"Surely there has to be a better way—"

"No." It was sharply said, with an air of finality.

And it made me suspect there was more to this pull between us—more than just assimilation—that worried him. But, as ever, he didn't deign to confirm or deny the thought—though I had no doubt he'd heard it.

Footsteps echoed softly on the highly polished concrete floor. I turned and watched Rhoan approach. His expression was grim as he stopped a couple of feet away. "We have ten minutes."

He spun and walked back to the lifts. I hurried to catch him. His tension and anger stung the air and snatched at my breath.

"What do you mean by that? And why are you so angry?"

The doors swished shut behind the three of us, and the lift dropped rapidly to the basement levels.

"I'm angry because I hate having to bring you in on a Directorate case, and because Riley is going to kick my ass over it. Not that I have *any* choice. And what I meant was, we have ten minutes to set you up for your meeting with our killer."

"Hang on—you never mentioned any of this."

"Because we didn't have the time. And I did tell you to hurry."

"Yes, but you told me he wanted me on the case, not that he wanted to meet with me again." My voice was defensive, hinting at anger but also fear. The very last thing I wanted to do was to meet the no-face stranger again.

"As I said, he's offering a challenge."

The lift came to a halt and the doors opened. The thick smell of vampire swept in, and my stomach began to knot.

Rhoan strode from the lift. I followed somewhat reluctantly. "So why ring to offer a challenge, and then demand to meet me? And where the hell does he want to meet?"

But even as the question left my lips, I knew. We'd meet on the astral plane again, where the Directorate could employ no traps and he could not be killed.

Rhoan confirmed what I was thinking, then added, "He wouldn't give us the details, Ris. He wants you, and only you."

I rubbed my arms and tried to ignore the trepidation that crawled through me. This could only end badly. I didn't know enough about the astral plane or hunting madmen to avoid the trouble I sensed I was stepping into.

God, as if I didn't have enough on my plate already.

I followed him silently through the maze of corridors. Though I'd never been down here before now, I'd learned enough over the years to be able to draw a rough floor plan of the place. If the ten levels aboveground were the public face of the Directorate, then the five below were the heart. The majority of the guardians were housed and trained down here, and it was also where the liaisons—the people who made the guardians' reports legible, who catered to their everyday needs, and who gave them their assignments—operated.

Rhoan slapped his palm against a scanner, and the door slid open. Three other people were already there, but only two looked up as we entered. The first—a brown-eyed, heavy-jowled woman in her mid-fifties—was a stranger. The second, a tall, dark-haired werewolf with handsome features, was Harris West, who'd been recruited by the Directorate after he'd helped Riley out of a deadly situation; I had met him before.

But it was the third man who caught my attention, even though he wasn't anything out of the ordinary to look at. He sat at the far end of the table, the bright glow of the com-screen in front of him casting a bluish light across his weatherworn features and bald head.

I'd never actually met him, but I knew him all the same. This was Jack Parnell, senior vice president of the

Directorate and the man in charge of the entire guardian division.

He was also Madeline Hunter's half brother, and *that* made him very, very dangerous, even if he didn't look it.

He finally looked up from the com-screen, then leaned back in his chair and studied me. There was little in his expression to give away what he might be thinking, but that was no surprise. He might be a few hundred years younger than his sister—an oddity due to both the long life span of shifters and the fact that they were born at either end of their father's life—but he was still a vampire and more than a little practiced at controlling himself. I guess with a sister like Hunter, he'd have to be.

"Risa," he said, his voice gravelly and holding the slightest hint of warmth. "Thank you for coming so promptly."

"It's not like I've got any other choice, is it?"

"Now *that's* the sort of comment Riley would make. You've been hanging around her and Rhoan too long." A half smile teased his lips, but it faded quickly as his gaze ran past me. "And this is your reaper?"

He's not my anything. He'll never be my anything. I swallowed the hollow bitterness that accompanied the thought, and simply said, "His name is Azriel."

Jack raised one eyebrow. "All reapers are called Azriel, are they not?"

"Yes." Azriel stopped beside me, his energy warm and intoxicating. "And you are well enough aware of the reason why."

"All names have power," Jack said. "Is that why Risa has you at her beck and call?"

I opened my mouth to refute the statement, but again Azriel jumped in before me. "You know the reasons I am here. Let us not play these games when life hangs in the balance."

Again a smile played briefly about Jack's lips. I glanced questioningly at Azriel, but he merely looked away. Which was frustrating, to say the least.

Rhoan motioned me to sit, then slid a mug of coffee in front of me. "Here's the deal. Our hunter wants to meet you on the astral field, where he will outline the details of his macabre challenge."

I wrapped my fingers around the mug, but it didn't do much to ease the chill from them. "So no one else can be there?"

"No Directorate personnel," Jack said. "But he did say the follower you had on the plane was permissible, as he would not interfere. We need to know who your follower is, and whether you can trust him."

Him. Not *her*, not *them*. In those bright depths, I saw awareness. He knew who was following me. Knew why.

But was that so very surprising? Hunter might not want the Directorate overall—and Rhoan and Riley in particular—to know about my dealings with her and the vampire council, but Jack was her brother *and* the vice president of the Directorate. It was doubtful she'd keep too many secrets from him.

Although I had to wonder what he thought of her plans to take over the council.

"My follower is someone who currently means me no harm." I hesitated, then half shrugged.

Rhoan frowned, his gaze flickering between me and Jack. He knew something was going on. "That's not exactly a ringing endorsement—who is he?"

"No one important." I took a sip of coffee, then added, "And we haven't the time to discuss this if our killer wants to meet me in a few minutes."

"True." Rhoan's gaze went to the woman. "Elga?"

She leaned her arms on the table, her gaze narrowing. "You have not had much experience on the plane, have you?"

A smile twitched my lips. "You can tell this by just looking at me?"

"There is a certain energy that radiates from those who travel frequently. How many times has your spirit walked free?"

"On the astral plane? Once. But I do walk the gray fields."

"That is something, I suppose." She pursed her lips and didn't look happy. "We must go prepare."

Jack nodded. "Take her. Harris, monitor all incoming energies and let me know the second there's any spike. Rhoan, you've got the sensors ready?"

He nodded and rose. I gulped down my coffee, scalding my throat in the process, then followed suit.

"This way," Elga murmured, her long skirts swishing as she strode past me.

I followed her out the door and down the corridor. The room she entered was small and dark, and reminded me somewhat of Adeline's room, without the thick padding underfoot. But the air was ripe with the scents of lavender and chamomile, and there was a comfortable-looking bed stuck in one corner.

It was also a room protected by magic. It caressed my skin, a touch that was warm and yet filled with power. It wasn't as strong or as ancient as the force that protected the Brindle, but it wasn't something anyone sane would want to mess around with.

Although I'd hazard a guess that our no-face killer didn't exactly fall into the sane category.

"Okay," Rhoan said, as he came into the room after me. "Strip off that dress."

I did as I was bid, suddenly glad that I'd had the foresight to tuck clean underclothing into my purse before I'd met Lucian. Rhoan carefully stuck seven sensors on me—one at the base of my spine, then the others at the top of my head, middle of my forehead, my throat, near my heart, solar plexus, then the final one below my belly button. The chakra points, I realized. They were monitoring my energy flow, not my vital signs. I glanced around to Elga.

"We need to detect incoming energies." She waved a hand to the bed.

I walked over and lay down. "And if you do detect them?"

"Then we will recall your astral body instantly." She hesitated. "It shouldn't be a problem, as this room is well protected. But it's better to be safe than sorry when we have no idea what—or who—we are dealing with."

With that, I could only agree.

"Now," she continued, "do you remember the process?"

"Yes, but I prefer it to be dark."

The lights went off instantly. Though it was pitch-black, Azriel's eyes seemed to glow, blue stars in a world that was otherwise black. He didn't say anything, didn't do anything, and yet, strength surged. He was here, and I was safe.

But on the astral plane it was a different matter entirely.

I closed my eyes and concentrated on my breathing, waiting until the sense of peace enveloped me. Then I imagined that cord hanging above me, and reached for it. This time, pulling free seemed faster and easier.

I didn't hang about, simply imagined the dark and grimy warehouse area where I'd first confronted the no-face stranger, and suddenly I was there.

The first person I saw wasn't our faceless killer but my Cazador follower.

Fancy meeting you here, I said, my voice dry.

He bowed slightly, amusement creasing the corners of his brown eyes. *You sound about as pleased to be here as I am.*

It's more accurate to say I'm less than pleased about my reasons for being here. A soft vibration began to stir the air, a sensation that crawled across my skin and made me shiver. I rubbed imaginary arms and added, *I gather you're still on a watching brief?*

Yes. His gaze swept me critically, one warrior sizing up another. Not that I'd ever be half the warrior Aunt Riley was, let alone go up against someone like him.

But your energy levels do not seem up to scratch right now, so I will step in if he threatens harm.

I frowned. *Why?*

Because Hunter would not be pleased if you were in any way hurt during this.

Yeah, because then I wouldn't be able to do *her* dirty work. The unpleasant vibration was getting stronger, making the hairs on the back of my neck stand on end. I turned and scanned the shadowy environs, glad that at least on the fields you couldn't actually smell anything. With the heat of the last few days, the rubbish and putrid-looking puddles would have been close to rank.

The sensations rolling across my skin seemed to reach a peak. Once again both the Dušan and the charm at my neck reacted, the latter burning so fiercely it cast the figure of the man who suddenly appeared into stark relief.

Fear stirred briefly. There was something very wrong with this man. Yet he wasn't evil. Just *wrong*.

I resisted the urge to retreat and studied him as intently as he seemed to be studying me. He still had no facial features, but lank hair that seemed to merge with the shadows around us covered half his brow, and he was dressed casually in faded jeans and an Adidas sweater. For some reason, that struck me as odd. I hadn't noticed his hair last time, let alone his clothes, and I suddenly wondered why I was doing so now.

Was it deliberate on his part? Because he certainly didn't look comfortable in them.

You came. His voice, as before, held little in the way of emotion, and yet I had an odd sense of amusement.

For the second time that day, I said, *It's not like I had any other choice.*

No, it is not. You, huntress, are the type determined to save. It is your failing.

Perhaps. The air continued to roll away from him, washing his darkness across me in fetid waves. I resisted the urge to step back, sensing I couldn't afford to show any form of weakness to this man.

If a man he was.

Right now, I wasn't so sure.

If I am the type to save, then what is your type? Because it wasn't me hunting on these fields, stranger.

He tilted his head sideways, and I had the sudden impression of a cat contemplating its prey. *I was not hunting when you found me. My prey had been well and truly ensnared by the time we arrived here.*

Why even hunt her in the first place? She was harmless—

No one who has the darkness within them is ever harmless, he cut in forcefully. The buildings around us shimmered, as if caught in a blast of heated air. *She had to die. They* all *have to die.*

I had a vague suspicion that if he'd had features I'd be seeing the glow of madness in his eyes right now. *But why? Because you say so? Or is there an actual reason behind this madness?*

There are always reasons. In this case, they are good ones. But they're not ones I wish to share just yet.

Meaning he intended to string me along just like he

was the Directorate. *So what has any of this got to do with me?*

Ah, he said, and once again his voice was even, without inflection or emotion. It was weird—almost as if he flowed between humanity and not. *The speed with which you found dear Dorothy impressed me. I thought it might be interesting if we had a little challenge.*

What is the point of another challenge if you're only going to kill your victims anyway?

What if I were to offer a guarantee that I would not kill my next victims until their allotted time?

Why would I trust a man who can't keep his word? A man too scared to reveal his face or share his name?

Just for a second, the vibration in the air halted, and I had an odd sensation of everything around me freezing—as if the astral plane itself held its breath. Then that moment passed, and the vibrations rolled on, little maggots of energy that crawled across my skin.

I cannot show what I cannot see. As for my name . . . His voice lowered, forcing me to lean forward a little to hear him.

But rather than continue, his hand shot out, something I felt rather than saw. I pulled back, Amaya instantly in my hands, an action that was more reflex than any spoken desire on my part. His fingers hit her blade rather than me, and his skin split. Blood flowed, though it was black rather than red. Purple fire leapt from the blade to his hand, and he jumped back, shaking his fingers in an attempt to rid his fingers of flames.

Amaya, release him.

Her grumbles filled the back of my mind, but the flames crawled from his flesh and dropped harmlessly to the ground.

I swung her lightly back and forth in warning. The stranger's features followed the movement, even though he had no eyes.

Do not attempt to do to me what you did to Dorothy, stranger. Amaya still burned with hunger and the need to attack, but her flames failed to lift the shadows around us. Whoever this stranger was, he seemingly had the ability to control how *I* saw the plane.

He didn't say anything for several seconds, simply continued to study me as he shook fingers that looked red and blistered. It was a clear indication that you *could* be harmed on the astral plane, and made me wonder what the hell he'd actually been trying to do.

But waiting for him to speak made my nerves crawl, so I said, *What is this challenge you're offering?*

It is a race, of sorts.

Define "of sorts."

I had an odd impression that he was smiling, but I didn't think it was a nice sort of smile. *Tomorrow I will send the Directorate a clue to help you find my next victim. You—and you alone—will conduct the search.*

And what will you be doing while I'm trying to save the next victim?

The sense of cat and prey suddenly sharpened. I shivered, and the buildings around me darkened even more. I swallowed heavily and thrust away the fear, but it didn't do a whole lot to ease the tense atmosphere.

What will I be doing? he repeated softly. *Well, my dear huntress, what I will be doing is hunting you.*

With that, he disappeared.

And all I could think was, what the hell was he going to do when he found me?

Chapter 6

I cursed mentally and swung around. *Any idea where he went?*

He has left the astral plane. Markel studied me for a moment, then said, *It is impressive that your sword works on this plane. Usually, such a weapon would not.*

Amaya is no ordinary weapon.

To which she practically preened. My sword was gaining a personality. Fabulous. *Not.*

Were you able to read his mind?

He shook his head. *Unless there is some form of physical contact between astral bodies, you can't.*

I frowned. *Is that what he was doing when we came across him the first time? Reading Dorothy's mind?*

I suspect he was doing much more than that, because mind reading usually does not leave a burned imprint.

I shivered, and the shadows around me trembled in time with the movement. *So basically, you got no more from him than I did?*

He half smiled. *Cazador or not, on this plane I am just another traveler.*

Somehow, I'm not believing that.

It was wryly said, and he acknowledged it with an almost regal nod. *Perhaps I do oversimplify.*

Perhaps? I seriously doubted there was any "perhaps" about it. I hesitated, then asked, *Just how closely do you follow me?*

Again that half smile appeared. It gave his almost stern features a softer edge, but didn't ease the impression of . . . not menace—not exactly. Perhaps it was more an underlying sense that the urban exterior was little more than a veil concealing a darker, more deadly soul.

I cannot enter your home, if that is your concern.

Surprise rippled through me. *So the vampire threshold rule applies on the astral plane?*

Yes. He hesitated. *I tail you everywhere else, though.*

Everywhere else? I repeated, a little mortified by the thought.

He cleared his throat, and I had an odd sense that he'd swallowed a laugh. This Cazador did *not* fit the image I'd created of them. But then, neither did Uncle Quinn. *Well, bathrooms are out of bounds, of course. As are boudoirs.*

Oh, thank God.

This time, he did laugh. It was a somewhat harsh sound, as if he didn't do it often. *You're an interesting person to talk to, Ms. Jones.*

Thanks. I think.

He bowed again. *You'd best return to your body. The weakness grows in you.*

Odd that he could sense that and I couldn't. But then, I'd become very good at ignoring my needs of late. *Chat with you later, Markel.*

Undoubtedly, he said.

I closed my eyes and imagined my body, and suddenly I was back there. I gasped at the shock of it and opened my eyes, but I didn't move, wary of causing a repeat of the sickness that hit me last time.

"Well," Rhoan said, voice impatient. "What happened?"

"Give her time to regain her full senses," Elga said crossly. "In fact, go get her coffee and chocolate. This poor girl needs some fat on her body; otherwise she's going to be of no use to anyone."

"I'm a werewolf," I murmured. "We're naturally lean."

But when even speaking hurt, I really *was* in trouble. I closed my eyes and rubbed my forehead somewhat gingerly. There was a low-grade throbbing deep inside my skull, and I knew it was a result of doing too much on too little sleep and food.

"Werewolves are lean, granted," Elga commented. "But you, my dear, are positively scrawny. You obviously need someone to sit you down and make you eat regular meals."

Is this one of those occasions where an "I told you so" would be appropriate? came Azriel's silent thought.

Probably. But I wouldn't suggest it because I might get nasty.

And that is supposed to scare me? The dry amusement in his tone swirled through me, sending warmth fluttering.

It would scare most men.

I am not a man.

True. You, reaper, are frustration personified.

Not unexpectedly, he made no reply. Rhoan came back carrying a large bottle of Coke and two chocolate-covered protein bars. I carefully hitched myself upright, but the room still spun around me. Elga was right—I couldn't keep risking the astral plane feeling like this. Not when we were hunting someone who was obviously very familiar with it, and also very dangerous on it.

Elga frowned. "Coffee would be better—"

"Trust me, it's not coffee that refuels her, but Coke. She was born with the stuff running through her veins, I think." He squatted beside the bed and handed me the Coke. "I know I'm rushing you, and I'm sorry, but we really do need to know what happened."

I took several gulps, felt the delicious fizz work its magic all the way down to my belly, then filled him in on all that had happened.

"Why in the hell would he want to play a cat-and-mouse game like this?" He tore open a protein bar and handed it to me.

"I don't think he's actually playing with a full deck, so who really knows."

"Whoever this person is, he's *very* adept at covering his tracks and keeping his identity secret—neither of which the insane tend to be." He hesitated. "Can you tell us anything else about him personally?"

"Well, he had hair this time." I frowned suddenly. "But oddly, it didn't really have any color."

"So it was gray?"

"No. There just wasn't *any* color. It merged with the shadows, as if it were part of them. It was weird."

"You know," Elga said suddenly, "he could be blind."

We both turned to look at her. "Why would you think that?" Rhoan asked.

"Well, if he was born blind, then he would have no understanding of color," she explained. "Of course, the blind *can* be taught to associate certain levels of heat with specific colors through the use of various colored-light filters, but they will never know colors as the sighted see them."

"Would that explain why he has no features on the plane? Because he's never actually seen his face?" I asked.

She frowned. "Not really, because while he may not see it, he *can* feel it. He would know the shape of his nose, mouth, and face, at the very least."

"Then why are his features missing on the field? I thought your soul wouldn't allow such deception."

"Normally, it doesn't. However, he may not be concealing it. What he may be doing is changing *your* perception of what you're seeing."

"Which means we're dealing with a *very* powerful individual indeed." Rhoan thrust to his feet. "Damn it, Ris, I like that you're involved in this even less."

"And you think I'm any happier?" I shook my head. "Trust me, if I could go home and leave you to it, I would."

"I know. It's just frustration speaking." He made a sharp motion with his hand. "Until we get our phone call, there's not much more we can do. I suggest you go home and catch some rest while you can."

I wished I could, but I still had a meeting with Jak to get to. I downed the rest of the Coke, then said, "He wanted me to chase the leads, not you."

"He can't get into this place, not even astrally, so he's not going to know who is doing what straightaway. And if he's as clever as I think he is, he'll know we'll be beside you every step of the way, regardless of what he orders. He simply doesn't think the Directorate is a threat. That's evident enough from his taunting phone calls."

I finished the last of the protein bars, then licked the chocolate off my fingers and got slowly to my feet. The room did a slow turn, so I pressed my fingers against the wall and said, "Have all his victims so far been women?"

Rhoan nodded. "Different ages, but all women."

"And they've nothing in common?"

"Other than the fact that they're all vampires, no."

"What about their makers?"

"Again nothing in common."

Meaning Stane's search for information on Dorothy's maker would be fruitless, because he wasn't the connection. Which, in turn, meant there was nothing to even remotely suggest who his next victim might be. Frustrating, to say the least. I pulled off the monitors and got dressed. "You'll ring me the minute the phone call comes?"

"I'll ring the minute we uncover anything useful. You, in the meantime, will get some rest. Promise?"

I nodded. He grunted, then swung around and offered me his arm. "Come on, let's get you out of here."

He escorted me back upstairs, then dropped a kiss on my cheek, reminded me to ring Riley, and left. I glanced at Azriel as I made my way out to Spencer Street. Though he walked beside me, he kept a careful distance between us. It didn't erase the awareness that stirred within, or the flow of heat that caressed my skin.

"How can the Directorate stop someone from entering that building astrally, and yet none of their devices even reacted to you?"

"Because I am not human. All the devices and magic are aimed at catching abnormalities in or on flesh-based rather than energy beings."

I frowned. "So it *should* have reacted to you."

"No, because this body is not real."

"It damn well feels real when I touch you." And it had certainly felt real when we'd made love. "Besides, you said you can find death in this form, so how can it not be real?"

"I bleed, and I can die in this form, true, but my being is energy, not flesh and blood." He hesitated, frowning a little. "That place would not react to you, either, if you were in Aedh form. Neither their technology nor their magic is attuned to what you and I are."

I frowned. "They're obviously aware of both reapers and Aedh, so why wouldn't they have some line of defense against either of you?"

"Because reapers interact with humans only on a soul-collecting basis, and why would anyone want to stop that?"

"But Aedh—"

"Have a long history of ignoring humanity, except

when it comes to their own needs—procreation, for instance," he said. "There is no major need for the Directorate to protect themselves against us, and they are well aware of that fact."

Which meant Lucian *could* have followed us into the building, if he'd wished. Though why *that* particular thought occurred to me I have no idea. And it wasn't like he could lurk in Aedh form anywhere nearby without Azriel being aware of him.

"So what if this person we're chasing is also not flesh-based?"

"He cannot be energy, as that would make him either Aedh or reaper. And no reaper can interact with those on the astral plane."

"That still leaves the possibility of another Aedh."

"Aedh have no need to use magic to transport themselves to and from locations. This killer did."

I grunted. I'd forgotten about that. "So what we need to do is uncover who in Melbourne sells powerful transport charms. It's something either the Brindle or Jak will know or can find out."

"What of Ilianna? And do you not think the Directorate would be already chasing that possibility?"

"I've involved Ilianna in enough dangerous shit already. She doesn't need this as well." I shrugged. "And the Directorate probably *have* investigated such an angle, but it doesn't hurt to ask the Brindle witches."

"Then why even bother with Jak?"

"Because I've got to meet him anyway, so it won't hurt." I eyed Azriel for a moment. "Has Jak suddenly become a problem for you?"

"No. I just think you risk his well-being needlessly."

"He's only going to ask around about charms, Azriel. I'd hardly call that dangerous."

He didn't say anything immediately, but then, he didn't need to. His disapproval stung the air. "And after this meeting, you will rest?"

"Yes." If nothing else came up, that was.

"Good. Because if you do not, I will be forced to make you."

"Try it, and I really *will* get nasty—" But I was speaking to air. He'd disappeared again.

Even though the bar was crowded with lunchtime patrons, Jak Talbott was easy enough to spot. It wasn't that he towered above everyone else, because at five ten, he was pretty much the average height for male werewolves. It was more that he exuded a raw masculinity that drew the eye. Or maybe it just seemed that way to me because I still wasn't entirely over the damn man, no matter how much I tried to convince myself otherwise.

He actually wasn't what I'd call handsome, but his rough-hewn features were easy on the eye and his body was well toned without being too muscular. His hair, like his skin, was a rich black, although there was a lot more silver glinting in the shaggy thickness of it these days. It gave him a genteel edge, which was something Jak would never be able to claim otherwise.

He leaned back in the chair as I approached, but his smile of greeting faded as his gaze swept me. "Damn it, Ris, you look worse every time I see you."

"Thanks." My voice was dry as I pulled out a chair and sat down opposite him. "You're looking swell, too."

He laughed. It was a warm, carefree sound, and the deep-down part of me that wouldn't entirely let go of the past, and this man, sighed wistfully.

"Yeah, lack of sleep does that to me," he said, a little too cheerfully. He obviously had news of some kind that he was excited about. "What's your excuse?"

"Same. What have you uncovered?"

His expression was one of resignation, but there was a twinkle in his dark eyes that had my pulse suddenly skipping. Once upon a time that twinkle had signified a sexual onslaught—one I'd always been willingly swept away by. "I thought we'd moved past this whole 'business only' deal with our rather erotic dance and kiss."

That rather erotic dance and kiss had actually been shared with Azriel, who'd taken Jak temporarily out of the picture—and taken on his form—to protect him. But because so many people had seen somebody they thought was Jak with me, I'd asked Azriel to supply him with memories of the evening. I just hadn't expected said memories to be *so* complete.

"Then you thought wrong, Jak. As I told you on that night, there's nothing left between us and there will be no repeat."

"Nothing left, huh?" His hand whipped out and snared mine. His grin was devilish as I tried—without success—to pull away. "So the racing pulse, and the desire that stirs the air, is nothing more than my imagination?"

"Nothing more," I said, and wished it was. Wished the past would just leave me the hell alone. But then, I'd invited it—and him—back into my life, so I had only myself to blame.

"And if I leaned across the table and kissed you," he said, in a voice so intimate it felt like a caress, "you would feel nothing more than the press of lips against lips?"

My gaze dropped to the lips I'd once known so well, and then I closed my eyes, drew back a foot, and kicked him. Hard. He yelped and released me, and I shifted out of immediate reach.

"Well, it's safe to say that was *not* the response I was hoping for." His grin was somewhat rueful as he rubbed his shin. "But do not think me defeated. If I breached your defenses once, I can do it again."

"Jak, give it up and just concentrate on business."

"I can't. I love a good challenge."

"Yeah, almost as much as you love a good story, and that's what wrecked our relationship in the first place."

"*That* is undeniably true." He caught the attention of a passing waitress and ordered a couple of beers. "So, business. I've been asking around about the murders of Frank Logan, his ex, and his secretary, and I'm afraid I'm getting nowhere fast. No one is talking."

"Not surprising, given that everyone who knows anything is ending up dead."

He nodded. "I did discuss Logan's murder with his partners, but other than sussing out who's handling his estate, I wasn't able to get anything helpful, either about Logan or Nadler."

I crossed my arms on the table and leaned forward a little warily. His spicy, woodsmoke scent teased my nostrils, warm and familiar. "Just as well I managed to get something, then, isn't it?"

He raised his eyebrows. "Like what?"

"Like the names of Nadler's three heirs."

"*Three* heirs? He's making damn sure we can't easily track him down again." He contemplated me for a moment, then added, "How did you manage that feat?"

"I talked to Logan's ghost."

He frowned. "I thought it was your mother who could talk to ghosts, not you."

"On this plane, yes. I talked to him on the astral plane. He died before his time, so he's stuck there rather than moving on."

"Huh. The things you learn." He gave the waitress a cheery smile as she arrived with our drinks. When she'd left, he added, "What are their names? I take it you're following them up?"

I gave him the three names, then said, "We've initiated searches, but haven't found anything yet."

"I'll see if any of my contacts can tell us anything."

"Good. Also, could you nose around and see if there's anyone in Melbourne selling transport charms?"

His eyebrows rose. "I may not know much about magic, but even I can tell you those things are rare. And expensive."

"Yeah. But someone used one recently, and I want to find out where it came from."

"This related to our quest?"

"Nope."

"Then am I allowed to know what it's related to?"

I hesitated. "It's a Directorate investigation—"

"The vampire drainings." His voice was grim. "Has to be. Not that we're allowed to print anything about them, which stinks."

"I can't do anything about that."

"Yeah, I know. I'll ask around, but don't expect much." He took a drink, then licked the froth from his lips, the simple movement raising memories of other things he'd done with his tongue. Desire stirred anew, and the heated spark in his eyes grew. But all he said was, "Now, to my news."

"And here I was thinking we'd have to dance around it some more."

He grinned. "I thought about it, but decided to take pity on you. You really *do* look like crap."

"Maybe I look that way because people keep saying it," I grouched, and downed half the glass of beer. Which wasn't a good thing to do on a practically empty stomach, but I was half were and it wasn't likely to affect me the same way it would a human. I waved a hand at him. "So, give."

"I think I may have discovered where the fake Nadler—if he *is* indeed our dark sorcerer—has his base of operations on West Street."

West Street being the street where Stane was located, and the area Nadler's consortium had bought up. But before I could say anything, Azriel popped into existence behind Jak and pressed two fingers against his temple. Jak froze instantly, but no one seemed to find this—or a half-naked, sword-bearing reaper—interesting. Azriel was obviously controlling what everyone saw again.

"What the hell are you doing?" I asked in exasperation.

Azriel raised his eyebrows, though his attention wasn't really on me, but rather Jak. "Getting the information he holds, of course."

"And you couldn't get it the old-fashioned way?" I said. "You know, by actually letting him tell us?"

"Why would I do that when this is quicker?" His differently colored blue eyes clashed with mine, as distant and matter-of-fact as his expression. "I will be back."

Before I could object, he disappeared again. I growled, but stifled the sound as Jak regained life. I said, "So how did you manage this minor miracle?"

"By keeping my ear to the ground." He took another sip of beer. "There's been some rumblings among the homeless in the area about being forcibly moved on—"

"The consortium has armed security patrolling the warehouses to stop the looters and taggers, so that isn't really strange." Especially in *this* situation, where the abandoned buildings surrounded one of the most powerful ley-line intersections in Melbourne. A sorcerer intent on using it wouldn't want anyone stumbling upon anything by mistake.

"Yeah," he said, his voice dry. "But these particular guards were dogs. Dogs that were big and black, with glowing red eyes."

I blinked. "Hellhounds?"

"If you believe in them, yeah."

"Oh, they're more than real. Tao and I barely survived an attack from a pair of them." And if Nadler—or whoever he now was—had hellhounds patrolling the area, then he sure as hell was hiding something *big*.

Which might mean our suspicions were correct. The sorcerer *had* used the power of the intersection to get onto the gray field and open the first of hell's portals.

"And just when did this event occur?"

I returned my attention to Jak. "What?"

"Hellhounds. You and Tao. Details, woman, details."

I waved a hand. "It's not important right now."

His growl of frustration practically echoed the one I'd stifled. "But you will fill me in later, won't you?"

"Maybe." I lightly bit my lip. "Did you uncover an exact location, or was it more general?"

"Exact. A warehouse on the corner of West and Reeves."

Which was the other end of the street from Stane. Maybe that was why the consortium had left him and the bar—the only two businesses in the area to remain in private hands—alone.

Azriel reappeared behind Jak. "I cannot access the site, but whatever is within, it is *not* the intersection itself. It lies farther down the road."

Jak jumped and swung around. "Fuck it, reaper, you could at least give some kind of warning before you pop into existence like that." Then he frowned. "How the hell did you even know about the site?"

"He can read any mind he chooses to," I explained, and switched my gaze to Azriel. "How come you can't get in?"

"There are wards similar to the ones your father once used set around the warehouse. I cannot enter when they are in place."

I frowned. "I wonder if the wards are set to repel all energy beings, or just reapers?"

"I cannot tell. The magic involved is beyond my understanding."

Ilianna would no doubt be able to tell us what it was, but I wasn't about to ask anything else of her unless it was absolutely necessary. She'd already placed herself in enough danger for this quest of mine. "We need to get into that warehouse to see what the wards are protecting."

"I'm glad you said 'we,'" Jak commented, "because you're not going anywhere without me."

I flicked my gaze to him. "Hellhounds are not something you want to tangle with."

"Probably not, but this is my story, remember, and I'm damned if I'm going to be cut out of it."

Do you wish me to tamper with his thoughts and send him home? Azriel asked.

I hesitated. *No. I don't want to go into that warehouse alone.*

If there are hellhounds, you will be better off calling your uncle. Jak will be of little use—you endanger his life for little reason.

We can't keep preventing him from taking risks. It's neither fair nor right when he's holding up his end of the deal.

Doing what is fair and right did not stop you from diverting him last time.

That was a different situation because the threat was di-

rect and real. Only it was Logan who the killer had been hunting, not Jak, as we'd presumed. *Besides, we won't be heading there unarmed.*

Naturally. Amaya is always with you.

I didn't mean Amaya. While I had no doubt Amaya could handle hellhounds, I wasn't about to walk into a possible confrontation with them without some form of backup. In this case, that was holy water.

I do not think this a wise course of action.

It isn't like I have many other choices. I wasn't going in alone, and if I called Rhoan, he'd cut me out of the investigation completely. Which meant I went either with Jak or with Lucian—and Azriel sure as hell wouldn't want me going *anywhere* with him. *But your disapproval has been duly noted.*

And ignored, he said, mental tones flat. *As you wish.*

He disappeared again—an action that was really starting to piss me off.

Jak cleared his throat. "Why do I have this feeling that there's a whole conversation going on that I know nothing about?"

"Because there is." I waved a hand at his beer. "Finish that. We have to go see a witch about some holy water."

Ilianna looked up from the magazine she was reading when I walked through the door of our home, but she jumped to her feet when she saw who was behind me, her expression suddenly furious.

Shit, I thought, as she muttered something under her breath and flicked a hand. I swore again and spun around—just in time to see Jak hit the floor face-first, then go slithering back toward the door. Which was shut. He grunted, then began to curse as his body plastered itself to the metal.

"Ilianna!" I spun back round to face her. "Let him go!"

"No," she spat back, her green eyes practically dripping with fury. "I *did* warn him never to darken our door again or there'd be consequences."

"I invited him here. Let him go."

"Why should I, after all the heartache he caused you? Damn it, Ris, he walked away unharmed *and* unregretful."

"Maybe, but that was the past. Let it go."

She snorted. "Is that what you're doing? Letting it go and forgiving? I thought you had more sense than that."

"Uh, hello?" Jak said, his voice a little hoarse. "Remember me? Still stuck to the door here, and it's getting rather uncomfortable."

I gave her a pointed look, and she sighed. "If you insist."

She made another flicking motion, and there was a *thunk* as Jak was released from the door.

"So nice of you," Jak muttered in a dark voice.

Ilianna snorted again. "Trust me, if it weren't for the rule that states whatever harm I do to you will be returned to me threefold, I would have done a whole lot worse than try to force you out the door."

He climbed slowly to his feet, then rotated his shoulders, as if trying to work out a kink. "Look, I can't take back the past—"

"And you wouldn't, even if you could," she snapped.

"True, but that doesn't mean I don't have regrets—"

"The only thing you regret is not being able to unleash the second part of that damn story because you were under the threat of jail time—or worse—from her uncle."

"Well, yeah, but—"

"Guys," I interrupted before things could get more out of hand. "Let it go. That's not what we're here for."

Ilianna gave me a somewhat cross look. "I don't care what *he's* here for."

I walked over and caught her hands in mine. "Thank you," I said softly, "for caring so much. But right now we need all the help we can get, and I'm afraid that means using Jak. Just trust me, okay? I know what I'm doing."

Her gaze searched mine, concern evident in those rich depths. "No, I don't think you do."

Unease slipped through me. I might have inherited clairvoyant abilities from Mom, but my abilities were nowhere near as reliable as either Mom's or Ilianna's. She could predict a sparrow's fart to the second if she wanted to.

"What's that supposed to mean?"

"Bringing *him*"—she cast another scathing glance in Jak's direction—"back into the fold is dangerous, for both the quest *and* you."

"He's not in my bed, nor ever likely to be." As for our quest, could it really get any more dangerous?

Somehow I doubted it. Yet even as the thought crossed my mind, I had to wonder if I'd just tempted fate. "And as far as my love life goes, it's surely *impossible* for that to get any worse."

"I wouldn't bet on it." She touched a hand to my cheek. "Just be careful, okay?"

"I will." It wasn't like I *wanted* another bout of pain and heartache—though I had a horrible suspicion that was exactly what I was headed for. Only the source wouldn't be Jak, but rather a stubbornly distant reaper.

"Good." She glared at Jak once more. "And if you do *anything* to hurt her again, I will cast a spell so strong that you'll never even fancy a woman again, let alone get it up."

Jak winced and held up his hands. "I promise. I don't intend to hurt her or write another story about her or anyone else related in *any* way to her."

"Good." She tossed her hair, her eyes sparkling. A mare enjoying her victory. "Now, tell me what you need."

"Holy water," I said.

"Of course you do." Her voice was dry. "Because it couldn't be something easy like demon deterrent, now, could it?"

"You have demon deterrents on you?" Jak asked, walking a little closer to the lounge.

Ilianna cast him a look that stopped him in his tracks. "Not on me, no."

"But you *have* got them?"

"I can make them—"

"Holy water," I interrupted, in an effort to keep the conversation heading in the right direction. "Have you got any?"

"Of course. Given the shit that has happened of late, I thought I'd better keep a good supply at the ready." She paused. "What is it this time?"

"Hellhounds. Maybe."

"Oh, *fuck*." She shook her head. "Why are you two tackling hellhounds?"

I gave her a quick update, then added, "We need to get into that warehouse and see what we're dealing with."

"Which means you actually need me—"

"No," I interrupted forcefully. "Absolutely not."

"Ris, I know magic. You don't—"

"I don't care. Azriel said the warehouse *isn't* on the ley intersection, so until I know for *sure* that's what we're dealing with, you're not going anywhere near that place."

"You don't have to be in the intersection to use the power of it," she said. "There's going to be magic there, trust me."

"Yes, but we don't know if it's been leashed or not."

"If the sorcerer *has* used the intersection to hit the gray fields and open the first gate, it's been leashed." She paused, her concern deepening. "And if he *has* leashed the magic, then he'll have more than hell-hounds protecting it."

"Undoubtedly. Which is why I don't want you in the middle of it until we're sure what we're facing."

"So why does *he* get to go, when he knows jack shit about magic?"

"Because risking his life means less to me than risking yours." I flashed him a smile to take the sting out of the words.

"I love you, too," he muttered, but there was amusement in his eyes.

I snorted softly and returned my attention to Ilianna. "I need you to do a couple of other things, too, if you wouldn't mind."

"Like?"

I hesitated. "There's two things I need."

Actually, there were three, but one I couldn't—wouldn't—ask with Jak present. I wasn't about to give him that much information about the current state of my love life.

"So tell me," Ilianna said.

"The first—can you contact the Brindle and ask if they've sensed any dark magic at work on or near the intersection? If he *did* use it, they'd have to know about it. Maybe they can tell us about either the magic or the man behind it."

She frowned. "Not necessarily. It depends what sort of protection circle he's using. It could be inclusive—keeping the magic and the spells within the circle and undetectable beyond it."

"But surely the ley line itself would not be contained so easily?"

"I don't know. I'll ask. The second task?"

I hesitated. "Tao's struggling to pull himself together

after the accident in the kitchen yesterday. I was wondering if there was some sort of potion or charm that might help him."

She frowned. "Whatever I give him would be more illusion than reality. I've told you before, there's no magic beyond time that will help him heal."

If he ever does. She might not have said the words, but they nevertheless hung in the air between us.

"The illusion of help might be all he needs right now."

She slowly nodded. "I'll see what I can brew up."

I hesitated again. "Good."

Her gaze swept me shrewdly. She'd guessed that neither of my requests was what I'd really wanted. But all she said was, "The minute you sense *anything* magic related, you ring me. At the very least, I can advise you long distance."

"That I can agree to."

"Then go get something to eat before you collapse on your feet."

"I do wish people would stop ordering me to eat," I muttered, but nevertheless headed for the kitchen.

"Someone has to," Ilianna said. "You seem damn determined to run yourself into the ground lately."

"Which is an echo of what Azriel said not too long ago."

"You should listen to him more often."

I glanced back at her. "How much is he paying you to say that?"

She rolled her eyes at me. "Speaking of our reaper, where is he?"

"Sulking."

"What have you done to the poor man?"

I snorted softly. "He's neither a man nor poor, and you should be on my side, not his."

She shook her head, amusement tugging at her lips as she headed for her bedroom. I opened the fridge to study the contents, then decided on lamb sandwiches.

I glanced up at Jak. "You want a sandwich?"

"Yep." He propped his butt up on the counter. "What sort of accident did Tao have?"

"*That* is none of your damn business." I slapped thick slices of lamb between slices of bread and handed it to him.

"Huh." He bit into his sandwich, then added, "So what is going on between you and Azriel?"

"Nothing. He's a reaper." I squashed my sandwich down with a little more force than necessary. "They don't do love *or* life."

"Which, interestingly enough, does not preclude them doing sex."

I pointed the knife at him. "Drop it. Now."

He grinned and held up his hands again. "A little too close to the mark, huh?"

"More wide of the mark, and still none of your business."

Thankfully, Ilianna chose to call me into her bedroom at that moment. It was a cool green and normally very calming, but it didn't do a lot to ease the tension suddenly coursing through me. She closed the door, then crossed her arms and said, "Out with it."

I plopped down on the edge of her enormous bed. "Is it possible that some sort of attraction spell has been placed on me?"

Surprised flitted across her features. Whatever question she'd been expecting, that obviously hadn't been it. "Why on earth would you think something like that has happened?"

"Because it would explain my unrelenting need to be sexual with Lucian whenever I'm with him."

The surprise gave way to amusement. "Why does a spell have to be involved? I mean, he's a hot and sensual man and you're a werewolf—unrelenting need comes with that sort of combination, doesn't it?"

I was shaking my head before she'd finished. "This is something else. It's almost a compulsion. It takes a huge amount of effort to say no to the man, and I've never been like that with *anyone* before now, werewolf heritage or not."

She frowned and walked across to me. She raised her hands and skimmed either side of my body, not touching me but close enough that I could feel the sudden tingle of energy flowing from her fingertips. *Reading my aura*.

She stepped back. "I can't sense any obvious spell, but that doesn't mean there isn't one on you. It could be a *geas* of some kind, which tends to be subtler and harder to trace."

"Damn." I thrust a hand through my hair. "Have you got anything that might be able to counter such magic?"

She hesitated, then went over to the huge, walk-in

floor-to-ceiling cupboard that housed all her magical bits and pieces. She opened one side, revealing shelves stocked with all sorts of bottles, herbs, various tools, and other stuff I had no idea about, and fished around for several minutes. Eventually she returned with what looked like a thin rope bracelet entwined with dead leaves.

"This isn't strong enough to totally counteract any spell or *geas*, but it will mute the force of it and allow clearheaded thinking."

"Which is all I really need." Sex with Lucian might be extraordinary, but I sure as hell still wanted the option of saying no occasionally.

She slipped the bracelet over my left hand, but as it settled on my wrist, the Dušan came to life, its head whipping around as if to study the intruder. Its tail lifted from my skin, curled around the bracelet, then returned to my flesh. And the bracelet went with it, prickling and itching as it leached into my skin. After a few seconds, it was little more than a leafed tattoo that encircled my wrist, one that was entwined by the Dušan's serpent-like tail.

My gaze shot to Ilianna. "Was that supposed to happen?"

Ilianna's eyes were wide. "Hell, *no*."

"Azriel?"

He appeared and I shoved my hand at him. "Any ideas about this?"

He studied my newest tattoo with a frown. "Unfortunately, I do not know enough about the magic that created the Dušans, let alone understand what they are fully capable of. I *had* thought they were unable to be active on this plane, but that is patently untrue when it comes to the one that resides in your flesh." His gaze met mine. His expression was flat, giving little away, and yet I felt the turmoil in him. He was fiercely glad that this had happened, and just as annoyed by the strength of that reaction. "This is not a bad thing, though."

No, it wasn't, though I suspected his reasons for thinking that stemmed more from a hope that I'd now stay totally away from Lucian rather than merely being less compelled in his presence.

Ilianna tentatively touched the tattoo. "The magic is still alive within it. Amazing."

"Let's just hope that if there *is* a compulsion, it works, because it looks like I'm stuck with it."

But if there *was* a *geas*, and this bracelet *did* work, did that in any way imply that Lucian had meant me harm?

He'd made no secret of his desire for revenge, and definitely no secret of the fact that he would do any-thing—use anyone—to get it. Having a *geas* placed on me might be nothing more than his way of ensuring a continuing supply of the information he needed to hunt down the Raziq, especially since the only time he could fully read my mind was when we had sex.

Or was I simply trying to excuse the behavior of someone I liked, *geas* or not?

There was no easy answer to that one—or at least not one I wanted to confront right now—so I pulled the sleeve over the tattoo and said, "Holy water?"

"Ah, yes."

Azriel stepped to one side as Ilianna returned to her

cupboard. She came back a few minutes later carrying a purple satchel and a knife. "There's six bottles in here. If you need any more than that, you get the hell out of there."

"And the knife?"

"That," she said grimly, "is for Jak. And no, I'm not going to stab him, as much as I might want to."

I grinned, slung the satchel over my shoulder, and led the way back to the kitchen. Azriel made himself scarce again, although the heat that caressed my spine suggested he hadn't gone far.

Ilianna handed Jak the sheathed knife and said, "This is for you, though you don't deserve it."

He took the knife tentatively. "I'm not much into weapons, you know—"

"If you're tackling hellhounds, you'd better be," she retorted. "And it's not just a knife—it's a *blessed* knife. It'll work when other weapons don't, so use it. I don't want Risa hurt protecting your useless ass."

"Thanks for the concern," he muttered.

I restrained my smile and glanced at Ilianna. "Are you and Mirri still having dinner with your parents tonight?"

Mirri was Ilianna's girlfriend, though like many mares she was bisexual rather than just a lesbian like Ilianna. She was also very open about her sexuality, whereas Ilianna kept hers a closely guarded secret—at least where her parents were concerned. She and Mirri had been in a steady relationship for a while now, but it was only very recently that Ilianna had acceded to Mirri's requests to meet her parents—as friends, nothing more.

She grimaced. "Yes. And Carwyn will be there."

Carwyn was the stallion her parents were trying to set her up with. According to Mirri, he was rather hot—in bed and out—but given Ilianna's preferences, she was either going to have to be honest with her parents or get stuck in a situation that could only end badly.

"Oh," I said, well aware that Jak was rather avidly listening in. Once a newshound, always a newshound. "Good luck."

"Yeah, I'm going to need it." She grimaced. "Just make sure you ring me if you find magic."

I nodded, then picked up my sandwiches and headed out. Jak followed so close on my heels that his breath washed the back of my neck. Unfortunately, it *wasn't* an unpleasant sensation.

"You can drive," I said, as the front door slammed behind us.

"Color me shocked," he said. "Here I was thinking you didn't trust me to keep my hands to myself when you were in the same vehicle as me."

"I don't. Which is why you're driving."

He snorted softly, but opened the passenger door of his red Honda Accord, ushering me in before running around to the driver's side.

It didn't take us long to get to West Street. We cruised slowly past the warehouse, then turned into Reeves Street. Halfway down the block, we stopped and I climbed out of the car, then leaned against it, my gaze sweeping the building. It was one of those old two-story, redbrick places that had become so popular with inner-city renovators. The iron roof was rusted and covered in bird shit, and the regularly spaced windows were small and protected by bars as rusted as the roof. But considering its age, it still seemed surprisingly solid. Like many of the other buildings in the area, it had walls littered with graffiti and tags, and rubbish lay in drifting piles along its length. It looked and felt abandoned.

Only it wasn't.

Though there was no sign of guards or movement, there was an odd, almost watchful stillness about the place. In fact, the whole area was unnervingly quiet. Even the sound of traffic traveling along nearby Smith Street seemed muted.

Azriel reappeared, but the heat of his presence did little to chase the growing chill from my body. "I can sense no human life inside."

My gaze swept the building again. It was waiting. Ready. Trepidation shivered through me, and I rubbed my arms. "What about *un*life? Or hellhound-type life?"

"There is nothing in there other than vermin."

"So why does it feel like a predator is about to pounce?"

"I do not know."

"Well," Jak said, from the other side of the car, "we're not going to find out what's going on by standing here."

"No." I hesitated and glanced at Azriel. "You really can't get in there?"

"The wards are set just within the building walls. Destroy them, and I can enter."

"If I do that, whoever set them will likely feel it."

"Yes." He half raised a hand and, just for a moment, he leaned closer, as if to kiss me. Then he stepped back. "Be careful."

"Coward," I muttered, then spun and walked away.

"So." Jak's voice was conversational as he fell in step beside me. "There's absolutely nothing going on with that reaper and you, is there?"

"Just drop it, Jak."

"Thought so."

"Then you thought wrong."

He chuckled softly. I ignored him and kept walking. There were no doors on this side of the building, and all the bars—despite their rusted appearance—were solid. But there were two entrances on West Street— one of them heavily padlocked and apparently leading into an old office area, and the other a roller door over what once must have been a loading bay. The door itself was battered and coated with grime, and the bottom edge had been torn away from the guides. Obviously, this was where the homeless had been getting in.

I took a long, slow breath that didn't ease the tension knotting my stomach, then squatted and squeezed through the gap.

The room beyond the roller door was still and quiet. I shifted to one side so Jak could enter, and studied the immediate area. A platform ran around three sides of the dock, and there were stairs down at the far end that led up to it. I could neither see nor smell anything or anyone out of the ordinary, and yet there was something here. Something that crawled along the edges of that other part of me—the bit that saw the reapers and was sensitive to the feel of magic.

Jak hunkered down beside me. "Anything?"

His voice was little more than a whisper. Maybe he felt the closeness of something, too. *Azriel? Can you hear me?* There was no response. Obviously, the magic was broader than he'd suspected. I shook my head and said, "You?"

"Just rats and rubbish."

"Yeah." I pulled the satchel around and gave him a couple of Ilianna's little blue bottles. "Put these in your pocket. If there are hellhounds here, pop the cork and use the water. It'll deter them."

"So holy water really does work?"

I glanced at him. "You investigate paranormal events and happenings, and you don't know this?"

"Reporters are natural skeptics. Until I see it, I don't believe it."

"You haven't seen ley lines or the gates to heaven and hell, yet you believe in those."

He raised his eyebrows in amusement. "No, I believe *you* believe. I'm still holding out for proof."

I snorted softly. "You may regret that."

"Yeah, I usually do. It never stops me, though."

A truer sentence had never been uttered. I rose and padded forward, still drawing in the scents around us, trying to find some hint of the magic I sensed was here. It might not be related to the ley line, but something was definitely going on in this place.

We followed the loading bay to its end, then carefully went up the steps and headed to the left. Several doors lay ahead. I paused and glanced questioningly at Jak. He hesitated, then pointed to the one in the middle. It was as good as any, I supposed.

I reached for the handle and felt the shimmer of . . . not energy, something else. Something darker. I said, "Be ready. Whatever is going on, I think it's happening on the other side of that door."

He nodded, his expression a mix of excitement and wariness as he drew Ilianna's knife. I hoped like hell he'd use it if we got into trouble.

I took a deep breath, released it slowly, then opened the door. The room behind it was deep and dark, and the air still. The sensation that had briefly caressed the door handle wasn't evident in the room itself, yet my uneasiness increased, and I wasn't sure why.

I took one step into the room. The flooring was wood rather than concrete, which seemed odd. I paused, waiting.

Nothing happened. No one and nothing jumped out at us.

I took another step. Still nothing. Yet tension continued to crawl across my skin, and the feeling that something watched—waited—was growing.

"I can't smell anyone or anything unusual." Jak stopped beside me. His words seemed to jar uneasily against the still blackness of the room.

"That's the problem." I took another step.

It was one step too many.

With very little warning, the floor collapsed and we fell into deeper darkness.

Chapter 7

Wood and dust rained around us as the blackness swallowed us whole. There was no light, no stirring of air, no sound except the harsh rasp of our breathing.

After what seemed an eternity, I hit the dirt feetfirst and stumbled forward a couple of steps before falling on my face. Pain shot up my legs, then raged through the rest of me, until even the mere act of breathing hurt.

Jak landed with a grunt and slightly more balance, ending up on his knees rather than his face—a fact I knew simply because the sharp rasp of his breathing was close but not ground-close.

For several seconds neither of us moved. My breath was caught somewhere in the middle of my throat, and tension wound through my limbs as I waited for the axe to fall.

Nothing happened.

"You okay?" Jak asked eventually. Dirt stirred, and then his hand caught mine. I gripped it gratefully.

"Yeah. You?"

He helped me to a sitting position. "Winded, but okay. Can't see a goddamn thing, though."

"No." I dusted my hands, then reached back and drew Amaya from her shadowy sheath. Flames flared along her blade and spread across the darkness in lilac waves.

"And where the *fuck* did that come from?" Jak asked.

"Long story."

My gaze swept our cage. The pit was about ten feet square, and smelled of earth and age. I squinted up. Even if I stood on Jak's shoulders and jumped, I wouldn't be able to catch the edge and haul myself out. And I doubted I'd be able to take my energy form. If the magic in this place prevented Azriel from entering, it was a fair bet it would also prevent me from changing into Aedh.

It was also a wonder both of us had come through the fall relatively unscathed. But then, I guess werewolf bones were stronger than human ones, even in those of us who couldn't actually shape-shift.

But our going through the floor was no accident—the concrete slab had been neatly cut, as had the timber that had covered this hole. It had held only long enough to catch the two of us.

"It can't be a traditional sword," he murmured, and reached out.

"Don't—" I said at the same time that Amaya hissed and spat tendrils of fire at his fingertips.

He quickly withdrew. "Shit, that thing is *alive*."

"Alive and aware."

His gaze jumped to mine. "How the hell is something like that even *possible*?"

"It's not—not in this world, anyway. She was born

on the gray fields—forged in the death of a demon—
and she has a life and a mind of her own."

"So you control her?"

I half smiled. "Only sometimes."

"You, my dear Risa, are becoming more and more
interesting."

I snorted softly and pushed to my feet. "Remember
Ilianna's threat."

"Oh, trust me, I am." He rose with a wince and
rubbed his left knee. "How the hell are we going to get
out of here?"

"I don't know." I used Amaya's flames to inspect the
walls more closely. The earth looked hard-packed and
solid. I didn't fancy our chances of digging ourselves
out.

But I didn't fancy waiting around for the creator of
this pit to arrive, either.

Not, Amaya said.

I frowned. *Not what?*

Solid. Not.

My gaze swept the walls again. *They look it.*

Not. Left go.

I walked to the wall on my immediate left. Amaya
flared, sparking brightly off the quartz in the dirt. *I
don't see—*

Magic. Touch.

I carefully extended the tip of her blade and touched
the wall. Only she didn't hit it. She went *through* it.

The wall was fake.

I reached out and ran my hand across it. Grit and
rock brushed my fingertips. I pressed harder. The wall

resisted briefly, then, with a slight sucking sound, my hand went through. Cold damp air caressed my fingertips.

I withdrew, then repeated the procedure a few feet on either side. Real wall, not magic-enhanced wall. The doorway was a foot or so wide. Enough for a human to squeeze out sideways.

Or a hellhound to get in.

I swallowed heavily and looked around at Jak. "There's a concealed exit here."

"To where?"

"Do you care?"

"Yes. But I don't fancy staying here, either."

"Keep your knife handy." I went through sword first. It felt like I was walking through molasses—the magic creating the illusion was thick and syrupy, and clung like tendrils to my body, resisting my movements and then releasing me with an odd sucking sound. I shuddered, my skin crawling with horror. Whatever—whoever—had made that wall was not into white magic.

I forced my hand back through the wall. Jak's fingers entwined with mine, and he came through as I had—shuddering.

"God, that's revolting," he muttered, shaking himself like a dog trying to rid his coat of excess water. "Where are we?"

"I have no idea."

I raised Amaya again. We were in a tunnel of some kind, and it was a tight fit—there was only an inch or two between my shoulders and the walls. Jak was forced not only to stand sideways but to keep his knees bent as well.

It wouldn't be a good place to be caught in. There was no room to fight.

I looked to the left, then the right, but couldn't see much in either direction—just the tunnel sweeping away into darkness. But as my gaze moved back to the left, the odd sense of unease increased. Something was down there. Something bad.

I shivered, then glanced up at Jak. "Does your nose tell you anything?"

"Can't smell much more than age and dirt." He hesitated, then glanced past me to the right. "It smells a bit fresher down that direction, though."

It did? I studied the lilac-lit shadows dubiously, then glanced to the left again. There wasn't a chance I was heading down *there*, so that left only Jak's choice.

With Amaya's fire lighting the way, we crept forward. The tunnel continued to narrow, until the bits of rock and debris in the soil were tearing into my shoulders and the scent of blood stung the air.

If there were hellhounds ahead, it would call to them.

I swallowed heavily and tightened my grip on Amaya. Her hissing ramped up, and I didn't know whether she was reacting to something I'd yet to see, or merely echoing my tension. I hoped it was the latter, but I had a horrible suspicion it was the former.

At least I was better off than Jak—even as awkwardly bent over as he was, he kept hitting his head against the roof.

"Fuck," he said eventually, "I really think we need to turn back."

"No. There's something down the other end of this tunnel—" I yelped as a particularly sharp rock sliced into my arm.

"At this rate," he muttered, "we'll bleed to death before we ever reach an exit."

"I think I'd rather bleed than chance whatever is at the other end."

"It can't be any worse—"

"I wouldn't bet on it."

The words were barely out of my mouth when I burst out of the tunnel like a cork being popped from a champagne bottle. I stumbled to gain my balance and took a quick look around, once again using Amaya for illumination. No hellhounds, nothing that appeared immediately dangerous—just two innocuous-looking stones that stood like petrified soldiers in the middle of a cavern. Which didn't mean we were out of trouble, but wherever the hell we were, it had to be better than the tunnel. Jak all but exploded out of it three seconds later and came to a halt beside me.

"Fuck *me*!" he said vehemently. He swept the sweaty strands of hair from his forehead with hands as bloody as mine and looked around. "Where are we?"

"I have no idea. And not in a million years."

"I'll remind you of those words the next time we make out—" Jak stopped, and his eyes widened. "What the hell are *those*?"

"I don't know."

It was somewhat absently said as I studied the two

pillars. They were about six feet tall and stood the width of a body apart from each other, so that they formed an odd sort of doorway that seemed to go nowhere. Though they were mostly gray in color, their surface was littered with quartz that Amaya's flames sparked to life, sending rainbow-colored flurries skating across the earthen walls. There were markings and weird symbols etched into each pillar, but it was no language I'd ever seen, and it felt ancient. No, not just ancient—*powerful*.

I stepped forward cautiously. Energy caressed my skin, similar to the magic I'd felt briefly when I touched the door handle. I swept Amaya's light across the floor. While it was mainly dirt, there was a series of wide, flat stones that formed a circle around the pillars. While there was no quartz within these stones for Amaya's flames to catch, there *was* writing. This time I recognized the language, even if I didn't entirely understand the spell. They were runes, meaning the stones were some sort of protection circle.

"You think it's a gateway of some kind?" Jak said.

"Of some kind." I walked around the pillars, making sure to keep close to the walls and well away from the runes. "Be careful where you step, Jak."

"I may be a skeptic when it comes to many things magic, but even *I* can sense the wrongness in whatever is written on those stones."

And that's *precisely* what it was. A wrongness. The magic in this place wasn't dark, it wasn't evil—it was just *wrong*.

Like the man without a face, I thought absently, though it was doubtful they were in any way connected.

Each rune in the circle was a little bit different from its neighbor, except at the north and south points, where a set of six identical ones appeared. Exit and entry points, perhaps?

I stopped when I reached the tunnel entrance again and studied the walls themselves. There appeared to be another exit to the left, but on closer inspection, it proved to be little more than a niche. Whoever had built this place obviously used it for storage, because it was filled with an odd assortment of things—including a shovel, a crowbar, a hammer, and various-sized jars of nails. The sort of stuff you'd need if you wanted to repair a floor or bury a body.

I shivered, and hoped like hell we got out of this damn hole long before we had to worry about either of those things.

"Now what?" Jak crossed his arms and stared at the pillars thoughtfully. "Do we attempt to breach the magic?"

"Nope, we use our 'ring a friend' option." I dug the phone out of my pocket, hit the vid-button, then called Ilianna.

"You found something?" she said by way of hello.

"Yeah. I need you to tell me what it is. Hang on and I'll show you." I turned the phone around and did a slow sweep of the cavern.

"Fuck," she said. "That's some heavy-duty magic they have happening there."

"But what sort of magic?"

"I have no idea what the script on the pillars is, but it's obviously some form of gateway."

"To heaven, hell, or somewhere in between?"

"I'd guess in between, if that's where earth falls in that little list."

I supposed that was *something*. At the very least, it meant we didn't have the immediate worry of hell-hounds making a sudden appearance. I walked around to the north point. "Does this signify an exit or entrance?"

"The pattern the stones are placed in suggest exit. The entrance should be the other side."

"How can identical rocks form a pattern?" I walked around to the other side.

"They're not identical to the trained eye."

I shoved the phone down so she could see the stones, and she added, "Yep, that's it."

"And is there anything in these runes that would stop Jak and me leaving via this gate?"

"Other than the fact that it would be sheer stupidity, you mean?"

I grinned. "Yeah, other than that."

"Um, Ris—" Jak said.

I made a "quiet" motion with my hand as Ilianna said, "I honestly don't know." She hesitated. "The runes shouldn't offer a problem, but as I said, I can't read the script on the pillars so I really have no idea just what might happen or even how to activate them."

"Ris—" Jak intervened again.

"What?" I said, looking up in exasperation.

He waved a hand at the pillars. Light shimmered between them, as if it were a mirror catching the first sickly rays of the day.

"Oh, fuck," I said. "The pillars just activated."

"Then get the hell out of there!"

"Love to, but we're stuck underground in a fucking cavern. Call you back."

"Wait—"

I didn't. I turned the phone off and met Jak's gaze grimly.

"I can't go back into that tunnel," he said. "It's too tight for *any* sort of speed. Niche?"

"Niche," I agreed. "And let's hope whoever—or whatever—is coming through that gate has neither good sight nor a strong sense of smell."

"Amen to that," Jak muttered, and lunged for the niche.

I squeezed in beside him, and watched as light continued to pulse and swirl between the pillars. Its color was a sickly green—the same color that now glowed within the runes. Amaya screamed, a battle cry that was audible both in my head *and* in the cavern.

Fuck, flame out and be quiet, I ordered fiercely.

No. Fight what comes.

Not yet. Flame out, Amaya.

Should fight. It was all but a snarl, but her light died. I wished I could say the same about her fierce screaming, but at least it was only inside my head.

The sickly light of the pillars spread tendrils across the darkness, lifting the shadows in some sections of the cavern but casting others into deeper darkness. Our niche fell between the two. Whatever was coming through that gateway had only to glance our way and we were gone.

Then, suddenly, the light stopped pulsing and a shadow stepped through. It was a man—a tall man, with broad shoulders and dark hair. As he strode toward the exit, the light between the pillars died, leaving only the sickly glow of the runes to lift the sudden darkness. It wasn't enough, and the stranger became little more than a shadow, hinted at but not fully fleshed out.

He paused at the north point of the circle and waved his hand over them. The light in the six runes died and he strode toward the tunnel, quickly disappearing. Oddly enough, though he'd appeared taller than Jak when he'd first come into view, I had no sense that he was in any way restricted by the tight confines of the tunnel. Maybe it was just the weird light that had made him seem taller.

As the sounds of his steps faded, Jak bent closer, his breath warm against my left ear as he murmured, "Now what?"

"We wait."

"But if he came through those pillars, why can't we use them to exit?"

"Because he'll sense the magic kicking in and will either give chase or send something after us."

"Either option is better than getting caught in this damn niche."

"Not when we have no idea if the pillars are both exit and entry. For all I know, the exit point here is nothing more than a ruse. It could be what I sensed down at the other end of the tunnel."

"But Ilianna said—"

"That she didn't understand the entire spell. It won't hurt to wait, Jak."

"It just might if that man comes back and sees us," he muttered. "Just because I have a knife doesn't mean I can use it."

"Then it's a good thing I can use the sword, isn't it?" I all but snapped.

"Yeah, I guess it is." His free hand slipped down my back and came to rest on my butt. "You have no idea how exciting I find that."

Actually I did, given how close we were standing. But then, he *was* a werewolf, and danger was an aphrodisiac to most wolves, even if they didn't actively seek it out. I grabbed his hand and shoved it away. "Behave."

He chuckled softly, but otherwise did as bid. I flared my nostrils and sifted through surrounding scents, trying to get some idea of the man who'd come through the gate. But no matter how hard I tried, I could neither smell nor hear him. Maybe there *was* an exit at the other end of the tunnel. Maybe he'd done little more than check what his trap had caught and then moved on-

A gruff voice cut the thought short. "Look, I'm telling you, there's no one here."

It was hard to tell just how close he was because his words seemed to echo in the still blackness. One thing was sure—his voice was unfamiliar, and *that* was something of a relief. I'd half expected otherwise—that it would, somehow, be Lucian. Azriel's distrust had a lot to answer for.

"Well, apparently vermin *can* set the trap off," the

stranger said. Despite the hint of exasperation, there was a deeper edge of wariness enriching his voice. He feared the person he spoke to. "As I said, there's no one in the hole."

He was definitely closer now, and tension wound through my limbs. I licked my lips, and once again tightened my grip on Amaya. Her screaming ratcheted up several notches, but at least she was restrained enough to keep it internal—although that didn't help the ache in my head any.

"Yes, I've released them." The stranger paused. "Yes, I'll head up now and move any cars that might be hanging about, just in case."

"Damn," Jak muttered. "If he damages—"

I stamped on his foot, hard. He hissed, but otherwise fell silent.

The stranger reappeared. He made a motion with his left hand, and the sickly glow reappeared in the runes. It wasn't strong enough to light the niche, but it did throw off just enough to make him a little more visible. He was about my height, with thick shoulders, muscular arms, and tree-trunk legs. He reminded me somewhat of a wrestler, but he was extraordinarily light on his feet. He passed close by our niche, but didn't see or smell us—he was human, not shifter or were, and for that I was suddenly grateful.

But as he passed, I noted the tats on his shoulders— one of a dragon with two swords crossed above it and the other a ring of barbed wire.

I'd seen both a number of times over the last few months. The dragon and swords meant he was a Razan, and while I wasn't sure what the barbed wire tat represented, I'd seen it on the man who'd arranged the delivery of the Dušan that now resided on my left arm, as well as on one of the men who'd killed Logan's secretary. How the two were connected I had no idea, because while we suspected that my father was responsible for the Dušan, there was no logical connection between him and the murder of Logan and his secretary. In fact, we were pretty sure the person responsible for *those* was the man who'd been impersonating Nadler.

Which meant we really needed to question *this* man.

The stranger strode on, the light in the six runes dying as he approached. As it did, the pillars came to life again.

It was now or never.

I motioned Jak to stay put, then carefully squeezed out of the niche and padded silently forward, flipping Amaya around to hold her by the blade rather than the hilt as I did so. I suspected—given her generally shitty mood—that if I used her blade she might take matters into her own hand and kill our quarry rather than just knock him out.

I raised the sword, but he suddenly dropped and turned, and Amaya whooshed harmlessly over his head. He surged upright, but I spun and kicked him hard in the gut. He flew backward, hit the wall with a loud crack, and slithered to the floor. I flipped Amaya, holding her hilt once more, but the Razan didn't get up. After another moment or two, I stepped forward and pressed two fingers against his neck. His pulse was steady and strong, so I hadn't done much more than knock him out.

"Now what do we do with him?" Jak came out of the niche and stopped beside me.

"We find out who he is and who he was talking to."

I knelt beside the Razan and went through his pockets. I found the phone and tossed that to Jak, then continued the search until I found his wallet.

"According to his license," I said, "his name is Henry Mack, and he lives in Broadmeadows."

Jak grunted. "The phone is locked. Any ideas?"

My gaze went to his birth date on his license. It was a long shot, but a lot of people used such things for passwords. "Try one-four-oh-four."

He did so, then shook his head.

"Reverse it."

He pressed the appropriate buttons. "Nope."

I gave him the year; then, when that also proved a bust, glanced at our last hope—the post code—and said, "Three-oh-four-seven, either way."

"Bingo to the latter."

I placed his license on the stone near his hand, then pulled out the other cards. There were four credit cards—two in the name of Henry Mack, and two in the name of Jason Marks—a transit card, and various receipts from shops. Mainly for clothes and grocery items, although interestingly, there was a small receipt from a place called Esoteric Supplies, which I knew from Ilianna was one of the main suppliers of wiccan items in Melbourne.

There was little else in the wallet except cash, so I placed the remaining cards on the stone, took a photo of both them and our stranger, and shot both off to Stane with a quick note to see what he could uncover.

"Well," said Jak, "he's only got a couple of numbers in his address book, and his last call came from a blocked number. I don't suppose we can take the risk and call it back?"

"And let whoever is behind this know we have his Razan? Not a good idea."

Jak flicked through other screens. "They're going to know something went on, anyway. I mean, you knocked him out."

"True." I hesitated, awareness suddenly prickling across my senses.

And suddenly remembered the Razan's last words. *Yes, I've released them.*

I spun around. The stones' circle was complete again, and its fading glow did little to light the immediate darkness. The pillars had fallen completely silent. There was no escape that way—not unless we could get the gate open again.

A low growl reverberated around the darkness, raising the hackles along the back of my neck.

"What the hell was that?" Jak's voice was filled with trepidation as he studied the tunnel behind us.

"That"—I grabbed his hand and dragged him toward the northern end of the stones—"is a hellhound. We need to get out of here—fast!"

We reached the northern entrance and stopped. The

runes didn't react to our presence. They just continued to glow that same sickly color.

"Now what?" Jak's voice was grim and there was fear in his eyes.

"I don't know."

I remembered the gesture the Razan had made when he'd reentered the cavern, and repeated it as best I could. Nothing happened. The runes continued to glow ominously.

Fuck, fuck, *fuck*!

The air began to stir, became a thick scent of malevolence. They were coming.

I grabbed one of the bottles from Ilianna's satchel and popped the cork. It flew toward the still-glowing runes but never made it across them. There was a sharp report, a flash of fire, and the cork was little more than cinders falling harmlessly to the stone floor.

That would be us if we weren't very careful.

The smell of death, decay, and ash began to fill the air. I licked dry lips and looked around wildly. There was no decent place to stand and fight. Our best bet was to try to keep them in the tunnel.

And the only way to do that was to use the holy water as some sort of barrier.

But I'd barely taken two steps when evil flowed into the room. The creatures were big, bigger than the ones I'd seen previously, their large heads held low and their red eyes glowing brightly in the shadowed darkness. Thick yellow teeth gleamed eerily as the pair of them snarled. The sound echoed like a death knell.

I flung the water at them.

It flew across the air like a silver ribbon, hitting the first one on the snout and splashing across the coat of the other, sizzling and bubbling where it struck.

The first hound twisted and howled as its face began to disintegrate. Flesh dropped from its cheeks in chunks, until all that was left was bone. Soon that began to crack and shatter, until nothing remained of that half of its face.

But it didn't die. It was disfigured, but still very much alive.

It would be just my luck to get a stronger breed of hellhound this time around.

And then I remembered that Azriel had killed the hounds with his sword when they'd been distracted by the burning water.

I had no choice but to do this the hard way.

I switched Amaya to one hand and carefully reached for more holy water. Her *kill, kill, kill* chant was fierce and rapid, matching the pounding of my heart.

"Jak?" My voice was little more than a murmur, as I had no idea just what would set these creatures into motion. Right now, they didn't seem to be doing anything more than watching us, but I doubted that would last. I suspected that once we moved, they would.

"What?"

Though I could smell the fear on him—as he could no doubt smell it on me—his voice was amazingly steady. But then, I guess he'd seen more than his fair

share of dangerous beings in his years as an investiga-
tive reporter.

Just not *this* dangerous.

"Use the holy water to form a wide half circle around
yourself, then press back against the wall."

"What are you going to do?"

"Kill them."

"Ris, if the holy water works as a barrier, why don't
we both just wait behind it?"

I carefully opened the bottle. The cork hit the dirt
near my feet and bounced a little before settling. The
hounds' eyes gleamed a fiercer red in the darkness, and
tension rippled across their sleek black hides. They
were getting ready to pounce.

"Hellhounds have one design function, and that's to
kill. Holy water might work as a short-term deterrent, but
it's not strong enough to provide long-term protection."

"It only has to last long enough for us to ring for
help. Your uncle—"

"Will not get here in time. No one can. Hellhounds
aren't stupid, and they're not going to wait around
while we ring for help."

"Oh."

"Use the knife if a hound decides to ignore the holy
water and attempts to get at you." God, how did that
come out so calmly when my stomach was twisted into
knots and my hands were shaking? "And good luck."

"Yeah, you, too."

We were both going to need it. I took a deep breath
and gripped Amaya tightly. Her desire to kill was so

fierce it was almost blanketing, and suddenly not only was she in *my* head, but I was in *hers*. In the steel, at one with her.

I didn't question it. I just threw the second bottle of holy water and followed it up fast. The creatures split, one flowing to the left of the runes and the other to the right. The silver ribbon of deadly water flew harmlessly between them, hit the wall, and dribbled down to the floor stones.

Shit, I thought, and swung Amaya. Her steel was little more than a blur as she cut through the air. The hound snarled in response—an action made grotesque by the fact he had only half a face—and slashed with a viciously barbed paw. Claw and steel crashed together, the sound reverberating across a darkness that was no longer so silent. One of the creature's claws hit the top of my hand, slicing skin even as Amaya's flames leapt from steel to flesh and burned with fierce joy.

I jumped back and swung Amaya again. Blood sprayed across the ruined remains of the hound's face, and the gleam in its eyes grew stronger. It ducked the blow, then leapt. I had no time to move and took the full brunt of its weight, staggering backward but somehow avoiding the snapping, slashing teeth. One of its claws hooked into my right shoulder, and a scream tore up my throat. I flung Amaya over its head, then caught her with my free hand and brought her down on the creature's spine. The force of the blow reverberated up my arm, but it did little more than cut the hound's flesh. She didn't sever muscle or bone, as I'd hoped she would.

Will, she screamed. *Time need!*

And *that* was the one thing we didn't have a whole lot of.

I clawed at the creature's remaining eye. It snarled and shook its head, its breath fetid, washing my skin with the smell of death. The movement dislodged its claw from my shoulder and I fell backward with a grunt of pain. Energy washed across my spine and I realized with horror that I was near the runes. Then air stirred, and the scent of malevolence grew stronger. The hound was in the air, coming straight at me.

I became one with Amaya again—felt the fierceness of her spirit rush through me. We leapt to one side. One foot skimmed the edge of a rune and sent a warning ripple of sickly green light across the darkness. We raised the sword, brought her down hard. Hit the creature's spine even as *it* hit the runes. The runes didn't react, didn't flare, didn't cinder.

It didn't matter.

This time, the combined strength of both Amaya and me drove the sword, and it burned and flamed swiftly through the hellhound's flesh, cutting through skin and bone with the ease of butter.

The hound screamed as it flopped to the floor, but it still had movement. It dug its claws into the stone and dragged itself around, snapping at my legs with its remaining teeth. I leapt back—separated from Amaya's spirit once again—then swung the satchel around, dragged out another bottle of holy water, and poured it over the creature from head to foot. The rancid smell of burning flesh filled the air as the creature twisted and howled in fury and pain. I raised Amaya again and brought her down—point first—with as much force as I could muster. This time she didn't sever, she consumed. Purple flames erupted, swept swiftly across the hound's hissing, disintegrating flesh, until there was no skin, no bone, no sound, just purple fire and the wretched smell of death. Then, with a sharp report, the flames and the hound were gone, and Amaya suddenly felt heavier in my hand.

Which didn't mean she was in any way satisfied.

I swung around. Jak *had* created a protective ring using the water, but it wasn't as secure as we'd hoped. It stopped the bulk of the creature, but it hadn't stopped the creature's slashing attacks with wicked-looking claws.

I spun and ran around the runes, coming up on the hellhound from behind. It sensed me—it was always going to, as I was making little effort to sneak and Amaya was screaming her heart out—and twisted and leapt in one smooth motion. I threw myself forward, turning as I fell, coming up under the creature as it flew above me. Amaya's screaming was at fever pitch— wanting, needing bloodshed—so I gave it to her. I drove her blade into the creature's belly and ripped her along its length. Blood and gore splattered across my face, stinking to high heaven and stinging like acid. These creatures may not be truly flesh, but god, when their innards spewed it damn well *felt* real.

"Jak, you okay?" I scrambled to my feet, Jak's circle at my back and Amaya held out in front of me like a baton.

"No worse off than you—watch out!"

It wasn't a warning I needed. The creature had barely hit the stone when it was in the air again. I threw the last bottle of holy water, but the hound somehow twisted, and the water hit trailing innards, not flesh. I swung the blade, slicing across the creature's snout, then twisted out of its reach. It had barely smacked down on the stones when it leapt again. But as it did, Amaya and I once again became one. All her fury, all her energy and her vicious need to kill became mine, and I screamed as she screamed. Together, we severed the creature's head clean from its neck even as it managed a last, desperate slash with its claws. I sucked in my gut, felt clothing and skin part, but little else, still held by the fury that was Amaya. As the hellhound hit the stone in separate parts, her fire leapt from the blade and covered both. In very little time, there was nothing left but ash.

I lowered Amaya's point to the stone and leaned against her, suddenly weak with relief. We'd done it. Somehow, we'd beaten them.

All we had to do now was get out of here.

Jak's hand slid around my waist as he leaned next to me. "You okay?"

I took a deep, somewhat quivery breath, and released it slowly. "Yeah. You?"

"Scratched, bleeding, and fucking glad to be alive."

I smiled, as he no doubt intended, then straightened and stepped away from his touch. "I don't think we can get out via these gates. I think we need to go back through the tunnel."

"Then we'll have to leave our prisoner. It'll be next to impossible to drag him through it."

I grimaced. "But we can't afford to leave him. The last thing we want is him reporting back to his masters. At least if we get him upstairs, Azriel can alter—"

I stopped as once again awareness swept over me.

Someone else was in the tunnel, and they were coming our way.

Chapter 8

I half raised Amaya, then stopped as fear gave way to realization. It wasn't a foe who walked toward us; it was a friend.

Uncle Quinn—Riley's moon-sworn lover, and the half Aedh who'd taught me how to use my own Aedh skills—to be exact. He was also a former Cazador, and one of the few who not only survived the experience but walked away virtually unscarred. And that, to me, only emphasized just how deadly he could be.

It was a damn shame he hadn't turned up five minutes earlier. He would have handled the hellhounds with one hand tied behind his back and very little bloodshed.

"Risa?" The muffled confines of the tunnel made it hard to judge how close he actually was, but the Irish lilt usually evident in his voice had all but disappeared—a sure sign he was ready for battle. "You okay?"

"Yes." I sheathed Amaya.

"Then why do I smell blood?"

"I guess because I'm bleeding."

"You guess? You, my dear, have been around Riley entirely too long."

So people kept saying. "Which isn't a bad thing when it taught me to survive situations like this."

He squeezed out of the tunnel a damn sight more elegantly than either Jak or I had, and strode toward me. While no half-breed got the wings of the Aedh, many did inherit their mesmerizing looks, and Quinn was no exception. He was, in every way, angelic, from his beautiful face that was framed by night-dark hair to his well-toned body.

His dark gaze swept me, then moved on to Jak. What he thought of *his* presence I couldn't say—Quinn was a very old vampire, and well practiced in keeping emotions contained.

Rather like Azriel, I thought absently.

"That may be the case, but she's *not* going to be pleased that you not only failed to call in help but got wounded in the process."

"It looks worse than it is," I said, then remembered I was talking to a vampire. He'd know *exactly* how much blood I was losing. "And it's not like you have to tell her."

"As if *anyone* can hide secrets from that woman." Undercurrents of amusement and love ran through the comment. He ripped the sleeve from his shirt, tore it into strips, then roughly bandaged my shoulder. "She already suspects the worst, given the rather frantic state your reaper was in when he appeared to fetch me here—"

"Azriel?" I interrupted, surprised. "Frantic?"

His gaze jumped to mine. "You didn't send him?"

"No." I hadn't even heard from him, simply because the magic was still in place. They couldn't stop our chi connection, however, so he would have understood the danger we were in. But frantic? He knew I had Amaya, and besides, while I'd seen him angry, I couldn't imagine my often uptight reaper showing anything more than mild concern.

"Does that mean Riley's here as well?"

"No, because I took Aedh form to get here fast."

It also enabled him to get around the usual sunlight restriction, although as one of the old ones, he could actually stand huge amounts of daylight.

"So where is she?"

"Waiting at home, medi-kit in hand." His gaze moved to Jak, and his voice lost some of its warmth as he added, "Are you all right?"

"There's nothing a Band-Aid and a stiff drink won't fix." Amusement ran through Jak's voice. He'd obviously noted the temperature change, too.

Quinn's dark gaze swept the room, and narrowed slightly as it settled briefly on the pillars. *He knows what they are*, I thought. But he said nothing, and looked down at our captive instead. "Who's this?"

"According to his ID, he's either Henry Mack or Jason Marks, and he's a Razan."

His gaze leapt to mine again. "A Razan? Whose?"

"That, indeed, is the question." I shrugged. "We suspect he was talking to his master before we knocked him out, but the number was blocked and we dare not call it back."

A wry smile touched Quinn's lips. "In other words, you want me to read his thoughts."

"Well, yeah, that would be nice."

Quinn considered me for a moment, then said, "As long as you agree to come back home with me, so Riley can reassure herself that you're alive and well."

"And then tell me off."

"Undoubtedly. But seeing as you refuse to seek help from those of us who have more experience with things such as hellhounds, it's well deserved."

A point I didn't argue with, although I could have. Easily. He and Riley had been through enough shit in their time together—they didn't deserve to get hit with mine now that their life was relatively sane and quiet. Besides, I'd already lost my mom. I wasn't about to lose anyone else I was close to. It was bad enough that I'd involved Ilianna and Tao as much as I had.

"You have a deal."

He nodded, then glanced at Jak. It took me several moments to realize that awareness had slipped from Jak's eyes.

I raised an eyebrow. "There was no need—"

"There was. You trust him too much."

Yet another comment people kept making. "Jak's under threat from Rhoan. Trust me, he's not going to print anything without clearing it first through him."

"And now he can't even *consider* writing about it because he won't even be aware of it." He knelt beside the Razan and appeared to be doing nothing more than simply looking at him—although I knew from past experience that he was riffling through the man's thoughts.

Then his gaze met mine again. "An Aedh has been active in this man's thoughts."

"Meaning what?"

"Meaning that while he knows the name and location of his master, any effort on my part to access it would immediately notify said master of the intrusion."

"Well, damn."

"Yes." He paused. "It is possible to circumvent such blocks, but it takes time."

"Which we don't have. I suspect that if he doesn't report back soon, it'll make our quarry suspicious."

"Which might just draw him out."

"He's not that type. He's more likely to cover his tracks and start somewhere fresh."

Although the ley intersection was near here, so he wasn't likely to go too far from it. Still, we needed to avoid warning him just how close we were. "You can't get anything useful from him at all?"

Quinn hesitated, and glanced down at the Razan again. "There's three of them left. They live together in an old warehouse in Dawson Street, Brunswick West, and he's more than a little pissed about running these sorts of errands when he was trained as a soldier. He believes he could take care of any intruders and be a hell of a lot less conspicuous about it than hellhounds."

But hellhounds didn't need to eat or drink or go to the toilet—they were on watch twenty-four/seven, until ordered otherwise.

"Where did he serve?" Although he didn't look that old, Razan were linked to the life force of their masters and could live for centuries. Knowing which war might be handy to track down his real identity, because I very much doubted that the license and cards he carried were actually his.

Quinn hesitated. "He's a Middle East army veteran. Retired about eighty-five years ago."

Not very old in Razan terms at all. "And his name?"

"Mark Jackson. I can't tell you at what point he became Razan, because that memory lies behind the shield."

Damn. I squatted down beside the Razan, rolled him onto his side, and pointed to the barbwire tat. "Have you seen one like this before?"

Quinn shook his head. "But it is not usual for Raziq to mark their Razan with their own unique brand."

"This particular brand has been seen on Razan who we are fairly certain belong to different masters."

He half shrugged. "That is not unusual, either. There were Razan who served the Aedh priests at the gate temples who belonged to all. Maybe this tat signifies a joint venture of some kind."

Which again lent weight to the idea that my father and this dark sorcerer were in cahoots, but I just didn't think that was the case. Not now, at least.

Although it wasn't like I could be sure of anything when it came to my parent.

"What about the pillars?"

Quinn raised his eyebrows. "What about them?"

"Well, can you ferret out any information about them—where they go, how they operate, that sort of stuff?"

"*I* can tell you most of that."

No surprise there, given his reaction—or lack of it— when he'd first seen them. "So you *have* seen pillars like this before?"

"Not exactly like these, no. But the writing on them is a variation of old cuneiform, and they were once used to summon Aedh."

I blinked. "Really? Why?"

"To bless crops or hunts, to garner favors, and in some cases, to offer one of their own to gain the blessing of the gods."

"But Aedh aren't gods." I could understand them being mistaken for angels, but gods?

"We know that, but the prehistoric world was a much simpler place."

I guess. "But these pillars aren't summoning devices. They appear to be some mode of transport."

He nodded. "They are."

"Can we use them?"

He half smiled. "No, we cannot." He picked up the Razan's wrist and pushed up his sleeves. On the inside of his arm was a small tat that was a mix of cuneiform and scrollwork. "The magic within this allows the wearer to pass through such gates. But even if we could pass through them, I wouldn't let you."

"Why not?"

"Because you're still bleeding." He cupped a hand under my elbow and carefully helped me to my feet. "If you bleed to death before Riley can give you a piece of her mind, there'll be hell to pay."

I snorted softly. Right now, *him* being chewed out by

my aunt was the least of my worries. "What about Jak? And our captive?"

"I will give both appropriate memories. You start back through the tunnel."

I hesitated, then did as he bid. It wasn't very long before I heard them behind me, Jak cursing like a trooper as he once again scraped his way through the tunnel. Quinn had left rope dangling into the pit earlier, so even with my various aches and pains, it was fairly easy to climb out.

I'd barely crawled through the gap in the roller door when Azriel took my hands in his and gently pulled me upright.

He didn't immediately say anything, just kept hold of my hands as his gaze swept me. His expression gave little away, but his anger and concern raged through my inner being, the sheer force of it rocking me back on my heels. Maybe Quinn *hadn't* been overstating when he'd said Azriel had been frantic. And while that thought warmed me, the snarky voice deep within couldn't help but note that if anything happened to me, his mission would fail. And in the end, his mission was everything.

"You cannot keep going like this," he said eventually. "It will be the death of you."

"Yeah, well, tell *that* to the bad guys who keep attacking us." I pulled my hands from his, even though all I really wanted to do was step fully into his embrace and let the heat and warm strength of him melt into my bones and make me feel safe.

And I didn't care if that feeling of safety was as temporary as the man himself.

"Ris—" He stopped.

I shifted briefly into Aedh form to stop the bleeding, then crossed my arms and regarded him steadily. "I'm glad you didn't bother denying the temporary situation, Azriel, because really, how can you *ever* be anything else? Especially when you don't *want* anything else?"

"You have no idea what I do and don't want." It was vehemently said.

"No," I agreed. "But to be honest, I don't really think you do, either."

I resolutely turned away, suddenly too tired to get into a fight with him again. It didn't help. Awareness of him whispered through me: the flex of his fingers, the slow release of breath, the close shimmer of heat as he reached for—but didn't quite touch—me.

I know what I want, Risa. His thoughts ran through my mind like whiskey on a cold night—warm, and yet with an edge that bit. *And for both our sakes, you had better hope I never decide to take it.*

That sounds like a threat, reaper.

It is nothing more than honesty.

And as usual, you being honest doesn't actually tell me a whole lot, does it? I shook my head slightly. *One of these days, Azriel, you might just regret your reticence.*

I do every day I'm in your presence. His words stabbed deep, but he continued relentlessly. *But it cannot alter my actions. It will not.*

No, because what he truly wanted was to become a soul guide again. And nothing, not this quest, and certainly not whatever this thing between us was, would divert him from his path. He'd never made any secret of it, either, but it was beginning to rankle *me* more and more.

Because I cared, more and more.

I was, I decided, an idiot.

I crossed my arms and watched Quinn and Jak crawl through the gap. Quinn kept within the shadows of the building, even though the midday sun had passed. Habit more than necessity, I thought.

"Shall I meet you back at your place?"

"Yes," Quinn said.

"No," said Jak.

I glanced at him, surprised. He waved the notepad in his hand. "I took note of the numbers in that man's phone book, and I want to chase them down just in case our sorcerer starts covering his tracks again."

"Good idea." It also saved me the hassle of having to explain to Riley his reemergence in my life. "You'll call if you find anything?"

Jak snorted softly. "Like I have any other choice, given your uncle's threat."

I half smiled, and he gave me a sketchy farewell wave and headed back to his car. Once he was gone, I met Quinn's gaze. "What does he remember?"

"Nothing more than my arrival, and me rearranging the Razan's memories."

At least he hadn't rearranged *all* Jak's memories.

"I wouldn't," he said mildly; then, as shock shivered

through me, he smiled. "The micro-cells do provide some measure of protection against most vampires— even the ones as strong as Madeline Hunter—but they create little more than a mild barrier for someone as telepathically strong as me."

"And Riley?" I asked, even though the answer was obvious. She was stronger than even *him*, after all.

His smile widened. *Oh, fabulous*, I thought, and pointlessly tried to remember everything I'd thought since his arrival. Undoubtedly he'd caught more than a few interesting ones—though generally, both Quinn and Riley had strict rules regarding mind reading, and rarely indulged in casual telepathy. According to Riley, the thoughts of most people weren't worth it.

I cleared my throat, hoped I didn't look as embarrassed as I felt, and said, "I'll see you soon."

He nodded, then melted into mist and disappeared. I shot Stane another quick note, asking him to add Mark Jackson to his search, and then Azriel's arms were around me and we were whisking through the gray fields.

We reappeared in the middle of Aunt Riley's living room. She was, as Quinn had said, waiting for us.

"About fucking time." Her gaze swept over me and her expression became grim. "What the *hell* have you been tangling with?"

"Hellhounds." I stepped free from Azriel. "There were two of them, and two of us."

"Unfair odds in anyone's book. Those bastards fight nasty." She waved me toward the bathroom, then glanced at Azriel. "You can wait here. Or you could do something useful and help Quinn in the kitchen."

The thought of Azriel making coffee struck me as funny, but he merely offered a short bow and headed for the kitchen. But then, very few people ever argued with Riley when she used *that* tone.

I stripped my clothing off as I walked into the bathroom, and dumped the bloodied remnants of it in the bin rather than the laundry chute.

Behind me, Riley sucked in a sharp breath. "What the hell happened to your back?"

I cursed mentally. I'd forgotten about the damn scar. "I fell off my bike and hit a pole." Which was the truth, just not the reason for the scar. "Both the bike and I got smashed up pretty badly."

"I can imagine." Her tone was dry and suggested she didn't believe my excuse, but she motioned me toward the shower without further comment. The water came on automatically as I entered, the water hot and the spray sharp and massaging. It felt sensational against my battered and bruised body.

"Who else was with you in that tunnel today? Azriel obviously wasn't."

I hesitated, but there was little point in lying. Especially since Quinn already knew. "Jak."

"Have you lost brain cells or something?" There was an edge of incredulity in her voice. "Why the hell are you messing around with him again?"

"Because I needed someone who knew the streets and who could mix it up with street scum without raising suspicions." I couldn't quite hide my irritation. I'd really had enough of people questioning my judgment today. "He's a source, nothing more."

She studied me for a moment; then a warm grin broke loose. "Spoken like a true daughter of mine. Your mother would be horrified."

I smiled. "She always did blame you for my wild ways."

"Yeah, she did." Her grin faded. "So tell me about the hellhounds."

I did so. Once I was out of the shower, she sealed the few wounds that were still bleeding, patched up the rest, then fetched me some clean clothes. When I was dressed, she dragged me into her arms and hugged me fiercely.

"Ris, we're here if you ever need help. Remember that."

I blinked back sudden tears. "I know, but—"

"But you are incredibly stubborn and want to do things your way." She stepped back, a slight smile twisting her lips. "You really *could* have been mine, we're so damn alike. Which is why I'm reminding you. I don't want you making the same mistakes I did."

"I won't."

Her gaze searched mine for several seconds, and her smile become stronger. "You won't seek help, you mean." Her voice was wry. "Not unless you absolutely have to."

I didn't say anything. She laughed, then caught my hand and tugged me toward the living room. "Let's go get you fed, before you fade away into nothing."

I'd made it through three meat and salad sandwiches and was feeling a hell of a lot more sociable when the phone rang. The ringtone told me it was Rhoan, and trepidation tripped through me.

I swallowed to ease a suddenly dry throat, then hit the vid-phone's ANSWER button. Rhoan's expression was grim. "He's made contact."

"And?"

"We have a name—Vonda Belmore."

I frowned. "Why would he give you her name? It makes the hunt far too easy."

"Yeah, that's what's got us worried."

"So what do you want me to do?"

"Where are you?"

I hesitated. "At your place."

He groaned. "Don't tell me Riley's listening—"

"Yes, she is," Riley said mildly, over my shoulder. "And she's very interested in the reason why you're involving Risa in Directorate business."

"Because I have no other damn choice, that's why. Look, I'll explain everything later. Right now, we have a murderer to hunt, and Ris *has* to be in on it."

"Is this something I can help with? I have more experience than Ris—"

"Yeah, but that's not going to help in this case. She made contact with the killer on the astral plane before she knew we were after him, and now he won't deal with anyone else."

"He's a murderer. He should be dead, not dealing with anyone, least of all Risa."

"The problem is, he's a fucking ghost and we can't find him. We have to use Risa to have any hope of tracking him down, but trust me, we'll take good care of her."

"I trust you, Rhoan. I just don't trust the killers you hunt."

She squeezed my shoulder, then walked away, leaving me feeling warm deep inside. I might have lost my real mom, but in very many ways, I still had another.

"I'll send you the address," Rhoan said. "Meet me there in twenty minutes."

"Will do."

I hung up, then grabbed the last sandwich as I stood.

"To repeat myself, be careful," Riley said, her expression concerned.

I smiled grimly. "As Azriel has already noted, I've lost more than enough blood for one day. I'm not intending to lose any more."

"I don't think it's your intentions she's concerned about," Quinn noted.

I half smiled, then walked around the table, kissed them both, and said, "I'll be fine. I won't do anything stupid. I promise."

And I hoped like hell it was a promise I could actually keep.

The address Rhoan sent me was for a small house in Campbellfield. It was off a busy main street, on one of those long blocks that had been subdivided years ago, with a second dwelling built at the back. That was the one we were interested in.

I sat on a brick fence on the opposite side of the road.

The rumble of trucks and cars going past was so damn loud that the clatter of a helicopter overhead was almost lost to it. The air was an unpleasant mix of exhaust, rubber, and the various scents coming from the fast-food shops down the road, and my nose twitched against the need to sneeze.

I glanced at my watch. We still had a couple of minutes to wait, and frustration swirled through me. It was tempting—very tempting—to just head in myself, but I'd promised Riley to be careful and that wasn't exactly careful-type behavior. Besides, I wasn't at the top of my game right now—in fact, a gnat could probably overpower me with very little effort. I needed sleep, and I needed more food despite everything I'd already eaten. But most of all, I needed the bad guys to be sensible and give me a break.

And seeing as I couldn't control *them* in any way, shape, or form, I guessed the sensible had to come from me.

I sighed wearily and leaned against Azriel's shoulder. He didn't move, didn't react, didn't wrap his arm around me and pull me closer, but the skin-on-skin contact was still oddly comforting.

"Is there anyone inside?" I asked eventually.

"A woman, a man, and a child in the first house. No one alive in the second." Amusement warmed his otherwise formal tones as he added, "And before you ask, there's no one dead, either."

"So if this *is* the next victim's address, he might already have her."

"That is more than possible."

I glanced left as a black Ford turned into the street. Rhoan. Given the Directorate plates, it couldn't be anyone else.

The car slid to a halt in front of us. There were two men inside, but only Rhoan climbed out. He didn't look happy.

The trepidation that had been up until now little more than a muted background buzz suddenly sharpened. I straightened. "What's up?"

"This whole setup. He's deviating from his previous MO and I'm not liking the possible reason."

"You think it's some sort of trap?"

"It can't be anything else," he growled. "We've done a quick background check on Vonda. She turned vamp about one hundred years ago, and has been leading a relatively low-profile life ever since. She works the night shift at the Ford vehicle factory in Broadmeadows and doesn't socialize much."

I frowned. "What about feeding? How does she cope with that if she doesn't socialize much?"

He shrugged. "She probably uses synth blood. They've gotten better at manufacturing it in recent years."

A fact he knew because his vampire half sometimes demanded blood, even if he didn't have the teeth to go with the hunger. "So Vonda has nothing in common with the other victims?"

"Other than that she seems the least likely target for a serial killer, no." He spun around and studied the houses on the opposite side of the road. "She lives with her sister, who also works at Ford. We had an infrared-equipped helicopter sweep the area a few moments ago. There's three people in the first house, but no one is at home in our target house."

He was half vampire and had infrared vision himself, so he didn't really need the helicopter to tell him that. Maybe he just didn't want to get too close to the house and spook our quarry—not that he was inside from the sound of it.

"It's not much of a trap if there's no one inside."

Rhoan glanced at me. "Just because we can't detect any form of body heat doesn't mean there's nothing waiting."

Like a spell of some kind. I shivered and rubbed my arms. "What did he say when he rang?"

"He gave us the name, and said for you to be in the house—alone—by two p.m. if we wish to save his next victim."

I glanced at my watch again. "Then I'd better get moving. We've only got a few minutes left."

"I know." He studied me, expression worried. "Are you sure you're up to this?"

I touched his arm. "I'm fine. Azriel will be with me, and he can't afford to let anything happen to me."

Rhoan's gaze went past me briefly. "Okay. But you're wearing these, so I know what is going on."

He pulled two blue stones out of his pocket, and I studied them with interest. "I'm gathering they're not just earrings."

"One is a camera, the other is a mic. Until this case is over, I want you to wear them."

My gaze jumped to his. "Um, you know I love you and all, but there's certain parts of my life I have no desire for you to see or hear."

"And I'm sure I wouldn't want to know about them, either." Amusement briefly crinkled the corners of his gray eyes. "You can turn them off easily enough—you just press the left stone once. Two presses activates them again."

"What about when I shower? Do I have to take them off?"

"No."

"Oh. Okay."

He pressed the two stones onto my earlobes. They had to be some form of nanotechnology, because the stones warmed the instant they touched my skin, and they clung to my earlobes without anything to actually secure them. He lightly squeezed the right stone, then stepped back. "Karl, you getting the picture?"

"Yeah," the man inside the car said. "Sound, too."

"Good." His gaze came back to me. "At the first sign of trouble, I'll be in there."

"I'll be fine. Really."

He didn't say anything, but he didn't need to. He wasn't worried about my ability to protect myself; he just didn't want to see me hurt.

I headed across the road. My gaze swept the first building, but came to a halt at the security camera.

"Azriel, you might want to become invisible."

He did so immediately, then said, *You suspect he might have hacked into the security system?*

Well, not him specifically if he's blind, but someone working for him certainly could. It's safer for me if they don't know about you.

You're considering your own safety? His mental tones held an edge. *This has to be a first.*

Sarcasm doesn't become you, reaper. Even if it was true.

I walked down the side of the first house. Though I couldn't see anyone, the curtains twitched, a clear indication that someone was watching.

It is the woman, Azriel commented. He hesitated, then added, *Her thoughts are odd.*

Odd how? I scanned the second house as it came into sight. There was another security camera perched on the side of this house and metal protection bars on the windows. Obviously Vonda and her sister didn't trust either their neighbors or the neighborhood.

They are vacant. It is like she has nothing else to do but look out the window.

Maybe she hasn't. Or maybe she's been made to take something. I doubted her behavior was a coincidence, given the reason we were here.

I rounded the corner of the first house and headed for the front door of the second. The security door was thick and heavy, just like the bars on the windows. I twisted the handle and it opened, as did the wooden front door. My stomach began to churn. This was *way* too easy.

Possibly, Azriel said, and it took me a mental moment to remember what he was replying to.

What about the man and the child in that house? Are they okay? I pushed the door open with my fingertips. The air inside was fresh and cool, and ran with the scent of femininity.

They sleep. He paused. *Deeply.*

Something in the way he said that had me looking around before I remembered he wasn't actually visible. *What do you mean?*

Just that it does not appear to be a natural form of sleep.

So they're all drugged up? I took a cautious step inside.

I do not know much about drugs, but as I have said, this sleep is not natural.

And he didn't like it, which no doubt meant there was something wrong. Something we should check out.

I stopped just inside the door, my bottom lip caught between my teeth as my gaze swept the room. The furnishings—though sparse—were of good quality. The main living area was L-shaped, with a kitchen tucked in the shorter end of the room. There was a hallway to my right, with a number of doors leading off it.

I couldn't see anything out of place, nor could I hear anything or anyone. Which I guess wasn't surprising; Azriel had already said there was no one here. I flexed my fingers, then headed into the hallway. A quick check revealed two bedrooms—one messier than the other—a bathroom, and a small laundry with a door leading out into an even smaller courtyard. There was nothing odd to be found, and no sense that Vonda had, in any way, feared for her life.

But then, neither had Dorothy Hendricks, and our hunter had been bleeding her to death here while burning a brand into her forehead on the astral plane.

I retreated back through the living room and went into the kitchen. It was small, neat, and filled with the latest in cookware—which was an odd thing for a vampire to have.

I crossed my arms and walked over to the front window, staring at the back of the first house. The back door was ajar and there was no security or wire door in place. Which seemed odd with a small child in the house, even if he was asleep.

Is the woman still standing where she was? I asked.

She has not moved since we appeared on the other side of the street.

Which was *not* normal behavior. Not for the mother of a small child. Sitting, I could understand. Even catching a nap. But simply standing there like a zombie? I'm sure looking after a young child made mothers the world over sometimes feel like the rambling dead, but this was definitely something stranger.

I swung around and headed for the front door. "Rhoan, I'm going to talk to the people in the first house, and see if they can tell me about Vonda's recent movements."

"Be careful." His voice reverberated inside my earlobes and made me jump. I hadn't actually realized the connection was two-way. Which meant he could tell me off if I did something wrong—*just* what I needed.

I crossed the little patch of sunshine between the two houses, then pressed my fingertips against the rear door and carefully opened it. The small laundry was filled with clothes—some in clean stacks on top of the washer, others in sorted piles on the floor. The door of the front loader was ajar, and half filled with dark clothing. She'd obviously been in the middle of loading when she'd decided to move into the living room and stare out the window.

Odder and odder.

I stepped over the piles and stopped at the next doorway. The only sound to be heard was the gentle ticking of a clock coming from the right. The air was rich with the scent of humanity, but underneath it ran something else—something sharper.

Fear.

Tension tightened through me. I flexed my shoulders, but it did as little as flexing my fingers had earlier. To the left was a hallway with several doors leading off it. If the layout of this house was similar to the other, then they'd be the bathroom and bedrooms. I hesitated, then padded softly to the first door and carefully pushed it open. A small child lay still and silent on a cot. For a moment I thought he was dead, and it felt like someone had punched me in the gut. Then I noted the slow rise and fall of his chest. Asleep, as Azriel had said. Whether it was natural or something else was the question that needed to be answered.

I closed the child's bedroom door and stared at the next one. Though I had no doubt that the father would also be asleep, I couldn't escape the notion that I had to check. That I *had* to confirm whether this sleep was natural.

Of course, if it was, I'd feel like a complete and utter

idiot. Not to mention how furious *he'd* be about being woken by a complete stranger.

Trust your instincts, Azriel commented. *There is something odd here, as I have said. Their minds have been . . . touched, although whether by drugs or telepathic intervention, I cannot say.*

But you usually can sense it, so why not here? I walked to the other bedroom door and opened it. A fully clothed man lay stretched out on the queen-sized bed, his hands—resting on his chest—rising and falling with each breath.

If this is telepathic interference, it is only very minor, and that is often hard to catch or define.

Meaning what? That someone has simply forced them to sleep? Why in the hell would anyone want that?

He didn't answer, but I really wasn't expecting him to. I walked over to the bed and lightly touched the man's shoulder. He didn't react in any way.

I pinched his cheek. Nothing. I pinched harder, but the result was the same. This definitely *wasn't* a natural sleep. "You seeing this, Rhoan?"

"Yeah. And I'm liking it a whole lot less. Check the third person."

I spun and headed down to the kitchen. It was less tidy than Vonda's, with baby bottles in various states of cleanliness scattered over the sink and a half-made sandwich sitting on the counter.

I kept walking into the living room. The woman was still standing at the side window, but as I entered, she slowly turned to face me.

Shock hit like a hammer, and I stopped.

Burned into the woman's forehead was a raw and bleeding K-shaped mark.

It was the exact same mark that had been burned into Dorothy Hendricks's forehead just before she'd died.

Chapter 9

My fingers twitched with the need to feel Amaya in my hands, but my sword was, for once, quiet. Whatever was happening here, she didn't sense an immediate threat.

I forced a smile, then walked toward the woman and held out a hand. "I'm sorry to intrude like this, but I'm looking for Vonda Belmore. I don't suppose you know where she is, do you?"

The woman didn't shake my hand—she didn't even look at it. Nor did she immediately respond to my question. She just stared at me in an oddly dead way.

I let my hand drop to my side and stopped just beyond her reach. But it was still close enough that I could smell the wound on her forehead, and it was rank. It was almost as if her flesh had rotted away rather than burned.

My gaze swept the rest of her. She was statuesque, with fine, almost regal features and silvery hair that was cut short but well styled. She was also a vampire, which, when combined with the wound on her forehead, meant this was more than likely Vonda. But I wasn't about to admit that knowledge. Better to play the game, whatever the hell the game was.

"I do know Vonda," the woman said eventually. Her voice was whispery and, like her gaze, lacked any sort of life or warmth. "She faces you."

Vonda might be facing me, but she wasn't the one forming the words.

He was doing that.

He was in her mind, controlling her. Maybe even seeing what she saw.

It was certainly one way for a blind man to check out his adversary.

Azriel, are you able to get into her thoughts? Can you catch anything about the man we hunt?

I am only able to read the minds of those who are in the same vicinity. She currently has no thoughts of her own, and while he may control her, he does so from a distance.

I guess I should have known it wouldn't be that easy. I shifted my weight from one foot to the other, and barely resisted the urge to run from this freak show. Or at least run from the freak behind it. The only reason I didn't was because it wouldn't help—this was a game and, for whatever reason, it was one he wanted to play with me.

"And why are you here rather than in your own house, Vonda?"

"I knew you were clever. I just wanted to see how observant you were."

"So I've passed the test?"

"Yes and no."

"Meaning?"

"Meaning you found one, but you did not find the other."

I stared at him—her—for a moment, my stomach churning as I remembered that Vonda didn't live alone. "You've taken her *sister*?"

"You weren't paying attention, huntress. Did I not say *victims*, plural, last time we spoke?"

Like I was supposed to understand the nuances of every word spoken by a crackpot? "Taking two women at once doesn't follow your usual pattern, and I suspect you're a man who likes his patterns and rules."

"Indeed, I do. But I have never come across twins such as these before."

"What is that supposed to mean? And what have any of these women done to you?"

"They are not what they pretend to be. They are Kudlak, and therefore must be destroyed. That is my destiny, huntress. It is my task by birthright."

It was his birthright to hunt harmless women? Sanity and he really *weren't* on speaking terms. "I have no idea what a Kudlak is, but I know these women are vampires—and harmless ones at that. You're mistaken—"

"No, I am not. Nor am I about to argue." The words were snapped, the tone annoyed. "The sister has an hour left."

And with that, the woman collapsed.

I lunged forward and caught her just before she hit the floor. The mark on her forehead was even more putrid this close, and her breathing was shallow and uneven, even for a vampire.

"Rhoan, we need an ambulance." I lowered her

gently to the floor and looked up at Azriel as he materialized beside me. "Is she going to die?"

"Yes," he said. "He may not have drained her blood, but he has drained her spirit."

I closed my eyes and fought the useless rise of anger. Vonda's sister was still out there, and getting angry wouldn't find her any faster. "Is there anything left of her mind now that he has released her? Or has he drained that, too?"

"She is mentally present."

"Can you read her?"

He hesitated. "No. Her thoughts are blocked. I would damage her mind further if I broke past them."

She was dying anyway, so it wouldn't really have mattered, but I guessed it came down to reaper rules. He couldn't do anything that might harm an innocent.

Which meant I had to do this the hard way. I pinched her pale cheek as hard as I could. It was a mean thing to do to someone who was dying, but I really had no other choice. She might just hold the key to finding not only her sister but the crackpot behind these murders. "Vonda, wake up."

She murmured something that sounded decidedly unladylike, and made a weak movement with her hand, as if trying to swat me away.

I pinched harder. "Vonda, your sister is in danger. We need your help to find her."

Her eyes fluttered briefly open, but there was little life or understanding in the green of her gaze. "Dani?" she murmured. "No."

I grabbed her shoulders and shook her. "Yes, Dani. Where is she? Where did she go?"

"Club." It was so softly said it was little more than a sigh of air.

"What club, Vonda?" I looked around as Rhoan came in. He glanced from me to the woman, and motioned me to continue. "You need to tell us or Dani dies."

Distress ran briefly across her pale features. She made a couple of attempts to speak before finally saying, "Underground."

Underground? *Oh fuck,* I thought. Surely she couldn't mean *those* clubs—the ones that catered to vampires who were addicted to feeding from blood whores, humans whose whole life revolved around the ecstasy of a vampire's bite. The council had no intention of ever allowing the rest of the world to know about those clubs; the only reason I did was because one of the clubs was haunted by those who'd been killed there, and their anguish had summoned a Rakshasa— the same Rakshasa that had given me the scar down my spine before I'd killed it.

God, surely fate couldn't be so cruel as to send me into one of those places again, could it?

"What club, Vonda?"

Her mouth opened and closed again, and though I leaned closer, I barely caught her reply. It sounded like "the Crimson Dive," but I wasn't completely sure.

"Where was she planning to go after the club, Vonda?"

Her eyes rolled back into her head and a small sigh

escaped her lips. She was leaving us. I shook her again. "Damn it, Vonda! Who was your sister planning to meet? Where did she plan to go after the club?"

"Hartwell," she murmured. "Zane . . ."

Her words faded away and her head rolled back. Azriel touched my shoulder, but it was a warning I didn't need. I released her and closed my eyes. She was gone, and I really didn't want to see the reaper who'd come for her. Didn't want to see her soul—and any real chance we had of saving her sister—rise and walk away.

Rhoan squatted beside me and pressed two fingers against her neck. "Damn."

"Yeah," I said. "Hartwell and Zane aren't much to go on, either."

"It's better than what we had, and at least we now know the reason behind the forehead branding." His gaze met mine grimly. "I've called in a cleanup team. We'll sort out the father and son, and go through the sister's room—maybe we'll find something to clarify what she meant."

"We only have an hour." I rose and rubbed my arms. "Do you know what a Kudlak is?"

"No, but I will soon enough." He eyed me thoughtfully. "Did you catch the name of the club?"

If he was asking that, it meant the mike on the earpieces hadn't been strong enough to catch Vonda's whispered reply, and for that I was suddenly grateful. "I think it was Red something or other, but I couldn't guarantee it."

"We'll run a scan and see if we can find anything

that matches." He thrust a hand through his short hair. "Can you hang around, just in case we find something?"

"I'll wait outside, where it's warmer." I paused. "Does Dani look like her sister?"

He nodded. "They're identical twins."

Which might explain our killer's statement that he'd never come across two such as these before. Identical twins who were also blood-whore-addicted vampires surely had to be a rarity.

Rhoan walked out. I pressed the left ear stud to deactivate the earrings, then headed back across the road to watch the sudden influx of Directorate people from a safe distance.

"Why did you not tell him about the club?" Azriel asked as he sat down beside me.

"Because of Hunter. I'm not going to risk giving him information that may well get him killed."

"But it may help solve the case."

"It may. Which is why I'll ring Hunter myself and ask." It wasn't something I really wanted to do, as I was rather enjoying the brief respite from her overbearing presence in my life.

I dragged out my vid-phone, said, "Hunter," and watched the psychedelic patterns swirl across the screen as the phone made the connection.

"Risa," she drawled. "What a lovely surprise."

"Considering you've got Cazadors following me around reporting every little twitch, I seriously doubt that it's either a surprise *or* lovely."

Amusement gleamed in her cold green eyes. "They

do not report *every* little twitch—although Markel is more circumspect than some."

Which wasn't something I wanted to hear. With some trepidation, I asked, "Just how detailed do the others get?"

She gave me that smile—the one that reminded me of a shark about to consume its prey. My stomach sank. Obviously, they followed where Markel did not—and there wasn't a damn thing I could do about it, which was infuriating.

"Then you already know why I'm ringing now."

"Yes." She paused. "You were wise not to mention your knowledge of the clubs. Rhoan is an asset the Directorate would not like to lose."

I bet *she* was an asset the Directorate wouldn't like to lose, either, but I sure as hell hoped that one day, it would. In fact, the sooner the better.

"Is there a club called the Crimson Dive?"

"It's Dove, not Dive." She paused. "I've rung the manager, and both Vonda and Dani Belmore are members. As were the other victims."

And the bitch had known about the connection well before I'd gotten involved—she was just more intent on protecting the secrecy of the fucking club than in protecting its patrons.

"Have any of them killed while they were feeding?" If they had, it might explain our killer's insistence that they needed to be destroyed. It was a view I could almost agree with—although his time and attention would have been better spent chasing down those responsible for the clubs' existence than attacking the addicted who attended them—whether by choice or not.

"No." Hunter hesitated again. "The Dove is not like Dark Earth. It caters to those who are more lightly addicted."

I snorted softly. Addiction was addiction, and unless something was done about it, it would always get worse. But the vampire council seemed content to cater to the situation rather than cure it.

Damn it, these women *weren't* like the men and women I'd seen in Dark Earth. They weren't so far down the abyss of addiction that they couldn't function normally. Hell, they held down jobs, something the deeply addicted could rarely manage. They *could* have been helped, if they'd wanted it, and if that help had been available. So why these woman rather than those who drank from and sometimes killed blood whores in clubs like Dark Earth?

"The killer called them Kudlak," I said. "Is that another name for blood-whore-addicted vampires?"

"No. Kudlaks are something else entirely." She turned around, giving me a brief glimpse of stark white walls and a view out over the bay through ceiling-to-floor windows. She wasn't at her Directorate office. Maybe she was home—she was certainly old enough that even windows that large wouldn't be much of a threat sun-wise. "Kudlaks originate from Croatia and some parts of Slovenia. They are a form of vampire who are, at their core, evil."

"Define 'form of vampire.'"

"Both the Croatians and the Slovenians believed

them to be a form of energy vampire—someone who feeds off the emotions of others, and who does evil when alive, but who becomes an *actual* vampire at death."

I frowned. "But you have to undergo a blood ceremony to become a vampire. You don't just become one willy-nilly."

She smiled, though it did little to lift the darkness in her eyes. "You and I know that, but truths often get lost in the beliefs and myths handed down through time."

"So why would this man believe his victims are Kudlaks rather than plain old vampires? And why the hell would he think it's his birthright to kill them?"

"If he believes his victims are Kudlak, it is possible he also believes himself to be Kresnik."

Meaning we weren't dealing with an ordinary, everyday nutter after all, but something far worse. I rubbed my eyes wearily. "What's a Kresnik?"

"Ah, that's where this gets interesting. According to the myths, a person born with a caul—an embryonic membrane still attached to the head—is destined to become either a Kudlak or a Kresnik. It is said a person born with a red or dark caul becomes a Kudlak, but a person born with a white or clear caul becomes a Kresnik."

"And it's the destiny of Kresniks to go after Kudlaks?"

"Yes."

"So what else do these myths say about them? Do they have any special powers?"

"I have never come across either personally, but it is

believed Kresniks can leave their bodies to attack their foe, and are also capable of magic."

Which explained our killer's ability to harm someone both astrally and physically, as well as the hint of magic Azriel had sensed when we'd found Dorothy's body.

"Are Kresniks also vampires?"

She hesitated. "Some legends suggest they are enhanced by the goodwill of the community, and that in itself suggests energy vampirism rather than blood."

Which meant it was more than possible he could move around in daylight, since energy vampires often didn't have the same restrictions as blood vamps. The thought had trepidation shivering through me. "What kills them?"

"Kudlaks are killed by impaling them with a hawthorn stake, then slashing their tendons below the knees and letting them bleed out." Amusement touched her lips. "Of course, such actions would kill anyone, human or not."

Except, I suspected, her. Not because she was immune to such things, but because no one who knew her—or knew *of* her—would ever be stupid enough to attempt such a thing. "Is Dani Belmore still at the Dove?"

It wasn't likely, given that the man behind this madness had said she'd only an hour left to live, but it didn't hurt to ask.

"No. She hasn't been there for several days, apparently."

So why had Vonda believed that she was? Or was

that simply a belief our killer had implanted? "Did you get the club's management to check the security tapes, on the off chance she met someone near the club?"

Hunter raised an eyebrow. "She would not be foolish enough to meet anyone outside the club."

I snorted softly. "She has an addiction, and she'd just come away from feeding it. I seriously doubt she would have been too worried about what she should and shouldn't be doing as she left the place."

Amusement touched her lips again. "You would have made a good guardian, Risa, if you'd chosen such a path."

It sure as hell would have been an easier path than working for *her*. "Does that mean she *did* meet someone?"

"She caught a cab in Glass Street." I didn't ask how they knew this, because I knew she wouldn't tell me. She continued. "I will send you the details of the company and driver."

Hunter paused and gave me *that* face. The one that said I'd better do what I was told. And yet her face didn't even twitch—it was more a darkness that crept into her eyes. "Do not inform Rhoan where you got the information."

Or you'll both die.

The unspoken words seemed to hang in the air, despite the fact that the conversation was over a phone, not in person. But then, this wasn't the first time I'd heard that warning or seen that look.

"I know the drill," I said. "What about Dani herself? Could the manager tell me anything about her?"

"He did not know her personally—he had to look up her membership form to remember who she was. I will send you the relevant details."

"Thanks."

"Remember to check in when you uncover any new information regarding the keys." And with that, she hung up.

I sighed in relief, then glanced at my phone as it indicated an incoming message. Hunter was fast, I'll give her that. But then, she had been warned about the situation by Markel and had undoubtedly been waiting for my call.

There wasn't really much information about Dani—nothing more than her address and banking details, which suggested that at the Dove, members paid for the privilege of easing their addiction. But maybe they did that at all the clubs—if they were a moneymaking venture, it would certainly explain the council's reluctance to address the problem.

The taxi driver who'd picked Dani up was Charlie Tan, and the depot was in Tullamarine, which was only about ten minutes away.

"You wish to go there now?" Azriel asked.

"No, I don't," I all but snapped. "But it's not like I have much of a choice, is it?"

He raised his eyebrows at me. I sighed again, and waved a hand. "Sorry. The anger isn't aimed at you."

"*This* time."

I half smiled. "Yeah. No guarantee about the next time, though."

Amusement touched his lips, and warmed places

deep inside me. "Something would have to be very wrong for you not to be angry with me at least a couple of times a day."

"Oh, come on, it's not that bad—"

"Oh, but it is." The smile still tugged at his lips, and took away some of the sting of the words. "But then, you are not alone in feeling frustrated by the situation we find ourselves in, Risa."

I guess that was true. He just seemed to control it better than me. I double-pressed the ear stud and said, "Rhoan, I need to disappear for a few minutes. Give me a call if you find anything."

"I won't ask where you're going, because I have a suspicion you won't tell me," he replied. "But if you find anything and *don't* tell me, there will be hell to pay."

"I'm just going to check in with a hacker friend. He might be able to help find either this club or what the hell Hartwell is."

Rhoan grunted. Whether he believed me or not was anyone's guess. I turned off the earpiece again and glanced at Azriel. "Let's go."

He wrapped his arms around my waist and zapped us through the gray fields. We reappeared in the middle of an industrial estate. The place across the road was some sort of auction building, and the parking lot to one side of it was filled with cars of all makes and models. I spun around, spotted the cab company, and headed for the office. Azriel fell in step beside me, then opened the door and ushered me inside. The receptionist gave us a warm smile, but I couldn't help noticing it was mostly aimed at the man who stood beside me. Which niggled, but also made me wonder what the hell she was seeing. If the intensity of her gaze was any indication, there might well have been nakedness.

No. There was amusement in Azriel's mental tone. *Although that can be arranged if you so wish.*

If you get naked for her before you get naked for me, I'll be more than a little annoyed.

I have already been naked with you.

Not nearly enough, I'm afraid.

"How can I help you?" the receptionist said.

"I need to speak to Charlie Tan," I said, a touch more tartly than I probably should have. "We're trying to trace the location of a woman who was recently a passenger in his cab."

She frowned. "I'm afraid I can't—"

Azriel made a small movement with his hand. "It is vital we find her."

"Oh," she said. "Okay. Hang on a sec."

She spun away and picked up the phone. I glanced at Azriel. *And just what happened there?*

I made her believe we were police.

I didn't think you reapers were supposed to intervene in the thoughts of others.

We aren't. But I am Mijai, and we do whatever must be done.

Something ominous crawled down my spine at the emphasis he placed on "whatever." I shivered but refrained from saying anything as the woman turned back toward us.

"If you just go through the door to your left, Francis will be able to help you."

Azriel gave her a high-wattage smile. "We appreciate your help."

She blinked and all but stammered, "My pleasure."

He turned and walked toward the indicated door. I followed, torn between amusement and annoyance. *You handled that a little too well. Done it before, have you?*

As I said, I do what must be done. In this case, it's getting the information we need quickly so we can solve this and move back to our real quest.

Then why not just pluck the information from her mind? Why flirt? And why flirt with a damn stranger and not with me?

Because she does not know where the cabdriver is, nor can she connect us to him.

He opened the door and ushered me inside again, one hand pressed against my back. The light contact chased away the ominous sense of trepidation that still lingered, but did little to ease the niggling annoyance.

A woman—Francis, I gathered—glanced up from a com-screen as we entered, and gave us a pleasant smile. And once again, it was mostly aimed at Azriel.

"Sue says you need to speak to Charlie urgently." Her gaze swept him, and interest sparked deep in her brown eyes.

I felt a sudden urge to grind my teeth. The only reason I didn't was because it wouldn't have done any good.

"If it wouldn't be too much trouble, yes," Azriel replied, his voice warm enough to melt ice.

If it wouldn't be too much trouble, I grouched silently. *Good grief.*

Azriel glanced at me, amusement crinkling the corners of his eyes. *And you were accusing me of jealousy?*

I crossed my arms and regarded him steadily. *It's not.*

In the same way as mine is not?

This is different.

I do not believe it is.

You'd believe the sky was green if it suited you.

That is an incongruous statement.

But true.

His smile increased, but he returned his attention to Francis as she pressed several buttons, then swished a finger across the screen. The face of a man appeared. He was bald and chubby, with red cheeks and merry blue eyes.

"What can I do for you, officer?"

I opened my mouth to reply, but Azriel beat me to it. Perhaps he thought politeness wasn't in my current repertoire given my sudden bout of grouchiness. And to be honest, he might have been right.

"We believe you picked up a woman in Gable Street a day or so ago. Can you remember where you took her?"

He frowned. "Listen, I get a lot of passengers—"

"This woman was regal-looking, with silver hair, a thin face, and a hooked nose," I interrupted. "She might have appeared high on something."

He grunted. "Yeah, I remember that one. She smelled funny—like old paper. I dropped her at some abandoned industrial building in Brooklyn. I did ask her if she had the right address, being a woman and alone and all, because it wasn't a nice-looking place." He looked suddenly worried. "Has something happened to her?"

"No," Azriel said, in a reassuring voice. "We simply need to talk to her. Can you give us the address where you left her?"

"It was Cawley Road. I don't know the actual number, but the place had a stack of old shipping containers on the premises. You can't miss it."

"Thank you very much for your assistance, Mr. Tan."

"My pleasure," he said, and then the screen went blank.

Francis swiveled in her chair and gave Azriel a somewhat sultry look. "Anything else I can do for you, officer?"

I rolled my eyes and left him to it. I gave the woman at the desk a nod of thanks, but she was paying as little attention to me as the woman in the control room had. Which I could totally understand, but it still rankled.

I waited outside in the cool air, and Azriel appeared a few minutes later.

"So," I muttered, "you all set for later tonight?"

He raised his eyebrows. "I do not understand what you mean."

My ass he didn't. *That* was obvious from the mischievous twinkle in his eyes. But I bit back my annoyance *and* my reply, and glanced at my watch. Even though he'd zapped us here, we'd still lost valuable time inside, and the clock was ticking down. Time to stop being so idiotic and start concentrating on what really mattered—saving a woman's life. A reaper who was becoming more and more of a frustration could be dealt with later.

"We need to get moving."

He nodded and stepped close, but this time he didn't immediately wrap his arms around me and dissolve us into mist. Instead, he caught my chin between his fingertips and said softly, "You are an idiot, Risa Jones."

Then he kissed me.

It was fierce yet gentle, everything and yet nothing. It was energy and spirit and desire, and it made me soar even as it made me hunger for things I knew could never be.

And it was insanely, infuriatingly brief.

His lips left mine and he wrapped his arms around my waist, but I barely even saw the gray fields as we zipped through them. My head was still dizzy from the power and the promise of the kiss. From the knowledge that it would never go any further unless *he* wanted it to.

What I wanted apparently didn't matter.

We reappeared in the middle of a road. He released me and stepped back, his expression restored to its usual distant self. Like we hadn't just kissed. Like the kiss meant nothing.

And yet I knew, deep down, that was far from the truth.

"Damn it, Azriel—"

"There is magic here," he cut in, obviously not

wanting to discuss his actions. He indicated the high wire fence to our right. Behind it stood dozens of old shipping containers in various states of repair. "Over there."

Fine. Play your games. But don't expect me to be happy or to play along.

Once again, he gave no indication that he'd heard the somewhat surly thought. I released a frustrated breath and reminded myself yet again that there was a life at stake here. "Can you sense anything behind it?"

"No life, if that's what you mean." His gaze met mine. "But no death, either."

I frowned. "If you can't sense any life, maybe she simply met our killer here and they went elsewhere."

"No. There is something here. It is similar in feel to the magic near Dorothy."

I swung around and studied the battered, abandoned containers. I couldn't see anything that jumped up and screamed magic, but then, I wasn't as sensitive to the stuff as he was.

"Where, exactly?"

He pointed down the road, to the right. "It appears to be located near the containers behind that warehouse."

The warehouse in question was big, old, and had been in disuse for some time if the state of the place was anything to go by. The remnants of the sign over the main entrance said HARTWELL SHIPPING in what must once have been bold red lettering.

"This is definitely the place."

"It would seem so."

We hurried toward the entrance. My shoes clicked noisily on the road surface and the sound seemed to echo across the odd hush that held the immediate area. It was almost as if the old buildings around us were holding their collective breath, waiting for something dramatic to happen. Trepidation continued to crawl across my skin, and I slowed.

"What?" Azriel said immediately.

"I don't know."

The nearby cyclone fence was topped with razor wire, which seemed a little extreme given the state of the entire area. It wasn't like there was a lot here beyond rusting remnants, but maybe they were simply left over from the days when this was a thriving business park. There didn't seem to be any other security measures present, either. And yet something about the place still felt off.

I heard a slight *tick-tick*, and walked closer to the fence. A piece of razor wire had been cut and swayed regularly in time to the breeze, and every time it touched the fence, it ticked. The damn fence was electrified. I walked down to the main gate. It was similarly protected.

"The gate doesn't provide much of a barrier for the likes of us," Azriel commented.

He touched my arm and drew me lightly toward him again, but this time I resisted. "Thanks, but I'll get in there under my own steam."

"I do not mind—"

"Yeah, but I do." I wrapped my fingers around my purse and phone—they wouldn't change unless there was skin-on-skin contact. "Especially if you're going to keep using those moments to steal kisses."

"That was wrong of me—"

"Yes, it was," I cut in, then closed my eyes and called to the Aedh within. I was still pushing my limits strength-wise, and this was really the last thing I needed to do. But I wasn't about to keep relying on Azriel to zap us around. Enough was enough. If he wanted distance, he was damn well going to get it.

The heat and energy that was my Aedh half surged with the defiant thought, numbing pain and dulling sensation as it invaded every muscle, every cell, breaking them down and tearing them apart, until my flesh no longer existed and I became one with the air. Until I held no substance, no form, and could not be seen or heard or felt by anyone or anything who wasn't reaper or Aedh.

I swept in under the gate and headed toward the back of the warehouse building. Even though I had no flesh in Aedh form, I felt heavy and movement was slow. It was just as well I didn't have far to go, because I wasn't going to be able to hold this form for long.

I'd barely reached the rear of the warehouse when my energy gave out and I hit the ground with an undignified splat. I stayed there for several minutes, my head booming and my breath a harsh rasp that burned my throat. Azriel, wise person that he was, didn't say a word, although he was standing so close that the heat of him washed over me, chasing the worst of the tremors away.

I took a deep, somewhat shuddery breath, then released my grip on my purse and phone and climbed slowly to my feet. The world did a couple of mad turns, then settled. I swept the sweaty strands of hair from my forehead and, with some determination, walked on.

Azriel followed closely. I had a suspicion he was ready to catch me should I fall—a distinct possibility considering how shaky my legs still felt.

My gaze swept the old building as we neared the rear entrance. It was covered in grime, and there were cracked and broken windows along its entire length, but the roof—or the bits I'd seen of it—seemed in far better condition than what I'd expected. Once again I couldn't escape the notion that someone was using this place—and that there would be more than just electrified fencing waiting if we dared go inside.

Something I really didn't want to do.

"There is no need," Azriel commented. "The magic comes not from within the building, but from a container over to our left. This way."

I followed him through the maze of rusted and rotting containers, although my strides were a whole lot less elegant and assured. In fact, I was amazed I was even still walking, given how crappy I felt.

"And it still feels like the magic you sensed when we found Dorothy?"

"Yes."

"But he's not there?" I knew he wasn't, because otherwise Azriel would have mentioned it, but I still had to ask. After all, we were dealing with a man who was apparently capable not only of leaving his body to attack his foe, but also of transporting spells and god only knows what other type of magic. And Azriel *could* be stopped by magic, though I doubted our killer would have that sort of knowledge, let alone have ever come across someone like our Mijai before now.

"No, he is not. The magic resonates from the blue container up ahead." He came to a halt. "It prevents me from reading what lies within it."

"So much for me thinking our killer didn't have the necessary knowledge to stop you." I stopped beside him. It was tempting to lean against him and let the warmth and strength of him chase away the worst of the aches—if only for a moment—but I resisted. *Give him what he wants*, I reminded myself fiercely. Even if it was the last thing in this world that *I* wanted.

"It is not designed specifically against me. It appears more tuned to stopping *anyone* sensing what lies inside."

I frowned. "Does it just prevent psychic sensing?"

"No, it's olfactory as well." He glanced at me, his expression blank but his blue eyes angry. "I fear someone lies dead inside, even if I cannot immediately feel it."

Meaning that once again our killer had not kept his word. But then, had I really expected him to?

I flexed my fingers, then stepped forward and grabbed the container's latch. It was heavy, rusted, and it took a lot of strength to wrench it open. When I did, it opened with such force that the door slammed against the side of the next container. The sound echoed across the hushed stillness, a deeply resonant noise that was almost a death knell.

That's what waited in the container.

And it wasn't fresh.

I tried breathing through my mouth, but it didn't really help. The smell of rotting flesh had permeated the air, and it wrapped around me like a shroud, clogging every breath and clinging to my skin.

I ignored the churning in my gut and forced my feet forward. Dani lay on wooden boards that spanned two forty-four-gallon drums. Her arms hung limply from her sides, her fingertips stained with the dried remnants of blood. The tendons in her calves had been cut, the wounds no longer clean but flyblown. Bile rose up my throat. I swallowed heavily and stopped beside her. She'd also been staked, but, like Dorothy, had apparently died without pain, without fear. The expression forever frozen on her face was peaceful. Accepting.

My gaze rose higher. She also bore the K-shaped burn on her forehead, but unlike the other wounds on her body, there was no fly infestation. Maybe even they found the mark distasteful.

"Goddamn it!" I all but exploded. "Why is he doing this? Why tell us we can save her when he's already killed her?"

"Did not Rhoan say he taunted the Directorate? Perhaps this is just more of the same."

"But it's pointless! What the *hell* does he gain by any of this?"

Azriel shrugged. "It is often hard to discern the motives of those who derive pleasure from the kill."

I glanced sharply at him. "You think he does this for fun?"

"No, I think he truly believes that this"—he indicated

Dani—"is his calling. But it would seem he gains immense satisfaction from being the puppet master. After all, it is not everyone who can give the Directorate—and now you—so many clues and yet successfully avoid their grasp."

"If he thinks they'll let *that* continue unchecked, he doesn't know the Directorate very well."

"And therein might be your answer."

I frowned. "What do you mean?"

"I mean, cut off his pleasure."

I had a sudden vision of nuts being hacked off, though that obviously wasn't what Azriel meant.

"No," he agreed, amusement briefly tugging at his lips. "I mean, perhaps it would be better *not* to chase."

"But that would mean letting people die."

"They die anyway. You were never meant to save any of these women."

"I guess." I let my gaze sweep Dani one more time, then spun on my heel and walked out.

Once I was free of the stinking confines of the container, I stopped and sucked in large breaths of the crisp, clean air. But it didn't do a whole lot. The smell of death still clung to my skin and clothes.

With some reluctance, I tugged my vid-phone out of my pocket and rang Uncle Rhoan. "I found her," I said the minute he answered.

"Fuck it, Risa, I told you to contact me when you found anything. This is a Directorate investigation—"

"And one that *you* dragged me into," I snapped back, "so don't get all snotty when I chase a lead that may or may not have gone anywhere."

"You have definitely been hanging around my sister for far too long," he muttered, and thrust a hand through his hair. "What have you found?"

"We followed the Hartwell name, and it led us to an abandoned warehouse in Brooklyn. Dani's here."

"Dead, if your expression is any indication."

"Very. There's maggots, so she's been here a while."

He swore softly but vehemently. "Damn it, this bastard's death will be neither quick nor pleasant when I get my hands on him."

"Good." I hesitated. "You might want to investigate the warehouse, too. I don't think it's connected in any way to these murders, but someone has electrified the fencing, so there's obviously something here worth protecting."

"What, you haven't investigated? Color me shocked."

I grinned. "See, there is some common sense left in me after all."

"Apparently so." He glanced away briefly as someone murmured something behind him, then said, "I'll get another cleanup team out there. There's no need for you to hang around."

"Good, because I need to go home and shower."

"Ring me if you happen to chase down either the club or the man Vonda mentioned," he said. "Don't go off investigating them by yourself. This bastard is too dangerous."

I knew that. Not only had I seen the rotting evidence of it in the container behind me, but I'd confronted him on the astral fields. It was *not* an experience I wanted to repeat in real life.

"I won't—don't worry."

"The more you say that, the more I will," he muttered, and hung up.

I shoved the phone back into my pocket, then raised my face to the sky, letting the sun bathe the chill from my flesh. After a few minutes, I said, "This is not getting me home."

"No."

Azriel's voice held a slight edge, and I glanced at him. "What?"

"I am just wondering if you're going to be sensible enough to let me take you there or not."

"Given your somewhat dour expression, I'd say you've already guessed *that* particular answer."

He sighed. "There is no need to tax your strength when I can very easily—"

"Azriel, I can't keep doing this. I can't touch you, or be kissed by you, without wanting more. I understand the dangers you've mentioned—I do—but if you want resistance, then that *has* to mean *complete* distance."

He studied me for a moment, then gave a quick, sharp nod. "Perhaps you are right. It is shortsighted of me to expect such control from you when I am not able to find it in myself."

And with that, he disappeared again. And this time I couldn't even feel him in the immediate vicinity. He had obviously gone back to watching from a distance.

Not what I'd wanted at all.

I made my way back through the containers to the main gate. In Aedh form, I slipped under the fence, but re-formed in human shape almost immediately. The pounding in my head was far worse the second time around, and I stumbled to the nature strip and lost everything I'd eaten that day.

Then I called a cab and went home.

"Hey, stranger," Tao said from the kitchen as I slammed the front door shut. "Sounds like you need coffee."

"I need coffee, sleep, and a shower, and not necessarily in that order." I headed for my bedroom, stripping my clothes off as I went. "Did the electricians and gas people come to the café today?"

"Yeah. Everything has been checked and cleared. I pulled a few strings to get the council inspector in tomorrow, so we should be able to reopen on Friday."

"Fantastic."

I kicked off my shoes as I entered my room, then noticed a pale blue envelope sitting on my bed. It didn't appear to be a bill of any sort, and while the address was typed, there was no return address on either the front or the back of the envelope. I raised it to my nose and sniffed, but couldn't smell anything more than crisp paper, ink, and the faintest wisp of exotic wood and oriental spices—Tao's scent. Whoever had handled this envelope before him had done so very carefully.

I half wondered if this was yet another letter from my father and flipped it over, sliding a nail under the rim to open it.

The sheet inside was the same blue color as the en-

velope. Obviously, whoever sent it liked matching sta-
tionery.

I tugged the sheet out and unfolded it. And discovered it wasn't a letter, but rather a warning.

I know where you live, it said.

And I know what protects you.

Chapter 10

For a minute, I felt nothing. Absolutely nothing.

Then fear set in and I began to shake so badly that my legs wouldn't support me and I dropped onto the bed.

He knew where I lived!

Fuck, oh *fuck*.

I stared at the letter for several more minutes, then, without warning, started to cry.

Fiercely.

Uncontrollably.

The sobs were so bad my whole body shook with them and though I was gulping down air like a fish, it caught in my throat and made it even harder to breathe.

Tao was suddenly on his knees in front of me. He wrapped his arms around my body, making soothing noises low in his throat as he pulled me onto his lap and rocked me as gently as a father would a terrified child. It felt like a furnace had wrapped itself around me, and it went a long way toward chasing away the chill that had enveloped my body.

But the tears continued to fall. In anger, in fear, and in

frustration. For everything that had happened, for everything I'd lost, for all those who had died because of me, and for all those who might yet die because of me.

Because I was sick of monsters chasing me and sick of people using me.

And because I knew, no matter what, there was no going back. This path, this journey, was leading me inexorably into darkness, and I knew with every fiber of my being it was a darkness from which I would not escape.

My mother had sensed this destiny long, long ago. Had, in fact, told Aunt Riley when I was still a child that I would be involved with angels and demons and god knows what else, and she hadn't been sure if that involvement would be for the side of good, or for evil. She'd never actually said anything to *me*, of course, but I'd known. She'd had her secrets, but this was one I'd uncovered fairly young—too young to understand the true depth and cost of such darkness.

I understood it now.

Understood, and feared it.

I'm not sure how long we stayed like that, but it was certainly long enough that Tao's legs had to be cramping. He never said anything, just continued to hold me long after the tears had stopped falling. Eventually, I lifted my head from his shoulder and said, "You wouldn't have a tissue on you, would you?"

"No, but I can produce a handy sleeve."

He offered me his left arm. I made an odd sound that was caught between a laugh and a sob. "Thanks, but it's too nice a sweater to ruin with snot."

"Snot can be washed off." He gently thumbed away a remaining tear, then placed his hands on my hips and lifted me onto the bed. "Now, do you want to tell me what that was all about?"

"It was this."

I handed him the letter. He read it quickly, then met my gaze again, his expression curious. "Who is it from? It doesn't seem the sort of thing the Raziq or your father would send, and they're the only crazy people currently in your life, aren't they?"

"Well, there's Hunter and the vampire council, but this isn't from them. It's from someone who brings a very fresh approach to the business of being insane."

"Well, you do seem to attract them." Amusement ran through his voice, but there was concern in his eyes.

"Yeah, I do." I rose, stepped past his legs, and walked around the bed to grab a tissue, blowing my nose before adding, "I met this one on the astral plane. Apparently he's been killing people and taunting the Directorate for a week, but now he's decided to turn his attention to me. Why, I have no idea."

"The insane rarely need a good reason to do anything." He studied the note for a moment, then threw it on the bed and rose. "Have your shower and then pack. We're getting out of here."

"Why? I mean, this place is more secure than just about anywhere."

But even as I said that, I remembered that *this* foe could astral-travel and was apparently able to interact with people on both the plane *and* the real world while in that astral state.

And though we had the latest in security gadgets in our apartment as well as wards designed specifically to keep Aedh out, it wouldn't keep out a human in astral form.

He knew where I lived.

All he had to do was wait until I was asleep and vulnerable. And because Azriel couldn't interact with the astral plane, he wouldn't be able to stop him.

Azriel.

I wanted the comfort of his presence so badly it hurt, and it was rather surprising that he hadn't appeared, given the stress I'd been under. But then, he was a man fighting for control and warring against need while trying to do the job he'd been sent here to do. And as our all-too-brief kiss had proved, it was a war he was losing.

And while part of me *did* want him to lose that particular battle, I knew in the long run it wasn't for the best. Whatever my fate might be, whatever my future might entail, it wouldn't involve Azriel. It couldn't. He was reaper, I was a half-breed werewolf-Aedh. We were two very different species physiologically, if not emotionally.

Even if, right at this point in time, what we both secretly hungered for was exactly the same thing.

"This place might be secure," Tao said, dragging me out of my thoughts, "but if this guy is as bad as you say, then we must go somewhere he doesn't know about. Stane's."

I frowned. "But I don't want to drag Stane into danger—"

Tao cut me off with a snort. "Oh, trust me, Stane is more than able to take care of himself. Besides, his place is almost as well protected as this apartment, especially with the wards Ilianna gave him still online."

I *had* forgotten about those, though I doubted that even wards designed to keep demons out would deter astral travelers. "But that doesn't mean we should risk—"

Tao touched a finger to my lips. "No arguments. I was going to Stane's for the night, anyway, as it's game night and we've planned to shoot the shit out of people online. So, get ready while I go ring Ilianna."

He walked out. I gave in to the inevitable and went to have my shower, lingering long enough to get prune skin. Once dressed, I packed several days' worth of clothing and other necessities, then slung the bag over my shoulder and headed out.

"Ilianna's going to stay at Mirri's. She's not happy about it, though."

Mirri lived in an apartment building in Carlton, and while it was well enough protected magically, there were apartments both above and below Mirri's and they weren't well soundproofed. Ilianna hated the sensation of so many people surrounding her, as well as the fact that you could hear every little movement in the other apartments.

"I'll ply her with her favorite ice cream when we all return home," I said. "That'll ease the grumpiness."

"You'd better make it a couple of tubs, then." He ushered me out, then set all the various locks and alarms. "Oh, and she said to tell you that the Brindle witches haven't noticed any unusual activity along the ley lines, which means the magic is being contained."

"Did she say if they were going to follow up the possibility of containment?"

"No." He opened the car door and ushered me in. "But you'd think they would. I mean, they wouldn't want anyone controlling that sort of magic, would they?"

"I wouldn't think so." But then, when it came to the Brindle witches, who really knew what they would or wouldn't want? Certainly some of their actions so far had surprised the hell out of me.

Stane greeted us with a cheerful hello and several boxes of pizza. He kissed my cheeks, then waved his free hand toward his bedroom. "It's all yours. I've even changed the sheets."

"You didn't have to do that. I mean, you don't use the thing, do you?"

He grinned. "I do tend to sleep on one of the couches, granted, but that doesn't mean the sheets were clean. I don't dust and it was thick on the bed."

I laughed, then rose on my toes and kissed his cheeks. "Thank you. And enjoy your pizza and online destruction."

"What, you're not going to join us?"

I shook my head. "Right now, all I really want is to sleep."

"We'll try to keep the noise down." Tao squeezed my arm gently, his touch light but comforting. "Yell if you need anything."

"I will. And thanks."

I turned and walked into Stane's bedroom. It was very much like the rest of his apartment—filled with all the latest gadgets, and there was little in the way of dust, despite his claim to the contrary. Which wasn't really surprising—dust could ruin the innards of expensive gadgets, after all, and there were lots of them up here.

I closed the door, shed my clothes, then tucked Amaya under the pillow and climbed into bed. It was big and warm and comfortable, and I was asleep in no time.

The sensation of movement woke me. For a couple of minutes I did nothing more than lie there, dizzy, confused, and feeling oddly transparent. Like my body had somehow disappeared and I was nothing more than particles drifting in the air. When I tried to wake, tried to move, I couldn't do either. But as panic surged, the movement stopped, and suddenly I was full-bodied and fully aware.

I wasn't in Stane's bed.

Not unless it had suddenly turned to cold stone.

No, no, no! It *can't* be happening again. They *can't* have taken me again.

I opened my eyes. Realized my fears were all too real.

They *had* taken me.

The last time I'd been in this place the heavy blanket of darkness had been lifted only by Amaya's lilac flames. This time there were torches on the wall. Why they were there I had no idea, but they sputtered and spat and threw an angry light, as if they had no desire to be in this place.

It was a desire I fully understood.

Because this was the place where the Raziq had torn my molecules apart to place the tracker in my heart.

My heart began to race so fast I could have sworn it was trying to tear out of my chest. But fear wouldn't help me get through this. Truthfully, nothing would. They'd do what they wanted to regardless of what I said or did.

But I could at least face it with dignity and strength. If nothing else, it would make me feel better afterward.

I forced myself upright. I couldn't stand—the ceiling in the cavern was far too low to allow that. The air was as stale as ever, and the torches only made it harder to breathe.

The Raziq were little more than a faint shimmer in the shadows, but the electricity of them crawled across my skin. This time, it was different, though—stronger. There was someone else here, someone I hadn't met before. Someone more powerful than the other five combined.

And I was without Amaya.

Fuck, fuck, *fuck*!

Once again I shoved aside the panic that threatened to overwhelm me and hugged my knees close to my chest.

"So," I said, somehow managing to keep my voice conversational, although it wouldn't have mattered if it wasn't. These Aedh had about as much understanding of human emotion as a brick wall. "My posse has gained a new member—how lovely."

"I am not new." Though I'd been expecting a male, this voice was not only decidedly feminine, but surprisingly pleasant. "But I am here due to past actions, both yours and ours."

"And do you have a name?"

She didn't answer immediately. I had the odd impression she was considering the wisdom of doing so, as she no doubt knew I'd ask my father about her. But then, they *wanted* me in my father's presence so they could capture him, so there was little harm in telling me.

It was a conclusion she must have agreed with. "I am called Malin."

"And what do you want from me this time, Malin?"

"We want what we have always wanted—your cooperation."

"And as I seem to be saying a lot lately, it isn't like I have much of a choice to do anything else." I considered the shimmer that was her presence. "How did you get past Azriel?"

"The distance the reaper kept between you was foolish." There was a hint of smugness in her voice. The Aedh might be unfeeling creatures, but they were *not* above feeling superior. "He did not realize the danger he had placed you in until you were in our grasp."

And he couldn't rescue me, either. For some reason, earth inhibited a reaper's ability to track souls, so being this deep underground meant that not only would Azriel be unable to find me, but our chi connection wouldn't work.

If he'd been frantic when I'd been confronted by the hellhounds, I could well imagine his state right now. And he'd no doubt blame himself for my capture. But even if he had been close, he wouldn't have been able to stop this kidnapping. They'd wanted me, and one solitary reaper could not have stood up to the number of Raziq currently in this place. No matter how fierce a fighter Azriel was, it would have been six against one, and the death I'd feared at the train station would have been real and devastating.

"Look, my father sensing your damn device was *not* my fault. I didn't warn him. I did what you asked."

"We realize this. The device placed within you was somewhat hurried in its creation. I plan to rectify this now."

Horror crawled through me. "Rectifying" was surely just another word for pulling me apart to adjust the thing in my heart. I'd lived through that once. I wasn't entirely sure I could do so a second time.

"My father is no fool, and he's managed to remain one step ahead of you lot all along. He'll expect changes to be made to the device."

"Undoubtedly."

"Then what is the point of making the adjustment?"

"It will provide a nice piece of subterfuge. He'll see what he expects to see, and will not go looking for any other changes."

Any other changes? I was *not* liking the sound of that at all. My voice shook slightly as I said, "Meaning what?"

"Meaning I plan to interweave the strands of our beings."

I could only stare at the flame-lit shadows in horror. Weave her being through mine? What the hell did that mean? How the hell was something like that even possible?

"When you can pull apart the atoms of a being as easily as a human might a tapestry, such a task is relatively simple."

"But—" The rest of the sentence got stuck somewhere in the thickness of my throat. I swallowed heavily and tried again. "But what does it actually *mean*?"

"It means that not only will you carry the threads of your father's heritage, you will also carry mine."

Was "thread" the Aedh word for DNA? Is that what she was going to do—insert her DNA into mine? What the hell would that do to me? Make me more Aedh? Make me more like *them*?

"Yes," she said. "And no."

"Well, that fucking answers the question, doesn't it?"

She didn't react to the anger in the statement. No surprise there, I guess. "You will become more fully Aedh than you currently are, and your skills will therefore be stronger, but it will not affect your overall humanity."

The way she said "humanity" made it all too clear that she meant "emotion," and *that* was a huge relief. As much as I'd enjoyed being with Lucian, I didn't want to be like him emotionally. Hell, the only thing *he* seemed passionate about—aside from sex—was revenge.

"But won't my father sense such an insertion?" I was his daughter, after all, and he could trace my whereabouts thanks to that fact. Surely that same connection would inform him that something had been altered within me.

"Your father cares as much for the human part of your nature as any Aedh ever does. As long as that is retained—however minor it might be—he will not notice the change." The tone was still smug, and yet oddly kind. Like a parent talking to an obtuse child.

I guess if she intended to weave her DNA through mine she technically *could* be considered a parent.

"But he can read my thoughts as easily as you lot. It's illogical to think he won't know."

"Which is why you will not remember exactly what we have done," she replied. "In fact, we bet your life on this."

Fuck, they were going to alter my memories. Then the rest of her words sank in and my gut began to churn even harder. "What do you mean, you're betting my life on it?"

"Hieu will not risk our regaining control of the keys, so if he *does* notice the insertion, he will kill you."

Maybe. Maybe not. After all, my father seemed overly determined to get the keys for his own nefarious reasons, and I was his only way of doing that when he had no physical form here on earth.

But then, what did I really know about the man who was my parent? He'd been one of the Raziq, had worked with them to create the keys. They surely had more of an insight to his character than I did.

"How will this insertion help you capture my father?"

"As you have noted, your father has always been one step ahead of us. Now that he knows of the device, he will work on a way to mute it."

"Yes. And?"

"By threading my DNA through your lesser being, I will be aware of your movements, no matter where you are. If the device within your heart becomes subdued, I will still be able to find you."

I stared at the energy of the Raziq, and felt ice crawl through me. There was more to this than that. It would *do* more than that.

"If the keys were so damn important, how the hell did you lose them in the first place?"

"We did not expect treachery."

I snorted. "More the fool you, then. Treachery comes with any attempt at power."

"The keys were meant to end our servitude to the portals by closing them permanently. They were not a means of power."

The person who had control of the keys had control over the gates to heaven and hell—how could that *not* be considered a means of power? Hell, maybe *that* was the real reason Hunter wanted the keys. It wasn't about the high council using hell as their own private prison—a stupid idea if ever I'd heard one—but rather yet another means of Hunter solidifying her power base.

"Can I remind you that it's the reapers who have been guarding the gates? The priests who were actually supposed to guard them died out long ago." Or rather, had died out or become Raziq.

"Just because we no longer serve or guard the portals does not mean we are free from them."

Another statement that didn't make a whole lot of sense.

God, I thought, dropping my head onto my hands. Why in hell didn't someone wake me? Surely this couldn't be happening. Surely it *couldn't* be real.

But it was. And it was a nightmare from which there was no escape. I very much suspected that not even death would help me. After all, beings who could unravel the threads of humanity could command a being to life as easily as they could kill.

"What about the device in my heart? What are you going to do to that?"

"Little more than mute its power and make it a less tangible presence. Hieu will still sense it, but only because he already knows it exists within you."

I closed my eyes and took a deep breath. "Do what you have to." My voice was flat but not truly steady. It couldn't be when I was all too aware of what was about to happen. "It's not like I can do much to stop you anyway."

"That is refreshingly compliant of you."

I snorted. "Fighting you bastards didn't achieve a whole lot the last couple of times, did it?"

"No, but it is in your nature to fight regardless of the wisdom of such an action. We were expecting nothing less."

"Which just goes to prove that even those of us with

thick heads get sick of constantly knocking ourselves out against brick walls." I rubbed my arms, and felt a flicker of warmth run through my fingers. I glanced down. The Dušan's eyes glowed with deep, angry fire. She might not be able to react against whatever the Raziq were about to do, but she was here, with me, and they could neither remove nor alter *her*. And suddenly I didn't feel so alone.

"Then let us proceed."

As she spoke, dark energy began to swirl around me. I braced myself, expecting the worst, but this time was very different from the last. Maybe it was simply a matter of accepting rather than fighting, but it didn't rip through my body, tearing me apart cell by cell, until every atom felt like it was on fire and screaming in agony. *This* was more like a slip into Aedh form. The energy wove through me like a summer storm, powerful and yet oddly warm, numbing pain and dulling sensation as it invaded every muscle, every cell, breaking them down and tearing them apart, until my flesh no longer existed and I became one with the air. Until I held no substance, no form, and was little more than thousands of tiny particles floating aimlessly in the air.

Then I felt it.

A sharpness, like a knife being inserted into flesh. Pain rippled through my being, a burn that got fiercer, brighter, sharper. Silver flickered across the edges of awareness. The foreign line of particles was finer than a hair, but bright, shining, and cold. They wove through the tapestry of my being, stitching themselves to me and forever altering what I was.

Then the dark energy began putting me back together, piece by piece, until I was again on the stone, quivering and shaking and gasping for air.

For several minutes I didn't say anything. *Couldn't* say anything. The change into Aedh might not have been of my choosing, but it still affected me exactly the same.

In some way, that was a comfort. They may have altered strands of my DNA, but I was still reacting as I always had. At least for the moment.

My skin rippled as the Dušan crawled around my forearm, her claws creating tiny pinholes into my skin with each movement. I glanced down at her, and her head whipped around, her gaze meeting mine. There was displeasure and anger rather than concern in those dark violet depths.

I rested my fingertips against her gleaming body, gaining some measure of calm from her warm presence in my skin, then glanced up to the shimmer that was Malin and the other Raziq.

"Now what?"

"Now we return you and wait for your father to contact you."

"And if he doesn't?"

"Have no doubt that he will. Hieu wants those keys as much as we do."

"Only *he* doesn't want to basically destroy humanity by permanently shutting the gates."

"No," she agreed. "What Hieu wants would be far worse."

Trepidation crawled through me. Her words all but echoed my earlier fears. "And what *are* his motives?"

"Dictatorship over all realms."

"As in heaven, hell, and earth?"

"Yes."

Fuck. Which didn't really seem an adequate response to *that* bit of news.

Of course, given who was relating it, maybe I should be taking it with a grain of salt. They wanted my help to capture him, after all, and maybe imparting this bit of mind-blowing news was little more than an extension of their revised plans.

"Believe what you want," Malin said. "It is not important to us."

And with that, the dark energy swept around me again, shifting me from flesh to Aedh in the blink of an eye. It didn't re-form me in Stane's bed, but somewhere dark, cold, and wet.

It was rain, I realized, after staring at it running down my arms. I was kneeling in the rain. Why the hell did they dump me in the middle of a storm? *Because they didn't want to risk a clash with Azriel, even with greater numbers on their side.*

I sat back on my heels. The madman in my head was reacting less severely than usual, enabling me to at least look around without feeling like I was about to pass out.

Not only was I in the middle of a storm, but if the height of the moon was anything to go by, it was also the middle of the night. Obviously, I'd been in the hands of the Raziq for longer than I'd thought.

A heartbeat later, a hurricane hit, blasting my skin with heat. Azriel dropped onto his knees in front of me, his fingers cupping my cheek as his gaze met mine.

There was a whole lot of anger in those blue depths. A whole lot of guilt.

"I'm okay," I whispered, wishing he'd just wrap his arms around me and hold me like he never intended to let go. It might be a lie, but it was one I suddenly needed, if only for a few minutes.

"You are *changed*." The words came out tight.

"It didn't hurt. Not this time."

"*That* is not the point."

No, I guess it wasn't. And like the last time, it couldn't be undone. Not by him, and certainly not by me.

"Just take me home, Azriel. Please."

He swept us across the fields even before I'd finished speaking, but when we reappeared, it was in Stane's room, not mine.

"But—"

"No," he said, his voice sharp, almost vicious. "I allowed you to be taken once. I will *not* risk it a second time."

And I, for one, wasn't about to complain about that, even if I'd rather be home. I stepped back and rubbed my forehead wearily. "The Raziq won't snatch me again."

"I didn't mean the Raziq."

I stared at him blankly for several heartbeats, then fear struck anew and I began to shake again. God help me, with everything else that had happened, I'd forgotten about our faceless madman.

But he was still out there, still after me.

I couldn't do it. I couldn't cope. Damn it, why wouldn't everyone just leave me the hell alone? Was that too much to goddamn ask?

Azriel caught my hands and tugged me into his embrace. I closed my eyes and leaned my cheek against his chest, listening to the rapid pounding of his heart. It felt like heaven. Like I was home.

"Leaving you alone was what caused you to fall into Raziq hands." His breath tickled the back of my neck, ragged and warm. "That should not have happened, and I apologize."

"It wasn't your fault." I lifted my face and met his gaze. And while I ached to brush my lips against his, any move in *that* direction had to come from him. He knew what I wanted. He'd always known.

"If I had been here—"

"You would have been dead." Even saying the words had my stomach tightening. "I know you believe otherwise, but there were six of them, Azriel, and one of them was immensely powerful. She said her name was Malin."

He closed his eyes for a moment and said something in his own language. And though I didn't understand one word, I didn't really need to, given the anger in his voice.

"Malin is the leader," he said eventually. "She is the one your father betrayed when he stole the keys."

"Then what she did to me was as much about revenge as the keys." I hesitated, and suddenly realized I couldn't actually *remember* what they'd done. "Damn it, are you able to un-erase my memory?"

"No. And it is better that you do not know."

Which suggested he *did*. Frustration ran through me, but it was quickly forgotten when he brushed a fingertip down my cheek and rested it all too briefly on my lips. "But you are right about the revenge factor. Your father and Malin were lovers. Malin has commanded the Raziq for a very long time, and she is nearing the end of her life. She wanted to reproduce. Your father refused."

"But I thought that when the Aedh were at the end of their life cycles, breeding wasn't a matter of choice, but rather an imperative they couldn't ignore."

"That is true."

"Then why did my father turn to my mother when he had the option of a full-blood Aedh to breed with?"

He shrugged. "Your father is an uncommonly powerful Aedh, and one who has long planned domination. It would not surprise me if he foresaw the current problems and created you as a means of working around the Raziq and finding the keys."

"But if he'd known the keys would be lost, why the hell wouldn't he just ensure that they weren't?"

"Because there were other players involved, and Hieu could not control them all. And perhaps you were nothing more than just a backup plan."

Well, *that's* something every child wanted to hear— although when it came to my father, nothing should really surprise me. "How come you know so much about Hieu and Malin?"

"When one is a hunter, it helps to understand the prey."

"But I can't see either of them giving those sorts of details to their own kind, let alone a reaper."

"They didn't. But the Raziq are nearly a hundred strong. It was simply a matter of capturing one of the unwary, lesser beings, and questioning him."

Whatever it takes. Whatever needs to be done. The words rolled around the outer reaches of my mind, and though I didn't know if they were mine or his, I shivered. Because those words were like a death knell ringing in my future.

"Why would the lower-ranked Raziq be privy to information like that, though?"

"Aedh can read the minds of any who are in close proximity, and though Malin and Hieu are powerful enough to conceal information, they would have considered their relationship neither valuable nor important."

Because they didn't do emotions—although they *did* seem to have the whole revenge thing down pat.

I sighed wearily. "This is all becoming a nightmare."

Azriel raised an eyebrow, amusement briefly teasing his lips. "Becoming?"

I smiled. "Yeah, I guess *that* train left the station long ago."

"Definitely." He hesitated, his gaze sweeping my body before coming to rest briefly on my lips. Desire spun around me, but its sweet heat disappeared as quickly as it had appeared. "You need to rest."

I couldn't disagree with that. But I also didn't want to get into that bed alone.

"Azriel—"

"No," he said softly. "I want what you want, Risa, but it is better that we fight this. Assimilation *is* a very real threat."

"But it's not assimilation you truly fear, is it?" I said it softly, my gaze searching his. Looking for the emotions he was never going to reveal, but that I nevertheless knew were there. The hum of them echoed through the deeper parts of my being, warm and precious.

For a moment I thought he wasn't going to answer, but then he said softly, "No."

"Then for once tell me the truth, Azriel. What is it you truly fear?"

His hesitation was longer this time.

"What I fear," he said eventually, "is *us*."

Chapter 11

Of all the answers I'd expected, *that* certainly wasn't one of them. I reached for him, but he stepped away from me.

"You do not understand," he said, his mismatched blue eyes glowing with a fierceness that was part determination, part desperation. "I have a task to achieve, one that is vitally important to *both* our worlds. I cannot let emotion get in the way or cloud my judgment."

"But this isn't about emotion—"

"It *is*, and we both know it."

His words should have made me want to dance. Instead, they scared the hell out of me. Because he was right. Whatever this thing between us actually was, it was certainly more than just sexual attraction. It had the potential to be something far deeper, far stronger. It was something that could change both our lives, in ways I couldn't even begin to see or imagine.

But *he* obviously *could*, and that's what scared me.

I licked suddenly dry lips and said, "If you've feared this all along, then why did you give in to desire in the first place?"

"If I was without flaws, I would not be a dark angel."

"But it's only made things worse."

Because now we both knew just how good we were together. And we were both aware that what we'd shared was only a beginning, that there was a whole lot more left unexplored between us.

"I understand that now, but I cannot undo what has been done." He paused, then added softly, "Nor would I want to. When all this is over and we resume our separate lives, I will at least have something to cherish, even if it is only a memory."

Tears prickled my eyes. Goddamn it, I did *want* an end to the madness. I *did* want life to resume normalcy. But at the same time, I couldn't even begin to imagine my life without Azriel's presence in it.

Which only testified to just how much I'd come to care for my stubborn reaper.

"We both hunger for things that should not be," he said, his voice gentle. "But for the sake of our worlds, it *cannot* be."

It was very tempting to just say *fuck our worlds, what about us?* I'd always been one to fight for what I wanted, but this was a very different situation. What I wanted—what he wanted—really didn't matter in the bigger scheme of things. It never had.

God, I wanted to scream about the unfairness of it all. But that wouldn't help anyone. I guess I just had to pull on my big-girl britches and deal with the situation as best I could.

"That is all the fates can expect of either of us," he agreed softly.

"The fates need to be fucking shot," I muttered, then thrust a hand through my hair. "I guess I'm going to bed alone, then."

"I guess you are." His words were as flat as his expression, but behind the facade, frustration burned, and it was every bit as deep as mine.

I forced myself to turn around and climb into bed. Drew the covers up and told myself to sleep.

Which I did.

Eventually.

And not before a very long battle against the urge to get up and claim what we both desired.

The phone woke me hours later. I groped for it blindly, then realized I'd actually left it in my bag, which was still sitting on a nearby chair. But before I could muster the energy to move, it appeared in my right hand.

I opened a bleary eye, and came face-to-face with Azriel. "It is Rhoan," he said, rather unnecessarily. The ringtone informed me of that much.

"Let's hope he has some good news for a change," I muttered, then hit the ANSWER button. Rhoan's face appeared onscreen, and the high-pitched wail of a siren just about blew my eardrum out. I hastily turned down the sound and said, "Please tell me you're on your way to catch the bastard."

"We hope so." If the dark circles under Rhoan's eyes were any indication, he'd been getting even less sleep than me. "And not only do we have a possible location, we have a name."

"How the hell did you discover *that*?"

"Do you remember suggesting we investigate the warehouse?"

"Yes."

"Well, inside we discovered a marijuana crop that had to have a street value of at least four million. Naturally, there was all sorts of security to protect this investment, including cameras." He smiled. "Actually, your presence must have spooked them, because they were in the process of dismantling and bagging when we arrived. We caught all of them."

Well, at least some good had come out of Dani's death. "I'm gathering the cameras also picked up the coming and going of our killer?"

"Yes. And he wasn't alone."

"If he's blind, it makes sense he'd have an assistant." I paused. "He *did* have a face, didn't he?"

"And a butt-ugly one it is, too. Actually, that could apply to him as a whole."

Which made you wonder how he was hooking his victims. But then, sometimes it wasn't about looks. Sometimes it was about aura and power. And from what I'd seen on the astral plane, our killer had *those* in spades.

"So who is he?"

"He's going by the name of Zane Taylor, but we can only trace his existence back about five years, which is when he landed in Australia. We're currently checking the Croatian and Slovenian databases to see if we can find a match."

"What about his buddy?"

"He's a man by the name of Jason Bright. He's an IT specialist with a history of hacking into high-profile companies and then selling their information on the black market. He's served a smattering of time, but he's been flying under the radar since he was released five years ago."

If he was an IT specialist, why wouldn't he have done something about the cameras to stop them from recording their presence? It wouldn't have been that hard for someone who knew what they were doing— Stane could have managed it with his eyes shut.

"Meaning the two of them somehow hooked up when Zane arrived in Australia?"

"More than likely." He glanced sideways, said something to whoever was in the car with him, then added, "We're on our way to Bright's last known address now."

"What about Zane?"

"The address listed in the system was for an apartment that was torn down years ago. But his bank records show activity in the same vicinity as Bright's house, so we're hoping they share a residence and we can nab them both."

It wouldn't be that easy. No way, nohow. Our faceless killer might now have both a name *and* a face, but he seemed way too smart to leave such an obvious trail.

"You'll call me after you raid the place?"

"Yes. But I'm sending through pics of both men, just in case this is little more than a diversion and they're actually coming after you."

A shiver ran through me. He *was* coming after me. I knew that for a fact, but at least knowing what he looked like would give me a small advantage.

Not that it would matter if he came in astral form.

"Be careful, won't you? I'd hate to see—"

"Risa, I've been doing this for more years than you've been alive." Amusement and warmth filled his voice. "Even if Taylor and Bright were aware of the cameras and have done a runner, they won't have had time to clear away all the evidence. We'll find them."

I wasn't worried about Rhoan and the Directorate finding them. I was worried about our killers finding *him*. After all, he was the one who'd pointed out how little respect Taylor seemed to have for the Directorate—and maybe that was because he was always one step ahead of them.

I had a horrible suspicion he was still one step ahead of all of us.

"I know," I said. "Just . . . good luck."

"Stop worrying about me, dear Risa, and just make sure *you* keep alert until we catch this bastard."

"I will."

"I'll be in touch when we have him."

He hung up, but the phone beeped immediately as two messages came in. I opened them to discover the faces of both my hunter and his assistant.

As Rhoan had noted, Zane was one hell of an ugly man. His face was round and puffy, the left side so scarred that it almost looked like it had melted. His hair was sparse and the same nondescript brown as his eyes, and his nose large.

Jason Bright, his companion in crime, had thin features, thick-framed black glasses, and dirty blond hair. He was the sort of man you wouldn't look twice at on the street. The sort of man who looked totally and absolutely harmless.

And yet it was no doubt thanks to him that Zane had discovered my home address. If he could hack into the systems of high-profile companies, it would have been easy enough to gain access to the security company that monitored Vonda's and Dani's homes.

And maybe *he* was the reason the Directorate hadn't been having much luck tracking Zane. If he was so damn good, then it wouldn't have been too hard to get into the Directorate system and see what they were up to. After all, Stane could do exactly that—though he hadn't recently because the Directorate had increased security and he preferred to stay out of jail.

I took one more look at the killer who was hunting me, then dumped the phone on the nearby pillow and closed my eyes. Weariness still rode me, but it was nowhere near as deep as it had been. I half wondered if Azriel had given me a little energy boost while I'd slept.

"No," he said softly. "It would not have been wise."

To touch you. The unspoken part of that sentence swam through my thoughts. Frustration rose like a wave and threatened to swamp me yet again.

Get it under control, I reminded myself fiercely. *Accept the reality and just move on.*

But saying that, and actually doing it, were two entirely different things.

"What time is it?" I asked eventually. I could have opened my eyes and looked at the nearby clock—hell, I could have picked up my phone and looked—but right now either required too much effort.

"Four o'clock."

"A.m. or p.m.?"

"P.m."

That *did* wake me. "So I've slept for over *twelve* hours?"

"You needed it. You were running far too close to the edge of exhaustion, Risa."

"Hard to do anything else considering what keeps getting thrown at me," I muttered. I flipped the covers away from my face and sat up.

Azriel's gaze swept me briefly, then moved away. But not before I'd caught the flash of desire in his eyes.

"Tao has gone to the restaurant to deal with the council inspectors." His voice was back to its formal self. "Stane has coffee percolating, Coke in the fridge, and bacon and eggs on standby."

"I need all three. But I need a shower first."

I forced myself out of bed, raided Stane's closet for an old T-shirt to wear between here and the bathroom, then grabbed my toiletries and clothes and headed out.

Stane swiveled around in his chair and gave me an appreciative once-over. "That T-shirt looks a *lot* better on you than it does on me."

I smiled. "How did the game go last night?"

"We thoroughly thrashed the opposition, and moved up several levels in the process. What would you like to eat?"

"Azriel mentioned bacon and eggs."

"Done," he said, and practically bounced toward his kitchen.

I quickly showered and dressed. Though Azriel

wasn't present in body, he was still nearby, still keeping watch. The heat of him washed across my skin like a summer breeze, warm and sultry.

I once again forced myself to thrust away the growing slithers of desire, and followed the delicious aroma of fried bacon back out into the kitchen portion of his open living area.

Stane slid both a Coke and a mug of steaming coffee over to me, then flipped the eggs. "I did that search for Henry Mack, Jason Marks, and Mark Jackson."

It took me a moment to remember that Mack, Marks, and Jackson were the aliases of the Razan we'd knocked out in the cavern where the hellhounds had attacked us.

I propped on the nearby stool. "And?"

"As you might have already guessed, neither the Mack nor Marks identity actually exists. The Jackson one does, although if it is the same man, he's over a hundred years old." He served up the bacon and eggs, then picked up his coffee and leaned his elbows on the kitchen counter.

"If he's listed as a Middle East war veteran," I said, alternating between speaking, eating, and drinking, "then it's the same man."

"Interesting, given that the photos of his recent incarnations suggest he's not more than forty."

"He's had a little magical help."

Stane snorted. "Then they should package that and make a fortune."

"Trust me, it's the sort of magical help you wouldn't want. It amounts to slavery."

"Oh, well, that they can keep." He grimaced and drank some more coffee. "The address listed for both the Mack and Marks identities is Railway Crescent, Broadmeadows, but I couldn't find them listed as tenants in the apartments there."

"Probably because he actually lives in Dawson Street, Brunswick West." If what Uncle Quinn had pulled from his mind was to be believed, anyway. "Any chance of you checking to see if there's a traffic camera nearby, and monitoring it?"

"I can check. Can't promise results."

"Thanks."

He grinned. "You know, a crate or two of Bollinger wouldn't go astray. I'm almost out of the last lot."

I choked down a laugh. "Done deal. And cheap at half the price."

"Then I shall double the price next time."

He could triple the price and it would still be cheap. The information he kept getting for us was invaluable.

I scooped up the last of the egg yolk with a piece of bacon, then pushed the plate away with a contented sigh. "That was delish. Thanks."

"You're lucky. I normally only stock frozen meals, but Mom insisted on having real stuff while she was here."

I grinned. "Mothers are funny like that."

"Tell me about it." His voice was gloomy, but there was a mischievous twinkle in his eyes. "She's even insisting I meet the daughter of one of her friends before she leaves."

"The daughter might be hot, you know."

He snorted. "It's not the hotness that matters, it's the nerd factor. Most women these days have absolutely *no* appreciation of either the fine art of hacking *or* black marketeering. And they always want to dust."

"Heaven forbid," I said, voice dry.

"I know! What is with that?"

I snorted, but didn't reply as my phone rang. The tone told me it was Lucian, so I excused myself and walked into Stane's bedroom to answer it.

"Well, hello," he said, his voice low and intimate. Just the sound of it had desire stirring, and though I suspected it wasn't entirely "real," it didn't seem to matter. Nor did Ilianna's leafy charm appear to mute that reaction.

But maybe it only worked for face-to-face confrontations. I had to hope so, because if I was going to continue my relationship with Lucian, I wanted it to be because I chose to, not because I was under some sort of compulsion spell.

"Hello, yourself," I said, keeping my voice as even as possible. "What can I do for you?"

Surprise flitted briefly through the bright depths of his eyes. Obviously, he'd been expecting a stronger response.

"Oh, I'm sure I can think of one or two things, but the point of the call is what *I* can do for *you*."

The emphasis he placed on *I* and *you* had all sorts of wicked images floating through my mind. I cleared my throat and said, "And what might that be?"

"Besides the obvious, you mean?"

I half smiled. "Yeah, besides that."

"Lauren believes she might have an answer to our dilemma."

My heart began to race a little faster. Now that the moment was here, I wasn't sure that I should go through with it.

"What sort of answer?"

"She didn't say. She just said she needs to run a test to ensure it works, and for that she requires your presence."

I hesitated. "Lucian, I don't think—"

"It can't hurt to check out what she has to offer," he interrupted, in a voice that wasn't about to brook any argument. "After all, it may not even work."

I had to hope so, because I really *didn't* want to be in debt to a dark sorcerer.

So why even bother going? Azriel's thought was knife sharp.

Because I need to know. About whatever magic our dark sorceress had come up with, and about the charm that now encircled my wrist.

And if the charm doesn't work?

Then I guess you have the choice of watching, joining in, or keeping your distance. My reply was somewhat tight. I might understand his reasons for keeping his distance, I might even agree that it was for the best when it came to the task still ahead of us, but that didn't give him the right to get pissy whenever I happened to be talking to—or was with—Lucian. Even if he *had* placed a compulsion spell on me.

I half expected Azriel to disappear in another huff, but he merely crossed his arms and gave me his impassive, not-thinking, not-feeling face.

"Earth to Risa," Lucian said. "You there?"

I blinked. "Yeah."

"But obviously didn't hear a word I just said," he said, amusement teasing the corners of his eyes. "That reaper giving you grief again?"

"No."

He sighed. "You're not a very good liar, my girl. I said, Lauren will be here at five, if you're free."

"Where's 'here'?"

"My apartment, not the club." He paused, then gave me a wide grin. My stupid hormones did a happy little two-step. "Although we could visit the club afterward, if you'd like. It's fancy-dress night."

"A fancy-dress night sounds a little too tame for your tastes."

"If you think that, then we obviously need to go. And it will be my extreme pleasure to teach you otherwise."

"One step at a time," I said, trying not to smile. "Let's meet with Lauren, and see how that goes first."

"So you can get here by five?"

I glanced at the clock. It was close to five now, but it wouldn't take me that long to get there by taxi. I *could* travel by Aedh form, but even though I felt a whole lot stronger after eating and sleeping, I wasn't about to waste energy uselessly. Lucian and his dark sorceress would just have to wait if I was late.

"Depends on the traffic," I said. "But probably."

"Good. See you soon."

I hung up, then tossed the phone in my purse and walked to the bed to retrieve Amaya from under the pillow. *Happy, not*, she said, as I slung her over my back. *Should not leave alone*.

It wasn't my choice to get snatched without you, I replied, then wondered why in the hell I was justifying myself to my own damn sword. Maybe I was going crazy—which would not be surprising given the mess my life was in at the moment.

I made the bed, then slung my purse over my shoulder and headed for the door.

"Risa, don't go," Azriel said softly.

Fuck it, Azriel, don't do this. I stopped. "Why not?"

"Because I do not want you to go."

I flexed my fingers, and found myself reeling between the desire to do what he asked and the knowledge that what he was asking was wrong. "You were the one who said this quest was more important than anything else. If talking to this dark sorcereress gets us closer to the keys, then we have to do it."

"I am not talking about the keys. I am talking about you and Lucian."

"Lucian has his place in this search, whether you like it or not."

"It is not so much his place in this search that I object to."

"Damn it, you *can't* say things like that. Not after everything you said last night." And while a deeper part of me rejoiced at the admission, it mostly only added to the deepening well of frustration.

"There have been a lot of things I should not have said or done, Risa."

Yeah, and showing me just how truly amazing we could be together, then snatching away the possibility of it ever happening again was certainly one of them.

"You said last night that I wasn't understanding the seriousness of the situation. Well, this time *you're* the one not understanding." I turned. There was very little in the way of emotion to be seen in his face. "I might be part Aedh, but I am also werewolf. Sex may not be the necessity for me that it is for others of my kind, but by the same token, I do not want to live my life without it."

"I am not asking—"

"Yes, you *are*." I said it fiercely, my fists clenched. "You're asking me to stay out of Lucian's bed, and right now he's the *only* sexual partner I have. And don't suggest I seek out others, because I can't afford to bring anyone else into my life with all the shit that is happening. At least Lucian is fully able to protect himself."

"But he is not to be trust—"

"Maybe not," I cut in. "But then, who the hell *am* I supposed to trust in this whole debacle? Every single person involved in this quest is using me for their own reasons—you, Lucian, Hunter, my father. Hell, even Jak's doing it to get a story, but at least with him it's a mutual thing."

"What about Tao, Ilianna, and Stane? They are not—"

"They're my *friends*, and only part of this quest because I've dragged them into it. They're not using me; they're trying to keep me alive."

"*I'm* trying to keep you alive."

"But only because you need me to find the keys. If it came to a choice between saving me and gaining the keys, we both know I'd be a goner."

He didn't say anything. And whatever he was feeling, whatever he was thinking, he was keeping it all locked down very tightly.

I sighed. "We can't keep doing this, Azriel. We can't keep arguing over this same point. Either you and I take the risk of deepening our relationship, or you accept the fact that I will take other lovers, be that Lucian or not."

He made a sharp "whatever" motion with his hand. "You are right. I will not mention it again."

"Good." I spun on my heel and headed for the door.

But as I reached for the handle, he added, "I told you once that reapers *are* sexual beings, that we mingle energies and recharge ourselves with other energy beings."

I paused, my fingers still on the door handle as I glanced over my shoulder. "Yes, so?"

His expression was as remote as ever. "So, we can only recharge with those who possess a harmonious frequency, and such compatibility is not widespread. When a connection is found, it is to be cherished."

I frowned. "I'm not getting the link between this and what we were discussing."

"The connection," he said softly, "is the fact that I can recharge with you."

I blinked. To say I was surprised was an understatement. Hell, I was flesh and blood, and he was energy. How was something like that even possible?

"I'm not a reaper. I'll *never* be a reaper."

"No, you are not."

My confusion deepened. "So what exactly are you trying to say?"

"Nothing. I merely explain what you see as unreasonable behavior." He hesitated, and something flashed through his eyes, something that resembled pain. "I once had a recharge companion, but she was killed while escorting a soul through the dark portals."

"I'm sorry—"

"There is no need for your sorrow. She died long ago, and was not my Caomh. While I regret her passing, it was not a life-altering event."

Caomh was the reaper equivalent of a life mate if I'd understood the little Azriel had said about them. "So, is the fact that you can recharge through me a sign that the assimilation threat is greater than you were admitting?"

"No. I am, as I said, merely explaining why I react to Lucian's presence in your affections."

Because he wanted to protect something that was rare and precious in his world. And yet, at the same time, he was desperate to avoid it because he feared that it might cloud his judgment when it came to his task here. No wonder he seemed all over the place when it came to the two of us.

"What happens to reapers who do not find someone who is compatible energy wise?"

He shrugged. "Their life span is shortened. Even energy beings eventually need some means of sustaining themselves."

"So recharging is as much about food as sex?"

"Yes."

"Then how did you survive so long without your recharge partner?"

"I survive because recharging for a reaper is not the everyday necessity that it is for flesh-and-blood beings. We can go eons before the lack affects us."

Thank god I wasn't a reaper, then, because I actually enjoyed the daily necessity of food and sex.

"Look, I'm sorry you've been put in this position, Azriel, but I can't stop living my life because you and I share what is rare in your world—especially when it's something you fear will endanger us both."

"I understand this now and, as I said, I will not mention it again." He hesitated briefly, and again emotion flashed through his eyes. This time, though, I couldn't really define what it was. "I just wanted to explain why I react as I do."

"Thank you," I said softly. "But you haven't actually explained why you can recharge with me, when I'm not a full energy being."

"No."

I waited for him to continue, but when it became obvious he wouldn't, I turned and walked out of the room.

It was the hardest thing I'd ever had to do, given that all I really wanted to do was to wrap myself in Azriel's arms and let the rest of the world go to hell.

Which was *still* a very real possibility if we didn't get to the remaining keys first.

*   *   *

I was half an hour late by the time I got to Lucian's. Even though we'd been going against most of the traffic to get into the city, it was still peak hour, and that generally meant madness no matter which side of the road you were on.

I climbed out of the taxi and stared up at the old Victorian building. There were still workmen on-site, despite the fact it was nearing five thirty. Maybe they were making use of daylight savings and trying to get ahead of schedule. My gaze swept the top floor, but I wasn't sure what I was searching for. The windows were covered by heavy plastic, so even if Lucian had been standing at one of them, I wouldn't have been able to see him.

I took a deep breath, then released it slowly, but it didn't do much to ease the tension slithering through me. And standing here wasn't doing a whole lot for it, either. I waited for a tram to pass, then crossed the road and made my way through the scaffolding into his building.

The old lift rattled upward and came to a bouncing halt at the top floor. The doors groaned open, but it took me several seconds before I could force myself out.

And I wasn't entirely sure whether the reluctance stemmed from not wanting to meet with the dark sorceress or not wanting to have my suspicions about Lucian confirmed.

Damn it, I *liked* sex. I especially liked having sex with Lucian. I *didn't* want a return to the nun-like state I'd been in before this madness had all begun.

Of course, confirmation that he'd placed a compulsion spell on me wasn't exactly a deal breaker, but it *would* worry me. If he was being dishonest about that, then what the hell else was he being dishonest about?

I walked through the clouds of dust that filled the room, my footsteps echoing softly in the vast emptiness. There were no workmen on this floor, just the sound of their jackhammers and whatnot echoing up from the floors below. Lucian's lemongrass and suede scent filled the sub-layers within the dusty air, but it was entwined with an energy that was uneasy and shadowed. His dark sorceress was here.

I snuck under a dustcover and entered the kitchen. Except for the addition of four folding chairs, the room hadn't changed since the last time I'd been here. Lucian and Lauren stood near the chairs, but there was nothing relaxed about either of them. In fact, the heat in Lauren's cheeks and her sharp gestures very much suggested I'd walked in on the middle of an argument. Hell, Lucian was all but hissing in her face.

And yet, something in the way they stood—in their very closeness—was oddly intimate.

Unfortunately, thanks to all the noise the builders were making, I caught only a couple of chopped-up sentences of his conversation with the sorceress—*it means nothing, I will have my revenge regardless.*

And while Lucian had made no secret of either aim, I had to wonder why he was now saying those words to a sorceress he claimed to barely know.

Because he is a liar. And have no doubt that he will not only lie, but cheat, steal, and kill to gain what he wants.

Azriel could have been talking about the weather, for all the emotion he showed, yet we both knew that was as far from the truth as you could get. *What we cannot be truly sure of yet is what, exactly, he wants.*

He says revenge, and that's the one thing I truly do believe he's being honest about.

Perhaps.

And perhaps he was just incapable of seeing the forest for the trees where Lucian was concerned.

That is an incongruous statement.

But true.

Possibly.

As I drew closer, Lucian swung around and gave me a wide grin of greeting. Any sign of anger had completely disappeared. My gaze flicked briefly from his face to Lauren's. She looked regal and composed—a woman certain of her place and power rather than one who'd seemed ready to tear eyeballs out just moments ago.

"You're late," Lucian said, the amusement in his eyes at odds with the rebuke in his words. "I was beginning to think you'd had second thoughts."

"Just because I'm here doesn't mean I don't."

"Of course."

He dropped an overly polite kiss on my cheek, and again I had to wonder if the argument I'd witnessed *had* been about sex. The only time he'd ever been so frugal with his kisses was when she'd been witness to them.

And while I was aware that he had a stable of bed partners, I certainly hadn't expected one of them to be a dark practitioner. Nor was I entirely sure how I felt about it.

But at least it *did* explain the heady scent of sex and blood I'd smelled when I'd entered the room at Maxwell's—it had come from *their* activities rather than from those on the main dance floor.

"Would you like something to drink?" he asked.

"A Coke would be good."

He tsked. "And I had my best champagne on ice, too."

"Save it for when we've got something to celebrate."

"Later, then."

"Perhaps."

My reply was somewhat absent as movement caught my gaze. Lauren folded gracefully onto a chair and crossed her legs. The bright lights gave her dark hair a purple sheen but shadowed her face, softening her stern, somewhat matronly features. Once again I had that odd sense of familiarity, but I still couldn't place who she reminded me of. Although she *did* remind me somewhat of a spider. A big black one, sitting in the middle of her nest and contemplating the world around her as she waited for her prey to fall into her web.

"Take a seat," Lucian directed. "I'll grab your drink."

I claimed the chair nearest to Lucian's, and Lauren gave me a thin smile. "And still you distrust me."

"It's not so much you as your profession."

She raised one thin eyebrow. "Which is not saying much given my profession is who and what I am."

I wasn't quite sure how to take that statement, so I

didn't say anything. Lucian returned and handed me a can of Coke, then sat down between us.

"So," he said, picking up his glass of wine from the floor. "As I said on the phone, Lauren believes she has come up with a possible answer."

My gaze flicked to hers. Those icy depths watched me closely, and the hairs on the back of my neck rose. Not because of the intensity of her gaze, but rather the hatred so very evident in it.

Why the hell would someone I'd barely even met hate me so much? Or was it not so much me, but the fact that she considered me a sexual rival?

If she thought *that*, then she didn't understand Lucian. But maybe she hadn't even known he was Aedh until he'd told her about the device in my heart. She might be knowledgeable about the dark arts and the denizens of hell, but that didn't mean she had any expertise when it came to the beings who inhabited the gray fields.

"I'm not committing to anything until I know exactly what we're talking about."

"Of course."

He said it soothingly, like a parent talking to a spooked child. Irritation swirled, but I forced myself to ignore it and kept my gaze on Lauren.

"It is not a spell, so you have nothing to fear along those lines," she said easily. A little too easily for my liking. It sounded like a well-rehearsed line more than anything approaching sincerity.

I took a sip of Coke, but it failed to help the sudden dryness in my throat. Despite what I'd said to Azriel earlier, I really *didn't* want to be here discussing magic with a dark practitioner. And yet, it was an avenue that had to be explored. *We do what we have to do*, Azriel had once told me. It was that statement that had driven me to enlist Jak's help, and if it also meant enlisting the help of a sorceress, then so be it.

"Then what is it if not a spell?"

She glanced at Lucian. And *that* had all sorts of alarm bells ringing, if only because it suggested they'd discussed just what she should and shouldn't say before I'd gotten here.

Had that been another part of what they'd been arguing about? I knew Lucian was desperate to gain revenge on the Raziq, who'd stolen not only his wings but also his ability to shift into Aedh form, but was he so desperate that he would advise a dark sorceress what to say—and not say—to convince me to use her magic?

I briefly studied his angelic face and saw a determination that bordered on ruthlessness. Yes, I thought, he was.

Lauren took a sip of her wine, then casually said, "It's a ward."

I waved the statement away. "You and I both know there's a million different kinds of wards."

She smiled. It didn't do a whole lot to ease the tension. Quite the opposite, in fact. "This one is designed to prevent magic escaping its boundaries once it has been activated."

So, similar to the wards Ilianna had used when we'd attempted to read the clues in the book my father had sent me—a book that had been subsequently destroyed when the elementals had attacked. "How is it powered?"

"Not by blood magic, if that is what you fear."

"Then how does it get its power? You felt the energy of the thing in my heart. You know it's not a creation of this world."

"Which is why I do not use the magic of this world."

I stared at her, my stomach twisting into knots. "You exploit the power of *hell* to create your spells? That is a very dangerous practice—"

She snorted, the sound unladylike and at odds with the image she was projecting. "I think I understand better than you just what it is I'm dealing with."

Somehow I doubted that. I might not have had much experience with hell and its denizens, but I did have a healthy respect for just how dangerous they could be—something Lauren appeared to have lost.

"Look, I really don't think a ward powered by the energy of hell is something I should be handling." Especially not when I had a sword at my back eager to kill all things related to hell.

"You cannot make that judgment without at least looking at it," Lucian commented. "I have handled it without harm, and its magic seems no better or worse than what the Raziq use."

I cast him a somewhat wry look. "You *would* say that, given how desperate you are for revenge."

"I cannot deny I have a stake in this device working. If we get the remaining keys, we can force a confrontation with the Raziq." He hesitated, and something flickered briefly in his eyes. Something that was altogether too dark for my liking. "That is something I have long desired."

"If you confront the Raziq, you'll be dead. There's too many of them."

"I am not suicidal, dear Risa." He slid his hand under my skirt and gently squeezed my thigh. His fingers were warm and familiar, but there was no must-have-you-now-or-I'm-going-to-melt hormonal attack. Which didn't mean it had *no* effect, just that my response was basically normal when being intimately touched by someone who was as sexy as all get-out. The charm, it seemed, was working. He added, "I plan to be around to devastate your bed long after the keys are history and the Raziq are little more than a bad memory."

Anger stirred the air, a sharp burst that was quickly contained. I glanced at Lauren. Her expression was as calm and as regal as ever. The only sign that the flash had come from her was the whiteness of her knuckles as she gripped her wineglass. But the moment she caught the direction of my glance, her grip eased. I resisted the temptation to smile. Lauren was in for one hell of a shock if she thought Lucian would ever stay with just her.

Although it had to be said, if they *were* lovers, then Lucian was playing with fire. A sorceress wouldn't be someone you'd want to make an enemy of.

"Which is presuming I'd actually *want* you in my bed by then."

Amusement crinkled the corners of his eyes. "Of course you will. I'm a magnificent lover, and we both know it."

"What you are is conceited, Lucian Dupont."

"It is not conceit when it's the truth." But he removed his hand and took a drink of wine. His gaze, I noted, went to Lauren, almost as if he were daring her to react.

She didn't.

"However," he said, after a moment, "we are not here to discuss my bedroom skills, but rather the ward. And I reiterate, it cannot harm you to simply look at it."

That statement should not be taken at face value when dealing with someone involved in the dark arts, Azriel commented.

I know that, Azriel. I'm not a total ignoramus about magic, so please don't treat me as such.

I merely comment. It was not a rebuke.

Well, it sure as hell had felt like one. I drank some Coke, then met Lauren's gaze and said, "I thought you said it had to be fine-tuned?"

"It does. To work fully it has to be tuned to your energy."

Energy, or aura? I very much suspected the latter, and that had my doubts rising even higher. "Where is it?"

"In my purse. Lucian?"

He rose and walked over to the bench. I put my Coke down and followed. I wanted some distance between me and Lauren when I studied her creation.

Her purse was black leather, and was about as far from feminine as you could get. In fact, it looked more like an over-the-shoulder briefcase than an actual handbag. Lucian gamely delved into it, and his hand came out holding what looked like an oversized die. Only there were no dots on its black surface, which held an odd sort of oiliness that gleamed in the sharp overhead lighting. He set it down on the counter in front of me.

I leaned closer, but didn't immediately try to touch it. Despite the oddness of the surface, there was no sense of energy radiating off the black stone. It really could have been nothing more than a numberless die.

"It won't bite," Lauren said, amusement clear in her voice. She hadn't moved, but I had an odd sense that she missed nothing, despite the fact that I had my back to her.

"Forgive me for not taking you at your word." I shifted around to study the other side of the die. It didn't look any different, and I wasn't entirely sure why I'd bothered moving.

"Here, look." Lucian picked up the die and deftly tossed it from hand to hand. "See? Nothing bad happens when you touch it."

"Agreed, nothing bad happens when *you* touch it," I muttered, my unease growing as I watched the toss of the stone. "But this thing is supposed to tune itself to me, and I'm not exactly believing everything will be fine and dandy when it does."

"Oh, for the love of . . . Nothing is going happen." Exasperation rode Lauren's voice. "Lucian would not allow it, even if I *had* wished you harm."

I glanced at her sharply. "Since when does a dark sorceress take orders from someone she barely knows?"

Lauren's smile was thin and unamused. "Come

now, Risa. You saw us arguing and you are no fool. Please do not take me for one."

"So you *are* lovers?" My gaze went to Lucian. "Why didn't you say that up front?"

"Because it wasn't pertinent."

I snorted softly. How could the fact that he was fucking a dark sorceress *not* be pertinent information? "And just how did you come to that conclusion?"

"Who I spend my time with is nobody's business but my own." The comment was decidedly barbed, and I couldn't help glancing at Lauren. If his words annoyed her, she wasn't showing it. *This* time. "The only reason Lauren is here now is because she *is* powerful."

"Maybe, but it does make me wonder what else you're not telling me, Lucian."

"It's no secret that my life revolves around the need for revenge—"

"Yeah," I interrupted, "and it's what you'll do to get it that has me worried."

"You have nothing to fear—"

"Meaning you're not behind the compulsion spell that's been placed on me?"

My voice was matter-of-fact, and his sudden grin was warm and unrepentant. "I feared my Aedh charms might not have been enough to hold you, so I stacked the odds in my favor. But the spell is harmless, Risa."

"Maybe this one is, but the next one might not be."

He held up his right hand. "I promise, I will place no more spells on you."

And you can trust every word out of a liar's mouth, Azriel commented.

Have you ever heard the saying "If you can't say some-thing nice, say nothing?"

I do not believe so. Nor can I help commenting when he makes such blatantly unbelievable statements.

It was pointless saying anything further when I was never going to convince him that Lucian was remotely trustworthy, so I didn't bother. Especially since I wasn't one hundred percent sure of it myself.

I crossed my arms and said, "And what about getting other people to place spells on me?"

"I promise I won't do that, either."

"Does that mean there's no other spells on me?"

"I did not need more than one."

Which wasn't actually confirmation that there were no other spells, just that he hadn't actually needed them. I eyed him for a moment, then sighed softly and waved a hand. "Fine. Give me a closer look at the ward."

He pushed it toward me. I studied it dubiously for several minutes, then gathered together the threads of my courage and reached for it.

No touch! Amaya screamed, the sound so high-pitched it made my eyes water.

At the same time, the Dušan swiveled around in my flesh, its head near my knuckles as it snarled at the ward.

I snatched my fingers away.

"I can't," I said, and stepped away from the counter.

Anger exploded around me, the force of it so fierce it stole my breath. My gaze snapped to Lucian's. There was no anger to be seen in his expression, not even the merest hint, but it had come from him nevertheless. "Why the hell not?" he said, his voice as flat as his eyes.

I might as well have been looking into the eyes of death. A shiver that was part fear, part foreboding, rolled through me. "What do you mean? Didn't you see that?"

"See what? What the hell are you talking about?"

I frowned, my gaze searching his. "The Dušan. It reacted to the ward."

He glanced at my wrist sharply. Now that I'd stepped away, the Dušan had resumed her normal position on my arm. Amaya, however, was still eager to bite into whatever darkness Lauren had employed to make the ward, and she was letting me know it. Banshees had nothing on the noise she was currently making inside my head.

"Impossible," he said.

"Not in this case." I crossed my arms. "I can't use the ward, Lucian. I *won't*."

He contemplated me, his expression still remote, then turned and faced Lauren. "It would appear you have wasted your time and energy. I'm sorry."

Lauren rose and moved toward us, her long dress flowing around her legs like the gray tendrils of a web. *Definitely a dangerous, dark spider,* I thought with another shiver.

But one who wasn't entirely surprised or annoyed by my actions, if her expression was anything to go by. My gaze returned to Lucian. Maybe she wasn't worried because she would still extract the price of the ward from him.

"A foolish choice, but one that she nevertheless has the right to make." Her gaze came to mine. "You may yet regret this decision, however. There are worse things in this world—and the next—than this stone and the magic within it."

"I'm more than aware of that, believe me."

She wrapped her fingers around the ward, then raised it to eye level and contemplated the oily black surface. "It is a thing of beauty, is it not?"

I didn't reply, but then, she didn't seem to be expecting me to. She dropped the stone into her bag and then, with a glance at Lucian, turned and left.

I heaved a silent sigh of relief. One problem down, one silently seething Aedh to go. I hesitated, watching him, wondering if it was better to keep my distance, then shook the thought away. He might be angry, but he surely wouldn't hurt me. After all, he needed me alive just as much as everyone else did. I walked around the counter. "Well, I can't say I'm sorry to see the back—"

The rest of the sentence was cut off as Lucian's hand shot out and his fingers closed around my neck in a vise-like grip.

Chapter 12

Shock held me immobile for too many seconds. By the time my brain *did* start working, my lungs were burning and my head was pounding—a result of not only lack of air but Amaya's scream of fury.

But there was also fear. Not because of the sheer and utter fury in his eyes, but because, for one instant, it felt like his fingers were going *through* my flesh. That he would, at any minute, rip my throat apart from the inside out.

"Do you know what you've just done?" He shook me with each word, as if to emphasize the point. "You just let what might be our one chance to win this race walk out the door!"

I made a gargling sound and kicked him. The blow was weak, ill aimed, and went unnoticed. *Amaya*, I thought, and flayed my hands back, trying to reach her. I couldn't. I didn't have the strength.

It didn't matter. She burned through my flesh, answering my unspoken need.

Hurry, I thought, as spots began to dance in front of

my eyes. Only they were spots that burned like fire. Furious, red-tinted blue fire.

Valdis, I realized dimly.

"I have been looking for an excuse to kill you for some time now, Aedh," Azriel said softly. "If you do not immediately release her, I will have one."

For a moment Lucian didn't respond. Then the fury melted from his eyes and he blinked. A second later, I was a heap on the floor, coughing and spluttering and sucking in great gulps of air.

But I wasn't on that floor alone for long—Amaya had finished her journey through my flesh and had appeared in my right hand, her shadowed steel spitting dark purple fire as she hissed her displeasure and need to kill. I gripped her, then surged to my feet and aimed her point at the middle of Lucian's brow. My whole arm shook as I fought the urge to press farther, to let steel taste flesh and blood.

Amaya did *not* appreciate my restraint.

"And here I was thinking you'd do as I ask and not bring your sword into the company of a dark sorceress." His voice was calm, and there was little fear in his expression. The bastard knew I wouldn't kill him. That I couldn't—not in such a cold-blooded manner, anyway.

"Then you don't know me as well as you thought." I pressed Amaya's point to the bridge of his nose. A thin stream of blood trickled from the wound. "I may be many things, Lucian, but I'm not stupid. That's what meeting Lauren without some form of personal protection would have been."

"I would have protected you."

I resisted the urge to let Amaya bite just a little bit deeper. "I think your actions just now show where your true allegiance lies, and it's certainly not with *me*. Or even, I'd hazard a guess, with Lauren."

"You've known for some time just how deep the well is when it comes to revenge." He reached out, but I snapped my head back and his caress hit my arm rather than my cheek. He let his hand drop again, but there was a brief flash of annoyance in his eyes. "I *am* sorry for the anger. I didn't mean to harm or frighten you."

He'd done both. But, more important, he'd shattered the trust I'd had in him.

His reaction had been deep and unthinking. He hadn't seen me as a lover, or even as a person. I was just some *thing* that had sidetracked a means of gaining what he wanted.

And he'd *hated* me for that.

Hated me enough to want to kill me. He might not have meant to, but that would have been the end result if Azriel hadn't turned up.

Of course, I had no doubt he would have regretted the momentary lapse of sanity, given that both he and everyone else needed me alive to find the damn keys. But regret after the fact wouldn't have done *me* a whole lot of good.

"You and I are finished, Lucian." I stepped back and sheathed Amaya. Her grumbles filled the back of my thoughts, and though the noise had dropped from banshee territory, it was still sharp enough to bring on yet another headache. "I can't be with someone I can't trust."

"Risa, don't be stupid. I apologized and I meant—"

"It's not what you *meant*," I interrupted testily. "It's what you *did* that matters. Damn it, Lucian, I saw the *hate*."

"What you saw was not aimed at you." Perhaps he saw my disbelief, because he added, a little more sarcastically, "There is only one person I actually hate in this room, and he can lower his sword. I really do *not* intend you harm."

"I *could* lower it, true," Azriel said. "But Valdis rather likes the taste of your flesh."

"We both know she will bite no further, as her master has no desire to flaunt reaper rules and thereby jeopardize becoming again what he once was."

"I would not be so sure of that, Aedh."

"So we're all just going to stand here like this?" he asked, the sarcasm stronger this time. "That could get a little tedious, don't you think?"

"What I think," I said, taking another step away from him, though my retreat wasn't just physical, "is that Azriel was right. You will lie, cheat, steal, *and* fuck to get what you want. Nothing and no one else matters—it's all about you and your endgame. And while I might have been able to forgive the lying, I can't forgive the attack. I don't *want* that sort of violence in my life. Not now, not ever."

"Risa—"

He reached for me again, but I slapped his hand away.

"No. I mean it, Lucian," I said, anger and perhaps a touch of regret in my voice. Whatever else he was, he'd been a good lover, and I mourned the loss of that if nothing else. "You and I are finished."

"As lovers, perhaps, but you will need another sword when it comes to finding the keys. Our last attempt proved that."

"I would rather fight alone than fight with someone who plays this game for reasons he has not yet fully disclosed," Azriel commented.

"I don't believe I asked for your opinion, reaper," Lucian snapped, then flexed his fingers and added, "I intend to remain part of this quest, Risa."

"Well, I'm afraid that's an option no longer open to you."

My voice was resolute, but deep inside, doubt stirred. There was a saying about keeping your friends close, but your enemies closer. If Lucian *was* playing a deeper, darker game than mere revenge, it might be far better to keep him around and keep an eye on him.

That is a very dangerous game to play with one such as him, Azriel commented.

Perhaps, but I just get the feeling that there's more going on here than what we think.

Have I not been saying that? It was wryly said, even if there was a hint of rebuke embedded within the words.

You've said a lot of things, reaper, most of them nasty in regard to Lucian.

He deserves nothing less.

"I will not be kept apart from this quest, Risa." Lucian's voice was resolute. Dark. Almost as dark as the gleam in his eyes. "Whatever it takes, whatever I have to do, I *will* be there when you search for the keys."

"If you get in our way, if you attempt to harm or spell or do anything else to me or my friends, I'll kill you myself," I said flatly.

And there went any idea of keeping a close eye on him.

"Warning heeded," he said. The madness and hate flared again, so strong I could taste it. And while he appeared to have it under control, it nevertheless scared the hell out of me. I'd been sleeping with that darkness. It could have overtaken him—and me—at any time. "And now, heed this. Vengeance is *mine*, and the keys play a major part in that. I will not be deterred."

"Then we both know where we stand." I grabbed my purse and slung it over my shoulder. "It was fun while it lasted, Lucian."

With that, I turned and walked out.

And I didn't stop walking until I was out of his building and well down the street.

That's when the shaking began.

I leaned back against the nearby shopfront and sank down, wrapping my arms around my knees as I sucked in great gulps of air. I felt like crying like a baby again, and all I wanted to do was scream, *why, why, WHY?* to the heavens.

Just this once, it would have been nice to catch a break, to have my suspicions proved wrong. Why the hell couldn't fate play nice for a change? Just one break—surely to god that wasn't too much to damn well ask?

"It would seem that it is," Azriel said softly. He sank down in front of me and placed his hands on my thighs. His touch was like fire, and it chased away the shivers and lent me strength. "I am sorry that it has come to this."

"No, you're not," I shot back, taking offense where none was intended. "You wanted Lucian out of my life, and now he is."

"That is undeniably true," he agreed. "But I do not wish to see you in such pain. Believe that, if nothing else."

I *did* believe it. Just as I believed that the pain I was feeling now—a pain that came from betrayal rather than any emotional depth—was only just the beginning.

I rubbed my eyes wearily. "This has all become so totally fucked, Azriel. All I've ever wanted is an ordinary life, and that seems so far beyond me now I'm not sure I'll ever get it back."

"There was never anything ordinary about you or your life, Risa, however much you might have convinced yourself otherwise."

"That's where you're wrong. The restaurant was ordinary, falling in love with Jak and then getting my heart broken was ordinary, wanting kids and a family sometime in the future is very, very ordinary. That's what I want back, and yet all of those things may now never be." My gaze pinned his. Deep in those turbulent blue depths I saw the acknowledgment of my words. "And you know it."

He wrapped his hands around mine and squeezed

lightly. Longing shivered through me, but sadly, *he* was just another desire that was never meant to be.

"Nothing is ever written in stone, Risa. Fate is a fluid thing that changes with every decision and action. The future I see and the one you fear might never be."

"And just what fate do you see?" I asked softly.

He hesitated. "Death. Many deaths."

I closed my eyes again. There were some things better left unknown, that was for sure. And yet I couldn't help asking, "Who?"

"That is uncertain and depends on our actions going forward."

"Me? You?"

He half shrugged. "There are always casualties in a war, and you and I are front-line soldiers. The possibility is always there."

I knew that. I'd *always* known that. But somehow, having him say it made it seem that much more inevitable.

"I don't want to die, Azriel."

"That is not an outcome that would please me, either."

I couldn't help smiling. "Really? I mean, it would at least free you from my bothersome tendency to do what I want rather than listen to your good advice."

Amusement briefly crinkled the corners of his eyes. "Is there not a saying about challenges being the spice of life?"

"Actually, it's variety that's the spice of life."

"And you are nothing if not variable," he agreed solemnly.

I laughed, then leaned forward and brushed a quick kiss across his lips. "Thank you."

His hands clenched briefly against mine. I had no doubt he was fighting the urge to reach for me and deepen the kiss, because I was fighting the very same battle. "For what?" he said, voice controlled and very, very even.

"For making me laugh when all I want to do is cry."

A shadow fell over us both and my stomach twisted in sudden fear. I glanced up hurriedly, but it wasn't an angry Lucian, as I'd half expected. The man was thin, rat-faced, and *not* a stranger. He was the shifter my father had used previously to courier packages and notes to me. We'd cornered him in the basement of an abandoned apartment building, but he hadn't provided a great deal of information, thanks to the fact that my father had erased his memory. As had Azriel, once we'd finished questioning him.

"James Larson," I said, my gaze dropping to the simple envelope he held in his hand. It was the same sort of paper that my father had used in his previous notes, and my stomach began to twist even harder. "What a pleasure it is to see you again."

He stopped and frowned. "How the hell do you know me?"

"You've delivered stuff to me before."

"Huh," he said. "Can't remember it."

Good. It meant Azriel had been successful and my father would not be aware that we'd found his courier.

"How did you know I'd be here?" Surely to god my father wasn't tracking me *that* closely.

"Didn't," Larson said. "Not exactly. I was told to keep an eye on the building being renovated up the road, because you'd be there sooner or later. Missed you going in, but saw you exit."

So my father knew about Lucian. Through reading my thoughts? Or had he been aware of Lucian way before I'd even entered the scene? It was an intriguing possibility, and one that raised all sorts of questions, especially when Lucian's fierce need for revenge was factored in. Maybe it was a bit of a leap, but it was altogether possible that Lucian wasn't after only the Raziq and the keys. Maybe he'd been using me to get to my father as well.

"How long have you been waiting for me to appear?"

"A few hours." He shoved the letter at me. "This is yours."

I took it rather warily, then glanced at Azriel. He rose in one swift movement and touched Larson lightly on the forehead. The shifter stilled and his face went slack. Azriel closed his eyes and I watched the passersby, checking that no one was getting too interested in just what Azriel was doing.

Then he opened his eyes again. "Your father had his Razan deliver the note and, this time, he did not accompany him."

"You've picked the Razan's image from Larson's brain?"

"Yes. And the good news is, Larson picked the Razan's pocket." He reached inside the rat-shifter's jacket, slid a wallet from the pocket, and handed it to me.

I flipped it open and pulled out his driver's license. The Razan pictured was average-looking with blond hair, blue eyes, and a scar running down the left side of his face. Even in the picture, he didn't look like the sort of man you'd want to double-cross. "According to this, the Razan's name is Pierre Danton, and he lives in Southbank."

Which meant he had some money, because that area was expensive, thanks to its close proximity to the city.

"I do not believe the identity will be real," Azriel commented. "And he has no doubt realized by now that this rat has been through his pockets. He may not be there if we check it."

"I doubt a rat picking his pocket will overly worry him, other than the inconvenience of having to replace all his cards." I waved the license lightly. "How come the Raziq's Razan live in sewers, and my father's live in plush apartments? And who the hell does the Razan working for the dark sorcerer belong to, given that they all bear the same sort of ownership tat?"

"I cannot explain why one group lives in luxury and the other not, especially as your father is not known for his generosity when it comes to Razan. As to the other question—" He hesitated. "There are many possibilities."

I raised a querying eyebrow when he didn't go on. "Such as?"

"It is always possible that either the Raziq or your father works with the sorcerer."

I frowned. "Both were pretty damn pissed that he got the key rather than them."

Azriel nodded. His fingers were still resting on the rat-shifter's forehead, keeping him still and compliant. "But working with the sorcerer does not mean they ever intended him to get his hands on the keys."

Then the sorcerer had outsmarted them all, and *that* made him doubly dangerous. "You didn't mention the third possibility."

This time he raised an eyebrow. "I was not aware there was one."

"Lucian."

"I had not forgotten. I merely discounted him on the basis that the Raziq tore away his power. Thus mutilated, he would not be capable of creating Razan."

Meaning he *hadn't* lied to me about everything. I guess that was something to be thankful for. "So you're certain he hasn't got full Aedh powers?"

"I'm certain, yes." He hesitated. "But that does not preclude the possibility that remnants survive. It is far easier to kill an Aedh than to strip them completely of their powers."

So maybe I *hadn't* been imagining his fingers going through my flesh, after all. I shivered, and wondered what the hell else we didn't know. A lot, I was beginning to suspect.

I shoved the license back into the wallet, then handed it to Azriel.

"You do not wish Stane to check his identity?" Azriel asked, surprised.

"Yes, but I can remember the name. It's better if our rat-faced friend doesn't suspect we went through his pockets." I slid a fingernail under the seal and opened the envelope. The note inside was brief and to the point—*Go to the station*. It didn't say when, so I presumed it meant immediately. I sighed. "You'd better release him."

He did so, and the rat-shifter blinked. "What about a tip?"

Don't pick the pockets of scar-faced men who work for would-be dictators. I reached into my pocket, dragged out a two-dollar coin, and flipped it to him.

He sneered. "Oh come on, a chick as classy as you has to have more than that on her. I went without coffee to deliver that note."

"Take it or leave it," I said, a touch irritably. I mean, a fucking courier telling me off for being stingy? He was lucky to even get a damn tip considering this wasn't America and tipping certainly *wasn't* the norm. "You were paid well enough to deliver the note, and we both know it."

"Bitch," he muttered.

And got a clip over the ear from Azriel for his trouble. "*That* is not polite language to use in the company of a lady."

It was a comment that earned another sneer, but Larson wisely refrained from saying anything else and walked away.

"Since when have I been a lady?" I asked, amused.

Azriel held out a hand. "I didn't say you were a lady; I just said it wasn't the correct language to use when in the company of one."

"Ah, that's all right, then." I gripped his hand and let him pull me up.

He didn't release me immediately, and there was concern in his expression as his gaze searched mine. "Are you up to facing your father right now?"

"No, but it's not like I have any other choice. Besides, the sooner we find the remaining keys, the sooner the madness destroying my life might just go away."

"Do you wish me to take you there?"

Yes, I thought, *I would*. If only to soak in the heat of his touch for a few precious moments. But it would also sharpen the gathering tide of frustration and, right now, I really didn't need that. "I thought we'd agreed that wasn't a good option."

"We had, but the note implies haste is required, and traveling the fields is faster than walking. It also taxes your strength less than you taking Aedh form."

All of which was true. I hesitated, torn between desire and sanity, then shook my head. "Walking will clear my head. But you could go get the locker key for me. It's on the dresser—"

"I am aware of its location."

He winked out of existence. I went into a nearby café, grabbed a can of Coke and a couple of sausage rolls, then started walking. I didn't actually feel like eating, but I had a suspicion that I was going to need the fuel over the next couple of hours.

And it was premonitions like *that* I could really do without.

Azriel reappeared as I was halfway through my second sausage roll, and handed me the key. " 'Tidy' is not in your vocabulary when it comes to your jewelry, is it?"

"No, but I thought you said you knew where it was."

"I knew the location. I did not know it was hidden under a multitude of twisted chains and charms. Do you not have a better method of filing them?"

"I do, but it involves walking into the closet. It's easier to simply dump them on the dresser as I'm taking off my clothes."

"That is not logical."

"A rather common problem with me, I'm afraid." I finished the sausage roll and dumped the paper in the nearest bin as we walked past it.

"True." He was close enough that his shoulders occasionally brushed mine and, as I'd feared, every brief touch had longing coursing through me. But as much as I wanted to step away, I didn't. I needed the comfort of those too brief moments, if only because the heat of contact went some way toward combating the chill of gathering fear.

It took nearly ten minutes to walk down to Southern Cross Station, which was a riot of noise and bodies thanks to the fact that peak time was approaching. We made our way through the crowd, but my footsteps slowed as I neared the locker room.

"Your father is not waiting within," Azriel said.

Something I already knew because I couldn't feel the power of his presence, but that didn't erase the churning in my gut. "What about Razan?"

"There are a number of humans, but no one else."

I took a deep breath that did little to bolster my flagging courage, then forced my feet forward. No one looked at us, let alone attacked us. I'm not sure why I'd expected otherwise—Azriel had already said there was no one dangerous here. Paranoia, it seemed, might be becoming a staple in my life.

I stopped in front of the locker and stared at it. Which wasn't exactly getting us anywhere, but I just couldn't force my hand up to shove the key into the lock.

Azriel gently took it and did it for me.

What we discovered was another square ward roughly the size of a tennis ball.

This one was white rather than black, but its surface was just as slick and ran with the colors of the rainbow.

"I cannot feel any dark energy coming off this one," Azriel commented.

"Did you feel it coming off the other one?"

"Yes."

I glanced at him. "Then why didn't you say something?"

"Because you wished to explore the option."

Against my advice. He might not have said the words, but they swam through my mind nevertheless. The link between us was definitely getting stronger.

"So what sort of energy has this one actually got?"

"It is Aedh, and therefore neither light nor dark."

My gaze returned to the stone. It sat there, all shiny and harmless-looking. Yet I suspected there was nothing harmless about the magic that went into the creation of this thing, whatever Azriel might think. "Does the Raziq magic also sit between the two?"

It certainly hadn't felt like it, but after what they'd

done to me every time they'd used it, it was probably fair to say I was a somewhat biased judge.

"Their magic *is* darker, but it is not powered from the dark path; rather it springs from darker desires." I felt his gaze on me. "Trust *me*, even if you do not trust your father. You will not be harmed if you pick it up."

I took a deep breath, then reached inside and gingerly picked up the stone. It was a little too warm against my palm, suggesting that it was more than mere stone. But I knew that already.

"There is a piece of paper with it." Azriel reached in and took it out. "It says, *The ward will be activated by a drop of the blood we share. Use it in a secure place.*"

"If this thing is activated by blood magic, how can that *not* be a bad thing?" Misgivings filled me as I stared at the stone in my hand. I didn't like it and I didn't trust the magic within it. It came from the hands of my father, after all, and he was one of the bastards responsible for the evil that was the keys.

"The ward is not created from blood magic," Azriel said. "Using a drop of blood to activate it would merely be a precaution to ensure that if it fell into the wrong hands, they could do nothing with it."

I guess that made sense—except for the fact I had a body filled with blood and absolutely no doubt that the Raziq would use every last drop if they felt it would be in their best interests.

"Then my next question has to be, where in the hell are we supposed to find a secure place?"

"Your home is as secure as you are likely to get."

"I'm staying at Stane's for the very reason that it isn't."

"Against one who can astral travel," he agreed. "But Ilianna's wards ensure the Raziq cannot enter without difficulty."

"Maybe, but my father is also Aedh, so how will that help?"

"I suspect he will have accounted for that in the creation of this ward." He shrugged. "The only other truly secure place is the old ritual site on Mount Macedon. I doubt the magic within that place will allow you to enter with this ward, because its magic is Aedh based and that site is blocked to all things Aedh or reaper related."

I studied the stone for several more seconds, then shoved it into my purse. The heat of it burned into my hip, despite the leather and fabric that now separated us.

"I'll meet you at home, then."

He didn't argue. Didn't offer to wrap his arms around me and transport me there. He simply disappeared. He was sticking to his word, and keeping his distance as much as possible.

And while I appreciated the effort, part of me still wanted to rant and scream and tell him where he could stick his restraint, because I certainly didn't want it.

I have no more wish for restraint than you, came his thought. *But the fate of both our worlds hangs on our actions.*

I know, I know. But knowing it, and getting through it, were two very different things. I shoved my phone into the waist of my jeans to ensure that it touched flesh, then reached down for the Aedh half of my soul. Despite my utter weariness, it answered with such a surge that it surprised me. Once I was nothing more than particles drifting in the gentle breeze, I gathered myself together and flowed through the streets, enjoying the freedom of my alternate form even though tiredness quickly began to pulse through me. I still wasn't fit enough to hold this form for very long, so I practically cheered when my street came into sight.

But as I neared our warehouse, my particles began to tingle. And the closer I got, the worse it got. It was almost as if there was a force trying to stop me . . .

Ilianna's wards, I realized suddenly. In this form, I was as susceptible to them as any other Aedh. But it was good to have confirmation that they were actually working.

I couldn't get near the front door, so I scooted through the small gap between the garage door and the pavement, then re-formed and splattered rather inelegantly onto the floor. One of these days, I thought, as the headache kicked in and my stomach threatened to revolt, I was going to practice re-formation until I could land with at least some semblance of elegance. Of course, being fit, healthy, *and* strong would also be a good first step.

It took at least five minutes for the headache and shaking to subside to acceptable levels, and I was finally able to move. Azriel appeared beside me, one hand half outstretched, obviously ready to catch me should I fall back down.

"I'm okay," I said. And wondered whom I was trying to convince—me or him.

"Of course you are." His fingers caught my elbow as I walked up the steps to the heavy metal door.

I gave him a somewhat amused sideways glance. "You sound disbelieving, reaper."

"Maybe that's because both you and I know the truth."

"But what good is admitting the truth? It's not like it's going to help any."

"Being stubborn or refusing help when you need it is not overly helpful, either."

"It's not like I *never* accept help, Azriel."

"It is interesting that you make no comment about being stubborn."

I smiled. "That's because I fully acknowledge it's another of my failings."

I looked into the scanner, waited until the retina reader did its business, then typed the code into the keypad. The door slid open and we stepped inside. I dumped my bag on the couch, then moved into the kitchen to raid the liquor cabinet.

After a large glass of bourbon and Coke—heavy on the bourbon—I grabbed a knife, then sat down in the middle of the living room floor and placed the ward in front of me. The rainbow colors seemed to run faster through it, as if it knew what was coming. Which was daft, because it was an inanimate object.

At least until I dropped some blood on it, anyway.

Azriel sat opposite me and placed Valdis across his knees. Blue fire dripped from her blade to the floor, then ran around us, creating a living barrier.

I raised an eyebrow in silent query.

"It is not a protective circle," he said, "but there will be few able to get past the burn of Valdis. Your astral traveler certainly won't."

Something within me relaxed just a little. "So why haven't you used her like this on other occasions?"

"Because it taxes us both, and it is generally better for you that we remain fighting ready." He nodded toward the ward. "Activate it."

I picked up the knife and jabbed the point into my finger. As blood began to well, I turned my finger upside down and let the blood drip onto the ward. As the droplet hit, the rainbow stopped moving, and everything was still. Silent.

Then light erupted from the center of the stone and briefly blinded me. When I was able to see again, I was encased in a cylinder of white. I couldn't see Azriel, and Valdis's fierce blue flames were little more than shadow. Which meant I hadn't actually been transported anywhere, even though I'd half expected to be.

"Now what?" I said it out loud, though I wasn't sure Azriel could hear me.

"He cannot," my father said.

I jumped and looked around wildly. Normally I could sense my father's presence the second he entered my vicinity, so why the hell hadn't I this time?

"Because I am not in your vicinity," he answered. "This is little more than a communication sphere. It allows you and me to talk without interfering with the energy of the device within your heart."

I snorted softly. So my father was once again ahead

of the game when it came to the Raziq. "Where the hell are you, then?"

"It is unwise for you to know." He paused. "I see you have been in Malin's presence. She plays a dangerous game."

"No more dangerous than you, apparently."

"Ah, so she has outlined my intentions. Or what she knows of them."

"She did. And I have to ask, why lie? Why say you wanted the keys destroyed when the opposite is true?"

"I thought a gentler approach might be wise."

I snorted. Yeah, that whole throwing-me-around-the-bathroom episode could definitely be described as gentle. "So *can* the keys be destroyed? Or was that also a lie?"

"It is not a lie, but it is also not possible. Not unless you wish to destroy existence."

Of course, I thought wearily. Why on earth I'd actually expected the destruction of the keys to be a simple thing with few repercussions, I have no idea.

"Why would destroying the keys destroy the gray fields *and* earth?"

"Because blood was used in their creation, and it now links the keys to the structure of the portals. Destroy the keys, and you will more than likely shatter the power of the portals."

"How is this different from the sorcerer forcing the gates open or the Raziq wanting them closed?"

"In either event, the link shared between portals and keys is not altered or disrupted. But destroy them, and the portals—which are woven into the very fabric of existence—are endangered."

Well, *fuck*. What was I supposed to do now? Let a dictator win? Or worse still, the Raziq or the dark sorcerer?

"Am I not the better option for humanity? At least the portals would still remain viable."

Until *he* decided it was better for him that they weren't. Whatever else my father might be, I very much doubted that he'd be a benevolent dictator.

But that was not an argument I was going to get into. "Malin did something to me, but I can't tell you what. She erased the memory."

"She more than likely sharpened the frequency of the device so that its call would be more instantaneous. That's what I would have done in her place."

"Maybe." Maybe not. I wasn't trusting an Aedh to do the expected, my father included.

"Nor should you." He paused. "I see that you have had a parting of the way with the Aedh. That *is* unfortunate."

It was, but why the hell would my father think that? Had I been right in my earlier suspicions? And did I really want to know just how much Lucian had played me for a fool?

No, I thought. But I asked all the same. "What Aedh are we talking about now?"

"You are not stupid, Risa. Please do not act like it."

"Lucian." God, I thought, had *every* single moment with him been filled with nothing more than lies and schemes?

"As you have partially guessed, he and I are adversaries." There was cool amusement in his voice, and I wasn't sure why. "But what you do not know is that once we were allies. In fact, he was my *chrání*—what you would call either a student or protégé."

Shock coursed through me. "You and Lucian? *Allies?* Then why in the hell does he hate you so much?"

"Because I never intended to share domination. Once the keys were safely in the possession of *my* Razan, I betrayed him to make my own escape."

He was the reason Lucian had been stripped of his powers. Fuck, the hate I'd seen *had* been aimed at me as much as the Raziq—not only because I was Hieu's offspring, but because I'd *also* betrayed him by not using his sorceress's ward.

"Then how did you get caught? Or was that another lie to get me to do your bidding?"

"The *chrání* knew more than I thought, hence I was captured. I was stripped of my flesh form during Malin's attempts to gain the location of the keys, but I could not give what I did not have."

"Why did they keep you alive? After all, I was born by that time. They didn't need you to get to me."

"Yes, but I was the only one who knew the clues. Malin, for all her power, could not take that information from me."

And then he'd somehow escaped his prison. But thanks to his capture, he'd missed his meeting with his Razan—who had, as he'd ordered, killed themselves to protect the earthly location of the keys. "Why was Lucian left alive?"

"As I said, he was my *chrání*. I have no doubt that Malin thought I might attempt to contact him again."

"Well, *that's* a stupid thought given how much he appears to hate Raziq."

"She would not understand such emotion. Few of us do."

Because they didn't *do* emotions. And yet Lucian did. Was it simply a result of being made less than he was, or were there deeper reasons?

My father was obviously following my thoughts, because he said, "For an Aedh, being less than you were is a far worse fate than being dead."

Which explained the fierceness that drove my father. He wanted domination—particularly over those who had made *him* less than he was.

"Even as I am, I am far more than Malin and her rabble will ever be." There was no conceit in my father's voice, no hint of boasting in his words. He merely stated a fact as he saw it. From the little I'd seen of the two parties, he *did* seem the stronger. And he was certainly more cunning.

"Why didn't you warn me that Lucian was an adversary? He's linked sexually to my thoughts, and no doubt tracking your intentions through me."

"As I was tracking *his* movements and thoughts—and therefore the movements of the dark sorceress he plays with—through you."

I frowned. "Why would you be tracking her movements? She's not the one who took the keys."

"You are sure of this? Because I am not."

"Her energy wasn't the same." It was almost stubbornly said. I knew what I'd felt, and Lauren's energy *wasn't* what I'd sensed when the key went missing.

So why did she seem familiar to me? I didn't know, and that niggled.

"I still would not erase the possibility that she is involved, especially considering the *chrání*'s liaison with her. Everything he does, he does with intent."

"Like master, like student," I muttered.

"Indeed," my father agreed. "I taught him well."

Too fucking well. And the worst thing was, he was yet another person who was going to create trouble for me in the weeks ahead.

I rubbed my forehead wearily. "Look, you called me here for a reason. What is it?"

"What else would it be? You need to find the next key."

"You still want me to find it after the shitty mess I made of the last attempt?" It was a stupid question, but I couldn't help asking it all the same. I mean, miracles *did* occasionally occur, and there was always the faint hope that my father would decide I was useless and try to find someone else.

And by tomorrow, pigs will have flown.

"You are my only child, and therefore my only option."

Meaning if he'd had another option he probably would have taken it. And as much as I'd always longed for a sibling, I was suddenly glad that I was an only child. It was bad enough risking the lives of my friends; I couldn't imagine doing it to a brother or sister.

"Okay, so hit me with the clues."

"As I said in the book you destroyed, the second key bears the semblance of a dagger. It was sent to the northwest, where the alluvial fields run deep and the soil is stained by rebellion."

He stopped, and I waited. He didn't go on. "That's it? That's all you've got?"

"That's all I dared give my Razan. I could not be more specific in case I was captured—which I was."

I thrust a hand through my hair. "It doesn't give me a lot to go on."

"That was the whole point. But you found the first one; you will find the others."

I was glad someone had confidence in me. Although I wasn't entirely sure I *wanted* my father's confidence.

"What am I supposed to do when I get it?" Especially now that I knew I couldn't destroy the keys—*if* my father was telling the truth, that is. He *had* told me previously that they could be destroyed, and Azriel seemed of the same opinion as well.

"Use this stone to contact me. I will give you further directions."

"What about Azriel?" He wanted the keys destroyed—or at least in Mijai hands, and I had no doubt he'd take it the minute we found it. Especially given what had happened with the first key.

"Do not let the reaper gain possession of the keys. Whatever it takes, whatever you have to do, do it. Otherwise, your friends will not live to see another dawn."

Fury, fear, and frustration swirled through me, and I clenched my fists. Uselessly, because there was nothing and no one here to hit. "Damn it, how the hell am I sup-posed to stop a reaper? I'm only human—"

"You were *never* human. You are a creation of *my* flesh, and that well runs deeper than you realize." He paused, and the energy in the cylinder became so elec-tric the hairs on my arms stood on end. "Do what I say, Risa, or face the consequences."

And with that, the white light died and I found my-self blinking furiously against tears as I stared at Azriel.

"What happened?" he asked, concern in his voice.

I brushed away the solitary droplet that trickled down my cheek. "You weren't following events through the chi connection?"

"No, the ward severed the connection."

I guess that was no surprise—my father was more than aware of Azriel's presence in my life. "He gave me the clues to find the second key, and then gave me a fucking horrible choice."

Azriel studied me for a moment, his expression giv-ing little away, then placed Valdis on the floor and rose in one smooth movement. He disappeared into the kitchen, but was back within minutes, a large glass of bourbon and Coke in one hand. "Drink this, then tell me."

I half smiled. "With the amount of booze I can smell in this glass, I'd normally think you were trying to get me drunk."

"You're a werewolf—is that not impossible?"

"Oh, I can get drunk. It just takes a hell of a lot of time and booze, and it usually doesn't last long enough to make the effort worthwhile." I took several large gulps and felt the burn of the bourbon all the way down to my belly.

"What happened?" Azriel said softly.

I briefly closed my eyes. "How sure are you that the keys can be destroyed?"

"As sure as we can be. The keys are not part of all creation, as the portals are, so therefore we should be able to destroy them without overwhelming effects to our worlds."

"My father says otherwise."

"It would be in your father's best interest to have you believe so." But a frown marred his usually calm expression.

"He says the keys were created in blood, and that blood now links them to the fabric of the gates. If we destroy the keys, we risk destroying the gates."

"I do not think that is possible."

"But you don't know for sure?"

"No, but there are those who will." He hesitated, his gaze capturing mine. "That is not all, is it?"

He *knew* it wasn't. I gulped down more alcohol, and swallowed the subsequent burp. "If I let you take the remaining keys, he will kill Ilianna and Tao."

He didn't say anything. He didn't have to. I could read his thoughts as clearly as if they were mine. Anger surged, so fierce and bright that Valdis's flames flared in reaction.

"They will *not* be casualties in this cause, Azriel. I'd rather give the keys to my father than let either of them die."

"The fate of our worlds rests—"

"I don't fucking *care*!" My grip on the glass tightened. How it remained intact I have no idea. "This *isn't* negotiable, Azriel. If what my father says is true, then you won't be getting the keys. End of story."

Red flickered through the tips of Valdis's flames. It was an indication of her master's emotions—emotions he was otherwise very carefully controlling.

"Then I had better check the legitimacy of his comments as quickly as possible," was all he said.

"Yeah," I agreed. "You'd better. And while you're at it, ask what can be done if the keys can't be destroyed."

"If they cannot be destroyed, we are all in trouble. Neither the Raziq nor your father will rest until they possess them." He eyed me critically. "Ilianna's and Tao's fates hang in the balance no matter what option you choose, Risa."

I knew that. I'd always known that.

But it didn't alter the fact that I wasn't willingly going to do anything that would place them in the direct path of either my father or the Raziq.

Azriel sighed. It was a frustrated sound. "What is the clue?"

I repeated what my father had said, and he frowned. "That does not tell us much."

"Which is exactly what I said. And *he* basically said 'tough.'"

My phone rang, the ringtone telling me it was Rhoan. I dug it out of my pocket and hit the vid-answer button. No picture came up, which was odd, but maybe he didn't want me to see what was going on around him.

"Uncle Rhoan," I said. "Please tell me you've caught the bastard."

"Indeed I have," a familiar voice said. "He's currently tied up tighter than a turkey at Christmas."

Ice entered my body.

It wasn't Rhoan on the other end of the phone.

It was Zane Taylor, my faceless hunter.

Chapter 13

For too many minutes I couldn't speak. All I could think was, *He can't be dead. Please, God, don't let him be dead.*

"What the hell have you done to him?" It came out a hoarse whisper, because my throat was locked tight with fear.

"Nothing that will kill him *just* yet."

I closed my eyes in relief, but it didn't last long. Not when the madman at the other end of the phone had Rhoan's life in his hands—and no doubt wanted mine.

"How did you even know—" I stopped, suddenly realizing the answer to my question before I'd asked it. "The cameras at the warehouse. You deliberately revealed yourselves so that we could find you."

"Yes," he said. "I had worried that the Directorate might catch on to our little trap, but, as usual, I overestimated them."

Because no one in his right mind would expect a suspect to deliberately parade about in front of security cameras. But then, Taylor and sanity weren't exactly chummy.

"Rhoan isn't the one you were hunting, so why are you even bothering to keep him captive?" My voice shook as I spoke, and I took a slow, deep breath in an attempt to remain calm. Clearheaded thinking was what this situation needed, not panic, not fear—even if there was plenty of both.

"He and I were playing this game before you came onto the scene, and would no doubt have arrived at this situation sooner or later." He paused, and I could almost feel the satisfaction oozing from his pores, even though the screen was blank and he was nowhere near me. "As to why he is still alive, that's simple. I believe he might be a much better lure to capture you than any-thing else I could have come up with."

He had *that* right. God, if anything happened to Rhoan, I wouldn't be able to live with myself—let alone face Aunt Riley. He might be a guardian, and this might not be my fault but rather a danger Rhoan willingly faced every day, but that still didn't alter one fact. I was involved, and I'd bear the brunt of guilt if he was hurt. Or worse, killed.

Oh please, don't let it be worse.

I took another deep breath that did nothing to ease the queasiness threatening to overwhelm me, then said, "So what do you want?"

"Why, dear huntress, you, of course."

I closed my eyes. Even though I'd expected the an-swer, the thought of willingly walking into this man's trap horrified me. "Why? I'm not one of your so-called aberrations you're destined to destroy. Why hunt me, when your calling gives you so many other options?"

"Good question." There was an edge in his voice that spoke of amusement. This bastard was sick. *Sick, sick, sick* . . . I thrust the mental chant away. *That* way lies madness. He continued. "The simple answer is boredom. That is why I originally started playing my game with the Directorate. In a life as long as mine, a challenge is sometimes needed."

"You're killing these women because you're *bored*?"

He sighed. "Huntress, that is not what I said. I kill the women because *that* is my calling. I taunt the Directorate because it is fun."

He was definitely a fruitcake. He had to be, because taunting the Directorate was stupid and dangerous.

"So where do I come into the picture?" I knew where well enough. I'd defied him on the fields, threatened him, marked him. For someone who obviously considered himself beyond the Directorate's reach, that *had* to be galling.

"You intrigued me, huntress. You, and the one who guards you both. I have not come across your likes before."

A chill ran through me. How the hell could he know about Azriel? "I'm not sure what you mean—"

He tsked. "Come, huntress, let's not play this particular game."

I swallowed heavily. If he knew about Azriel, then he probably also knew how to stop him. My reaper might not be of this place, but he *could* be blocked and killed here. That might be in this madman's plan. After all, what bigger buzz could there be for someone as sick as Taylor than killing a celestial guide?

God, this situation was getting worse and worse.

"How do you know about him? Few can see him."

"He did do a good job of concealing himself, but the astral plane is *my* world, not his, and there are few there who can hide themselves from me."

Markel. He was talking about *Markel*, not Azriel. Thank *god*.

"What does it matter who I have following me around? This is between you and me."

"Oh, the end battle will be, for sure, but that does not dampen my wish to see just what your guardian can do."

Markel couldn't do half of what Azriel could, but that didn't make him any less dangerous. Not that Markel would actually be getting involved—not unless it was absolutely necessary. Especially when Azriel could project any human form he desired.

"So," I said in a flat voice, "you wish to challenge us. How do you plan to do that *this* time?"

"Oh, the game hasn't changed; the stakes are just a little higher."

The stakes being Rhoan's life. I closed my eyes again and tried to control the rush of panic. I could do this. I *had* to do this.

"Just tell me what you want me to do."

"This time it is easy. I give you an address; you and your guardian go to it."

"And?" I asked, when he didn't go on.

"Inside, you will find Rhoan Jenson. You will lie down beside him and take astral form. From that point on, you and I will begin a battle from which only one will return."

It was too simple, too easy. For a man who claimed to love his games, there *had* to be more than this. My grip on the phone had become so tight my hand was beginning to ache. I flipped it over to my left hand, then flexed my fingers. It helped with the ache, but not the overall tension.

"What aren't you telling me?"

"I'm shocked that you don't trust me, huntress."

I very much doubted it. "If that's all you want me to do, why do you want my guardian along?"

"Well, there *are* one or two things I forgot to mention." His voice was still jovial, but this time it held a darker edge that had horror crawling down my spine. "The first being the fact that your uncle has been injected with hemlock. So far, it has done little more than rob him of speech and movement. However, the suppression of movement will soon spread to his respiratory function, and death will result."

Oh fuck, oh fuck. I gulped down air and tried to keep calm. But my heart was racing and there was sweat dribbling down my spine and all I wanted to do was run into the bathroom and throw up. Only sheer force of will—and fear of what might happen to Rhoan— kept me on the spot and on the phone. "That still doesn't tell me why you want my guardian there."

"Your guardian is there because you have a choice to make. He can keep your body safe, or he can save Rhoan Jenson. He will not be able to do both."

"Why not?"

"Because if you wish your uncle to live, he has to be taken to hospital. But doing so will leave your physical form unprotected."

Trepidation crawled across my skin, but I had no intention of worrying about what he'd planned in the event I was left unprotected. I wouldn't be, as simple as that, even if it meant calling in not only Markel but the whole damn Directorate.

"And do not think to call in aid from the Directorate," Taylor said, seemingly reading my thoughts. "Because the place you walk into has been wired with explosives. The minute my people see anything out of the ordinary, they will detonate. And that, dear huntress, would be an inglorious end for one such as you."

And it sure as hell wasn't the way I wanted to go, either. I shivered, feeling colder and more helpless than I ever had before.

He does not know about me, Azriel said, his words warm and comforting as they whispered into my mind, *and he will not know I am there unless someone attempts to harm you.*

But it means we have no choice but to involve Markel.

I do not think he will mind.

Maybe not, but his boss might. Hunter had put him on watch duty, and she was the sort to expect exact compliance with her orders.

But she does not want you harmed, unless she is the one doing the harming. She will allow this.

I guess. But it meant Markel was yet another person

being drawn into the web slowly closing around me. And while he might be an elite killer for the high council, that didn't mean I wanted his death on my conscience any more than I wanted Rhoan's on it.

"That isn't really much of a test for my guardian, Taylor. It's a choice for me, not him."

"True. But you will not choose death, huntress, and we both know it. Therefore, your guardian will remain and he will be tested."

And things would attack. Undoubtedly nasty things. While I had no doubt Azriel would cope, that didn't make me feel any better. I rubbed my forehead wearily, then said, "How do I know you won't explode the place when I win?"

"You don't," he said. "That's all part of the game."

Some fucking game. "What address do I have to go to?"

"Ah, so eager to begin. The address will be sent to you, huntress. And do not bother to trace the phone, because it will not be anywhere near my person by the time you find it."

"Fine. See you shortly, then."

"I look forward to it."

He hung up. I did the same, then threw the phone at the nearest wall. It hit with a satisfying thud, then clattered to the floor. It didn't make me feel any better.

"That," Azriel said calmly, "probably wasn't wise given that you need the phone to receive the address."

"I know. But I doubt I did any real damage—the cover is thick enough to protect it."

As if to prove my point, the damn phone rang. This

time I didn't recognize the tone, so it wasn't a call from anyone in my contacts list.

I climbed to my feet and walked over to retrieve the stupid thing. "Risa Jones."

"Risa, it's Jack from the Directorate," he said, voice brusque. "I'm afraid there's been a—"

"I know," I interrupted. "I just got a call from our favorite psycho."

"Rhoan's still alive?"

"For now. I'm just waiting for his location to be sent to me."

"Good." There was relief in his gravelly tones. "We need to get you here—"

"No," I interrupted again. "He wants a showdown on the astral plane—just him and me. And if you or anyone else gets involved, he's going to blow our bodies to kingdom come."

"He won't even fucking see us coming, let alone get the chance to blow you both up."

"Bright is an IT specialist. They'll be watching from a distance, and they'll detonate the same way."

Jack was silent for a moment, then said, "Fine. We'll play it his way, at least for the moment. The minute you get a location, you contact me. We'll start scanning the area for rogue frequencies and start blocking. Once we have the place locked down, we can storm his location and kill the bastard." He paused. "You'll be all right until then, won't you?"

"Yes." I had to be. There was no other choice except death, and I wasn't going *there* willingly. "But I very much doubt Taylor is going to be in the same location as me and Rhoan. He's not that stupid."

"Oh, I know that. But I doubt he'll be far away from either the location or his lieutenant. He'd want the pleasure of watching Rhoan burn after the fight he undoubtedly thinks he'll win."

And Taylor wasn't the only one who thought that the odds were on his side. As another bout of foreboding shivered down my spine, the phone indicated an incoming text. "Hang on, Jack—I think he just contacted me."

I switched screens. It was the address from Taylor. "Okay," I said, switching back to Jack. "His address is Twenty Keeshan Court, Altona."

"We'll begin the scanning process immediately. Take your time getting there, because the more time we have, the better it will be for you." He paused, then added, "And be careful."

"I will be." Whether it would be enough was another matter entirely. "What about Aunt Riley? Shouldn't she be involved? Or at least informed?"

"Riley contacted me a few minutes ago. I've told her the situation is in hand."

I snorted softly. "I can imagine what she said to *that*."

"Yeah, she may be older, but she certainly hasn't mellowed." His tone was wry. "Avoid contact with her. I can't stop her from searching for her brother, but we need to get this done before she finds him. There's already been enough people hurt today. I do not want her on the list as well."

God, I hadn't even given a *thought* to the men and women who would have been with Rhoan in that house. "I hope there weren't any deaths."

"Two, I'm afraid. We didn't get them to the hospital in time. It's only thanks to the comlinks that we knew they were in trouble."

The comlinks were small disks inserted into the earlobes of all guardians, and they worked in a similar fashion to the earrings I wore—only the comlinks had a "panic" button that sent out a distress signal when things went bad. "Have an ambulance waiting nearby. If I can get Rhoan out before I step onto the astral plane, I will."

"Do not jeopardize your life to save his," Jack warned. "Rhoan would not appreciate it."

No, he wouldn't, even though he'd do exactly the same for me. I hung up, only to have the phone ring yet again. I glanced at it, but the number was blocked. Trepidation surged anew, but I hit the ANSWER button and said, "Hello?"

"Risa, it's Markel. I overheard your conversation with Taylor from the astral field and have returned to flesh. I will be able to meet you at the location Taylor gave you."

"You've cleared it with Hunter?"

"Yes. Neither she nor the council currently has any desire to lose your services, so I am to do whatever needs to be done."

Considering he was a Cazador and could basically do anything he *liked* to get the job done, that was a pretty chilling statement. "The only thing I need you to do is to get Rhoan out of there."

"I'm sure that is not what Hunter—"

"In this case, I don't *care* what Hunter wants."

He hesitated, then said, in a distinctly cooler voice, "If that is your wish."

"It is."

"I shall be there in fifteen minutes."

"See you then."

I hung up a second time, then met Azriel's steady gaze. "I have a really bad feeling about all this."

He half raised a hand, but let it drop before he ever touched me. And at that particular moment, I almost hated him. I certainly hated the reasons he was distancing himself almost as much as I hated the madman I'd soon have to face. Right now, I *didn't* want distance and I certainly didn't care that those reasons made perfect sense. I just wanted the comfort of his arms wrapped around me, the heat of his body pressed against mine, the tease of his lips against my ear as he whispered everything was going to be all right.

Even if we both knew it was a lie.

Something flicked in his eyes, but he didn't move or otherwise react. "You are not unprotected on the plane, Risa. You have Amaya, and she will do all she can to keep you safe. As I will."

"I know. It's just that—" I hesitated, and rubbed my arms. "He's not sane, Azriel. He'll do the unexpected."

"Undoubtedly." He hesitated, and a flash of frustration ran across his otherwise impassive expression. "I wish I could do more, Risa. I really do."

My gaze searched his for a moment, and I suddenly realized he wasn't talking about fighting, but rather the desire to comfort me as I longed to be comforted. I clenched my fists against the increasingly familiar urge to rant and scream in the face of the unfairness of it all. There was no point in saying anything, let alone ranting. We'd hashed this all out a hundred times and there was nothing more to be said unless he changed his mind. And I couldn't see that happening anytime soon.

"You'd better remain invisible until we get the lay of the house," I said, somehow keeping my voice even. "I don't want Taylor setting off a damn bomb because he spots you."

"He will not."

I thrust a somewhat shaky hand through my hair, then said, "I guess I'd better take the car. I don't think it would be wise to let Taylor know I'm something more than a werewolf."

"I agree," Azriel said. "And him not knowing might also give you the advantage—especially if you travel near the umbra."

The umbra was the area where the real world and the gray fields merged, but I couldn't see how that actually became an advantage.

"The Dušan," he said. "She can take full form in the umbra."

"Then all I have to do is get the bastard there and let her loose." But how did I do that? How would I even know when I was getting close to it?

"The plane works in much the same way as your atmosphere," Azriel said. "The closer you get to the umbra, the thinner or more distant this reality will be."

I frowned. "So all I have to do is imagine myself flying up toward it?"

"It is not that simple. Nor would Taylor allow it to be even if it was."

"Then how the *hell* do I reach it?" Frustration, and perhaps more than a little panic, edged my voice. I didn't want to do this, even if I would never be entirely alone on the astral plane.

"The plane is separated from the gray fields by a series of—" He hesitated. "Layers, I suppose they can be called. The umbra is the fourth and last of these layers. Most astral travelers are only able to access the first two. The very seasoned can access the third and see the umbra. Psychics such as your mother and yourself can access the umbra itself and interact with the beings there."

I frowned. "But I thought you said most psychics only interacted with ghosts."

"I did. Ghosts inhabit the umbra, which is why even those who astral travel are rarely aware of their presence."

"So I was in the umbra when I met Taylor the first time?"

"No. You were in the umbra when you talked to Logan, but retreated to the base level when you went to rescue the woman."

Ha. The things you learned. "So all I have to do is lure Taylor through the levels until we're in the umbra?"

"Getting him *there* will be the problem. He will be wary of astral traveling too close to the umbra. Most seasoned travelers are."

I frowned. "Why?"

"Because while a soul generally cannot be killed on the astral plane, that rule doesn't hold on the umbra portion."

I digested that for a moment, then slowly said, "That's what he plans. He said only one of us will be coming back from this battle."

"Make sure it is you, Risa. I could not—"

He cut the rest of the sentence off, leaving me wondering just what he'd been about to admit. The part that hungered for his touch desperately wanted to believe it was something along the lines of not being able to live without me, but that was stupid, given that he had a totally different physiology. More likely, he was simply going to remind me that he couldn't continue the quest without me.

Which he'd reminded me of often enough.

I waved a hand toward the front door. "We'd better get going."

Because the sooner we got to that house and whatever delights Taylor had waiting, the sooner we could get on with the business of finding the next key.

But even as I made my way down to my car, a dark voice within was whispering, *You'll be finding nothing but the afterlife if you lose this battle. And you could lose it. Very easily.*

And if I kept thinking along *those* lines, I'd be defeated long before I ever made it onto the astral plane.

It didn't take all that long to get across to Altona, thanks to the fact that peak hour had pretty much passed. I parked under a streetlight at the top end of

Keeshan Court—there was little point in hiding—then climbed out and studied my surroundings. It was a typical middle-Melbourne suburban street, filled with tidy-looking brick houses and neat front yards. The sort of street I could imagine kids playing in happily, never realizing there was a psycho in their midst.

I shivered, then reached back into my car and grabbed my coat.

"So, we meet in the flesh at last," a deep voice behind me said.

I bit down a squeak and spun around. A tall man dressed in dark jeans and a black sweater stood in front of me. My gaze traveled up the long, lean length of him, and clashed with the darkness of his. Recognition stirred.

"Markel Sanchez," I said, relief evident in my voice.

"Indeed." He bowed slightly. "It is a pleasure to finally meet you on this plane."

"I wish it was in better circumstances," I muttered, and pulled on my jacket.

"Indeed." His gaze moved from me to the street. "I have done a brief reconnoiter. Number twenty bristles with hardware, some of which is cameras."

The rest no doubt being the bombs Taylor had mentioned, as well as other nasty stuff. "How many people are inside the house?"

"Only one. I presume it is the guardian, Rhoan Jenson."

I hesitated, then asked, "Is he still alive?"

Markel's dark gaze returned to mine. "At this moment, yes."

I released the breath I hadn't even realized I'd been holding. "What about the other houses in the court? Have you checked those?"

He raised an eyebrow. "Of course. I *am* the professional here, remember."

Yeah, he was. But it was my life on the line, not his. "So did you find anything unusual?"

"No. Taylor and his accomplice are not in this street as far as I was able to discern. That does not mean he is not nearby."

"He *will* be nearby." Watching, waiting. Anticipating.

I shivered again, then shoved shaking hands into my pockets and began walking toward the house.

Markel fell in step beside me. "What of the reaper, Azriel? Is he here?"

"I am," Azriel said, his voice coming from the opposite side of me to the vampire. Not that I needed to hear his voice to know exactly where he was.

Markel didn't seem altogether surprised, either. Maybe he'd asked the question simply to confirm what he'd already sensed.

"Good." He paused. "Do you really think this madman will allow us to rescue Jenson? I cannot see it myself."

"I don't think he'll expect it, but I don't think he'll stop it, either. Either Rhoan dies or I'm left unprotected, so he wins either way."

"But you are not unprotected."

"He doesn't know that."

Markel nodded and continued to study the house we were all too quickly approaching. It was almost as if he were trying to read the mind of an enemy who wasn't even present. His movements were fluid, easy, and there was absolutely no sense of danger emanating from him. It was oddly disturbing, but not entirely surprising. Cazadors might be the most efficient and deadly killers ever trained by the high council, but very few people knew they existed. And that, no doubt, was helped by the "wouldn't-hurt-a-fly" feeling Markel was currently emitting.

Which, in my estimation, only made him—and them—more scary.

Except, I'd bet, to people like Hunter. I don't think that woman feared anything, alive *or* dead.

"Jack's got an ambulance standing by," I said, my gut churning more and more the closer we got to the damn house. "It shouldn't be hard to—"

"I am aware of the ambulance's location," he cut in. "I will deposit Jenson into their care and come back."

"But Azriel—"

"Taylor is no fool." Markel's gaze met mine briefly. In the flare of the streetlights, red glinted deep in the dark depths. Not anger, not bloodlust, but something else. Something deeper—more remote and dangerous. I resisted the urge to step away from him as he added, "He undoubtedly has plans for your body once he thinks you are left unprotected. He will also have his people watching what is going on, and they will not react favorably when they realize you are not as unprotected as they thought."

"I doubt they'll react favorably to you coming back into the house, either."

"That is a risk we must all take." Thankfully, his gaze returned to the house. "I have my orders, Risa. I will obey them."

Meaning it was pointless to argue. We reached the end of the court. Number twenty loomed in front of us, dark and silent. While the surrounding houses might be well cared for, it was obvious that this place had been left empty for a while. The grass in the front yard was long enough to brush my knees, and there were trees sprouting in the gutters. Metal shutters covered all the windows, making it impossible to steal a glimpse inside, but the front door stood slightly ajar.

It was an invitation to enter that I wished we could refuse.

I flared my nostrils, sucking in the air and sorting through the scents as Markel pressed his fingertips against the door and pushed it all the way open. The house smelled of age and damp, but underneath these ran teasing scents of humanity and wolf. The latter undoubtedly belonged to Rhoan, but did the other belong to Taylor or his assistant, or someone else?

There is no one other than Rhoan inside, Azriel commented. *As Markel has already said*.

But they've been here, and very recently. If the strength of that scent was anything to go by, at least.

Naturally. They had to set their trap.

A trap we were willingly walking into. I shivered again, and rubbed my arms as I forced myself to follow Markel inside. With the windows shuttered, the only light coming into the house was from the door behind us, and it did little to lift the deeper darkness of the hallway. Rhoan's scent was coming from the room at the far end of the hall, but we approached cautiously, peering into each of the rooms we passed even though there was little enough to see. Markel and Azriel might be certain that no one else was here, but neither of them was taking any chances. For that, I could only be thankful.

Markel pushed the door at the far end of the hall open. The light that hit us was so fierce and bright that I had to blink back tears.

It revealed a room that was stark, white, and empty. Or rather, almost empty. Rhoan lay on the tiles in the middle of the room, his arms crossed across his chest and his face deathly white. Panic surged.

No, God no! I pushed past Markel, but he caught me before I got more than a step.

"Damn it," I said, twisting violently against his grip in a desperate attempt to rip free and get to Rhoan. "Let me go!"

"Your haste will kill us *all*," he said, and pointed at my legs.

Or rather, the trip wire that waited only inches away from my shins.

It felt like someone had tipped a bucket of ice water down my back. That one moment of panic reaction *could* have killed us all.

Think, I reminded myself fiercely. *Don't react blindly. That's what he wants.*

And while I doubted he'd actually want us dead *just* yet, I was betting he wouldn't have minded having Markel, at least, incapacitated.

"Follow me—carefully," Markel instructed.

He stepped over the trip wire and proceeded forward with caution. I did the same, practically stepping on his heels.

"Trigger plates," he said a few seconds later, and pointed at the tiles directly ahead.

I peered around him. "How can you tell?" They looked exactly the same to me as all the other tiles.

"The edge is fractionally raised. The trap waits above."

I glanced up. The trap was four rows of long, wickedly pointed metal stakes. They might not kill a vampire—only wooden stakes to the heart or decapitation could really do that—but they would still make a goddamn mess. "This is no seat-of-the-pants trap. He's been planning this for some time."

"From the moment you clashed on the astral plane, I would suggest."

He stepped over the tiles, then offered me his hand. I accepted it gratefully. Four rows of tiles might not be much of a leap, but if I became unbalanced and fell backward into one, I'd be dead. Those stakes *would* kill me.

We continued moving forward carefully, but there were no more traps and we were soon by Rhoan's side. Markel motioned me to remain where I was and knelt beside Rhoan. I flexed my fingers, fighting the urge to drop down, press my hands against his pale, still body, and feel the life within him even though I could clearly see he was breathing.

It seemed to take forever for Markel to pat Rhoan down, but eventually he glanced up and gave me a nod.

I dropped down beside Rhoan and touched a hand to his cheek. It was clammy and cold, and though he was definitely breathing, it was becoming labored. That could only mean the hemlock was beginning to fully kick in.

I glanced up. Markel regarded me steadily. It was oddly unnerving. "If we don't get him to hospital soon, he'll die."

He must not die tonight, Azriel said. *No reaper waits.*

And that meant he'd be one of the lost ones if we couldn't save him. I closed my eyes and fought the rush of panic. It wouldn't happen. He wouldn't die. He *wouldn't*.

I reached across his body and gripped Markel's arm. "Get him to that ambulance," I said fiercely. "Make sure they know he's been injected with hemlock. And be careful, because I wouldn't put it past Taylor to have some sort of backup attack on the off chance I *did* decide to save Rhoan's life rather than protect myself."

Markel's sudden smile was fierce. "Oh, he's very welcome to try an attack. It would be a pleasant way to stretch the kinks from my body after the inactivity of following you via the astral plane."

I found myself hoping Taylor wasn't that stupid, if only because I didn't want my uncle caught in the cross fire between Taylor and Markel.

He scooped Rhoan into his arms, then rose. "Tread carefully on the plane, Risa Jones. Hunter will not be pleased if your life was ended before her plans have come to fruition."

"Like I really care," I retorted, then saw the amusement crinkling the corners of his eyes. "You have a warped sense of humor, vampire."

"To remain sane in my profession, it pays to," he commented, then headed out.

I watched him leave, and prayed like hell that Rhoan would be okay. Then I took a deep breath, gathered the fading strands of my courage, and lay down.

Three minutes later I entered the astral plane alone.

Chapter 14

There was nothing to be seen except gray. There were no vague outlines of buildings, nothing to hint that anything existed beyond the fog. The astral world was still and quiet, and an odd sense of peace enveloped me.

It didn't last too long.

Air began to roll past me like waves receding from a distant shore.

It meant Taylor was here, somewhere.

I flexed invisible fingers, scanning the grayness, waiting for him to appear. I had no doubt that he would. He was the type to want to taunt me before he got down to the business of killing me.

Or at least, trying to.

Noise began to stir the fog—a soft, steady sound, like the rhythm of a heart at rest. It grew in tempo, getting louder and louder, until the fog churned with the force of it and the fibers of my being vibrated in violent harmony.

Game, Amaya said. *Play not*.

She was right. This *wasn't* some weird storm on the

astral plane. This was little more than foreplay, designed for fear rather than pleasure.

And it was certainly something I didn't have to stick around for if he had no intention of appearing.

I closed my eyes and imagined a beach, sunshine, and a calm, clear day. There was a brief sensation of movement and, when I opened my eyes, I was standing on the edge of an ocean as stormy as Azriel's eyes. I had no idea *which* ocean and, in the end, it didn't really matter.

Stop hiding and show yourself, Taylor, I said, my gaze sweeping the deserted sands around me.

He appeared at the far end of the beach, a thin form who cast a shadow that devoured the distance between us, stealing the heat in the air and the warmth from the sand.

Goose bumps ran across nonexistent skin, but I didn't say anything.

Welcome to your doom, huntress. His soft voice carried as easily as thunder.

If that is my fate, then so be it. My voice was even. *But you should know that fate and I are well acquainted, and I don't think she has plans to release me from her grip just yet.*

His shadow drew closer, though he hadn't physically moved. I resisted the urge to step back. Resisted the desire to call Amaya into hand and swat at the creeping darkness near my toes.

Fate is a fickle friend, huntress. I would not be so sure about her intents if I were you.

Ah, but that's the benefit of being a strong clairvoyant—surety of the future. Which was something more than a white lie when it came to my talents, but he wasn't to know that. *Death will find me sooner than it should, but it will not be via your hands.*

His shadow inched over my toes. It felt like oil, slick and dangerous, and my skin crawled at the sensation.

Kill, Amaya screamed. *Touch you not.*

Not yet. He was too far away. Too watchful.

I flexed my fingers, but otherwise didn't react as his slimy darkness began to twist itself around my ankles. It was nothing but shadows. Nothing to fear, despite appearances.

Taylor laughed. The sound grated across the stillness around us. *I see you will not be rushed into foolish action, huntress. I'm glad.*

Making you happy is not my intent, I replied, voice still despite the darkness creeping farther up my legs. *Why don't you give this game up, Taylor, and just turn yourself in?*

And what? Avail myself of the Directorate's mercy? We both know there is no such thing for someone like me. No, I prefer to play the game my way. At least then I am surer of a favorable result.

Then let the game begin, I said, and called Amaya.

She appeared in a blaze of furious lilac fire, eager to taste flesh, be it real or astral. I swung her across my legs, severing the darkness that clung to me. Her flames dripped onto Taylor's long shadow and raced back down its length, but they never reached his body, stopping abruptly several feet away.

Come, huntress, he said, his tone mocking. *You can do better than that.*

All I intended was to release your leash, I said. *This is your game, Taylor, not mine. I think the first shot should be yours.*

As you wish, he said, then disappeared.

I'd half hoped he would make an all-out frontal assault, but it was obvious the bastard was going to make this battle long and slow. Which didn't mean *I* had to play it that way.

I closed my eyes and imagined myself standing next to him. Though there was little sensation of movement, I suddenly found myself at the far end of the beach. Taylor's footprints marred the white sand, but Taylor himself was nowhere to be seen.

I frowned and half turned, my gaze searching the emptiness around me. There was nothing—nothing except the sensation of air recoiling. It wasn't from Taylor, but rather from something else. Something that was approaching *really* fast.

Then I remembered that Taylor could alter the way I saw the astral plane.

I ducked and flung Amaya upward. She connected with something so hard the force of it reverberated down my arm and made imaginary teeth rattle.

White ash, she screamed. *Hate!*

White ash was used by witches to repel all manner of darkness, demons included—which meant that Taylor knew what my sword was.

Fuck, fuck, *fuck*!

I dropped her away from the invisible ash staff and scrambled backward. Taylor laughed, an eerie sound that came out of the emptiness surrounding me.

I didn't bother hanging around to see what he was

going to do next, but lunged forward, using the tremor of recoiling air as a guide as I attempted to slice him in half. Azriel might have said it wasn't actually possible to do that on this level of the astral plane, but I *had* hurt him last time I'd called Amaya into action, so it was worth a shot.

It was a shot that proved futile, because her blade hit nothing but air. I paused, Amaya held at the ready, my gaze searching the immediate area as I tried yet again to pinpoint his position.

And in doing so, I realized the beach was *different*. It was fading. Or rather, a fog was devouring it—the same sort of fog that had greeted me when I'd first stepped onto the plane. But why? What advantage did it give him when I couldn't see him now under the fierce sunshine I'd imagined.

The thought died as awareness prickled my skin.

He was *behind* me.

I raised Amaya and spun around. Caught a glimpse of Taylor's wickedly pointed staff swooping toward me before the fog whisked him from sight. I lunged forward, under his blow, attempting to skewer him with Amaya's point. Once again I stabbed nothing but air. I swore and caught my balance. Felt the wash of movement against my skin and jumped back.

But nowhere near fast enough.

Taylor's staff whacked my left arm with such force that it knocked me sideways. The pain of the blow reverberated through every fiber, as sharp and as real as if I was wearing flesh. Warm stickiness flowed from the impact point and I glanced down quickly. There was no blood, no indication that I'd even been hit, nor should there have been since I wasn't here physically.

And yet the blood still flowed.

Imagination, I reminded myself fiercely. He was playing with my mind.

The fog crept over the remnants of my beach, obliterating it completely. Again I had to wonder why. Was it something to do with his blindness in real life? Did he think the fog gave him some advantage over me? It wasn't as if he didn't already have enough of those— The thought stopped as I suddenly realized what he was doing.

Taylor wanted me dead, and to do that he had to get me up into the umbra. He had no idea how skilled or not I was at astral traveling, so he was using the fog not only to disguise his movements, but to hide which level we were on.

I swished my sword back and forth. The fog boiled away from her flames, and I caught a glimpse of Taylor moving to my left. I imagined standing behind him, unseen, unheard. Moved in an instant, and swept Amaya left to right. Made contact, though where or what I hit I couldn't say. It could have been Taylor; it could have been his staff. He made no sound to give me any indication either way.

Yet the smell of blood suddenly seemed to permeate the air.

His or mine?

And how was something like that even possible, given that Azriel had said a soul could be killed only in the umbra?

Killed, yes, a voice inside me whispered—a voice that sounded suspiciously like Azriel's—*but remember Adeline's warning. What happens to you on the plane can become reality if the illusion is powerful enough.*

Taylor's illusion was certainly powerful enough.

To repeat a favorite phrase, fuck, fuck, *fuck!*

Which meant it really *was* time to stop playing the game his way. I needed to start moving up the levels, but I doubted he'd follow easily. He wanted to play, and I very much suspected he'd want me far weaker—bloodied and bleeding and on the edge of exhaustion—before he stepped onto the umbra and attempted to finish me off.

I had to convince him that I'd reached that state—that I was scared and on the run—long before I *actually* reached that point. And that meant I had to take far more blows than I already had.

Not something I really wanted to do, but I had little choice.

I gripped Amaya a bit tighter. Her hissing ramped up a couple of notches, an echo of the tension that gripped me. I swung her back and forth and watched the recoiling fog, trying to catch another glimpse of Taylor. For several heartbeats there was nothing; then air caressed my skin.

Once again, the bastard was behind me.

I waited until the last possible moment—until my nerves were a mess and the need to move so fierce it felt like every piece of me quivered—then twisted around and lashed out with Amaya.

She hit something solid and screamed in pain. I

jumped back, releasing her from the ash, and heard the whip of air coming in from the right. I bit my lip, and once again waited until the very last moment to jump out of the way.

Something thin and leather-like snapped across my spine and bit deep. A scream was torn from me and blood flowed, on the field and no doubt in real life.

And while the wounds might be nothing more than a product of imagination and Taylor's will—here on the astral plane, at least—they damn well *felt* real.

But I couldn't do much about *any* of the wounds that were appearing on my flesh, either here or in reality, simply because I needed to make Taylor believe I was scared enough to run. No hard task, as it was becoming the truth.

But I wasn't hurt enough yet. Taylor had nicknamed me huntress, and he wasn't likely to believe I'd be panicked into running so quickly. I had to take at least one more serious hit.

I watched the fog roll away from Amaya's point, feeling the backwash that was the plane reacting to Taylor's movements, but not actually reacting to them myself. The coward was coming in from behind again. My skin crawled as he drew closer and closer, until the itch was so bad I could have sworn I'd have to react or go crazy.

Staff! Amaya screamed. *Up!*

I didn't move, didn't obey. I just waited, my body tense, as the *whoosh* of air came down hard and fast. Amaya hissed and spat her fury. The flames that roiled from her steel crawled upward, as if seeking to incinerate the staff before it reached us. As her lilac fire began to wrap itself around the oncoming weapon and her screaming ramped up to fever pitch, I threw myself sideways.

The blow that was meant to split my head hit my shoulder instead, and once again it bit deep. I yelped in pain and there was nothing false or forced about it. As an odd weakness began to wash through my astral being, I closed my eyes and imagined myself on the second layer of the plane.

I opened my eyes, registered the lack of the enveloping grayness, then heard the air snap with sound. The whip slicing toward me again.

I imagined my fingers wrapping around the thin end of the leather weapon. Imagined it coiling around my hand as I stepped onto the next level of the astral plane. Felt the sudden shift in the air, and opened my eyes to see a beach that was far darker and more faded than before, and one that remained free of Taylor's fog. The third level, if all had gone according to plan. All I had do now was hope Taylor took the bait and followed. He should, since he actually wanted me in the umbra as much *I* wanted him there, but the insane often don't do the predictable.

Pain rippled across my fingers. I glanced down and realized I was still holding the whip in my hand. It was long and wicked-looking, and it was eating into my flesh with needle-sharp teeth.

I yelped again and flung it away without thought, then realized leather couldn't actually do that. It was Taylor, altering reality as I saw it. Which meant he was here, somewhere.

I did a slow turn and scanned the darkened beach. No Taylor, no creepy, oily shadow, but that didn't mean much. He was here somewhere—the quiver in the air told me that, even if it didn't seem to be giving away his location. Maybe he'd worked out that I was using it to track him.

I swung Amaya back and forth, and imagined her flames wrapping around the unseen and revealing their presence.

Fingers of lilac fire immediately swept across the empty beach, the arc wide at first, then gradually narrowing, until they formed a fist around emptiness.

Only it wasn't empty.

Very few people have such control on the plane, huntress, he said, as he reappeared. The flames cast an odd purple light across his skin, and made it look like he was wearing a bejeweled death mask.

It was a death mask that held no features.

I shivered—an action that reverberated across the faded beach. Taylor smiled. *I smell your fear, huntress. It is a fine scent.*

Him so pleasant, Amaya commented.

Amusement ran through me, though it did little to lessen the tension. My sword seemed to be gaining a sense of humor, and though I wasn't sure if this was a good thing or not, it was certainly better than her continual screaming for a kill.

Kill good.

Maybe her bloodthirstiness was rubbing off on me, because I could only wholeheartedly agree that killing

Taylor *would* be good. But it could happen only in the umbra, and we weren't there yet.

Fear is a useful tool, I commented. *It sharpens the reflexes.*

I wondered if Amaya's fire was capable of dragging Taylor onto the next level, if only because it would be a whole lot easier—not to mention less painful—if I could. I briefly imagined her flames dragging him closer, and though they rippled and moved, nothing changed—certainly not Taylor's position.

Which in turn meant her flames might not actually have him contained. Maybe he was simply pretending to be so in an attempt to lure me into a false sense of security.

God, the bastard had me second-guessing everything I did.

But is it so useful? he said. *Perhaps we should test this theory of yours, huntress.*

He threw something into the air, but I ignored the instinct to follow the movement and see what it was. I wasn't *that* green.

He chuckled, the sound grating down my spine. I shifted my feet, readying for an attack, but for several seconds nothing happened. His eyeless features just stared at me through the glow of his lilac cage.

Without warning, something hit me side on and threw me into the air. I twisted around, landing in a rolling tumble, then bounced back to my feet.

There was *nothing* there. Nothing I could see or feel, anyway.

Amaya?

Something, she replied. *Hides.*

Obviously. *Where?*

Everywhere.

Oh, great.

I swished her back and forth, but her flames didn't reveal anything—sinister or not—hiding.

I glanced over my shoulder at Taylor. He was still encaged, but an odd sense of satisfaction oozed from him. *Bastard*, I thought, and imagined myself standing next to him. The minute I was, I lashed out with a clenched fist. I should have hit nothing but air, but his head snapped back, as if I *had* hit him.

Then he disappeared again, and the lilac flames fell to the ground, landing in tight coils that writhed and burned.

Seems you could do with a little fear yourself, I said.

It was certainly a blow that should never have hit. I shall endeavor to restrain my confidence a little bit longer.

His voice was so close to me I felt the brush of air past my cheek. I spun around and lashed out with my sword, but hit nothing.

Then something hit *me* again.

I staggered sideways, then caught my balance and swung around, sweeping Amaya from left to right. Still nothing but air.

Another blow, this time to my right side. I twisted, lashed out. Caught nothing.

What the fuck were these things?

A growl rolled across the silence. I swallowed heavily. Damn if that didn't sound like a hellhound . . .

This time I felt the stir of air. I leapt up, twisted around, and stabbed downward. Hit something so hard my whole body shuddered with the impact. Amaya's flames fanned outward, encasing a hound-like shape.

Whether it was actually *was* from hell or just another product of Taylor's twisted mind, I had no idea—and right now it wasn't important. I pulled Amaya free and slashed at the hound's neck. It exploded, sending me tumbling through the grayness.

They come! Amaya's shriek was so fierce and loud I could have sworn it echoed across the plane, not just in my head.

Oh, fuck! I had no time to think or do anything else, because they were on me. Invisible beasts that snarled and slashed and tore at skin that didn't exist on this plane. Pain burned through me on all levels and blood flowed, until I was slick with it. I fought, god how I fought, but there were too many of them. Far too many, even for Amaya.

Run! the voice that sounded so much like Azriel screamed.

Instantly, I reached for the level that divided earth and the astral plane from the gray fields. Imagined myself there, free from the teeth and claws that rent my skin. Felt the plane shift, and then blessed silence. I didn't immediately move. I just lay on my back, panting madly, desperate to regain equilibrium and strength.

Finally, I opened my eyes. The umbra was a place of shadows and darkness. I could see only a little of the beach on this level, but this was the dividing line between earth and the fields, and that was to be expected.

Something moved. I tightened my grip on Amaya, then realized that this time the movement held no threat.

The Dušan had stirred to life.

She coiled up my flesh, then moved across my shoulders and down my right arm. Her eyes glinted in the distant, smoky surrounds of the umbra, and her teeth shone. She wanted out, wanted action.

Not yet, I murmured. *Not just yet.*

I agree. Taylor's voice was so close beside me I jumped. *Death shall not find you just yet, but it will come, huntress. Even now, your flesh weakens. Soon, your heart will stop, and you will find yourself trapped in this place of nothingness, never to move on or be reborn.*

Panic surged and I scrambled upright. Or tried to. My legs were like jelly and they refused to support my weight. One heartbeat later, I was on my knees. Which was stupid, because the wounds *weren't* real. The hounds hadn't chomped and chewed; I was whole and unhurt and *fit*.

But no matter how much I repeated that to myself, it didn't seem to make one jot of difference. Maybe the umbra didn't work that way.

Nevertheless, I took a deep breath, imagined it flowing through my being like a sweet breeze, blowing away the hurt and the pain as it refilled the wells of my strength.

Then slowly—and somewhat unsteadily—I climbed to my feet, Amaya clenched tightly in my hands. Her fire dripped from the end of the steel and formed a wide circle around me, as if drawing a line in the sand and daring Taylor to cross.

He didn't accept the challenge. He remained where he'd appeared, his arms crossed and satisfaction oozing from his pores.

Standing there watching me die seems a bit anticlimactic after all your huff and puff, I commented. *I was under the impression you wanted to kill me yourself.*

I wanted a challenge and you certainly provided it. But I am no fool. I have you here now, and here you'll stay.

I snorted. *You can't stop me from returning to flesh, Taylor—*

On the contrary, he interrupted. *I can.*

Fear slithered through me. I was playing into his hands, I knew that, but he was far too watchful for me to release the one ace I held up my sleeve. Or on my arm, as was the case with the Dušan.

No one has that much power, Taylor. Not even someone like you.

His amusement swam around me, taunting and stinging. *Do you remember Dorothy?*

Yes. I continued to swing Amaya back and forth, watching him warily. The Dušan had settled into my right forearm, her glow fading but not her readiness. She felt like a coiled spring, ready to explode from my flesh the minute I gave the word.

She was screaming, unraveling, and yet she did not return to her flesh. I prevented that, as I will prevent you.

That's what you were doing when you touched her forehead, I replied, suddenly realizing what had happened.

He nodded. *By touching her, I not only marked her with what she was, but I pinned her in place while I drained her, both in real life and on the plane.*

Well, he wasn't going to be touching me, that was for fucking sure. *So basically, you're a coward.*

Anger snapped around me, thick and fast. *I am no coward, huntress. As you can see.* He made a motion with his hand. Silver spun out of the darkness, slashing toward my torso. I raised Amaya and steel clashed with steel.

Coward, I spat. *Everything you do is from a distance, Taylor. Why? Do you fear getting close to someone who can actually defend herself?*

More steel came out of the shadows. I slashed and parried and battered it away, calling him a coward at every blow. His anger grew, and the attacks became more furious, until all I could see was silver and all I could feel was blood and pain.

Now, I said to the Dušan. *Do it* now.

She ripped free with a scream that seemed to echo all the pain and fury that filled me, and formed shape, growing and expanding as she hurtled toward Taylor.

I felt his shock as strongly as if it were my own; then the steel assault stopped and he began to fade—but nowhere near quickly enough to escape. The Dušan whipped across the shadows and wrapped around him, coiling so tightly she would have snapped bones if he'd actually been wearing flesh.

He screamed then, and began to struggle, but to little avail. The hunter had finally been snared.

I blew out a relieved breath, and lowered Amaya as I walked toward him. Fury battered me, but it was tinged now with fear. His fear, not mine.

It felt good.

There's one thing you don't know about me, Taylor, I said softly. *I'm not human.*

His fear increased. God, it was *so* sweet. *No, you're not. You're a werewolf.*

Oh, I'm much more than that, I'm afraid. I'm what the reapers are—a being of energy rather than just flesh and blood. Remember mentioning that my control was greater than most on this realm? Well, that's because this place is far more mine than it will ever be yours.

If he'd had a face, I think his eyes would have been wide and staring. I stepped closer to him and stopped.

This is for Dorothy, I said. *As well as Vonda and Dani Belmore, and all the other countless women you've killed over your many years of hunting.*

He snarled and spat at me. I sidestepped, and the globule landed near Amaya's point, hissing like acid.

Do your worst, he snapped. *I will be reborn, and I will remember. Fear for the future, huntress, because I will be back.*

I snorted. *I may fear for my future, Taylor, but it won't be because of anything you might or might not do—because you won't be doing anything. We're in the umbra, remember. Death here is final.*

He screamed then. Screamed long and loud and fearfully.

I raised Amaya and killed him.

Chapter 15

I rose through the levels of consciousness slowly, gradually becoming aware of the sounds and scents that surrounded me.

They were *not* pleasant scents. Not to the sensitive nose of a wolf, anyway. Antiseptic mingled with the smells of the dying and the diseased, creating a veil of misery and pain that permeated not only the air but the very foundations of the building. The minute I became aware of them, they became a weight that pressed down on my chest and made it difficult to breathe.

I was in a goddamn hospital. God, I had to get out of here, had to move—

A hand caught mine. Warm, familiar, feminine hands. Ilianna, not Azriel.

"It's okay," she said softly. "You're okay, Risa."

"No, I'm not." My voice cracked, and my throat felt raw. I opened my eyes. Ilianna smiled, but there was little disguising the worry in her expression. Not out of the woods yet, obviously. "I'm in a goddamn hospital, so how the hell can I be okay?"

"You're alive, and that's pretty amazing considering all you've been through."

She poured a glass of water, then offered it to me, straw first. I tried to lift my head, but it suddenly seemed heavier than a thousand bricks. She tilted the cup a little more, and managed to get some moisture down my throat.

I closed my eyes for a moment, then asked, "Where's everyone else?"

"Tao and I have been taking turns sitting by your side. He headed to the café about twenty minutes ago."

I frowned. Even that hurt. "How long have I been out?"

"Five days—longer than Rhoan, in fact."

Relief hit, so thick and fast tears stung my closed eyelids. "He's alive?"

It was an inane question—if he was awake he was obviously alive—but I still wanted her to say the words.

"Not only alive, but home. He got the all clear yesterday."

"Thank *god*."

"Yeah. Riley had Quinn stationed in here so she could get constant updates on your condition while she was beside Rhoan."

I glanced past her, for the first time seeing Uncle Quinn sitting in the corner. His warm smile crinkled the corners of his dark eyes. "Riley says to hurry up and get well, because she intends on knocking both your and Rhoan's thick heads together."

I laughed, which hurt, but at that particular moment

I didn't really care. I was alive, Rhoan was alive, and Taylor was dead.

"Now that I have seen for myself that you are awake, I shall leave." He pushed to his feet. "I'm afraid I need to eat."

I half smiled. "I'm sure there would have been more than a couple of nurses willing to offer their services."

"Ah, but there is only one neck I desire." He walked over to the bed and dropped a kiss on my forehead. "Do not lapse back into a coma. Riley would be most displeased."

If he thought I was in any danger of lapsing, he wouldn't be leaving. "Give her a kiss for me."

"I will."

He left, and my gaze returned to Ilianna. "So why was I out so long? Even if I'd lost a lot of blood, I shouldn't have been out for five days."

"It was the poison."

I raised my eyebrows. "Poison? What poison?"

"From the hounds that attacked you on the astral plane," Azriel replied, and suddenly appeared on the other side of the bed.

I very much suspected he'd been there the entire time, though I hadn't actually sensed him. But there was more than one reaper in this place, so maybe I was suffering some sort of temporary sensory overload.

My gaze met his. Anger and relief vied for dominance in the turbulent depths of his blue eyes. "But they weren't real. They were just a product of Taylor's imag—"

"No, they weren't," he cut in. "And because these

particular beasts were little more than plague bearers, the wounds became poisoned."

"I wouldn't have thought the hospital would have known how to cope with *that* sort of poisoning."

"They didn't," Ilianna said. "Kiandra did."

"*She* was here?" Holy shit!

"And I didn't even have to call her." Ilianna wrinkled her nose. "She didn't have an easy time of pinning down the particular branch of poison, though. It really was touch and go for a while there."

"Meaning Taylor was close to winning anyway."

"But he didn't." Ilianna rose suddenly from the bed. "And on that cheery note, I'm off to the canteen to grab a bite to eat. Don't do anything daft while I'm gone."

"Damn," I muttered, "there goes my idea of line dancing down the hall with all the other reapers."

She laughed, collected her purse, then headed out into the hall.

"That," I said, amusement teasing my lips, "was a very obvious exit. Your doing?"

"Yes." He sat down on the bed and caught my hand in his, entwining our fingers. Heat pressed into my skin, and warmed far more than it should have. "I'm sorry."

I frowned. "What for? It's not like you could have done anything to help me on the astral plane."

"No, but if I had not been so foolishly stubborn, I *could* have done something once your astral being had returned to flesh."

I stared at him, confused. "But what? It's not like you can heal me anymore."

"Ah, but that's not entirely the truth."

I closed my eyes for a moment. Though I wasn't really surprised that he hadn't been honest with me—even with something as simple as that—it still hurt. I thought we'd at least gotten past the lies—

"I did not entirely lie," he interrupted. "I currently can*not* fully heal you. Not against major wounds or the infection the hounds caused."

"Then what—"

"I cannot heal because I no longer have the energy."

I blinked. "What?"

"I need to recharge," he said softly. "I have gone a long time without doing so, and it is beginning to show."

"But you and I made love," I said, my confusion growing. "Couldn't you have recharged then?"

"I could have, but I didn't." His fingers tightened around mine. Pain rippled, but I didn't say anything. He could have crushed my hand and I don't think I would have said anything. My gaze—and my attention—was on his face. A face that did not reveal his emotions, even though the turbulent force of them ran like quicksilver through my being. "I erroneously believed it was better for the mission and us both that I hold myself apart, and not take what I needed."

"But why?" I hesitated, then said, "It increases the risk of assimilation, doesn't it?"

"Yes. And at the time, I feared that more than I feared not being able to heal you."

"And now?" I asked, my gaze searching his, seeking an admission, wanting to hear that he cared even though it was obvious that he did. More than he should, more than was wise.

"And now," he said softly, "I know there is a fate far worse than remaining a dark angel for time eternal."

Tears stung my eyes. While it was an admission I'd ached to hear, it was nevertheless a dangerous one for us both. We both had dreams of a future once this quest was ended, and what now lay acknowledged between us was as dangerous to those dreams as the quest itself.

"So where does that leave us?" I asked.

"I don't know. The only thing I *do* know is that I could not ever relive the horror of the last five days. Fighting to protect your body while you were battling for your life on the astral plane was bad enough, but being able to do little more than watch you weaken from wounds I should have been able to heal . . ." He paused and took a deep breath. "Not again. Not *ever* again."

Just for a moment, the control vanished, and emotions were there for all to see, so deep and dark and raw that it made my heart ache.

I tugged him toward me, wrapped my free arm around his neck, and just held him. The press of his body felt so real and right that tears trickled down my cheeks. Because it might be real, but it *wasn't* right. Not really.

"I'm willing to risk assimilation if it helps us both," I whispered. "But the decision has to be yours. You're the only one who truly understands the consequences either way."

He didn't say anything immediately; then he sighed and pulled away. His gaze, when it caught mine, was troubled.

"Then we take the risk," he said. "And may fate be gentle on us both."

Don't miss our special preview of
Darkness Unmasked, the next
book in Keri Arthur's fantastic
Dark Angels series

Coming soon to Piatkus

The office phone rang with a sharpness that jolted me instantly awake. I jerked upright, peeled a wayward bit of paper from my nose, and stared at the phone blankly. Then the caller ID registered and I groaned. The call was coming from Madeline Hunter, the bitch who was not only in charge of the Directorate of Other Races, but a leading member of the high vampire council. She was also the very last person in this world—or the next—whom I wanted to hear from right now.

Unfortunately, given that she was now my boss, she was not someone I could—or should—ignore.

I hit the vid-phone's answer button and in a less than polite voice said, "What?"

She paused, and something flashed in her green eyes. A darkness that spoke of anger. But all she said was, "I have a task for you."

A curse rose up my throat but I somehow managed to leash it. "What sort of task?"

Even as I asked the question, I knew. There was only one reason for her to be ringing me, and that was to track down an escapee from hell. She had not only the Directorate at her command, but a stable full of Cazadors—who were the high council's elite killing force—and they dealt with all manner of murderers and madmen on an everyday basis.

I even had one following me around astrally, reporting my every move back to Hunter. Trust was not high on her list of good traits.

Not that I think she had all that many good traits.

"A close friend of mine was murdered last night." Her voice held very little emotion, and she was all the scarier because of it. "I want you to investigate."

Hunter had friends. Imagine that. I scrubbed a hand across my eyes and said somewhat wearily, "Look, as much as I absolutely adore working for you, the reality is the Directorate is far better equipped to handle *this* sort of murderer."

"The Directorate hasn't your experience with the denizens of hell," she snapped. "Nor do they have a reaper at their beck and call."

So I'd been right—it *was* an escapee from hell. Not great news, but I guess it *was* my fault that these things were about in the world. It might have become my task to find the three lost keys that controlled the gates to heaven and hell, but the only one I'd managed to find so far had almost immediately been stolen from me. As a result, the first gate to hell had been permanently opened by person or persons unknown, and the stronger demons were now coming through. Not in great numbers, not yet, but that was only thanks to the fact that the remaining gates were still shut.

Of course, given the choice, I'd rather *not* find the other keys. After all, if no one knew where they were, they couldn't be used to either permanently open or close the gates. But it wasn't like I had a choice, not any more. It was either find them or die. Or there was the choice given to me by my father, who was one of the Raziq, the rogue Aedh priests who'd helped create the keys, and also the man responsible for having them stolen: Watch my friends die.

"Azriel isn't at my beck and call," I said, unable to hide the annoyance in my voice. "He just wants the keys, the same as you and the council."

Not to mention the Raziq and my goddamn father.

"*This* takes priority over finding the keys."

I snorted. "Since when?"

That darkness in her eyes got stronger. "Since I walked into my lover's house and discovered his corpse."

I stared at her for a moment, seeing little in the way of true emotion in either her expression or voice. And yet her need for revenge, to rend and tear, was so strong that even through the vid-phone I could almost taste it. That sort of fury, I thought with a shiver, was not something I ever wanted aimed my way.

Yet, despite knowing it wasn't sensible, I couldn't help saying, "I'm betting the rest of the council wouldn't actually agree with that assessment."

I think if she could have jumped through the phone line and throttled me, she would have. As it was, she bared her teeth, her canines elongating just a little, and said in a soft voice, "You should not be worried about what the rest of the council is thinking right now."

The only time I'd stop worrying about the rest of the council was when she achieved her goal of supreme control over the lot of them. Until then, they were as big a threat to me as she was.

But I wasn't stupid enough to actually come out and say *that* to her. "Hunting for your friend's killer is going to steal precious time away from the search for—"

"And," she cut in coolly, "just where, exactly, is your search for the keys?"

Nowhere—that's where. My father might have given me clues for the next key's location, but deciphering *those* was another matter entirely. We figured it was somewhere in the middle of Victoria's famous golden triangle, but given that *that* particular region encompassed more than nine thousand square kilometers of land, it left us with a vast area to explore. It was fucking frustrating, but all Azriel and I could do was keep on searching and hope that sooner or later fate gave us a goddamn break.

"It's probably in the same place as your search for my mother's killer."

The minute the words left my mouth, I regretted them. Hunter really *wasn't* someone I needed to antagonize, and yet it was her damn promise to help find my mother's killer that had made me agree to work for her and the council in the first place. And while I'd kept my end of the bargain, she hadn't.

For several very long seconds, she didn't reply. She simply stared at me, her expression remote and her eyes colder than the Antarctic. Then she said, her voice so soft it was barely audible, "Tread warily, Risa, dearest."

I gulped. I couldn't help it. Death glared at me through the phone's screen, and she scared the hell out of me.

I took a slow, deep breath, but it really didn't help ease the sense of dread or the sudden desire to just give it all the fuck away. To let fate deal her cards and accept whatever might come my way—be that death at Hunter's hand or someone else's.

I was sick of it. Sick of the threats, sick of the fighting, sick of a search that seemed to have no end and no possibility of our winning.

Death is not a solution of any kind, Azriel said, his mind voice sharp.

I looked up from the phone's screen. He appeared in front of my desk, the heat of his presence playing gently through my being, a sensation as intimate as the caress of fingers against skin. Longing shivered through me.

Reapers, like the Aedh, weren't actually flesh beings—although they could certainly attain that form whenever they wished—but rather beings made of energy who lived on the gray fields, the area that divided earth from heaven and hell. Or the light and dark portals, as they preferred to call them.

Although I had no idea whether his reaper form would be considered handsome—or even how reapers defined handsome—his human form certainly was. His face was chiseled, almost classical in its beauty, but possessed the hard edge of a man who'd fought many battles. His body held a similar hardness, though his build was more that of an athlete than of a weight lifter. Stylized black tats that resembled the left half of a wing swept around his ribs from underneath his arm, the tips brushing across the left side of his neck.

Only it wasn't a tat. It was a Dušan—a darker, more stylized brother to the one that resided on my left arm—and had been designed to protect us when we walked the gray fields. We had no idea who'd sent them to us, but Azriel suspected it was my father, who apparently was one of the few left in this world—or the next—who had the power to make them.

Of course, Azriel wasn't *just* a reaper, but something far more. He was one of the Mijai, the dark angels who hunted and killed the things that broke free from hell. And they had more than their fair share of work now that the first gate had been opened.

If you ask me, death is looking more and more like the perfect solution when it comes to the keys. My mental voice sounded as weary as my physical one. I wasn't actually telepathic—not in any way, shape, or form—but that didn't matter when it came to my reaper. He could hear my thoughts as clearly as the spoken word.

Unfortunately, it wasn't always a two-way street. Most of the time I heard his thoughts only when it was a deliberate act on his part. *If I'm not here to find the damn things, then the world and my friends remain safe.*

He crossed his arms, an action that only emphasized the muscles in his arms and shoulders. *Death is no solution. Not for you. Not now.*

And what the hell is that supposed to mean?

His gaze met mine, his blue eyes—one as vivid and bright as a sapphire, the other as dark as a storm-driven sea—giving little away. *It means exactly what it says.*

Great. More riddles. Another thing I really needed right now. I returned my attention to Hunter's death-like stare. "How did your friend die?"

"He was restrained, then drained."

"Drained? As in a vampire style, all-the-blood-from-the-body draining or something else?"

She hesitated, and for just a second I saw something close to grief in her eyes. Whoever her friend was, they'd been a lot closer than mere lovers.

"Have you ever seen the husk of a fly after a spider has finished with it?" she said. "That's what he looked like. There was nothing left but the dried remains of outer skin. *Everything* else had been sucked away."

I stared at her for a moment, wondering whether I'd heard her right, then swallowed heavily and said, "Everything? As in, blood, bone—"

"Blood, bone, muscle, intestines, brain. *Everything.*" Her voice was suddenly fierce. "As I said, *all* that remained was the shell of hardened outer skin."

A shudder ran through me. I did *not* want to meet, let alone chase, something that could do *that* to a body.

"How can human skin be hardened into a shell? Or the entire innards of a body sucked away? It had to be one *hell* of a wound."

"On the contrary, the wound was quite small—two slashes on either side of his abdomen." She hesitated.

"He did not appear to die in agony. Quite the opposite, in fact."

"I guess that's some comfort—"

"He's *dead*," she cut in harshly. "How is that ever going to be a comfort?"

I should have known I'd get my head bitten off if I tried sympathy on the bitch. "Where is his body? And is the Directorate being called in on this?"

If it was, it could get tricky. Uncle Rhoan worked for them—he was, in fact, second in charge of the guardian division these days—but he had no idea I was working for Hunter and the council. And I wanted to keep it that way, because the shit would really hit the fan if he and Aunt Riley ever found out. They'd always considered me one of their pack, but that protectiveness had increased when Mom had died. They'd kill me if they knew I'd agreed to work with Hunter—and once they'd dealt with me, they'd track her down and confront her. And *that* was a situation that could *never* end nicely.

I'd already endangered the lives of too many people I cared about by dragging them into this mad quest for the keys—I didn't want to make the situation worse in any way.

"Yes, they are," she said, "but Jack has been made aware of my wishes in this, and will ensure you get first bite at the crime scene."

Amusement briefly ran through me, although I doubted her pun had been intentional. "That really doesn't help with the problem—"

"Rhoan Jenson will not get in the way of this. You are a consultant, nothing more, as far as he is concerned."

I snorted. "A consultant you're using to hunt and kill."

"Yes. And you would do well to remember that you remain alive only as long as the council and I agree on your usefulness."

"And—" Azriel said, suddenly standing behind me. His closeness had desire stirring, even though I had little enough energy to spare. "—you would do well to remember that *any* attempt to harm her would be met with even more deadly force."

Hunter smiled, but there was nothing pleasant about it. "We both know you cannot take a life without just cause, reaper, so do not make your meaningless threats to me."

"What I have done once I can do again," he said, his voice stony. "And in this case, as in the last, I would revel in a death taken before its time."

Azriel, stop poking the bear. I've already antagonized her enough.

That is a somewhat absurd statement, given she is clearly vampire, not bear.

Amusement slithered through me again, as he'd no doubt intended. He'd grown something of a sense of humor of late—which was, according to him, a consequence of spending far too much time in flesh form. Whether that was true, I had no idea, but I certainly preferred this more "human" version to the remote starchiness that had been present when he'd first appeared. *You know what I mean.*

Surprisingly, I do. He touched my shoulder, the contact light but somehow possessive. *But her threats grow tedious. She must be made aware it gains her nothing.*

Hunter laughed. The sound was harsh, cold, and sent another round of chills down my spine. "Reaper, you amuse me. One of these days, when I'm tired of this life, I might just be tempted to take you on."

And she was crazy enough to do it, too.

"However," she continued, "that time is *not* now. I will send you my friend's address, Risa. The Directorate will arrive at his home at four. Please be finished with your initial investigation before then, and report your impressions immediately."

I glanced at my watch. She'd given me a whole hour. Whoop-de-do. "Where does he live, and what sort of security system has he got in place?"

"I've just sent you all his details."

My cell phone beeped almost immediately. I picked it up and glanced at the message. Hunter's friend—who went by the very German-sounding name Wolfgang Schmidt—lived in Brighton, a very upmarket suburb near the beach. No surprise there, I guess—I certainly couldn't imagine her slumming it with the regular folk in places like Broadmeadows or Dandenong.

I read the rest of the text, then glanced up at the main phone's screen again. "Is the security system just key coded?"

"Yes. Wolfgang is—*was*—a very old-fashioned vampire. He saw no need for anything more than a basic system."

And maybe, just maybe, that had gotten him killed.

While there was no electronic security system on earth that would actually *stop* a demon, it wasn't beyond the realms of possibility that something other than a demon had killed her vampire friend.

I mean, no one could ever be one hundred percent right all the time. Not even Hunter—although I'm sure *she'd* claim otherwise. And really, what sane person would argue the point with her when she wasn't?

Certainly not me.

And yet you do, Azriel commented, a trace of amusement in his mental tone.

I think we've already established I'm not always sane. To Hunter, I added, "You're not going to be there?"

"No."

I frowned. "Why not?"

"Because I have"—she hesitated, and an almost predatory gleam touched her gaze—"a meeting that needs to be attended."

If that gleam was any indication, the so-called meeting involved bloodshed of some kind. After all, the council—and Hunter—considered it perfectly acceptable to punish those who strayed by allowing them to be ripped to shreds by younger vampires.

Still, it seemed odd that she wasn't hanging around to garner my impressions, especially if she cared for the dead man as much as I suspected.

Like many who have lived for centuries, she has strayed from the path of humanity, Azriel commented. *For her, emotions are fleeting, tenuous things.*

But not all those who live so long find that fate. Uncle Quinn, for instance, was as emotional as anyone, despite the fact he could be as stoic and cold as any of them when the urge took him.

He is one of the few exceptions. It is very rare to live so long and hang on to humanity.

I glanced at him. *Does that apply to reapers as well?*

Reapers are not human, so we can hardly hang on to what we do not have.

But you are capable of emotions.

Again a smile touched his thoughts, and it shimmered through me like a warm summer breeze. *Yes, we are, especially if we are foolish enough to remain in flesh too long.*

In other words, I wasn't to read too much into what he said or did while he wore flesh, because when all this was over, we'd both go our separate ways and life would return to normal.

I wanted that; I really did.

But at the same time, it was becoming harder and harder to imagine life without Azriel in it.

He made no comment on that particular thought and I returned my attention to Hunter. "Once I've checked out the crime scene, what then? Are you going to tell me more about him or am I expected to work on this case completely blind?"

"Impressions first," she said, and hung up.

"Fuck you and the broom you rode in on," I muttered, then leaned back in my chair. "Well, this totally sucks."

"An unfortunate consequence of agreeing to work with someone like Hunter is being at her beck and call." He spun my chair around, then squatted in front of me and took my hands in his. His fingers were warm against mine, his touch comforting. "But there is little we can do until your mother's killer is caught."

I snorted softly. "Even if we *do* find her killer, do you really think she's going to let me go?"

"We both know the answer to that. But once the killer is caught, we will be in a better position to deny her."

"Maybe." And maybe not. After all, Hunter wouldn't have any qualms about threatening the lives of my friends if it meant securing long-term obedience.

"It does not pay to worry about things that may never happen."

"No." I leaned forward and rested my forehead against his as I closed my eyes. "I guess we'd better get moving. I want to be out of that house before the Directorate gets there."

"Do you wish me to transport us there?"

His breath washed across my lips and left them tingling. Half of me wanted to kiss him, and the other half just wanted him to wrap his arms around me and hold me as if he never intended to let go. Unfortunately, neither was particularly practical right now.

And it was a sad statement about my life when desire gave way to practicality.

"It'll be faster if you do." While I could shift into my Aedh form and travel there under my own steam, my energy levels were still low and I really didn't want to push it. Not yet, not for something like this.

He rose, dragging me up with him, then wrapped his arms around me. "Wait." I broke from his grasp and moved around the desk, striding out of my office and down to the storeroom at the other end of the hall. We kept all RYT's—which was the name of the café I owned with two of my best friends, Ilianna and Tao— nonperishable items up here, which meant not only things like spare plates, cutlery, and serviettes, but also serving gloves. It was the last of those that I needed, simply because I didn't want to leave fingerprints around Wolfgang's house for the Directorate and Uncle Rhoan to find. I tore open a box, shoved a couple of the clear latex gloves into the back pocket of my jeans, then headed back into the office. I grabbed my cell phone from the desk, then let myself be wrapped in the warmth of Azriel's arms again. "Okay, go for it."

The words had barely left my mouth when his power surged through me, running along every muscle, every fiber, until my whole body sang to its tune. Until it felt like there was no me and no him, just the sum of us— energy beings with no flesh to hold us in place.

All too quickly my office was replaced by the gray fields. Once upon a time the fields had been little more than thick veils and shadows—a zone where things not sighted on the living plane gained substance. But the more time I spent in Azriel's company, the more "real" the fields became. This time the ethereal, beauti- ful structures that filled this place somehow seemed more solid, and instead of the reapers being little more than wispy, luminous shapes, I could now pick out faces. They glowed with life and energy, reminding me of the drawings of angels so often seen in scriptures— beautiful, and yet somehow alien.

Then the fields were gone, and we regained substance. And though it involved no effort on my part, it still left my head spinning.

"You," he said, his expression concerned, "are not recovering as quickly as you should."

"It's been a hard few weeks." I stepped back to study the building in front of us, even though all I really wanted to do was remain in his arms. That, however, was not an option. Not now, and certainly not in the future. Not on any long-term, forever-type basis, anyway.

Which, if I was being at all honest with myself, totally sucked. But then, I had a very long history of falling for inappropriate men. Take my former Aedh lover, Lucian, for instance.

"Let's not," Azriel said, his voice grim as he touched my back, then lightly waved me forward.

Amusement teased my lips. "He's out of my life, Azriel, and no longer a threat to whatever plans you—"

"It is not the threat to *me* I worry about," he cut in, his voice irritated.

I raised my eyebrows. "Well, he can hardly threaten *me*, given he and everyone else wants the damn keys."

"His need for the keys did not stop his attempt to strangle you."

Well no, it hadn't. But I suspected Lucian's actions had been little more than a momentary lapse of control—one he would have snapped out of before he'd actually killed me. Although, to be honest, I hadn't actually been so certain of that when his hands had been around my neck.

I opened the ornate metal gate and walked up the

brick pathway toward the front door. Wolfgang's house was one of the increasingly rare redbrick Edwardian houses that used to take pride of place in the leafy bayside suburb. The front garden was small but meticulously tended, as was the house itself. I pulled out the gloves as I walked toward the house and said, "Lucian is no longer our problem."

"If you think that, you are a fool."

And I wasn't a fool. Not really. I just kept hoping that if I believed something hard enough, it might actually come true. I switched the discussion back to my health. It was far safer ground.

"You can't expect me to recover instantly, Azriel. I'm flesh and blood, not—"

"You are half Aedh," he cut in again. His voice was still testy. But then, he always did sound that way after a discussion about Lucian, whom he hated with a surprising amount of passion for someone who claimed it was only his flesh form that gave him emotions. "More so, given what Malin did to you."

Malin was the woman in charge of the Raziq, my father's former lover, and a woman scorned. My father had not only betrayed her trust by stealing the keys from under her nose, but had also refused to give her the child she'd wanted. Instead, for reasons known only to him, he'd gone to my mother and produced me.

"Meaning what?" My voice was perhaps sharper than it should have been. "You never *actually* explained what she did."

And I certainly couldn't remember—she'd made sure of that.

He hesitated, his expression giving little away. "No. And I have already said more than I should."

Because of my father. Because whatever Malin did had somehow altered me—and not *just* by altering the device the Raziq had previously woven into the fabric of my heart, which had been designed to notify them when I was in my father's presence.

My sigh was one of frustration, but I knew better than to argue with Azriel—at least when he had *that* face on. "It doesn't alter the fact that a body—even one that is half energy—can run on empty for only so long."

A fact he knew well enough—his own lack of energy was the reason he'd been unable to heal me lately. Of course, reapers didn't "recharge" by eating or sleeping or any of the other things humanity did, but rather by mingling energies—which was the reaper version of sex—with those who possessed a harmonious frequency. Unfortunately for them, such compatibility wasn't widespread, and Azriel's recharge companion had been killed long ago while escorting a soul through the dark portals. The good news was that he *could* apparently recharge through me—though *why* he could do this when I wasn't a full-energy being but rather half werewolf, he refused to say. Just as he'd so far refused to recharge. Up until very recently, he'd been more worried about the threat of assimilation—which was when a reaper became so tuned in to a human that their life forces merged and they become as one—than the lowering of his ability to heal me.

All that had changed when I'd almost died after a fight on the astral plane. Because, as I'd already noted, without me, no one could find the keys. My father's blood had been used in the creation of the keys, and only someone of his blood could find them.

Of course, making the decision to recharge and actually doing it were two entirely different things. Especially when I had barely enough energy to function, let alone have sex.

Which was another sad statement about the state of my life.

I punched the security code into the discreet system sitting to the left of the doorframe. The device beeped, and the light flicked from red to green. I opened the door but didn't immediately enter, instead letting the scents within the house flow over me.

The most obvious was the smell of death, although it wasn't particularly strong and it certainly didn't hold the decayed-meat aroma that sometimes accompanies the dead. Underneath that rode less-definable scents. The strongest of these was almost musky, but had an edge that somehow seemed . . . alien? It was certainly no smell that I'd ever encountered before, although musk was a common enough scent amongst shifters.

Was that what we were dealing with, rather than a demon? I had to hope so, if only because I then had more of a chance of redirecting the search to the Directorate.

The hallway that stretched before us was surprisingly bright and airy, and ran the entire length of the house. Several doorways led off it from either side and, down at the very end, sliding glass doors led out into a rear yard that contained a pool. Like the front yard, both the hallway and the rear yard were kept meticulously—there didn't appear to be a leaf out of place, and there certainly wasn't even the slightest hint of dust on the richly colored floorboards. Whoever looked after this place—be it Wolfgang or hired help—was one hell of a housekeeper.

I took a cautious step inside, then stopped again, flaring my nostrils to determine where the death scent was strongest.

"The body lies in the living area down at the far end of this hall," Azriel said. He was standing so close that his breath tickled the hairs at the nape of my neck.

I eyed the far end of the hall warily. Why, I had no idea. It wasn't like Wolfgang's husked remains would provide any threat. It was just that smell—the oddness of it. "Does his soul remain?"

"No. The death was an ordained one."

This meant that a reaper had been here to escort him to whichever gate he'd been destined for. It probably would have been comforting news to anyone but Hunter. "Does that also mean whatever did this isn't a demon? If this death was meant to be, then surely it can't be an escapee from hell."

He touched my back and gently propelled me forward. My footsteps echoed on the polished boards, the sound like gunshots in the silence. Azriel was ghost-like.

"Whether this death was the result of an attack from a demon has no bearing on it being ordained. If death is meant to find you, there is no avoiding it."

"Which doesn't actually answer the question of whether a demon did this."

"It could be either a malevolent spirit or some kind of demon, thanks to the first portal being open."

And *it* was only open thanks to me.

"*That* thanks belongs to us all," he corrected softly. "It is a blame that lies with everyone who was involved in that first quest."

But in particular, with one.

He might not have said the words, but they hung in the air regardless. And while it was now very obvious that Lucian had an agenda all his own when it came to the keys, I didn't think he was responsible for snatching the first one. He'd been as furious as we had been over its loss.

Of course, I had also been sure that he'd never harm me, and his strangulation attempt had certainly proven that wrong. Yet I still believed he didn't want me dead. Not until the keys were found, anyway.

I frowned. "I thought you said malevolent spirits were of this world rather than from hell."

"They are."

"Then why would the opening of the first gate affect them in any way?"

"Because the dark path is a place filled with dark emotions and, with the first gate open, these emotions have begun to leach into this reality."

"Meaning what?"

I slowed as I neared the living area and trepidation flared, though I still had no idea what I feared. Maybe it was simply death itself. Or maybe it was just a hang-

over from the hell of the past few weeks. Between escapee demons, malevolent spirits, and psycho astral
travelers, I'd certainly been kept on my toes.

Or flat on my back, bleeding all over the pavement,
as was generally the case.

"Meaning," Azriel said softly, "that it feeds the
darker souls, be they human or spirit."

"So basically, it's the beginning of hell on earth?"
Two steps and I'd be in the living room. My stomach
began twisting into knots. I flexed my fingers and
forced reluctant feet forward.

"Basically, yes."

"Great." As if the weight on my shoulders weren't
already enough, I now had the sanity of the masses to
worry about.

I entered the living room—and saw the body.

Or rather, the body-shaped parcel.

Because Hunter had left out one very important fact
when she'd described Wolfgang's death.

Not only had he been sucked as dry as a fly caught
by a spider, but he'd been entangled in the biggest
damn spiderweb I'd ever seen.

Do you love fiction with a supernatural twist?

Want the chance to hear news about your favourite authors (and the chance to win free books)?

Keri Arthur
S. G. Browne
P.C. Cast
Christine Feehan
Jacquelyn Frank
Thea Harrison
Larissa Ione
Sherrilyn Kenyon
Jackie Kessler
Jayne Ann Krentz and Jayne Castle
Martin Millar
Kat Richardson
J.R. Ward
David Wellington

Then visit the Piatkus website and blog
www.piatkus.co.uk | www.piatkusbooks.net

And follow us on Facebook and Twitter
www.facebook.com/piatkusfiction | www.twitter.com/piatkusbooks

piatkus